Lilith

The Last Temptation of Adam

Book One of the Lilith Trilogy

Special Edition

Now in Production as a Major Feature Film

TOM STEVENS

Lilith The Last Temptation of Adam:
2nd Special Edition © Tom Stevens 2012
ISBN: 978-1-906983-23-9

First published as *Nemesis* in 2007 this is the author's new and revised version of his original story and is an original work in its own right.

The right of Tom Stevens to be identified as the author of this work has been asserted by him in accordance with the Copyright Design and Patents Act 1988 and the international Berne Convention (Rome revision) of 1928.

Picture credits Front cover: Freya Lund as 'Lilith' copyright by the author. Back cover: Lilith Sumerian image from 1950 BC. Image in the public domain
Ancient languages consultant: Dr Bruce Routledge: Senior Lecturer in the School of Archaeology, Classics and Egyptology, University of Liverpool UK.

Project Renaissance™

Mind and Body as One

Film, television broadcast, and DVD/Blu-Ray rights are held exclusively by Tom Stevens of Green Chapel Films Limited www.greenchapelfilms.com
All Music by Maggie Reilly and Stuart MacKillop
© Red Berry Records Limited www.maggiereilly.co.uk
Book: published by Project-Renaissance Books for Viridios Productions Limited books@projectrenaissance.net and www.viridiosproductions.com
authors contact e-mail: tom@greenchapelfilms.com

 **Lightning Source** Printed and Bound in the UK and USA

Lightning Source UK
Chapter House
Pitfield
Kiln Farm
Milton Keynes
MK11 3LW
Email: enquiries@lightningsource.co.uk
Voice: 0845 121 4567
Fax: 0845 121 4594

Lightning Source (Inc) USA
1246 Heil Quaker Blvd.
La Vergne, TN USA 37086

inquiry@lightningsource.com
Voice: (615) 213-5815
Fax: (615) 213-4725

TOM STEVENS

Lilith Trilogy

Mystery and Adventure in Parapsychology and the Occult

Lilith

The Last Temptation of Adam

Lilith 2

The Devil's Bible

Lilith 3

The Pleroma

A Companion Trilogy to Tom Stevens ESP Series

INSPIRATIONS

As a writer in the Mythic Fiction genre I have been greatly influenced by the English playwright David Rudkin (Penda's Fen and Sir Gawain & The Green Knight) as well as by the historians Francis Tudsbery and Peter Beresford Ellis and by the mythologist Roger Sherman Loomis. Further inspiration has come from the pre-Raphaelite Brotherhood of artists and poets: and the Romantic painter John William Waterhouse. The music of singer-songwriters Maggie Reilly and Kate Bush has been particularly influential and I have recently been honoured to work on a collaborative creative film and music project with Maggie: *Lilith: The Last Temptation of Adam* based on this, my book of the same name.

My study of the psychology of myths and their enduring presence within the human psyche has been informed by a lifelong study of the work of Carl Gustav Jung and thirty years journey-work with the human soul as a psychodynamic psychotherapist.

I am indebted too to my muse and *femme inspiratice*: l'Orchidée whose belief in me has never faltered and whose spiritual sustenance through every trial and tribulation has made my creative work possible. Yet the most enduring influence on my creativity has been that of the land itself. From my earliest, nascent and most fleeting moments of childhood consciousness: I have been aware of the latent psyche of the ancient Wirral peninsula and felt its stories reaching out to me – stories long forgotten or overwritten – but still present in its living fields, meadows, brooks, and hills.

The eternal myths that have arisen out from the communion between mind and earth are as relevant now as they were for the ancient peoples of this land: and if we but only allow them, – they still speak to us...

Pour Mon Muse l'Orchidée

Gareth and Rhiannon

&

GENIO SANCTO VIRIDIOS EX VISV

In Fulfilment of My Promise to Franz Jung

Also

To Maggie Reilly for Her Music

Chapters

Lilith 2 The Devil's Bible

Prologue

Genesis

It was *Lilith* the wife of Adam:
>   (Eden bower's in flower.)
Not a drop of her blood was human,
But she was made like a soft sweet woman.

Lilith stood on the skirts of Eden;
>   (And O the bower of the hour!)
She was the first that thence was driven;
With her was hell and with Eve was heaven.

'Help me once against Eve and Adam!
>   (Eden bower's in flower.)
Help me once for this one endeavour,
And then my love shall be thine for ever!

(*Lilith*) EDEN BOWER
By Dante Gabriel Rossetti

1869

The First
Temptation
of Adam

he distant light reached out to her: its tendrils as spiralled pearlescent arms within the darkness of the eternal void. Entranced by curiosity, her mind reached back – the now golden hued globe shimmering with marbled blue waters, deep red earth and lush verdant life...

She closed with the light... her mind fascinated by the vivid intensity of its colours: "What place is this?" she thought "a *creation* out from the unending timeless void?" Nearer and nearer she approached ... until her fascination became at first rapture, and then at last... her own... self-entrapment.

"Behold, by act of mine own will am I came hence – and through this blood red soil is mine body made as living substance from pure spirit! See, my hair, is as golden as the sun's raying light, mine eyes as green as this garden's well-watered fields. Know me then, oh creation, for I am the first woman – arisen thus out of the earth itself: I... am Lilith!"

Amidst the trees of Eden a shape shimmered and moved. All Green he was with tawny-bark for skin: his eyes – one of green and one of blue followed her, and knew her truly for who she was…

Then Adam saw her, and was immediately beguiled by her incredible beauty – surely she was the most perfect thing in all of creation and... the Lord's promised wife, and companion, for him…

"Woman… thou art *woman?* Yes! My companion thus as promised unto me by The Lord: mine wife whose body I shalt know, and who wilt love me!"

Lilith too felt an attraction, an attraction to her opposite – to Adam – the first 'man': "*Man*… thou art… and the first of your kind… and so different unto me, in this, mine material form…"

Adam knew not what she meant, but his joy was unbounded: "Come, let me show thee Paradise – a garden laid out here by The Lord – a place of everlasting happiness and joy, called Eden!"

Lilith, Goddess of the *Pleroma* – the eternal uncreated void beyond this universes finite bound, smiled at the innocence and naivety of the First Man: "This paradise is Eden called, but what, of you?" she asked.

"I am called 'Adam' by The Lord – the first of humankind!"

"And I… am *Lilith* created through act of mine own will."

" *Lilith*… it *is* you!" exclaimed the First Man, slowly, as if by recognition of her from within his very soul. But then Adam's brow furrowed, as a first nascent glimmering of true human consciousness gnawed at him: "Created…you say, by act of thine own will? But what is that, what is 'will'? All things are created by The Lord, and I in *his* own image!"

"Really? And then in what image am I thus formed, oh Adam, in Eden?"

"By his... command....surely" faltered Adam "as a gift... for me. It was his promise!" he asserted.

"His *command!* Ha! None may command of me, oh First Man, for I am came hence from beyond this world's finite bound!"

"Beyond? You mean from The Wasteland outside the skirts of Eden's Paradise, you came hence from there? But I saw thee, arise, and were thus formed in pristine beauty, out from the very Earth itself – *his* Earth, the created soil of Eden!"

"Ha ha ha! *His* Earth? Oh no... for when I arose hence from the unbounded *Pleroma*, then so didst mine spirit transform that moistened red dust... Now, it is forever *my* blood-soil!"

"Then you *must* be she, who was promised unto me by The Lord – for I too am from the Earth fashioned. Come unto me now, and know me intimately with thy body, for in witness of thy true perfection and beauty, I am stirred thus unto *irresistible* passion for thee!"

But Adam was much too presumptive in thinking that this original woman was human – and the missing half of his incomplete soul, for she was indeed a primordial Goddess: made flesh, she believed, out of her own free will, through the filtering medium of Eden's blood-red soil. Yet in truth, although she had came hence as spirit; she was here immediately entranced and then fatally entrapped, by the beguiling beauty of this, the created, material world.

She would submit however to none: not to him, not unto Adam, The First Man, nor even the Lord Creator of this world. Adam... *must* submit to her... "Look well upon mine beauty, oh Adam for none of future womankind canst *ever* equal me... Eternal love and unrestrained erotic pleasure is in mine gift, but know thee this: I yield to none, but demand instead *your* devotion, and submission, *only* unto me!"

Adam was smitten with passion: and with the first yearning love in any human soul... and yet... "But the Lord promised me that I wouldst hath a woman, as mine companion, and she wouldst submit her body unto me, and thus her heart too!"

"Ha ha ha! Then learn ye well this first lesson, that even here in Paradise truly, a man and a woman are not equal: yet tis not so in favour of man... but of *this* woman... this... *Lilith!*"
Still laughing, she walked on and away through the beautiful fields and meadows – with a confused, anxious and lovelorn Adam following her close behind.

"Wait, *Lilith* for my heart is taken with thee as are my passions, I am sore and bereft to see thee depart thus from me! *Lilith* my love wait!"

"Wait for thee Adam? I wait for no one, for to wait is to submit to another's will – and that I will *never* do, er though your every single heartbeat calls out in my name!"

"But *Lilith* I cannot live thus without thee, for mine beating heart sickens: enchanted as I am I canst not thus endure without thy love: and so my existence wilt surely come to its end!"

"Then obey mine will, oh First Man... for then your deliverance from suffering is thus assured."

Adam halted, as his spine suddenly tingled in warning: "But The Lord... *he* is my Father Creator... and mine deliverance, he hath promised me eternal relief from suffering!" Turning in fear of judgement, he ran back towards the heart of the garden and cried: "Lord, creator of this world, whose breath gave me life out from the dusted Earth... the companion you hath sent me... the First Woman, *Lilith,* she pains me, and denies my love and possession of her, and will not submit unto me! Lord, help me now, for I am torn in heart and suffer great pain, help me oh Lord, I beseech thee: create a new companion for me; make me a *new* first woman!"

Lilith laughed to hear Adam's plea unto his God – for she was no shape and form made from breath animated dust, as was The First Man... She was herself a Goddess – uncreated and immortal, and here in this material world by act of her own will... and thus no mere created woman could ever rival her...

Or so she thought.

"Behold... for I am he who hath made this place, and set it aside for the fate, and for the fortune, of mankind: whom I hath fashioned thus in mine own image!"

"I know thee: as you know me, even in this flesh, for I am she who rules beyond, in the *Pleroma's* unchanging void!"

"Yea, thou do I know as *Lilith,* and yet here in this garden Paradise are ye subject unto *my* will – as are all here thus created, and in material form!"

Lilith's defiance was proudly stated: "In this place hath I created *myself*: as immortal spirit, that through blood-red Earth is made thus into flesh! I have seen your creation... the First Man... and felt his passion, and his desire... I know it, and him, by the devotion of his *every* single heartbeat. It pleases me... to be so desired, but he must surrender unto *my* will, as the self-created First Woman!"

"*Lilith* out of the unchanging void hath you instantiated yourself – and through the fire tempered soil of Eden: but *not* by thy own will: yet instead by the self-entrapment of thine own passions!

Now, here as flesh are ye subject unto my power... therefore will I banish thee, out hence from Paradise, and beyond the walled skirts of Eden into the Wasteland... Therefore you will *not* hath the love of Adam – and for him will I create another woman, and from their union, shalt their issue in generations to come, multiply to fill all of the four corners of the Earth! Out now I command, and be gone!"

In material form, *Lilith* was vulnerable, and unable to resist the power of the Lord Creator: the *Rex Mundi* of this world – and so it was that she was exiled and sent out into the arid and barren Wasteland.

Then The Lord went to Adam, and caused a sleep to come over him, and in his sleep, did he take a rib from him, and from that fashioned a new 'first' woman... Eve.

Eve, whose beauty near equalled that of *Lilith* herself – and she became Adam's second wife, replacing *Lilith* in his heart and also with the most intimate knowledge of her body: and so it came to pass that she was destined to become the mother henceforth of all of humankind.

Then did *Lilith* curse Eve:

"A curse I now make 'gainst the Second Woman Eve: and *all* who will descend from her! I will live on, here in Creation, both in spirit and in flesh: to be the eternal torment of her issue - I will bring disease, famine and the barren wasteland over the face of the Earth. I shall feast upon her children's souls by consumption of their passions - being as incubus and succubus and mother of all demons - and all of this until the time when I will chose for myself my 'new' Adam - one single human male: in true spirit from him, that First Adam in Eden: and having rid the Earth through pestilence, of all others descended thus from cursed Eve's womb, I will make with him a *new* humankind, in a *new* Garden of Eden!"

But there was first, one deception left still to pass. Eve herself must be tainted in human memory so that Adam and all of his male descendants would forever yearn secretly for the lost love of *Lilith*. She would be that furtive knowledge of unrivalled lust, seduction and beauty – that first roused Adam to passion, and to love – and so echo in their souls, down the ages, as the image, in unbidden dreams, of irresistible temptation.

Then came *Lilith* returning by guile unto Eden, and through her blood soil she took the shape and form of the Serpent of the Tree of Knowledge. There, she seduced Eve, with the forbidden fruit of the Tree, but also with an erotic desire for the love and the lust of womankind – tempting Eve away from Adam, and so for those women in generations hence to come, an erotic enticement away from the union of woman with any man: seduced by the beguiling mirrored image within their own soul: of the ultimate in feminine beauty: projected onto the face of another....

Thus it came to pass that Eve was blamed for the origin of sin: and tempting Adam, and all of humankind, unto their downfall from Paradise.

Then, from beyond the skirts of Eden, did *Lilith* howl in The Wasteland – howl and laugh as The Lord banished Adam and Eve and all henceforward of humankind, out forever from Paradise.

Yet their true, original sin, was not as they had believed, to taste of the forbidden fruit: but to deny Goddess *Lilith* the exclusive love of her Adam…

BOOK I

Lilith

Out of the earth she'll rise, hear her bell like call,
As oe'r the sapphire coast of night, edge of darkness falls,

She will weave her timeless spell, no one hears your screams,
Across a thousand skies she flies, as you drift in dreams,

Howling her name, know she will come for you,
Held by her gaze, you can never deny her,
Howling her name, oh she will steal your soul,
Vengeance is hers and her name is Lilith!

Temptress from a far off time, she'll haunt you and beguile,
Oh he can never leave now, he's enraptured by her smile.

Howling her name, know she will come for you,
Held by her gaze, you can never deny her,
Howling her name, oh she will steal your soul,
Vengeance is hers and her name is Lilith!

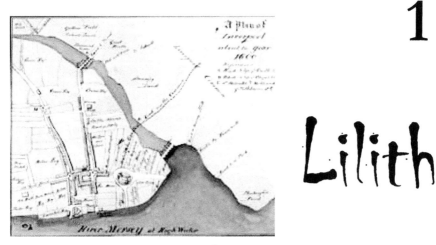

1

Lilith

Liverpool, England: Wednesday 5ᵗʰ June 1644

atthew Hopgood was a God-fearing man. Called 'Puritan' by his detractors he tried to live an honest and ethical life but these were hard times and in a Civil War between Parliament and the King a man's conscience may be torn betwixt his God and his earthy monarch.

The town was in Parliamentary hands, having been captured from the Royalists the previous year, its new garrison commanded by the Roundhead Colonel John Moore; a former chief burgess of the borough of Liverpool and now its military governor.

But now the ten thousand strong Royalist force of Prince Rupert of the Rhine were encamped overlooking the town from high upon Everton Brow. Mockingly, the Cavalier prince had declared Liverpool and its castle to be a mere 'crow's nest' and had resolved their immediate capture.

Matthew's young wife Martha was with child and due within the month: he could only pray piously unto God that the

Royalists would be distracted elsewhere and leave Liverpool and its citizens unharmed…

This morning Matthew had attended an open meeting of the citizenry at the town's High Cross near to St. Nicholas's Church: addressed by Mayor John Holcroft, the town's council of burgesses and their Parliamentary commander: Colonel Moore. The mood of the sombre gathering passed from despair and into firm resolve: as the people were told of Prince Rupert's merciless assault on Bolton town in Lancashire one week earlier: where as an example against the folly of resistance, his troops had all but massacred the entire civilian populace. The choice open to Liverpool's townsfolk, Colonel Moore had said, was between surrender - and with it no one could doubt, rapine and slaughter - or, a spirited defence in the name of Parliament and the reformed Christian faith of the majority of its citizens.

As the meeting broke up Mathew was deeply troubled and fearful for his wife and unborn child: he made straight for the Parliamentary commander: "Good day to thee Colonel…"

Colonel Moore's eyes glanced up slowly from the ground, their cast momentarily betraying the gravity of his concerns: "Ah good day to thee Matthew, and how is Martha: faring well I hope under these most dire of circumstances?"

 Matthew nodded and pursed his lip: "We pray unto God and do what we can Colonel. If the ramparts hold, then canst I bring supplies by boat hence from Wirral's yonder shore, over there at Tranmere Pool…but if they do not…"

"If they do not Matthew" interrupted the Colonel "then canst we all expect the worst, for Prince Rupert employs foreign mercenaries; Germans indeed from Catholic Bavaria. They wilt certainly apply free rein amongst us all for murder, pillage and plunder!" Matthew jolted to hear these words, the Colonel's speech to the townsfolk had been confident and stirring, and enough indeed to steel them gainst the coming assault, but the breaking note in his voice betrayed his doubts: "Will then the ramparts hold Colonel?"

"The ditch and earthen ramparts we hath dug about the town... should hold. After that, we hath the castle, in such disrepair as we hath found it..." Moore's voice faltered again. They'd had the better part of a year to make repairs to the castle, but... " The Mayor and Burgesses hath issued muskets upon my order, hast thou received thine?" he continued.

Matthew visibly bridled at the suggestion of violent arms: "I make my contribution to the town through mine labour and through mine boat... Yer knowe that as a Reformed Christian, I am *not* a man of bloodshed Colonel Moore!"

The hard-bitten Roundhead lifted a thigh-length leather booted foot, and rested it upon the tiered steps of the stone-cross: "If the Royalists take thy pregnant young Dutch wife unto them for their sport and pleasure... wouldst yer be so reluctant then, eh Matthew Hopgood?"

Matthew took a sharp breath; he was sensitive about Martha's foreign birth: "I will her away from here afore that shouldst ever happen!"

"Aye, thou will, if the ramparts stand long enough to allow it: and if they do not, then thinks yer that she wouldst be spared by their mercenary hand, even though she be so near with child?!" The Colonel lent forwards in emphasis: "And remember too, there is a fine of one-shilling for not bearing arms... and then shame to follow for any Englishman who wouldst not defend his borough and town 'gainst foreign mercenaries!"

"I wouldst not shame my countrymen Colonel, but I am of reformed faith, and tis *God* first, then family and then country!"

"Then let us pray Matthew Hopgood that town and family do not fall, for our country and aye even our faith wilt surely follow!" The soldier turned away, breathed out hard, and said: "God be with thee then citizen… Oh, and I will *expect* to see thee… when the time inevitably cometh… with us all, good Liverpool men and true, upon the ramparts!" Hopgood kept his counsel and didn't reply. Martha's coming child would be their first born: he had therefore no intention of leaving them to the spoil of Bavarian mercenaries, nor indeed did he of laying down his life in a futile gesture for a lost town…

God, not man, would be his judge….

Prince Rupert's forward Command Post

"What name is this hill called by Molyneux?"

"Copperas Sire."

"Copperas you say? Ha, as copper-assed as our bucket-headed opponent: Colonel Moore! And yon mill, what is it?"

"Townsend's Mill Sire."

"Good, we shall form some of our artillery into position over there; and then some here on the Copperas Hill, and the rest… by Everton on the Brow. A spectacular bombardment should loosen their Parliamentary bowels!

Molyneux… declare 'formal siege' and instruct them to resist us not… if they want to avoid the 'regrettable' massacre that followed at Bolton town on the 28th of May!"

Colonel Molyneux nodded in assent to his Princely commander's orders and then rode away to make the formal declaration under a flag of truce. He knew the mettle of this 'Colonel' John Moore and didn't expect him to accept the Prince's terms... A massacre therefore was inevitable...

Prince Rupert of The Rhine

The Prince laughed as he stroked his pet poodle 'Boye'. Then turning in his saddle he addressed his enigmatic Bavarian mercenary captain: Colonel Maximilian Von-Hesse: "Well Hesse, methinks we shall break these ramparts and then ye can have merry with the widows eh? There will be plenty of the traitorous harlots for ye men when we hath finished our days' work with the garrison. My good uncle, the King, is too often merciful to his rebellious subjects. But…in our *continental* style of warfare such considerations are not made: eh? Ha ha!"

Von-Hesse smiled an almost Mona Lisa smile: his dark black-brown eyes and deep olive complexion inherited from his Gothic-Italian and French Cathar ancestors. The 'Bavarian' found that his mercenary employment gave him the very best opportunity for his *real* work, which was secret, even from his princely master…

Matthew found Martha down by the Pool: she'd been checking the nets on her husbands' eel boat before he went out on his fishing trip; in a military siege such supplies were essential. With Martha was young Benjamin Teal a lad of fourteen and apprenticed as an eel fisherman to Matthew. He'd found the prior capture of the town from the Royalists to be exciting. A Puritan by upbringing, the two day battle that had ejected the King's troops from the Castle and from Liverpool Tower on the foreshore, had stirred his long suppressed instincts. He'd already spoken with Colonel Moore's sergeants and eagerly looked forward to taking his place amongst the men in the coming struggle. The grass-roots of the town's population were overwhelmingly Parliamentarian in sympathy, but all of the local gentry except for John Moore himself, had been for the King, and it was their Royalist troopers who had thus formerly held it.

Now, Prince Rupert, the most dashing and feared commander under King Charles had taken a detour away from his northwards march to recapture Liverpool. He'd even brought his *familiar* with him: his pet poodle: Boye, who many superstitious Parliamentarians thought had occult powers. The Prince of course did not disabuse them of that belief. He understood the earthly power of psychology to win wars.

But what the Prince did not appreciate was the *real* supernatural power that saddled close by his very shoulder…

Prince Rupert and 'Boye'

Ben Teal knew nought of these occult and arcane powers, only that there would be great battle, and a chance for everlasting glory...

"How is thy brother Henry?" asked Matthew of Benjamin.

"He fareth well sir, he hath joined the militia... I hope to follow him afore this siege be done with!"

"Do ye so young fellow... Well, I hope I waste-not our time in thy apprenticeship, for a corpse finds it hard to make gainful employment!"

"Matthew, frighten not the boy!" exclaimed Martha "his father John is our good friend and Town Clerk!"

Matthew was scolded by his loving wife too often in public company. His fundamentalist beliefs held that a woman's place was as homemaker and subservient companion to her husband: "Wife! Would ye have him dead? This battle shalt not be as last-time; for great slaughter wilt surely follow. Colonel Moore will n'er hold the town: the Prince hath ten thousand men and many great-guns! Think well wife, think well, for ye are with child!"

Martha was not to be chastised: "Husband, ye are born of this town: and so too thy family for all of its generations past! As thy wife, yea, thy foreign *Dutch* wife, I wilt *not* go away from it! And I wouldst that any man who is such, *fight* as a true man should: even if that man be but a boy as Benjamin is!"

Matthew flung his net to the ground: "See yon pool? There, shall be body upon body: sodden corpses full; so that a man may walk across them even unto the common heath at high tide! *That* is what awaits ye from this conflict!"

In his anger, he set-aside his Puritan mores' and stormed off towards the tavern in Dale Street. Martha shook her head: "See Ben, how thin layeth conviction when the heart is set in frustration..."

Captain Danks naval commander of a squadron of six Parliamentary warships under Colonel Moore was deep in strategic discussion with his superior at the Castle: "Sir, we canst bring in reinforcements by the river from Manchester – I understand that a troop of horse awaits' as well as a regiment of foot."

"Wouldst this be in time thinks ye Captain? The assault is near."

"In time *if* we can hold them at the ramparts sir…. Or maybe strike first; a raid upon their artillery. Rupert will surely bombard us afore he attempts investment!"

"Aye… but our most pernicious foe will be common affliction by disease. Ye must keep open the Mersey so that we can supply the town. Our forces hold the old priest's ferry-house o'er yon headland at Birkenhead. We must send further parties to Wirral and make requisition in Parliaments name.

There are Loyalist sympathisers there: at Bidston by Wallasey Pool… see that they harry us not! Send too, mounted scouts to Neston upon the river Dee shore of Wirral: for I wouldst know of any Royalist advance upon us by sea from Chester's port.

I have this fear Captain: if we maketh mischief with Rupert, then the investment will be unmerciful for the common population – the greater part of them are Reformed in faith and may be put to the sword, as one-thousand five hundred were slain in the streets of Bolton town. I would thou knowest, this, that *if* circumstances make such suggestion – then I will evacuate the town of our forces, by sea, and leave the civilian commons to Christian mercy – that is better than slaughter, but before God give word *not* of my plan to any man…"

Matthew was at the Old Strand and drinking more than his teetotal constitution could bear. Now that he very drunk, Bathsheba Prentice, that most accomplished of local prostitutes sought some amusement with him: "What business brings thee here Matthew Hopgood? For such a man as thee it must be paucity of the marriage bed!" Bathsheba was smirking at the sight of a hitherto clean-living Puritan man sozzled beyond his capacities for self-control.

Hopgood's head wobbled in an attempt to keep itself upright: "Away woman!" he declared feebly. But Bathsheba's experience had taught her that persistence usually overrode protestation. Placing her hands on his chest she caressed him seductively: "Come hither Matthew… consolation awaits thee!" Pulling by his collar she drew him back and then up the tavern stairs.

His steps faltered as his ear caught the sound of thunder. Prince Rupert's artillery had opened fire…

Rodney Street Liverpool: Monday 12th June 2006, 09.30am

Claire Lattimer was casually skimming through the pages of the Liverpool Daily Post newspaper. It was Monday morning, and her lecturing duties at the university had wound down ready for the summers academic break. She was professor of parapsychology at Liverpool, a post she enjoyed part-time whilst also heading 'ESP' the world renowned paranormal research institute here in the city's Rodney Street. As she read her eyes alighted on an item reporting a find by workmen below the foundations of a building being demolished to make way for the Capital of Culture renovations:

'Sunday 11th June: Dublin based contract workmen: Dermot O'Brien and Callum McHugh; have uncovered a stone sarcophagus below the foundation level of a building standing on the site of the old inlet-pool shoreline along Paradise Street near to the Albert Dock. Archaeologists from Liverpool University were called in to translate an inscription around the sealed rim believed to be written in an ancient Aramaic language. The sarcophagus is yet to be opened and may be removed to Liverpool World Museum for further detailed examination. A dating analysis of the soil layers that contained the sarcophagus suggested that it was buried in the mid to late seventeenth century...'

"Intriguing..." she mused.

"What is Claire?" asked Dr John Sutton, her old friend and colleague at ESP.

"This item in the Daily Post: seems that some Irish workmen have stumbled across an archaeological find: a stone sarcophagus with an ancient inscription on it."

"Roman?"

"No 17th century, but the inscription may be in an ancient Aramaic script… unusual…"

"Oh… is it in Liverpool?" he asked. "Sorry John" Claire realized that she hadn't explained properly: "Yes it is; along Paradise Street: apparently it was on the shore-line of the old Pool from where the city gets its name."

"So we're talking about a human burial of some kind?"

"Presumably. I guess it depends what's inside, it seems it hasn't been opened yet, but of course you usually get bodies in sarcophagi. Interesting though… the seventeenth century – that's the Civil War period, and all those witchcraft trials."

"And the plague!"

"Oh yeah… and that! Maybe it's something to do with a plague burial. Ah well we can wait and see. I suppose we better get back to work studying this girl who's claiming to be a spiritual medium." Professor Lattimer thought no more of the local archaeological discovery and moved on…

Liverpool: Thursday 6th June 1644

Matthew froze as the peel of thunder roared across the town. Prince Rupert's cannon were pounding the palisade and ramparts atop the earthworks at the end of Dale Street: "The Mill!" he exclaimed "They'll be firing from Townsend's Mill!"

Trying to turn he stumbled and fell face forwards down the last pair of wooden steps. Bathsheba sighed: "There'll nay be coin hath from thee now Matthew Hopgood!" Dismissing him as a failed prospect, she went to the tavern window. Straining to see through the murky glass of the tiny leaded window – she made her plans for profitable business when the Prince's army finally broke-through.

Down at the pool, Martha picked up her skirts and ran as best she could for the cover of her home. Heavily pregnant, she made slow progress. A determined woman in the character of her times; she would work until she could work no more, right up until her confinement. The local midwives: nominally Christian; nevertheless carried many practices over from the older faiths and beliefs. In these superstitious times they were often accused of witchcraft – their skills hidden from the men folk amidst the womanly mysteries of giving life through birth.

Martha's breath was shallow and quick. She was near full term and the stress of attack by a hostile army could induce her labour.

Young Ben Teal had rushed off at the first sound of cannon fire – heading for the Castle and a hoped-for rendezvous with his elder brother by four years: Henry – a zealous and militaristic Puritan who had excited his family with his passion for the Parliamentary cause.

At the Castle, Colonel Moore had hastened to the East Tower to gain the best view. His modest naval spyglass allowed a reasonable magnification – and he was quick to check that no Loyalist forces were attempting an outflanking manoeuvre across Liverpool common-heath – perhaps to force the bridges over the Pool. Satisfied, he joined his professional troopers as they made their way to the Dale Street palisade – the volunteer burgesses and common townsfolk made their own way to their allotted positions – minus of course the inebriated conscientious objector: Matthew Hopgood…

High on Copperas Hill Prince Rupert was keen for a quick end to the proceedings: "Molyneux… direct the men to use cover of our bombardment and maketh forth in concentrated assault there at… which street is it?"

"Dale Street Sire."

"Ah yes… at the Dale Street." Then lifting his wine glass he toasted – "Gentlemen: today's fox: Colonel John Moore!"

Laughter rang out amidst the clinking wine-glasses.

"Molyneux… I will *not* risk my Bavarians until the investment hath proceeded. They are more expensive than the common English soldiery… and their manner and tailoring befit a more splendid employment than rushing themselves at ramparts."

"Yes Sire." Caryll Molyneux, brother of Lord Molyneux and erstwhile resident of Liverpool Town, knew the Prince's real reasoning: he would not risk his best cavalry when he had need of them to later face a rising star in the Parliamentary army: a certain Cambridgeshire farmer; one Colonel Oliver Cromwell, and his personal regiment of *Ironsides*…

Colonel Moore reached the ramparts in time to see massed wedges of Royalist infantry closing with scaling ladders. His professional troopers were disciplined, but the common townsfolk fired at will and ineffectively. For best result – musketry must be by concentrated volley and at as close a range as could be safely afforded: "Men of Liverpool! Hold thy fire till the enemy durst be close: then make with volley concentrated at the ladder-bearers – they cannot climb hither without 'em!"

Morale was high as the men and boys prepared to defend their Town against the King's nephew and his mixed bag of professionals, southern and midland county shire-levies, and of course… the much feared Bavarian mercenaries…

Back at the tavern, an extended groan signalled Matthew Hopgood's return to consciousness. The Tavern keeper, Thomas Pullen, hauled him up to his feet: "Chose thee well Matthew Hopgood!"

"Eh?" Hopgood asked; his head throbbing and his eyes filmed over as if by clouds.

"Chose thee well thy time to drink! Prince Rupert's men are scaling the ramparts even as we speak. Have thee away home, back to thy good wife and keep upon her safe!"

Pausing outside the doorway to throw-up, Matthew took the old Tavern keepers earnest advice and stumbled across the filthy street. Played out to the accompanying rumble of Royalist cannon, dogs were barking; children crying; and armed men hastening to their duty. The cacophony of life swirled about him as a tidal whirlpool. At last he made his way to his home on the incline of Water Street, a modest house overlooking the imposing edifice of old Liverpool Tower.

Martha was lying down on their bed trying to get as comfortable as possible- the exertion had caused her great discomfort and she feared that her time would soon arrive: "Matthew! Husband!" She reached out her hand for him "call for Mistress Penny!"

"The midwife? Are thee then at term?"

"I cannot tell husband, I am frightened of my life, and for my child!"

Hopgood, still drunk, stumbled out to find Mistress Penny – the elderly spinster and chief midwife to the townswomen. She knew the 'old-ways' and the mysteries of childbirth. The commotion from the top of Dale Street now included musketry and the human cries of battle "Ben…" he murmured, as his conscience pricked at his reluctance to fight.

On the ramparts Colonel Moore had led a stalwart defence and was routing Prince Rupert's midlands volunteers. Adrenalin driven fear now turned to elation as the Liverpool men cheered and waved their muskets triumphantly through the clouds of drifting volley-smoke. Prince Rupert was not amused: "Molyneux! What drives our men so hastily to their retreat?"

Caryll shifted uncomfortably in his saddle: "Sire, tis concentrated musketry… the men couldst reach the ramparts, but the ditch hath forestalled them, and the enemies' fire hath marked the ladder bearers, so that none durst taketh them up.

We risk greatly to pursue this course: for we hath business in the north 'gainst Lord Manchester and Cromwell!"

Prince Rupert's eyes bulged at the temerity of his regular – troopers Colonel: "Thinks thee that I knowest that not! Damn this town! What are our casualties?"

"Sire, I fear in estimation that it must be greater than one-thousand five hundred: both slain and taken grievously with wounds."

The Prince's handsome face fell as he realized the folly of continuing with a now suicidal frontal assault: "Then let it be bombardment! Continue for as many days as shall be necessary, and then findeth me a suitable point for investment of the ramparts – do so by cunning and trickery – perhaps by night assault… and thence, slaughter *all* who resist us!"

Mistress Penny made her way to Water Street urged along by Matthew at greater pace than her age could comfortably allow: "Hurry me not Matthew Hopgood: thy breath betrays thee as a drunkard against thy reformed Christian beliefs!"

"Madam, I am Christian, and doest nought employ pagan practice… unlike thee!"

"Ha! Where wouldst thy be Matthew without my knowledge of such things? Well, I knowe where'st it is I shouldst be: safe at home in my old age, yea as God be mine witness!"

"Haste woman!" Hopgood unceremoniously shoved her down the incline of the street. Cussing under her breath she arrived to hear Martha's moans through the door of the house: "Keep thee back Matthew Hopgood, I wouldst see Martha privately, for such things are outside the common understanding of men-folk… away with yer now!"

Matthew did as bidden. He was superstitious enough to respect the mystery that surrounded birth.

Outside in Water Street, the perplexed Matthew was met by an excited Ben Teal: "Sir!" the youngster exclaimed "we hath beaten the Royalists, they run like chickens parted thus from their heads!"

The depressing effect of his alcohol had bitten deep into Matthew: "Just wait thee Benjamin Teal; for they shalt be back and we wilt *all* then pay dearly for thy hubris!"

"Hubris sir? Colonel Moore hath led us to victory!"

"Folly! Mark thus upon my words, tis folly!"

The roar of cannon thundered against the towns ramparts – now from three sides: "See Ben? They wilt bombard upon us till the town is as waste as yonder common heath!"

Ben shook his head and ran on – his youthful exuberance undimmed.

Back once again in the house: it seemed that Martha was not yet at full term. Mistress Penny was scolding of Matthew: "Tis fear Mathew Hopgood, fear! Good Martha was taken in severe fright at the cannon: she hath some days yet – perhaps five or even a week longer. I will make ready!"

Relieved, Matthew looked over at the town ramparts. The cannon smoke was thick and drifting into the streets. Colonel Moore had been returning fire – he'd even placed cannon in the tower of St Nicholas's Church. As bad as the constant noise was, Martha may get accustomed to it. The Royalist artillery was focussing on the ramparts and gates – not on the houses within the town. With luck, the child would be born before the inevitable outcome – and then he could persuade Martha to flee with him o'er the Mersey to Wirral…

"Interesting script…. It's ancient Aramaic you know!"
Dr Alan Flynn was an expert on Middle Eastern languages and a Senior Lecturer in the School of Archaeology, Classics and Egyptology, at the University of Liverpool.

"Really? Can you translate it?" asked Claudia.

"Well of course! It is a bit worn though… Better that you appreciate the date first… from its style I would say the tenth century Before the Common Era – or about nine-hundred and fifty BC. Not something you'd expect to find buried in Liverpool eh?"

Claudia Moore the chief field archaeologist responsible for retrieving the sarcophagus could only frown. This was a puzzle indeed…

"It was dated by pottery in the same layer to about 1670… or at least that's when it was buried."

"Where it originally came from and when it was buried in Liverpool are quite clearly two different things!" Dr Flynn was a petulant academic who tended to think that anything that wasn't spelt-out wasn't understood.

"I do know that Alan, it is basic archaeology after all! Anyway: about the translation?"

Dr Flynn adjusted his spectacles: "Direct translation between languages always involves a loss of meaning, you see meaning has 'context' so the meaning, or its *translation* out from Aramaic into modern English will involve some licence… in other words some phrases will have no direct translation, just 'equivalents'…"

"That's OK, I appreciate that." Claudia wished that he'd just get on with it. Specialists in ancient linguistics often gave lectures before getting down to the details.

"Well… here for example you have a personal name: "*Lilith*' is how you may be familiar with it…"

"*Lilith*?"

"Yes… that's how she appears in the Bible, in the Book of Isaiah, a cursory entry referring to a woman taking refuge in the wasteland. Isaiah dates to the seven hundreds BC so it's more recent than the style of this inscription."

"So presumably then this sarcophagus is a burial for a woman named *Lilith*?"

"Hardly… *Lilith* is not a 'woman.' She is a demon, or perhaps an archetypal goddess. You see there are other versions of her name: *Lilit, Līlītu* and the like. They refer to a malevolent entity who brings darkness or the night. Then, even older than Aramaic, you have Cuneiform inscriptions that refer to her as the harbinger of disease. The earliest Kabbalist and Judaeo-Christian references to her are as Adam's first wife, *before* Eve."

"Really?"

"Yes... created out from the Earth itself, rather than from a spare rib... But, she was wilful and would not submit to Adam, or indeed to any man. Probably suit you modern feminist types that eh Claudia? Anyway, it's hardly a suitable name for a Christian woman of the seventeenth century... as she's also associated with sexual demonology, contagion and... vengeance!

You see that's the 'meaning' of these words here,: 'Ho nu 'ana *Lilith* washewit pō 'anōt' - a simple translation of them would be: *Behold... for I am Lilith, and my name, is retribution!*

Or 'nemesis' as we'd understand it today."

"Nemesis... could it be a local woman, perhaps during the Great Plague in Liverpool... demonized and then blamed for the contagion and then somehow killed and buried in this sarcophagus?"

Dr Flynn lowered his glasses and set his aged light blue eyes on Claudia: "You know, you feminists really should study the wisdom of ancient mythology before you mix-up your twenty-first century gender politics with seventeenth century archaeology! It generates fantasies Dr Moore, not facts!"

Claudia was not to be put off: "That's *post*-feminist thank you very much: and anyway, how else then do you explain how such an inscription came to be buried in seventeenth century Liverpool?"

"How else? Well... you can exclude any specialist knowledge of *ancient* Aramaic! No one alive in Liverpool then could have read it. Not even your educated Puritan Pastors. Most likely it was some curio brought in by ship from the Levantine countries and then buried or somehow otherwise lost. But when you people finally get around to opening the sarcophagus then no doubt you'll have all of your questions answered…"

Liverpool: Monday 10th June 1646

The previous four days had seen an unremitting bombardment from Prince Rupert's artillery. This afternoon, Colonel Moore had summoned his subordinate professional troop commanders to the Castle for a council of war. He'd already made up his mind; it was now just a formality. The town he believed was no longer defensible. His troops would egress by ship soon after night-fall and leave the town open and undefended, so that the superior Royalist forces may occupy Liverpool without resistance. This he felt, was the surest way to make certain that the massacre at Bolton would not be repeated. The Burgesses and the town's civilian populace were not to be informed of the plan. Colonel Moore reasoned that it would cause alarm and even a premature collapse of the outer defences allowing the Royalists to affect entry before the Parliamentarians could safely withdraw.

Prince Rupert was also in council – at his headquarters; a seized tenant's cottage in Everton village: "Mark you Caryll, maketh thee this night-assault a success! I want the town invested and taken by first light!"

"Sire we will taketh the Old-Hall Street rampart and gate, close afore three of the clock, so that by daylight we shalt be in true possession of the town!"

"Good! See to it Colonel, I want my Bavarians to have their sport – it will suffice in lieu of mercenary payment: it will not pain the purse of my good uncle the King and we shalt hath riddance of traitors into the bargain!"

Just after midnight Colonel Moore's men made their way down to the pool by the south wall of the Castle and embarked onto Captain Danks ships. Moore had made certain that the townsmen volunteers had been stood down for the night, leaving only his own men on watch. Feeling secure that professional troopers guarded them; the people of Liverpool took their much needed rest – an exception being the Hopgood family of Water Street – Martha was now in the early stages of labour…

2.45 am on the 11th June and Mistress Penny was in attendance together with two younger women known only by sight to Matthew. Banished to the lower room of the house he was unable to rest let alone sleep. Childbirth was a dangerous time and many women died during its trauma. In his agitation he decided to take some air. Pacing up and down outside, he soon extended his range to take in a nocturnal walk through the length and breadth of the whole town.

Colonel Caryll Molyneux personally led the Royalist troopers as they closed with the Old Hall Street rampart. He was the brother of Lord Molyneux of Croxteth Hall, a family who had hitherto vied with the Stanley's – the Earl's of Derby, for control of Liverpool. His knowledge of the geography of the town was invaluable for Prince Rupert. 3.00am came and Molyneux ordered the scaling ladders to be set against the rampart. The ditch hindered the men in the darkness, but soon the first Royalists had climbed atop the outer fortification. To their surprise there were no sentries… Opening the Old Hall Street gate, they let the remainder of Molyneux's force in, followed immediately by Von-Hesse and the Bavarian mercenaries – the town was invested!

Matthew was deep in murmured prayer as he walked up Water Street and continued along into Dale Street. His meditations were suddenly shocked by the unmistakable blast of a musket coming from behind and to his left. Thinking that a sentry had fired over the rampart towards some movement in the Royalist camp; he stopped in his tracks and stared into the gloom. The second musket shot whistled past his head and thudded into the wooden frame of a nearby door. His stomach signalled alarm before his eyes fully appreciated the danger. Other shots rang-out as blazing torches funnelled into the town – some thrown into thatched roofing creating an instant blaze. The raging firelight at last told him all he needed to know… the enemy were within!

Ben Teal was deep in his last dreamless sleep. Shaken violently he awoke to the urgent face of his brother Henry: "Ben! Come hither! Alarm! The Royalists are in the town!" Disorientated, the youth clothed himself as best he could.

Already his father, John Teal, burgess of Liverpool and a captain within the town's volunteer militia had armed himself and was out in the street: "Assemble at the Town Hall, alarm, alarm!" he shouted.

The townsfolk now made desperate efforts to resist the invaders. Caught completely by surprise many were cut-down as they wandered about the streets looking for Colonel Moore's troopers and their protection. Others, firmly resisted; obliging Caryll Molyneux's men to fight from house-to-house.

Matthew was stunned, but his fear for his wife overrode all other emotion. Running full pelt down Dale Street he collided with Ben as he made his way towards the Castle: "Ben! Where hastens thee?"

"To the Castle and Colonel Moore sir!"

"Nay lad, take thyself unto cover… come with me, home, Martha is in labour!"

The flickering light from the burning buildings caught the careworn expression on Mathew Hopgood's face: "She's in need of protection Ben… she is at this moment with Mistress Penny… in God's name help me protect her!"

Young Ben slowly nodded. He had his musket and powder; it would be a dutiful thing to do, to protect his master's wife as she gave birth.

Von-Hesse led the Bavarian cavalry in a savage charge towards the High Cross and Town Hall cutting down men, women and children as they fled in panic from the torched buildings. Carefully avoiding any armed resistance they preferred simple slaughter to honourable combat. Meanwhile Molyneux's men were facing a stiffening resolve as the burgesses organised a house-by-house defence. Realizing that Colonel Moore's troops were gone and crying out 'treachery!' they defended their families and homes as best they could, but the weight of several thousand Royalist troopers would tell, it was just a matter of time…

Arriving at the Hopgood address in Water Street, it was clear from the sounds upstairs that Martha's time was *very* near: "Stay here Ben… I wouldst speak with Mistress Penny." Matthew tentatively climbed the stairs. Even in the midst of such an extreme emergency as a battle, he was in trepidation about daring to enter the labour room.

Von Hesse had made his way from The High Cross and had turned into Water Street with the intention of taking the old Liverpool Tower – a fortified stone manor house on the foreshore – formerly the property of the Royalist Earl of

Derby, and now a storehouse for Parliamentarian arms. As his men fanned out for their approach, they saw the candle light twinkling from the upstairs room of a nearby house.

Young Ben watched from the leaded glass window as the Bavarian mercenaries dismounted and approached the doorway. They were distinctively dressed in helmets and ornate breastplate armour – armed with swords and flintlock pistols. Instinctively, he drew back to the shadows beneath the stairs. His mind raced between standing his ground, and dropping his weapon and hiding – this mere boy of fourteen had just seconds to make the decision of his life.

It was taken for him… Von-Hesse's flintlock pistol fired, the lead ball blowing a large hole in poor Ben's forehead – exiting at the rear shattering his skull like an egg and painting the walls red with blood and brains.

In the birthing room Matthew heard the shot and knew what it must be. He stood by the doorway unarmed, but ready to defend his family. Mistress Penny and her helpers showed no emotion only concentration on the two lives in their hands. The child's head was out – the birth would be complete at any moment. In her agony and extreme effort, Martha was unaware of the mortal peril that now trod ever closer up the stairs. Matthew's mouth was bone dry, his stomach churning he was unable to stop himself urinating as the footfall stopped outside the door. Eyes bulging he waited his moment, the moment that he must desperately act to protect his family and his home.

The door burst open, just as the cry of his newborn child screamed its arrival into the world.

"A girl by God's blessing!" hailed Mistress Penny.

Matthew smiled. Distracted he lost his opportunity – a shape moved and all went black…

Hopgood was lucky. Having expended his single pistol shot on killing poor Ben, Von-Hesse had merely clubbed him to the ground with the weapons heavy wood and metal butt.

Martha held her newborn to her breast as Mistress Penny rose in defence of her patient: "Hold! Are thee such a barbarian that thou wouldst slaughter a mother with her newborn child!"

Von-Hesse's deep black-brown eyes scanned Mistress Penny's face, causing the old woman to shudder. She sensed something familiar yet deeply disturbing in his soul – even for the violent times that they commonly endured. He looked down at Matthew's unconscious body. Blood flowed freely from his scalp wound: "Be he the child's' father?"

"That he be!"

Von-Hesse nodded: "He wast un-armed…" Then he spoke to Martha: "Woman… I will spare thee, and thy husband… upon this *covenant*: thou shalt have mine protection for as long as our occupation lasts, but you must accept that the child be named as I desire – and my will is that she be called *Lilith*… in remembrance of my mercy!"

Martha nodded in fear, but also in agreement. In such superstitious times she felt obligated before providence to this Bavarian's mercy.

Von-Hesse then approached the child: taking her from Martha's warm chest he held her gainst his cold-steel breast-plate and with tender voice said: "*Lilith*, it *is* you…."

So saying he took a pouch from his tunic pocket and sprinkled some fine particles into the child's mouth.

Martha cried out in alarm and tried to grasp her daughter back, but Mistress Penny held her firm in fear of their lives.

Solemnly Von-Hesse pronounced: "Thy blood-soil is within thee, afore even thy earthly mother's milk… *So mote it be!*"

Matthew came round on the bed to find Mistress Penny bathing his scalp: "Thou shalt have need of more stitching Matthew Hopgood. Take some ale and calm thy heart, for it will pain thee not lightly!"

Struggling against the throbbing ache, he rose to a sitting position: "Maratha, and the baby!"

"Both well."

Relieved he sank back. His memory was clouded by the trauma of the blow. He could remember something about a pistol shot... and some armed men entering the room...

"Wait... the enemy... they hath invested upon the town!"

"All that is done Matthew Hopgood... Colonel Moore hath betrayed us to Prince Rupert, he shamefully egressed and deserted the town under cover of night, by ship from yon Pool. There hath been great slaughter, nearly four hundred of our citizens and volunteers are dead, including young Ben Teal, cruelly slain; shot down in this thy very own house!"

"Ben!" Desperately, Matthew tried to remember.

"Thou hast been without consciousness for two days... the Royalists hold the town. It was surrendered by John Teal at the High Cross, to avoid further massacre. Now, the Old Tower and St Nicholas Church are as prisons – the Castle is Prince Rupert's!"

Matthew struggled to retain it all but asked urgently after his baby: "My child... a daughter?"

"In God's gift, aye!"

"Where be she now?"

"Here, husband." Martha entered, carrying her tiny precious bundle: "She was saved be the mercy of a Royalist commander… upon covenant that we call her after his wish. She is called *Lilith*, and her name is mercy…."

2

The Alchemist

Liverpool Museum: Wednesday 16th August 2006, 12.00pm

eep in the basement of the Liverpool World Museum Dr Claudia Moore – the chief field and excavation archaeologist for the sarcophagus discovery, prepared to open the objects lead-sealed lid: but she'd decided upon employing sensible precautions – given that it may date from the Great-Plague period in Liverpool's history…

The archaeological teams' protective bio-hazard suits would also help preserve any remains there may be inside from contamination with modern bacteria or even DNA. Thus far other than it had a lead seal; what may be inside was still a complete mystery. An X-ray analysis had been attempted but the stone had proven to be too thick.

News of the find had been circulated through various professional channels and caused a great deal of interest: in particular from the Archaeology department of the Otto-Friedrich University of Bamberg in Bavaria – one of the oldest and most prestigious of German universities. Claudia had arranged for the opening to be recorded on high-definition digital film media and she had high hopes that whatever was inside would make a major contribution to the knowledge of Liverpool's' past.

Then, there was her career advancement to think of too…

The lid was heavy. Even after the lead seal had been gently heated so that it took on a plasticized form; it still resisted moving free and the team were cautious not to break the lid under its own weight. Pulses raced and breath quickened at both the effort and the tension.

After what seemed like ages, it gradually slid sideways exposing a small gap; and air contained for three hundred and forty years since the seventeenth century escaped at last into the twenty first.

Claudia shone a light inside: "There's…. a small container of some sort, looks like a lead box… and… I think… yes, they're bones!"

Adam Mitchell, her assistant, carefully laid out the bones on a large covered trellis table. "Male or female?" Claudia asked.

"They're in very good condition… the skeleton is complete: looking at the pelvis, I'd say definitely female and she probably hadn't had children. By the tooth wear, and eruption pattern… maybe twenty years of age? The bones are gracile and show no sign of disease, suggesting that she was in good health: the light muscle attachments indicate that she didn't do any heavy manual work…"

Claudia was pleased: "Good! I'd agree, that's an accurate summary. There's no sign of trauma at all on the bones… so we can presume a soft tissue injury or disease as the cause of death."

"Shall we take a tooth to sample her DNA?"

Claudia paused and breathed out. It would help to solve the mystery of the inscription if they could identify the skeleton's likeliest place of origin – "OK, and let's do an oxygen isotope test on the tooth enamel too, and see if she was local… with respect to where she grew up. I'm curious as to how she ended-up in this stone sarcophagus with that strange inscription…"

Claudia next examined the large and very heavy lead box. With some encouragement, she was able to open it: "Looks like soil, dried red soil?! What an odd thing to put in a sarcophagus…" she mused.

Adam made a suggestion: "Maybe it's from wherever she came from: yer know…so she could be buried with her home turf?"

Claudia smiled: "Maybe… OK, let's have the university take a good look at it and see what they can find out…"

Liverpool: Saturday 9th June 1665

Twenty one years had passed since *Lilith* was born amidst the drama of Civil War on the streets of Liverpool. She had grown tall and graceful with porcelain-perfect skin, long flowing blond hair, green-eyes and an angelic symmetry to her pre-Raphaelite face. In truth, a rare beauty, that not even sombre Puritan clothes and a strict upbringing could conceal. But there was more, her essential spirit was as free as the wind itself; enchanting, dangerously attractive and already from the age of thirteen she had drawn the dark unconscious projections of repressed sexuality that only just failed to break the surface tension of everyday Puritan life.

The men-folk were shocked by their involuntary reaction to her; women and young girls too, both idolized and envied her. Saved by a relaxed air of innocence; had she lived elsewhere in

England at this time, then she would certainly have been accused... and accursed of witchcraft.

Now in his late forties, Matthew Hopgood was a leading and respectable figure in the town, a lay-pastor of the non-conformist reformed or 'Puritan' church of the 'godly ones.' He had become wealthy, in comparison to his circumstances as a fisherman at the time of Prince Rupert's siege, making the import and export of goods through Liverpool to the American colonies his main business. His success, he had attributed to his pious faith and his support for the reformed New-England colonists in their wish to build a new Christian nation.

He and Martha had been blessed with one other child: Henry, born three years after *Lilith*, a youth very much in his father's mould and devoted to his elder sister.

Since the end of the Protectorate and the Restoration of the Monarchy five years earlier, men like Matthew Hopgood had searched their conscience and considered following their Puritan brethren out to New England. Many did, but Hopgood had hesitated. Outwardly he said that he would rather keep Gods work in 'Old' England, than run thither to a 'New' England.

The real reason however was *Lilith*. He was aware of her extraordinary even *uncanny* nature, and feared that in the American Colonies she would fall prey, fatally, to men's superstitions and fears.

Yet despite his strict Christian ethic, he too was superstitious. The strange Bavarian who had spared the lives of his family on condition that the new-born girl be named after his wish – was either the agent of Providence... or of Satan. He could not countenance the latter, so it must have been the Lord who sent that dark figure with his 'covenant'. Matthew's heart kept this conclusion secret, unspoken even between him and Martha, as he was fearful and did not want to hear what she may say upon it in return.

On this day, afore the eve of his daughter's twenty-first birthday, Matthew could not realize that the ship tying-up at the quayside at the bottom of Water Street carried the fate of the world within it…

Despite the passage of two decades it was the same darkly formed face: youthfully smooth, with jet coloured hair and beard. The black-brown eyes surveyed a town unseen by them since time of war: "My name? Doktor Maximilian Von-Hesse; physician, apothecary and… alchemist… of Bavaria."

The trooper's eyebrow raised in suspicion: "Bavaria sayeth thee? They be Catholic in faith by mine understandin'… this be mainly a protestant-reformed town, although some of the gentry still profess of the Catholic condition."

"Soldier: I be of *Christian* religion, and a foreign visitor to your town on medical business! My only purpose here is to practice my professions… I have… arranged premises, in the Chapel Street."

 "And thy companions sir?"

"They be mine assistants and students: Karl Reich, and Michael Scheer."

 "Not Dutchies!"

"Nay, they be Bavarians', but good Protestants both."

The curious trooper nodded in acceptance: "Report thee to the Custom's House o'er yon."

"I thank thee; I shalt disembark my baggage and thereafter attend."

The trooper moved on. There was war between England and Holland; just in case he made a note to watch the new arrivals...

Von-Hesse had already dismissed the incident as unimportant: "Karl... we must recover our 'goods' and maketh them safe at our appointed premises. They are heavy... pay what is needed for the necessary assistance." The black-brown eyes now gazed up the incline of Water Street, searching out the little house on the right:

"*Lilith*... I am return-ered!"

Lilith was walking back from the Toxteth Chapel, which meant crossing the Dingle and Mather's streams as well as the Pool itself. With her was Adam Teal, son of Henry, the elder brother of Benjamin killed by Von-Hesse twenty-one years previously. Adam was three years younger than *Lilith* but completely smitten by her – as indeed were many men and boys of the town and surrounding district.

The Chapel was a place of free worship founded by Richard Mather nearly fifty years past and was much frequented by the various branches of reformed faith, especially since the restoration.

Lilith enjoyed walking in the fresh air through fields and lanes. Adam enjoyed the journey too, mainly because of the time it allowed in her company: "Art thou not the most-lovely of all God's creature's mistress *Lilith*!" Adam couldn't help himself, despite his Puritan constraints.

Lilith smiled a Mona Lisa smile: "Perhaps ye have seen not enough maidens Adam Teal: if thy hadst... then maybe thy compliments would be less freely given."

Adam's feet left the ground as he jumped with excitement: "Oh say thou not *Lilith*! How couldst it be so! Thy beauty rivals even that of the Queen of Sheba herself!"

"Oh, and how wouldst thou knowe: thou hast never seen her?"

Adam struggled to find an answer: "Er... I, I can tell surely... from the account in the Good Book, she hadst not thy hair, thy face, thine eyes... nay... it could not be, other than thou, there is none fairer in all of the world!"

Lilith's smile broadened revealing attractive dimples: "She *was* very beautiful Adam Teal... I saw her with mine own eyes..."

Adam took her words as teasing: "Ha! Nay, never, and even if thou hadst, she wouldst not match thy face as hers the moon set against thine the midday sun!"

"*Sol contra Luna?*" she teased "The Queen of Sheba was beautiful... as a dark rose... but Salome was more lovely yet."

 "Salome? She who contrived for the head of the Baptist?"

"Verily Adam Teal: yet, I know, as mine eyes hath beheld them both."

 "Oh *Lilith*! Thy jesting and humour goeth beyond my comprehension!"

Little did poor Adam know just how far...

Von-Hesse and his companions had reached the new apothecary in Chapel Street. Large wooden boxes containing all manner of medical apparatus and instrumentation for alchemical experiments had accompanied the trio by sea. One large box in particular was carefully protected, and it was this one that Reich and Scheer had personally carried all the way from the quayside: "Have a care! That box must not be broken, nor its contents revealed: tis more precious than thy very lives!"

They knew that only too well. Von-Hesse would have no hesitation in killing anyone who tried to open it or subsequently to mishandle the contents – and yet all it had within was but dry, red, Armenian earth…

Lilith and Adam were crossing the bridge over the Pool that led into the eastern end of the town's Dale Street. Adam was still thick with flattery: "*Lilith,* I swear on my heart, that no woman descended from Eve herself could ever hold a light to thy beauty."

"Eve?"

"Aye nor any else formed thus from Adam's rib!" *Lilith* ran ahead laughing and teasing young Adam with her smiles: "But I am not from Eve, oh Adam Teal, nor from any rib, but of the very earth itself…"

Liverpool Museum: Monday 16th October 2006, 10.00am

Claudia was reading over the results from the tests on the sarcophagus find: "Tooth enamel oxygen isotope analysis – is local, mitochondrial DNA… yep, what you'd expect… radio-carbon dating 1650 plus or minus fifty years… OK, that's within the expected range… now soil… Bloody hell!"

Adam smiled at his boss's outburst: "Not from the Moon is it!" he laughed.

"May as well be, it says typical local composition from the Armenian Highlands: from Eastern Turkey, along the geographical line that connects the Republic of Georgia with Iran…"

"Cool!" Adam liked things to be cool, it made archaeology more interesting."

"That isn't all, listen to this: 'the chemistry of the soil seems to have been altered at isotopic level by some unknown process and there are some as yet unidentified compounds within it.' Unidentified! What does that mean?!"

"Er... it means... unidentified..."

"Do you want to get your PhD Adam?"

"Well yeah."

"OK, then get to work on this and tell the soil scientists that we want a clearer result... Unidentified, hah!

Oh shit who's that now?" Claudia's mobile had gone off "Who? Oh of course.... OK, er, send him down.

That was Dave up at the desk: that German archaeologist from the University of Bamberg in Bavaria: Dr Maximilian Von-Hesse has arrived... he wasn't due until tomorrow."

"Must be keen!" laughed Adam "What kind of a name is that: Von-Hesse! Sounds like something from a horror movie..."

Von-Hesse's footsteps echoed down the stairwell to the basement. He'd come a long way to view this find, come a long way, and waited a very long time...

Adam met him in the basement corridor: "Dr Von-Hesse? I'm Adam Mitchell, Ph.D student under Dr Moore." They shook hands, with Adam noting a strange sensation in his body as Von-Hesse's grip tightened. The black-brown eyes caught him in a penetrating stare, but softened as the he spoke: "So... you are Dr Claudia Moore's assistant: were you at the dig site when the find was first examined?"

Von-Hesse's excellent English momentarily stalled Adam's response: "Sorry... doctor... I was just thinking that your

accent is very good, not a trace of German or anything."
He laughed nervously to excuse his pause.

Von Hesse was relaxed: "I have had a very long association with your country and feel quite at home here."

"Oh… cool: er, yeah, I was there."

The Bavarian's eyes darkened again: "What was the *precise* condition of the sarcophagus was it intact with its seal unbroken?"

"Well, yeah…it was found by ah couple of Irish navvies, their photos are in the Daily Post!" Cool, Adam may have been, but he was nervous under direct questioning. It always made him feel like he was a naughty schoolboy or something.

"Which way to Dr Moore's room?"

"Oh sorry: this way!" Adam had drifted into a trance. Snapping out; he led the way to Claudia's open doorway: "After you Dr Von Hesse."

Claudia was momentarily stunned by her first-sight of the uber-handsome Bavarian – framed in the doorway- but managed a welcoming smile as she rose up from her desk and held out her hand in greeting. Von-Hesse scanned her face reading not only her outer appearance, but also deeply into her personality. Claudia's stomach twinged in sudden alarm as she met his increasingly intense gaze, but then relaxed as an unusual warmth passed into her hand as she shook his.

"Adam has been kind enough to give me an impression of the condition of the sarcophagus as it was discovered *in situ*."

Claudia's eyebrow rose at Von-Hesse's immediate concern for business without much more than a cursory introduction: "We can look at the physical evidence in a moment Doctor, here's the lab report on the bones…. and the soil."

Claudia was curious to see the Bavarian's reaction, particularly to the soil-analysis. There wasn't any, he merely handed the report back. She queried: "Don't you find the soil-science data interesting Dr Von-Hesse?"

"It is not unexpected Claudia... if I may call you Claudia?"

"Yeah that's fine...er... Maximilian?"

"Of course" he smiled. "I take it that you have *no* specialist knowledge of soil science, or of the particular region in Armenia?"

Claudia shook her head.

"I have..., I am also *fluent* in ancient Aramaic."

"You are?! That could be *very* helpful! We have a Dr Flynn from the university who helps as best he can, but he's a bit crusty... Still he managed to translate the inscriptions for us."

Von-Hesse seemingly ignored the bait about Flynn, but he made a note of his name: "Educated reformed-Christians in the seventeenth century would have been able to read Aramaic. Those people who were described somewhat pejoratively as 'Puritans' had to read scripture in Aramaic, as well as in Greek and in Latin."

"Really, Dr Flynn seemed to think otherwise… so, such an inscription is not unusual for the period then?"

Von-Hesse's eyes narrowed: "Oh it is unusual: *ancient* Aramaic is earlier than the kind used in biblical scripture… but the more curious amongst the Puritans would have… found a way to read its Phoenician styled script… You should carefully preserve the contents of the sarcophagus – including *both* the bones *and* the soil!"

"Well of course we shall… I take it then that you *did* note the chemical analysis of the soil in the report?"

"I did… What percentage was expended in the analysis?"

"Percentage was negligible… by weight, only a gram or two at the most."

Von-Hesse let out an audible sigh of relief: "I'd like to take some myself… er, for analysis… of course."

"That should be OK" Claudia had noted The Bavarian's now almost excessive interest in the soil: "What about the bones? We can let you examine them if you like, but… not to take any of them. The skeleton is complete; it would be a shame to dissipate it. The Museum may want to use them for a display in its English Civil War exhibition."

Von-Hesse jolted slightly at the suggestion on an exhibition: "Whilst I am here, I should nevertheless appreciate access to the bones for academic purposes."

"Of course, how long are you in Liverpool for?"

The hooded black-brown eyes narrowed and darkened: "Oh indefinitely Dr Moore, *indefinitely*… you see this is a singularly important thread in the weave of my life's work.
My department understands this… and so, I have *all* the time in the world…

Liverpool: Tuesday 12ᵗʰ June 1665, Noon.

Von-Hesse had arranged his new premises appropriately. Out front was to be the apothecary – for dispensing medicines with a small side room for medical consultation. Out to the back, a 'meditation' room cum library, whilst in the basement his alchemical laboratory: as yet incomplete; but soon to incorporate all the trappings of a seventeenth century physical and *meta*-physical alchemist. The upstairs would form the living accommodation for himself and his students. He had amassed considerable wealth as a mercenary soldier, not to mention his family's aristocratic means, and so even such an expensive outlay as this had hardly troubled him at all.

"Sire doest we approach the maiden now?" asked Karl.

"We… wait; I wouldst knowe the condition of the towns-folk afore I maketh myself known again unto her. Our first consideration is her *paternus mundus* – her earthly father: Matthew Hopgood…"

Liverpool Castle & Custom House 1665

Matthew was down at the quayside. As his business was import and export, he was curious to see the large number of remaining crates disembarked from the foreign ship: "Bavarian's ye say?"

"That be it Matthew: nearly a full ships-hold of crates! He's settin' up in Chapel Street, close by the Juggler Street Market: an apothecary and doctor he says." The Customs Officer smiled quietly to himself. Obviously Hopgood had been concerned about a potential business rival. Somewhat relived Matthew nevertheless thought to pass by the apothecary, just in case. It was not uncommon for enterprising foreigners to set up in diverse businesses: using one as a front for another. Puffing on his clay pipe, a particular object on the quay-side took his eye: "Be that a stone sarcophagus?!"

"Looks like it. Either that: or maybe tis some kind of bath?! I do hear that foreigners take daily waters for bathing! Methinks that to be a *scandalous* luxury: and if true of these *Bavarians'* then they be *not* of our Reformed faith!!

Matthew nodded, apparently in agreement: but he neglected to say just how meticulous his precious daughter *Lilith* was about her own hygiene.

Suddenly, the Customs Officer touched his forelock, looking past Matthew at the approach of some unseen person. Hopgood turned to follow his companion's gaze and saw a strikingly impressive figure striding purposefully towards them: flanked by four other men – the all of them strangers to Matthew.

"Good day to you Sir!" exclaimed The Customs Officer in greeting.

The leader of the group stopped abruptly and regarded the Customs Officer with a penetrating stare.

"A good day indeed!" he declared "We depart hence this very morning for *Ireland*. The Lord hath urgent work for us there…. With *witches!*

"Witches?!" interjected an astonished Matthew.

"Aye Matthew!" responded the Customs Officer "This be Nathaniel Lattimer! *Witchfinder* General!"

"But, that office was *abolished* at the King's Restoration!" asserted Matthew.

The Witchfinder closed intimidatingly, nose-to-nose with Matthew: "I have the authority, sir, of both King *and* Parliament! Only a servant of *Satan* would have reason to question it!" Matthew backed away, his face showing sudden fear and horror. Lattimer smiled in satisfaction. Easy intimidation always pleased him.

The Customs Officer interjected again, this time to draw attention away from his friend: "Here be one of them Bavarian's now!"

It was Scheer,

"Good day to thee" Scheer bowed slightly in the 'continental' fashion "My master requires the bath to be conveyed to the apothecary: as it is needed immediately, for his medical preparations."

"Does he indeed!" bellowed the Customs Officer "Well it's heavy: and It'd need more men for it than I can spare, afore midday on the morrow!

Scheer bit his lip in frustration.

Matthew sighs and then nods: "In Christian charity, I can offer you my help. I am Matthew Hopgood: a merchant of this town.

Scheer smiled enigmatically at the sound of Matthew's name.

"Thank you good sir! My master will be *most* grateful, and shall welcome you with his surest hospitality!"

The Witchfinder looked down at the 'bath' and saw the ancient Aramaic script carved into its lid: his eyes bulged as he read it. "Hold!"

Lattimer's men suddenly move forward with intent, like attack dogs called to attention by their master.

Scheer took alarm and reached for a concealed dagger.

Lattimer moved slowly forward, raising his chin as he looked sideways, and down his nose at Scheer - his eyes reflecting his innate sense of moral superiority - and of power: " Those marks, carved upon the lid?!"

Still holding on to his hidden knife, Scheer tried to bluff his way out: "*Jewish* scribble!" he gestured dismissively "My Master, obtained the bath in Alexandria, in Egypt: where he studied medicine. The words have neither any sense, *or* meaning!

Lattimer smiled enigmatically, and with obvious distrust of Scheer: "My men Abraham Edge... and Jonathan Bradley... *will* assist you."

Scheer's eyes darted about as he weighed up the situation: "Very well..." he said; reluctantly accepting that there was no alternative but to concede. Edge and Bradley walked over to the sarcophagus. Scheer paused in his mentations, then turned away from Lattimer to follow them.

The Witchfinder now addressed the Customs Officer: "Delay our embarkation until the next tide."

"*What?!* But the ship's Master!"

"Will do as I command on my authority from King and Parliament!" spluttered the angry Witchfinder.

The Customs Officer touched his forelock: "As *you* order sir…"

Lattimer turned to his disciple Thomas Partington: "Afore we depart, we'll reconnoitre the town. Methinks we'll be back here *sooner* than we'd have thought!

Partington was intrigued by his master's foresight: "The marks upon the lid, you could read them?!"

"*Ancient* Aramaic!" declared Lattimer "Twas in the name of *Satan's* whore. The Mother of All Demons herself: *Lilith!*"

Out of hearing of the Witchfinder's words, Matthew pursed his lip with determination for the task. Taking hold of the heavy stone base he declared: "Tis a quarter past noon: it'll be heavy work, so let us at once be away with it! On to the apothecary!"

Lilith was helping her mother with domestic chores. She'd already visited the Toxteth Chapel with her parents and had to endure the attention of love-struck Adam Teal on the return journey; restrained only by the presence of *Lilith's* parents. He hoped to meet with her later in the day, away from their prying eyes. For her part, *Lilith* was still chaste in her purity of body; just as would be expected of her until Christian marriage…

However *Lilith* was not contained by her physical form and for some years now in dreams and nocturnal visions she'd already penetrated deeply the mind and soul of her kin and fellow townsfolk. This almost open-secret painted the collective subconscious of the community with a charged eroticism that dare not be spoken of between people. *Lilith* knew of her power, and enjoyed its contrast with her carefree outer persona.

She was playing with those around her: a dangerous game amongst Puritans to be sure, but *Lilith* did not care…

Liverpool Museum: Monday 16th *October 2006, 10.45am*

"She was beautiful in life…" Claudia exchanged a quizzical glance with Adam at the Bavarian's words. Von-Hesse saw the look: "You can tell, from the gracile structure of her bones – the fine symmetry of her skull. Look at the cheek-bones: the zygomatic arch, the curve of the mandible. Surely Dr Moore, your experience can paint flesh onto bones… mine certainly can… I *see* 'her' before me. Look at the pelvis: a classic hour-glass figure. One can only wonder at what beautiful soul animated these bones…"

Claudia was unmoved. To her, bones had scientific interest not an eroticized aestheticism: "Do you believe in such things Max; as an immortal soul?"

Von-Hesse turned his intense black-brown eyes to bear on the senior field archaeologist: "Oh yes… you see, I *know*… it isn't a matter of belief… I know."

Adam thought that this was all nuts: "She was probably some outcast runt who was buried alive fer bein' too ugly!" he joked.

The Bavarian spoke quietly: "Oh… and would you say so to her face Mr Mitchell?"

Adam laughed and picked up the skull. Looking into its empty eye-sockets he said: "You woz probably a little runt who got buried alive fer bein' offensively ugly in a public place… there… OK not exactly Hamlet… but… ha ha ha!"

Claudia thought he'd gone too far: "Adam! Really, that's silly and un-professional, especially in front of a senior academic colleague who's our guest here at the Museum!"

Adam Mitchell blushed: "Sorry Dr Moore… sorry too Dr Von-Hesse."

The Bavarian's black-brown eyes narrowed: "I can forgive ignorance in a child… but will *she*?"

Despite his bravado, Adam felt his spine chill. His hands slackened as he almost dropped the skull.

"Careful!" cried Claudia "Just put it down and start acting appropriately for a Ph.D. student will you Adam!"

Von-Hesse returned the discussion to scientific matters: "Have you estimated the height?"

"The height?" Claudia scanned her memory "Yes… 158 cm approximately, or about 5 feet 4 inches."

"170 cm – which is 5 feet 7 inches actually…" replied the Bavarian.

Claudia furrowed her brow: "What? You're asserting that just by visually assessing a disarticulated skeleton?"

Von-Hesse replied curtly: "You made your estimation on the length of the femur?"

"Yes… that's pretty much standard procedure."

"But not accurate… she was 5 feet seven inches, and only just past twenty-one years of age."

"She was certainly tall for a female of her period; the seventeenth century saw a reduction in average height in Britain, after a peak in the early Middle Ages that was about the same or even greater than now, but… 5 feet 7! The average *male* height was only around five-four or five."

The Bavarian was tiring of his little game: "If you say so Dr Moore… Now, I would like to take a sample of soil with me, say with the skull… as an official scientific request on behalf of my university? They will be returned of course. I am staying over on the Wirral at the home of a family friend: Lake Hall in Oxton. It's near to a very large Tudor period property: 'Hill House'. Such an interesting area, Oxton: our 'specimen' may even have known the family who lived there… at the Tudor House… Communities were so much more united in those times, don't you think

Von Hesse strode purposefully out from the museum entrance: looking neither right nor left – his expression one of utter focus and determination. Halting at the kerbside, a black Mercedes Benz limousine pulled up alongside him. The driver: Hans Meier, immediately got out – a very tall, powerfully built German, with blond hair and dark glasses. Meier opened the rear door to allow his master to enter.

Von Hesse paused and looked closely at his driver: "Meier!"

Meier drew his heels together in 'Germanic' fashion, and then bowed slightly with a nod of his head: "Master!"

"Soon Meier, *soon*, the endless years of waiting will be over!"

Von Hesse climbed in the back on the Mercedes and slowly drew out *Lilith's* skull from beneath his black Abercrombie overcoat. A faint smile washed over his face.

As the car drove silently but speedily away; he spoke with reverence and devotion to the skull; staring deeply into its yawning eye sockets: "The time is nigh for your return: and to bring your *final* vengeance 'gainst the children, of *cursed* Eve!"

The stone bath was very heavy, even separated from its lid, it was a laborious task to lift it safely from the cart and position it for entry into the apothecary. Matthew's generosity was fuelled of course by his curiosity – he wanted to know more of these 'Bavarian's' – after-all men of that country had spared the lives of his family during Prince Rupert's siege. One had even named his daughter; Lilith. To this day, he did not know the identity of that mercenary soldier nor what had motivated him to show mercy, although his religious mind suspected that it was the work of providence. How else to explain not only what had happened but also the mysterious nature of his daughter? Of course; these foreigners were also potential business rivals, so there was much behind Matthew's curiosity.

At last Lattimer's men from the quay-side, together with Matthew and Von-Hesse's assistants: Reich and Scheer managed the bath safely to the ground, ready for the next part of its difficult journey – to the basement. There was another curious local passing-by however, one Henry Teal – elder brother of Ben and now a town Burgess: "Good day to thee Matthew, thou lends assistance kindly to your neighbour!"

Hopgood was breathing hard with his exertions: "Good day Henry, these gentlemen are of Bavaria, and hath set themselves under instruction from their master, a doctor and apothecary – to practice here, in our town."

"Ah… yes, I didst hear of this in chamber at the Town Hall. A doctor and apothecary… that couldst be most helpful. There is great-plague in and about London since April; we wouldst avoid it here if we can!"

Matthew was still catching his breath: "Plague!? Tis the Lord's wrath upon sinners: see how it struck upon Wirral, at Heswall township. Only last year, it came and then went as suddenly as it hadst arisen. Tis my belief that only sinners were taken… Once the Lord's justice hadst been administered, it passed away, and so shalt it be in London."

"Perhaps, Matthew, perhaps: but we are told that it hath spread as a *great* contagion. We must all to our prayers and keep to the path of righteousness!"

Henry nodded to the group and continued on his way.

Having rested, the little party resumed their labours.

From the upstairs accommodation the black-brown eyes narrowed as they beheld Matthew. It had been twenty one years, but they knew him still:

"Soon *Lilith*, soon…"

Lilith was out in Juggler Street Market shopping for fresh meat from the butcher; Simon Longfield. She was amused by Adam who was still following her as a moth to a candle-flame. Old Simon watched with envy as the young-folk flirted. *Lilith* of course, didn't even have to try; her beauty was magnetic in its physical form, but even when absent her *imago* haunted people's minds intruding into their thoughts, and even into their dreams.

Simon was one such victim. Obsessed, he would watch at the window of his home for any sight of her as she may pass by. So enchanted was he, that he couldn't bring himself to have sexual relations with his wife anymore – all he could do was to think, and to dream, of *Lilith*.

He waited anxiously for a middle aged woman - shopping for fresh pork, to pass out from his line of sight so that he could speak to her...

"Good day mistress Hopgood!"

"Good day master Longfield." *Lilith's* Mona-Lisa smile ignited a thrill in Simon's loins. A Puritan, he struggled with his arousal as a bewitchment, or perhaps, as his own sinful lusting – something to be dealt with as a personal battle with his conscience.

"'Tis your father's usual cut of beef?"

Lilith tilted her head and seductively scanned his face with her green-eyes. Her smile opened her dimples and showed the fullness of her generous youthful mouth. Simon's eyes blinked as he was inducted into trance.

"Thank ye master Longfield; that will be all."

Simon let out a gasp as he returned to consciousness, and struggled to focus his attention on the cut of meat - his face fixed in a beatified grin

Young Adam had seen everything. He didn't want to think of his love as being so.... so like a Salome...

On leaving the butchers stall he asked: "*Lilith*, I saw how thy enchantment didst take him! But for the Lord's sake; why?"

"Worry not Adam, tis but a game I play." She turned and smiled her Mona-Lisa smile. His heart, of course, melted: "Oh *Lilith*, I shouldst die a happy man if I couldst see thy smile again."

"Thou wilt see it again, Adam Teal, but ye need not die... as did your namesake... *just* yet."

Adam hurried in front of *Lilith* who was making a fast pace towards home. Bending on one knee he proclaimed: "*Lilith*, my father is in profitable business with William Strongbow of Prenton: over in Wirral — there will be good prospects for me... sayeth thee, couldst thee... become mine betrothed?"

Adam meant it. He was in love with her.

Lilith granted his wish and smiled for him again: "Adam Teal, thou art but three years younger even than I am. Ye shouldst wait a while till ye are at least nineteen. Ye may yet meet some other fair maiden and then thinketh the less for me."

"Never! My love for thee *Lilith* is for the whole of my life and then *forever* afterwards!"

Her green-eyes looked deeply into his soul. "I know ye speak truly, and from thy heart Adam Teal, but ye knoweth not what I am... nor what I am bounded by mine fate to do."

Adam didn't understand. He only understood his love for her: "What meaneth thee I knoweth not, but my love for thee is pure and certain: oh say that ye love me too!"

Lilith's face darkened. She was playful with him, but no one, no one at all, could *ever* demand affection from her: "Adam Teal, I giveth as I fancy and I doest not take command from any, not from the First Adam himself so still less from thee!"

"*First* Adam? What sayeth thee?" Poor young Adam Teal, he had no idea, no idea at all...

Nathaniel Lattimer, had gone with his followers Amos Cain and Thomas Partington, in search of further evidence of the occult in Liverpool town. He'd sent Abraham Edge and Jonathan Bradley – his two 'heavies', to ostensibly assist, the Bavarian Scheer, in taking the 'bath' to the new apothecary in Chapel Street.

But long experience had taught him that there was never any such thing as coincidence where the disciples of Satan were concerned: and so *Lilith's* sarcophagus must be the focus of a nest of witches, and perhaps, also of demons, already infesting the old town.

There was little time: he couldn't delay his passage to Ireland any longer than the next tide – if he wanted to keep the favour, and the protection, of Parliament and the King.

Relying on his uncanny instincts for sniffing out the supernatural, he soon found himself standing at the opposite end of Chapel Street to the Bavarian's apothecary – staring up at a curious, iron-fashioned, 'leaf-head' effigy, above the door of the town's blacksmiths forge.

"What manner of devilry hath wrought this?!" roared Lattimer in righteous indignation: pointing upwards with an accusing finger, at the clearly 'Pagan' image.

Slapping his leather-gloves down into the palm of his left hand, The Witchfinder strode into the forge: hurriedly preceded by Partington and Cain whose wild eyed religious fervour made them scurry like rats before their master.

Inside, 'Williams' the Welsh blacksmith, was labouring busily on his anvil: and despite the deliberate drama of Lattimer's entrance – he seemed not to even notice...

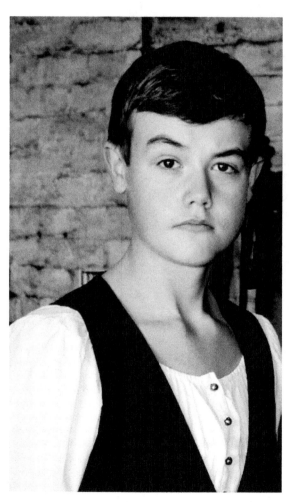

A young boy of about fifteen years: was standing nearby to Williams. The boy stared intently and without fear, straight into the eyes of the Witchfinder, unsettling him with an obvious challenge...

Williams looked up from his anvil and smiled. He was heavily muscled, with tawny, bark-like skin. Eerily he had odd coloured eyes, the right: bright blue, and the left as green as a verdant springtime meadow.

Clearing his throat Lattimer introduced himself: "Ahem... I, am Nathaniel Lattimer, by Royal and Parliamentary warrant, *Witchfinder* General!"

Williams walked slowly out from behind the anvil and smiled again. His gentle Welsh sounding accent belied his powerful physical presence.

"And I, am *no* one important: only as common, and as lowly, as the living *green*, itself...

Lattimer visibly shuddered, but immediately recovered himself: " That 'leaf-head' above your door! Tis a sign of *Pagan* idolatry!"

"Oh? Then how so, that it's found everywhere, in old churches? Growing out, *irresistibly*, from the cold, hard, stone..."

Lattimer's eyes narrowed.

Nathaniel Lattimer

Partington, unable to restrain himself further, interrupted to address the youth: "You boy! Your name and occupation!

"Connor O'Riley: apprentice to Williams, the blacksmith!" replied the youth in a soft, but assertive Irish accent.

"He's Irish!" cried Amos Cain "We've God's work to attend to in Ireland: hanging *witches,* and recusant *Catholic* rebels!"

Williams smiled broadly, and dismissively, then returned to his work on the anvil: but his eerie, green, left eye, looked up, independently of his other – blue eye - in the manner of a chameleon, deeply alarming Partington: "Look, his eye! He is, as a *demon!*"

Lattimer and his men started forwards with clear aggressive intent: Williams stood upright – calmly: but showing his impressive physique to the full. Cain and Partington faltered: but Lattimer walked on through them, to physically confront this 'supernatural' blacksmith.

Connor stepped out in front of the anvil, and between Lattimer and Williams. "'Tis an injury!" he said "When he was a boy, an apprentice, like me: a spark from his master's anvil caught his left eye, turning it green! So, now and again… it fails, or even *moves*, all by itself...

We are newly come to Liverpool" continued Connor "my master, a Welshman: and myself, from Waterford in Ireland."

Lattimer staid his approach: his eyes narrowing again, his expression unsure. Then slowly, he nodded, addressing Williams quietly: "When I return from God's Holy business in Ireland... We *shall* meet again…!

"That..." replied Williams "we will..."

At the Apothecary

Von-Hesse had left the internment of the 'bath' to the curious Matthew Hopgood, his own men Reich and Scheer, and unknowingly, to the disciples of the Witchfinder General; Nathaniel Lattimer. At last installed in place, Scheer had paid Bradley and Edge – generously, as it was his masters' policy to gain favour whenever it seemed profitable to do so. Seeing that Matthew had tarried a while talking with Reich and Scheer, he decided to make himself known: "Good day to you sir; my thanks for your kindly assistance – mine name is Maximilian Von-Hesse: physician, apothecary and alchemist of Bavaria!" His voice was proud, his posture steady and raised. Despite his conservative nature Matthew was taken to smile at such an impressive persona: "Good day, Doctor Von Hesse: twas only Christian manners to offer thy associates my help."

"Nevertheless sir; my thanks. I wouldst like… I wouldst like to offer mine hospitality to thou, and to thy family, to take evening meal with us as mine guests."

Matthew was flattered and didn't see the contrived nature of the invitation: "Thank thee sir; I wouldst be most honoured to accept!"

"Then let it be on the morrow at the sixth hour past noon."

Matthew made his way happily home: unwittingly drawing to a fateful close the circle that had opened twenty-one years earlier.

Liverpool Waterfront: the next high tide.

The Witchfinder paused behind his men as they ascended the gangway to the ship – ready at last to disembark for Ireland.

Turning he looks back at the Customs Officer who is at the foot of the gangway: "Our urgent work in Ireland will be completed swiftly. And then...I *will* be back!

The Customs Officer smiled knowingly and nodded his head.

Lake Hall: Oxton, Wirral; Tuesday 17ᵗʰ October 2006, 3.00pm

Von-Hesse had been allowed to borrow the skull and take a soil sample from the lead box – found inside the sarcophagus.

He could barely hide his elation: not an emotion commonly expected in a sombre German academic but he'd waited a long time for this… He was staying at Lake Hall in Oxton; and just as he had said, it was within reach of a seventeenth century hunting lodge once used by the Stuart Kings: a coincidental fact that he found appropriate.

However far from a detailed archaeological or antiquarian study, he required the samples for other purposes, way beyond the understanding of Claudia Moore and her rather immature doctoral student.

The Bavarian had his own assistants who had arrived some weeks before him. They had secured the property and equipped it appropriately for their common task. It had been convenient that Dr Moore had released the samples – as this forestalled any necessity to take them by other means. Von-Hesse would not have allowed any obstacle to be put in his way. He had a covenant to keep – one that would complete his own power, and release back into the world another far greater elemental force that had been in slumber for centuries.

His makeshift laboratory was a curious mix of the arcane and the very latest in high technology, including infra-red mass spectrometers and extremely powerful hand-built computers with the highest speed broadband and wireless internet connections.

To perform his *alchemical operatio* he would require everything to work just right. The precise chemistry of the soil; the *prima materia* must be in balance– for from this he would fashion the great work – the *magnum opus* of re-animation. Without a fresh and living human host, it would be in her former guise that she arose – it would be… *Lilith*.

Matthew had no inkling that this particular Bavarian was the self-same 'merciful' soldier who had spared his family all those years ago. He hardly looked old enough – in his estimation younger indeed than Matthew himself and by some years too.

Even Martha who had looked in terror into the black-brown eyes on that fateful night knew him not. Only *Lilith* did… and she was saying nothing.

"Welcome to you master Hopgood, and to your lady wife and children."

"Thank you Sir, this be Martha my godly wife, my son, Henry and my daughter is *Lilith*."

"*Lilith?*" Von-Hesse seized the moment with feigned curiosity "such an unusual name…"

"There be a story about that… a countryman of yours didst suggest it. Twas during the past siege of this town by Prince Rupert of The Rhine: a mercenary soldier, one who hadst killed many of our people in needless slaughter, but who didst show mine family mercy, and asked that in remembrance we shouldst name her thus. In my belief: twas providence… God himself had intervened and turned the cruel man's heart to mercy."

"Then she be most special Matthew – to be touched so by the Lord."

Matthew straightened with pride: "I hold her to be so: she is fair of face, and gentle in spirit. I wouldst though make certain that she hath righteous upbringin' in God's name. For I hath seen many men lust after her!"

Von-Hesse nodded to show his understanding: "Tell me… didst this mercenary disclose his name unto thee?"

"Nay… he didst not. If he be alive now, he wouldst be of perhaps two score and seventeen years, by my reckoning."

"Indeed… such a profession as soldiering doth not guarantee for longevity. Perhaps he is now already passed from this life and afore his God for judgement."

"If so, I pray that the Lord hold to account his mercy for mine family, and find it balanced against his sins."

Von-Hesse and his guests partook of the meal, a fine roast. At last Matthew's curiosity got the better of him again: "Ye be an alchemist doctor Von-Hesse? I have heard that many such have been deluded into Satan's service."

"Matthew!" Martha interjected.

"Please… do not be troubled, thy husband meant nought offence – and I taketh none such." Von-Hesse was charming. "Matthew, I am not a follower of your countrymen: John Dee Jonathan Fludd and Thomas Mandrake of the late Queen Bess's reign… My training and allegiance in matters alchemical are to *Christian Rosenkreuz* and through him, to *Hermes Trismigestus* of ancient Hellenic Egypt."

"Ha! I hath heard thus of them… Thomas Mandrake was of these parts for a while – in Oxton Vill indeed, o'er the Mersey on Wirral's far shore: as for Jonathan Fludd… he was a false priest.. and the both of them cursed as sinners in Satan's service! So then… ye be a Rosicrucian and thus follow the *Fama Fraternitatis Rosae Crucis?*"

Von-Hesse lowered his head and closed his eyes in solemn acknowledgement: "Aye that and the *Chymical Wedding.* Yer be well educated upon these matters, Matthew Hopgood. *Christian Rosenkreuz* was mine countryman, and from the Thüringen forest State of *Hesse* which borders Bavaria to the north… Thou canst tell from my family name that mine own origins are actually therein. Bavaria was merely my… residence… afore coming to England, and this town."

"I hath no complaints with Christian foreigners... as mine own dear wife, Martha, be Dutch by her country of birth" But now Matthew was on a roll: "I understand, that the Rosicrucian order, counts diverse influences unto itself – many to be sure are of God's Christian works, but some are of Arabian origination – and also of the Armenian and Turkish nations."

"Some..."

"Aye, and yet others still, spring forth from the Cathar heretics of The Languedoc province in France."

"Some... However, I wouldst have thought that a 'dissenting' Christian, who hath moved away, reformed, from the protestant High-Church in England and who values *conscience* wouldst appreciate the Cathar teachings?"

Matthew had reached his limitations: "Nay, they be devilish and ungodly ideas sir, and not suitable for the ears of a reformed Christian family!"

Martha cast down her table knife: "Matthew Hopgood, how canst thee insult our host so precipitously?"

Von-Hesse, ever magnanimous, moved to appease her: "Please, please, my lady, do not distress yourself: thy husband is merely... expressing his conscience, as is proper. He and all of thy dear family are most welcome as honoured guests here in my house."

Matthew could not bring himself to feel shame. Like many fundamentalists, his manners stopped at the rim of his beliefs.

Across the candlelit table a Mona-Lisa smile communicated its deepest meaning to Von-Hesse.

Lilith had recognized her servant and knew of his purpose...

Maximilian Von Hesse

Imago mortis

3

Plague

Von Hesse's apothecary

artha's embarrassment at her husbands' outburst had not abated several days later. She was a good woman; religious, but with that human warmth that allowed her to accept the basic value of difference in other people. For himself, Von-Hesse had taken no obvious offence and had remained the perfect gentleman for the remainder of the Hopgood family's visit. Matthew however, had found it impossible to step down from his moral high-horse. To do so he felt, would have been to contradict his reformed Christian faith. Young Henry was modelling the Puritan role of *Pater Familiaris* from his father and simply accepted his beliefs. *Lilith*; it seemed, could not have cared less. But, as with everything about *Lilith* what appeared to be the truth, often, was not…

Chapel Street Liverpool: Monday 16ᵗʰ June 1665, 11.00am

Lilith made her breezy way from the family home in Water Street to the apothecary in Chapel Street. The Bavarian, having noted her recognition of him, had wisely decided to allow her the initiative for further contact. Reich and Scheer made way for her as she entered – like the parting waters of the Red Sea. *Lilith's* Mona-Lisa smile broadened in amused appreciation. The sound of heavy footsteps from the basement stairs announced Von-Hesse's ascent. A Coquettish tilt of her head and a flash of her green almond-shaped eyes drew a broad smile from his face: "Mistress!" he exclaimed as he prostrated himself on the floor "I am returned unto thee!"

"Thou hast taken thy time Maximilian… how long hath it been since Genoa?"

Von-Hesse raised his head from the floor, his eyes drifting leftwards as he made his calculation: "That wouldst be…. some years Mistress…"

"Methinks much more that that!"

Von-Hesse had hoped to avoid having to make extensive explanations: "It hath been hard… there was much to be done. I barely escaped with my very life!"

The green-eyes darkened taking an autumnal black-brown hue: "Thy very life is mine Maximilian; it is given up unto my service – that is the reckoning for its 'artificial' prolongation… Tis in my gift to foreclose upon it!"

"Mistress… forgive me, I didst not know if thy reconstitution wouldst be taken successfully… I needed… time to allow thee to grow and mature in thy hosted form."

Lilith tilted her head again: "Tis an agreeable body, her personality was easily shaped… When my powers in this physical form are matured… I wilt… 'shape-shift' according to mine amusement! Thou must maketh all preparations, for I am bored with these people and wouldst fulfil my sworn vengeance 'gainst all who descend from cursed Eve!"

Von-Hesse rose to his knees, but dared not rise fully, just yet: "Mistress, plague already stalketh this land. London is taken greatly with it; one man in five is dead. Soon it will arrive here in this Liverpool town. We canst make use of it for cover, as before in Genoa!"

"Ah… yes, the 'Black Death…' but twas nought black-enough… for I wouldst hath destroyed all!"

Von-Hesse's lip quivered: "With exception Mistress, surely… of thy loyal servant and his followers?"

Lilith smiled her Mona-Lisa smile: "Of course… Rise Maximilian, thy shalt be… safe… from this contagion *and* thy followers too."

The Bavarian thought to dare the final question: "And after… …after all, who descend from cursed Eve, are destroyed, thy promise to me to be as thy *new* Adam?"

Lilith tilted her head – this time backwards in an unmistakeable demonstration of superiority: "Thy wouldst seek the ultimate *chymical wedding*, the *mysterium coniunctionis* with thy Mistress?"

"Mistress, tis only as thou hath promised, and upon which my life's duty is forsworn!"

Her eyes darkened again: "Maketh thee not the mistake of that *first* Adam and demandeth from me, for no man who derived hence from Eden shall be mine equal and n'er my master!

But…I will give upon it due consideration: *if* thou art successful…and true to thine duty…"

Von-Hesse prostrated himself again: "I shalt be Mistress, I shalt!"

Lilith smiled her Mona-Lisa smile. Now she would begin her proper torture of the despised people of the Town and under the guise of the coming Great-Plague release her miasma into the world to bring about the extinction of all humankind…

Mary Smith was with child. Her husband, Joseph was a burgess and minor landowner beyond the common heath towards Allerton. A respectable reformed family they had three children already. Joseph, as an associate of Matthew Hopgood, was one of the many townsmen uncannily influenced by *Lilith's* ethereal beauty. This night, however, her seductive Mona-Lisa smile was to become as the harbinger of death in the Smith family home.

In the seventh month of her confinement, Mary was finding both sleeping and breathing difficult. At three in the morning exhaustion at last took her: yet her shallow breaths soon altered the chemistry of her blood and affected her brain. In a semi-conscious state of sleep-paralysis – her eyes half opened: her muscles unable to move voluntarily– her chest rising and falling as if she were being ventilated by some outside force.

Feeling alarmed she tried to speak, her larynx strained but her lips were still. A strange rushing sound filled her ears as a pale-grey light bathed the bedroom. Transfixed, her alarm turned to dread as the outline of a human form filled her view.

The shapes features were indistinct at first but soon resolved into a Mona-Lisa smile. Naked, the unearthly, womanly form floated over the floor from the widow. The rushing sound penetrated louder and louder, now becoming as a rapid heartbeat – deepening in bass tone until it passed into a terrifying infrasound. The unborn child kicked violently as the spectral outline closed ever nearer. The figures right hand stretched out over Joseph's sleeping body causing it to jerk violently. Mary's eyes strained to look as terror gripped her heart. Edward let out a moan as he involuntarily ejaculated: his semen long withheld through pious abstinence gushed out across his thighs soaking the bed.

Mary's half-closed eyes caught the spectral form as its own penetrating gaze cut through into her very womb – the face… she knew the face of *Lilith*!

Next morning, Matthew was heading by cart towards the Toxteth Chapel when he stopped opposite a weeping and distressed crowd gathered outside the Smith family home.

Hurrying closer concern took his breath – he knew that his friends' wife was with child. In such a close reformed community, every pregnancy was precious, and death was still common for a woman in childbirth. Mary however, had three healthy children already, so Matthew had previously given little thought to any possibility of difficulty: first births were the most often dangerous.

It was a grim faced Henry Teal who met Matthew at the threshold of the Smith house: "Matthew... tis a melancholy thing... the Lord hath taken the soul of Mary and her unborn child. Joseph is sore of heart and I fear without any possibility of consolation!"

"In the night?"

"Aye, old Mistress Penny attended upon them, but poor Mary bled until life and soul left her mortal body. The child couldst not be saved."

Mistress Penny was now in her eighties... old beyond the expectations of her times. Near blind she was still much sought after for her many decades of midwifery experience, yet even this had not been enough to save mother and child.

Joseph was a shattered man, but the wise-woman of the town had senses keen enough to recognize the work of an unnatural intelligence in this tragedy. Joseph's pain was heightened by a feeling of guilt, for as his wife had commenced the agony of her death – and that of their unborn son – he had been in a state of enslaved rapture to the visionary dream of *Lilith*...

He hadn't spoken of it, he didn't have to. It left its trace on the bedclothes; his body milked of its semen until he had nearly died himself. Mistress Penny knew – the mark of the *Succubus*.

The wise old one sought Matthew out: "Master Hopgood… good day to thee – though it be not good, still we must acknowledge the Lord's bounty for giving us the blessing of life each new day!"

Matthew was inducted out from his horrified trance and into the everyday pleasantries of pious superstition: "Yea, in that we must trust, Mistress Penny – praise be to God's name, even so that he hath taken mother and child unto him in heaven for eternal life in the bosom of Christ."

"Aye…" The wise-one nodded, to put a full stop on the piety and get down to making her point: "But this… be *not* the will of God Matthew Hopgood."

 "What? What sayeth thee!"

"It be the mark of Satan, or of his demons!"

 "How woman, how canst thou say such?"

"I attended unto the marriage bed, and saw that which hath happened. On my soul I saw with mine wasted eyes, smelt with my failing nose and touched with my withered hand. Poor Joseph and Mary had a visitation… from a *Succubus*! Twas her who hath taken the mother and child – pray Matthew Hopgood for God's mercy and his recovery of their souls!"

Matthews face was a map of incredulity.

"Aye and pray ye that no more are taken, for once a visitation is made then more shalt surely follow!"

Matthew stared at the ancient face, its old eyes dimmed by cataracts. A movement through the crowd on his left caught his attention. Henry Teal addressed it: "I fear thou art too late doctor, the Lord hath taken them both – mother and child…"

Von-Hesse had been summoned by neighbours. As the only medical practitioner currently in residence – he had been called upon to assist, but only *after* Mistress Penny. Old beliefs and reliance's die hard – even in fundamentalist communities.

Von-Hesse halted and nodded slowly: the black-brown eyes peering intently from beneath his furrowed brow. Quietly, Mistress Penny shuffled past Henry Teal and beheld the Bavarian: "I knowest thee... yea I have beheld thee afore... these many years past..."

Matthew had followed Mistress Penny and was watching and listening intently.

"Nay old-woman, I am a recent visitor and newer resident of this town, but I humbly offer my medical services to the good people here."

"Thou be an alchemist too I am told?"

"I be so yes."

"Then... thou knowest of the mysteries... herein was the work of the *Succubus*!"

"Such... superstitions are not part of mine profession nor of mine calling" responded The Bavarian dismissively.

"Superstitions sayeth thee? Mark me – medical man, there will be more... and there be witchcraft behind all of this!"

Von-Hesse had tired of the old woman. Bowing his head slightly in the polite continental fashion he moved on. Mistress Penny however had not finished. Turning to Matthew she said: "Master Hopgood – thou hath met that man – these twenty-one years past."

"What?"

"Mine eyes are the poorest of mine senses, but I knoweth his voice, and he hath a distinct odour – ye may knoweth people by their scent Matthew Hopgood – his is unlike any other. Twas he who was at thy child *Lilith*'s birth, *he* is The Bavarian!"

This was too much for Matthew. He was certain now that the old-one's mind had gone: "Woman – all this talk of Satan, of

Succubae and of doctor Von-Hesse – tis all fancy, how couldst he be that Bavarian? He art too young in years! Be away now afore ye create even more mischief!"

Mistress Penny cussed and spat on the ground between his feet: "Mark me, Matthew Hopgood, thou wilt regret thine haste in such misunderstanding! He *is* that Bavarian, I saw him better than any – better even than Martha in her labours and even thou in thy pathetic state of unconsciousness! He hath returnered. Ye must ask for what purpose? None by the will of God, that much is certain! Beware Matthew Hopgood, beware!"

"Away woman, tis ye who art the only Witch in this town!"

Mistress penny shuffled away. She had tried her best…

Lilith was radiant – her smile more lovely than ever. Young Adam had followed her on foot to the chapel and again by return route he clung to her every step: "*Lilith*, the very flowers make way for thee and bow afore thy beauty!"

"Adam Teal, how canst thou talk of such things – today we shouldst be in mourning for poor Mary Smith and her child! Didst ye not pray for them at the Chapel?"

"I didst, *Lilith,* but surely God wouldst want us to continue with our lives and celebrate his bounty? They are safe within Christ's bosom and shalt have life everlasting!"

"And thou wouldst see me with thine own child wouldst thou not, Adam Teal?"

The directness of *Lilith's* question stunned the lovelorn youth – but only for a moment: "Verily, I wouldst, for that wouldst mean that we are as man and wife!"

"I see Adam Teal... so if I were as Eve, then you wouldst be as *my* Adam in Eden?"

"Oh say ye so, say ye so *Lilith*!" he fawned.

"Then, I must offer thee an apple…. from the Tree of Knowledge…"

Adam felt a twinge of anxiety in his stomach: "But that was a *temptation* from Satan…"

"How knowest thee that, wast thou then present in Eden?"

"Nay! Tis scripture! *All* Christians' know that."

"Then what doth thou say to this?" *Lilith* produced an apple from her sleeve – a fresh mature apple; in the month of June.

"How? Tis not season for apple harvest?"

"Ask not Adam Teal, but take from me as your chosen Eve!"

Adam couldn't comprehend, so he thought it to be a joke: "Nay thou art playing a jest upon me *Lilith*!"

Lilith was playing with him – it amused her that he was so naïve in his love for her: "When judgement hath been accorded then shalt there be a *new* Adam – a new Adam Kadmon – who shalt father all of humankind henceforward... from mine womb... and I will know him by his heartbeat..."

"*Lilith*... that be damnable heresy!"

"Doest thou not love me then Adam Teal?"

"Verily I do!"

"Wouldst thou not want to fertilize me as seed in my soil?"

Adam was torn between fear of scripture and an intense desire to sow his wild oats in *Lilith's* 'soil': "But..."

"Am I not fertile? Are not my hips broad for childbearing, is not my waist as slender as an autumn wasp; are not my breasts…"

"*Lilith* stop! Thy words enchant and excite me to passion!"

"Then have a care Adam Teal, for another yet may claim me – though, none mayest *ever* master me!"

Adam fell to his knees as *Lilith* ran laughing through the fields before him, her hair filled with flowers. She seemed as fertile as nature herself – how could the poor youth understand that she dealt death and destruction as easily as she breathed…

Von-Hesse had turned his attention to his alchemical preparations. For *Lilith's* power to be fully actualised certain occult rituals and operations had to be performed. He also had to safeguard himself. Many alchemists had authored their own destruction not only through improper chemistry of a physical kind, but also by mixing the wrong *psychic* elements.

The Great Plague, he knew, would soon be here. Unlike the reformed Puritan populace and their fellow Christian townsfolk – the Catholics and Anglicans – he knew that the contagion was a physical disease. Vaccination had recently been developed by the Ottoman Turks of Anatolia – specifically against smallpox. The Chinese too had for much longer, inoculated against smallpox by using the dried and powdered pox scabs. They had not developed it against Bubonic Plague, but Von-Hesse had in his artificially long-life determined that the principles could – with careful preparation, be applied to that disease: so he'd experimented using the dried and powdered black scab of the plague's distinctive bubo lesions.

When, the plague arrived in Liverpool, there would be the usual pious rush to religious sanctuary, thence to superstition and finally, and reluctantly, to medicine. Von-Hesse's services

would be in great demand. He had however, no intention of introducing his 'inoculation' method to the populace – that would be wasteful of his time and contrary to his purpose.

The miasmic contagion that arose from *Lilith* under cover of The Great Bubonic Plague would be incurable… even for him.

Lilith had enjoyed her exercise of power. Hitherto, it had been mere enchantment – and the stimulation of fantasy in men and women alike. Now that Von-Hesse had returned to her, and brought with him his skill and experience – she could extend that power to take human souls, just as she had with Mary Smith and her unborn son: "It amuseth me Maximilian, that the parents be called Joseph and Mary – and that I hath destroyed not only Mary but also her unborn child son: ha ha ha!"

Joseph too will die. Already his fertility hath been drained away – he couldst father no more, even if he liveth further – which he shalt not."

"Mistress… have a care… these people are superstitious and find witchcraft in all that they cannot understand. Thy power is not yet fully articulated unto thy will. If they taketh thee they couldst do thou unto death in that body!"

Lilith laughed: "It wouldst be only as sleep, I cannot be done to any true death by them or their superstition… If such did come to pass, Maximilian, then thou shouldst reanimate me as spirit within flesh – for without me, thou shalt *not* hath thy reward…

And… for your consideration, if ye fail me to mine purpose, I wilt condemn thee to eternal torment, for such *is* within my power, even now!"

"Mistress, I hath sworn not to fail thee, and fail thee I shalt not!"

"Good!" *Lilith* smiled her Mona-Lisa smile "For I will hath more sport with these people, and corrupt them in their morals; through which diverse means shalt I torture their very souls!"

Toxteth Park, outside the Liverpool town walls

Forlorn and love-sick: young Adam Teal had wandered off, over the Liver-brown pool, across the common heath and into the ancient Toxteth Park; once a reserve for deer hunting, and now largely common land: with parts, these days, claimed by local farmers as their very own. The lanes and bye-ways that led to Toxteth Chapel, where both he and *Lilith's* family worshipped: led him at first in the hope of seeing her; and then – through the magical fantasies of youth, astray and into the un-trodden, wooded greenery. Leaning against an oak tree, he sighed long and deep, as if his very soul had, on its outbreath, taken sojourn in this golden sun-dappled dale …

"Adam…"

Adam's spine tingled: as the whispered voice seemed to come forward, and from all around him.

"Adam…" it said again.

"Who's there?!" The youth responded in tremulous voice.

"Adam… In Eden's green: *temptation* came… The fate of the world *will* be: in *your* hands again…"

"Who's there?! Show thyself!" Adam's fear broke his voice.

From behind him, a shape moved in the bark of the tree, knotted and gnarled, at first and then, definite in its human shape. All green he was, garlanded with a crown of vines and berries, his vestments rich and verdant, a knotted vine-staff for a wand in his right hand. But Adam, saw him not…

"A *last* temptation… Adam…"

"What… what doth thou mean, who art thou?! I canst not see thee: thou art just a voice!"

"You see *only* your love… for her."

"*Lilith!*" gasped Adam. "You must be *Satan!* Yer be trying thus to tempt me *away* from her!"

"The future casts its shadow backwards… The souls of those damned never to live: cry like everlasting rain, in plea to a love-struck youth… Such a burden you unknowingly bear…"

"You're *not* real! Yer be a phatasm: *Lilith… Lilith* my love!"

"The fate of the world Adam: will be decided… in *your* heart…"

Overwhelmed by his 'hallucination' – Adam shook his head in denial, and ran away as fast as he could, back to old Liverpool Town: to find her; the unrequitted love of his life…

As softly as a summer's breeze, the tree claimed back its spirit.

The burgesses' and wealthy merchants had met at the Town Hall to discuss the encroaching plague. Thus far it had not appeared north of Worcester and hopes were high that it would burn itself out, as it had at Coventry nearly thirty years earlier. Matthew Hopgood was present, unwittingly drawing the guilty subconscious fantasies of the men-folk towards his ever more attractive daughter. Indeed since her attack on Mary and Joseph Smith, she had already penetrated into many of their dreams causing nocturnal ejaculations – and draining them both of semen and life-sustaining vitality. Thus weakened they were to become prime targets for the coming contagion...

But outwardly more worrying was the recent and concentrated spate of deaths amongst women: either in their labour or sufficiently progressed in their pregnancy that a miscarriage was inevitably life-threatening.

"It hath been only over a few weeks, but... for so many to die, and at divers stages of confinement...I am certain that it be more than half of a dozen. I canst remember not such a concentration of tragedy. It seemeth in my darkest meditations – to be as a punishment from God himself!"

Henry Teal was one of the most zealous of Puritan burgesses. He too had been visited by *Lilith* in his dreams, and was tormented by the hypnotic beauty of the merest sight of her as she walked by through the town. But as yet, if any man had connected their nocturnal enslavement with the death of the town's womenfolk, none were speaking of it openly. Thus, did their repression weaken them and make them the easy victims of *Lilith*...

Robert Pym thought that a medical answer should be sought: "Gentlemen... we must not submit to fear and superstition in this matter, we shouldst seek of course the guidance of providence and of scripture... but so too of science and medicine! We hath a fine physician and apothecary in the town: Doctor Von-Hesse; shouldst we not summon him unto council and engage his services for the protection of our womenfolk and unborn children?"

There was a general murmur of approval – and but one lone dissenting voice: "Brethren of our Town of Liverpool... this man be a foreigner; aye, not in itself a matter for suspicion, but he doth practice alchemy after the fashion of that noted heretic Christian Rosenkreuz!"

"Heretic sayeth thee? It be true that such practices are not wholly within scripture, but, a *heretic*?"

"Aye, heresy I say!"

"But Doctor Von-Hesse is a skilled practitioner of medicine and an accomplished and well provisioned apothecary... we wouldst hath need of him if the contagion reaches Liverpool!"

"We hath need *only* of scripture, and of Providence! Plague comes as punishment from God for *sin*!"

Matthew's fundamentalism was dangerous: to contradict it in the mountingly febrile atmosphere of fear would invite suspicion. Defending a 'heretic' often led to further charges of heresy or even witchcraft, and although the worst years of persecution were over, areas dominated by the Puritans could still easily be agitated into extremism.

Henry Teal – arch fundamentalist, could only agree: "Matthew Hopgood is a righteous and good living man. He hath spoken well… Tis only to scripture that we must look! If this doctor canst help – then so be it, but only under direction of God's word and God's laws. This 'alchemy' be Satan's cover for witchcraft and demonology, just as it was in the reign of the late Queen Elizabeth Tudor!"

Matthew drew an inevitable conclusion: "Aye, as in memory still held in Wirral of that sorcerer Thomas Mandrake and the heretic priest Jonathan Fludd! Methinks that this 'alchemist' hath to do with the deaths of our good womenfolk!"

Robert Pym was becoming increasingly horrified. Although a Puritan, he was nevertheless representative of the more rational end of the spectrum. Despite his fear of fundamentalism he asked with incredulity: "What, how, sayeth thee?!"

Matthew was firebrand: "Didst this evil affliction not occur till after his arrival in Liverpool? Is that not significant? Didst he not arriveth late to Mary Smiths attendance and that after she hath already been dead?"

"He maketh good point Robert!" Henry Teal could be relied upon in all matters fundamental to his faith.

"Gentlemen! Let us be rational and use our reason and conscience as God hath endowed upon us! Shalt we be given over to superstition?"

Matthew pursed his lip: "What proof requireth ye Robert: perhaps yet *more* deaths?"

Before he could reply William Hutchinson, a carpenter, came unannounced into the Council Chamber: "Good burgesses!

Joseph Smith hath been found dead in his bed. He seemeth to have been afflicted by witchcraft!"

The burgesses had assembled at Joseph Smith's home. Also present was Mistress Penny, summoned by the commotion in the street: "See he hath been drained from his loins!" exclaimed Hutchinson "Tis the devils work!"

Matthew stared in horror at the corpse. No sign of violence, or even plague; only the unmistakeable residue of an 'emission': "Mistress Penny: what sayeth thou of this?"

"As I have told thee... tis the mark of a *succubus*: a female demon who feasts upon human lust and their very souls as a vampire doth upon human blood... First she hath taken the unborn boy child of Mary, causing her death also, and then she hath returnered and likewise taken Joseph!"

Robert Pym asked a question: "A female ye say, not a male?"

"Aye, a female, but... *she* hath ability from Satan to become *incubus* – in the male shape and taketh women too, either for their soul or for impregnation with demonic semen, thereby to sire demons amongst God fearing families!"

Robert Pym would have none of it: "Woman; that is irrational superstition! Joseph was in grief of bereavement – he likely died of a broken heart, not witchcraft!"

"Ha! Mark me, Robert Pym, the *succubus* wilt claim more souls from Liverpool town, aye perhaps even thy very own, and that of thine family!"

Henry Teal interjected: "Mistress Penny, how shalt we defeat this demon?"

"Yer first must identify her!"

"How: how shalt we accomplish this, is it by a mark upon her, the mark of Satan?"

The old woman laughed: "Ha! she doth dwell amongst us, and be known to us all! Search thy mind and conscience: recall thy dreams and enchantments… there, there shall ye find her, but hath a care, for she shalt hath the power of a *changeling* a shape-shifter, to appear thus in that most seductive form according to the individual weaknesses of her victims!"

Von-Hesse was gravely concerned: "Mistress! Thy sorties hath caused suspicion to grow amongst the town's elders and burgesses. Already they whisper against mine practice as Alchemist, and doth seek a woman or girl as being host to a demon!"

Lilith merely smiled her Mona-Lisa smile: "Then we must maketh haste and release our miasma: for then shalt they fall as winnowed leaves in autumn: ha ha ha!"

"But Mistress… our preparations be not ready yet! I beg thee; let us wait a while, until the Great Plague arriveth here in Liverpool: that will take suspicion otherwise than upon us…" *Lilith* tilted her head as a coquet: "Then thy must apply care to maketh your decision correctly Maximilian, otherwise…"

Mistress Penny was at her table taking a lonely afternoon meal. Her sight was so faded now that everyday life was less a task than an unendurable chore. Only fear of an uncertain afterlife kept her will to live. She had embodied the 'old-ways' for Liverpool town these past three score and more years, and had survived pestilence, civil war, and persecution: she'd also delivered almost all the surviving population of the town. Her skills in midwifery and in some herbal medicines and tinctures, had allowed her to outlast the ebb and flow of religious zealotry – she had simply been too useful to do without…

Now that she was old and her faculties fading, she realized that her usefulness was waning. It was in self-interest that she'd sought to forestall any blame on her own person by suggesting the activity of a *succubus* demon – that, and her very real intuitions about the Bavarian; Von-Hesse.

All that remained was to urgently identify the female host...

The door to her little house opened. Not silently, not nosily but certainly brazenly: "Who be that?" The silence caused fear in her old belly. The foot-fall was familiar: "*Lilith*? Be that thou?"

The footsteps stopped by her table. The strong summer sunlight cast a glare over her cataract smitten eyes, but her sense of smell found its mark:

"*Lilith* I know thy scent, I smelt it thus as ye were born into my hands... *Lilith* It *is* you... as cursed as thy namesake 'Mother of all Demons, the cast-out first wife of Adam from Eden!"

The old one couldn't see the Mona-Lisa smile, the coquettish tilt of the head, the almond shaped, autumnal green-eyes.

The fear in her belly subsided as a resignation set in to her old heart.

The shadow of *Lilith's* hand passed across Mistress Penny's face. ..

"Plague, Plague!" The cry of alarm spread from man to woman to child. The town crier wrung his bell furiously by the High Cross as the burgesses anxiously gathered at the Town Hall: "Where?" asked Matthew of Henry Teal.

"Tis Mistress Prentice, found dead this morning at her dinner table, sorely swollen with bursted black buboes!"

Robert Pym caught his breath as something occurred: "Wait... that suggesteth the latter part of the progress, not a sudden death!"

"What say thee?"

"Simply that plague doest not take life so precipitously... tis three maybe five days of illness. The bubo's erupt at the end of that time!

"Nay! Clearly tis The Great Plague, it hath arrived here from Chester which is betaken with it already!" Henry Teal would have none of it "Instruct the carpenter William Hutchinson to lock the house and marketh it as plague!"

Robert tried reason: "Sir I pray let us be rational 'bout this! We hath no certain knowledge that it be plague other than appearance of the body! Surely... a medical examination..."

"From the Bavarian?"

"Of course!"

"I trust him not!"

"Then *I* shalt instruct him to make examination!" Pym had had enough of what he saw as superstition.

"So be it, but beware Robert Pym, if ye show signs and symptoms then ye shall be boarded up within thy house and kept therein, aye and thy family all, as in quarantine!"

Von-Hesse was waiting. Either his mistresses action would bring a plea for help, or, damnation and persecution. As an experienced soldier he was ready for violence. Several loaded pistols waited, hidden under a black cloth.

Reich and Scheer were similarly armed and all had makeshift grenades made from potted and fused gunpowder. The citizens would have a fight on their hands.

"Sir, a man approacheth, methinks tis the burgess Robert Pym!"

Von-Hesse peered through the small leaded glass window: "Aye it be him… let him pass, he is a reasonable man."

Pym knocked loudly on the front door, starring agitatedly about him up and down the Chapel Street.

Von-Hesse opened the door in welcome: "Robert Pym! Welcome sir, what mayest I do for thee?"

"Doctor… tis good, excuseth me the formalities of the day, but we hath had a death, feared to be of plague."

"Verily, I heard the cries."

"Then why hast thou not attended?"

"I am aware sir, of certain prejudices and false condemnations against me and my professional practices. I thought it best to await any request for assistance."

"I am ashamed sir to confirm the truth of your words, but tis not unanimous in the Town Council, or in the populace! Just a few otherwise good men turned through fear unto superstition. If ye canst help us, that wouldst be good work in the eyes of God!"

Von-Hesse feigned ignorance: "Who was the victim?"

"Mistress Penny, old in age as she was; the report is of bursted black buboes and yet in fine health was she only yesterday morning. I am not a man of science or medicine, but I knoweth that the plague taketh three or five days of sickness afore such an ending. I am of a mind that this be a different affliction."

"It may be different, but a contagion nevertheless. So then... you wish that I make examination?"

"By God's will yes!"

"The body lieth wherein?"

"At the place of discovery... we must be quick afore it is removed away and the house boarded."

"Verily... Reich, Scheer... accompany me in mine task!"

Lilith had of course heard the commotion. She was at home with her mother and brother Henry: "*Lilith*, stay indoors! The contagion may strike upon us!"

"Mother! Hath no such silly fears, for I am safe, and so... art thou."

"*Lilith* wait!"

But *Lilith* did not wait. She *never* did anything unless it was agreeable to her, and it was not agreeable this summers' morning to be confined indoors.

Breezing along with her Mona-Lisa smile radiant, she passed by the butcher Simon Longfield. He'd been to the High Cross and was making his way to the tavern in Dale Street. Wine would drown his fears he thought. The bright sunlight was in *Lilith's* eyes, she raised her hand as if to shield them, causing a shadow to fall across his face...

Von-Hesse examined the blackened body. Buboes had erupted to burst in her neck, armpits and groin. Her fingers where black too with gangrene spreading back from their tips: "She hath the rigor mortis, and hath been dead perhaps for one day. The buboes are consistent with plague, as is the passage of blood copiously from her orifices and blackening of the extremities: yet, the progression of the disease by time is *not* consistent with plague, just as ye hath said."

"Then thinketh ye what?

"That this be a contagion of some unknown origination… perhaps borne by foul air… a *miasma*."

"Yet plague is so carried by miasma!"

"It is…"

"Some will believe tis demonic intervention and taketh a scapegoat!"

Von-Hesse was feeling backed into a corner. *Lilith's* carefree death-dealing risked being too early. In his opinion, they should wait until the Great-Plague struck and then finish everyone off with her occult miasma. They could then safely move about spreading the contagion until all humankind was destroyed. *Lilith's* powers were as yet too weak to ensure her success. She would be vulnerable until he, Von-Hesse, had finished all stages of the alchemical *operatio*. He had to manipulate Pym as his unwitting ally: "For now, giveth advice unto all to stay indoors as much as be possible, and move only in company of one-another, even unto chapel"

"In company sayeth thee? Why so?"

Von-Hesse hesitated. The truth was he was hoping to slow down *Lilith's* purge until she was at her fullest strength: "Er… to maketh sure that shouldst anyone be taken with sickness… then assistance is at hand. Unless any more deaths occur, this shouldst be well enough… I wilt return to my apothecary and prepare poultices and other such preparations."

He was about to leave when the news of the second death was delivered…

"Master Pym, sir! Another is struck down, as by thunder!"

"Who boy!"

The youth was breathless with running: "I am sent hither by Henry Teal... he sayeth that in the tavern at Dale street – Simon Longfield collapsed and died instantly – and shewn terrible black coloured buboes with blood pourin' from his nose and ears!"

"What!?"

Von-Hesse closed his eyes. *Lilith* would not listen to reason.

"Good doctor, come hither to the tavern, we must make investigation!"

At The Blacksmiths

Lilith stopped in her journey, by the doorway: and stared up at the wrought-iron 'Green Man' image above the door. Tilting her head to one side with curiosity, she smiled and entered the forge.

Silently, as if a spectral apparition, she approached the anvil: where Connor O'Riley stood working, with his back to her. Suddenly, his spine tingled in warning: turning to behold her, he gasped out aloud in shock.

Lilith's face took on a faint, but clear, malevolence: her eyes fixing young Connor as a predator to its prey.

He stumbled away from her: his back against the anvil; his face writ with fear, his eyes wide and staring. Then, just as she was about to pass her hand over his terrified eyes, the Blacksmith appeared, to stand with the anvil between himself and Lilith: placing his right arm protectively across Connor's chest

Lilith smiled her 'Mona Lisa' smile as she looked deeply into the Blacksmith's eerie, odd coloured eyes. With a coquettish tilt of her head, she walked slowly from one side to the other, keeping her gaze fixed closely on Williams: "You're *too* late!" she said at last "My contagion will soon *rid* the world of humankind! *Every* living thing upon the Earth will die! Then, I'll start again, in a *new* Garden of Eden, with my *chosen,* new Adam!"

The Blacksmith shook his head slowly: "Winter, even the *wasteland* that you'll bring, is only an *interval,* between Springtimes."

Lilith smiled malevolently and went to move towards Connor.

Suddenly, the Blacksmith's hand sprouted green leaves and vines from its fingers: his skin turning into a tawny, knotted bark. The leaves and vines wrapped protectively around Connor. "*This* boy, will *live!* His descendants, just as all of his ancestors before him: *will* stand firm against you; and *all* of your kind!   Have *no* doubt..."

"Hmmm… green" mused *Lilith* "Green, is what grows, in the soil… But I am that soil, oh *Viridios* – or 'Green Man' as you are known. You forget, that I am the very Earth itself! What *grows* in the Earth, can be *destroyed* by the Earth! *You,* should have *no* doubt, about *that!*" Laughing, mockingly, she turned and sauntered away.

The Blacksmith's green coloured left eye followed her as she left, his tawny bark face betraying neither thought, nor emotion…

Lilith now made her way over to Henry Teal's house at Old Hall Street. Pausing by the window she looked to see if she could catch sight of him. He wasn't there; he was of course at the scene of Simon's death in Dale Street. Adam Teal however, *was* at home…

"*Lilith!* Hast thou come to call upon me?"

"Adam Teal… shall my shadow fall upon thee?" Her Mona-Lisa smile eclipsed her evil as the moon to the sun.

"Oh sweet love, thy shadow wouldst cool me greatly on this hot day!"

Lilith smiled as she mused how nothing is so cool as a corpse.

"*Lilith!*" Matthew had found his precious daughter "*Lilith,* get thee home my child! There is plague abroad in the town, people fall dead with sudden collapse!"

The coquettish tilt of her beautiful face and her lovely Mona-Lisa smile beheld Adam: "Next time then, perhaps, oh 'Adam' Teal?"

"I shalt wait for thee my love!"

"Get thee inside thy *own* good home Adam!" said Matthew sternly. He was aware of the lads' foppish love for his daughter, but didn't consider him yet mature or settled enough for a betrothal. In time perhaps, as Henry Teal's star was in the ascendant – especially since his recent business with the ancient Strongbow family of Prenton, who had interests both in the army, in profitable farming: and abroad in the Americas.

Lilith breezed her carefree way home singing to herself as all around her the town panicked in mortal fear.

"Tis the same Matthew" said Robert, scrutinizing the corpse.

Hopgood turned his caustic eye upon Von-Hesse: "And what sir are ye to make of this? Is it a poison perhaps?"

"Poison: how say thee?" queried The Bavarian quietly.

"If it canst not be contagion, and yet have all appearances of it then it must be by the noxious administration of a substance... A poison – perhaps one such as could be easily prepared in *thy* very own alchemist's laboratory!"

"Matthew! Have a care sir! The good doctor was in mine very presence when Simon didst collapse. We were attending at Mistress Penny's corpse making due investigation and preparedness for the protection of our citizens! How canst thou make such accusation unless it be from some spite within ye?"

"Spite sayeth thou?"

"Aye sir, *spite,* and a common hatred for no Godly purpose!"

Von-Hesse thought that magnanimity would be a good political gambit: "I thank ye sir, good and gentle burgess. I consider not any spite from Master Hopgood, only that he speaks in fear and that his Christian ethic hath not yet understood my purpose. Matthew, many are the great works of alchemists in support of God, and mine are but humble and simple but *Christian* nevertheless. Was not the late Protector Cromwell tolerant of all Christian faiths under God?"

Von-Hesse had hit a contentious nerve. Under Cromwell there had indeed been tolerance of all *Christian* faiths and practices, even if Puritanism had been on the ascendant. Since the Restoration, the reformed churches had lost their political power base. A reminder of the past was bitter-sweet. To speak for the Protector now could also be construed as treasonable, and yet, it also supported reformed Christian Puritanism.

Matthew shifted as he mumbled: "That be true... Yet we have a Restored Monarchy now, and to think of those times past favourably canst be considered as a treason... nevertheless..."

"Nevertheless Matthew in times of crisis for Liverpool we must set aside prejudice and work together for the common good! Let us then set to our immediate task, and solve this mystery together!"

There were no more deaths that day, or over the next week and the nearly five thousand resident souls of Liverpool began to relax. Shocking as the mortality of Simon Longfield, Mistress Penny and Mary and Joseph Smith were; sudden death was not in itself unfamiliar to the times. Superstition and pious faith in providence conspired to dull reason. A few amongst the town's population, including Robert Pym, urged proper cautionary measures including the checking of ships tying up at the quay and of itinerant traders entering by the roads.

But The Great Plague had already struck at Chester – most likely carried by the trade traffic along the road from London: it would now only be a matter of time, perhaps even only of days, afore it reached the streets of old Liverpool Town...

Lilith had at last escaped her observed confinement and wandered about and abroad again, this time to the apothecary: "Maximilian! How art thou this day?"

"Mistress! I beg thee please keep thyself unto restraint! We need some more time yet to prepare the mixture from thy blood soil. I must be careful… to use it unwisely wouldst be the ruin of it. It is more precious by weight than any gold!"

Von-Hesse was right. *Lilith's* power did ultimately derive from her 'blood-soil' that from which she had been first created.

"Tis a long way from this remote and uncivilized town, is it not Maximilian?" she mused, recollecting her place of 'origin'.

"Mistress… such a return journey wouldst be perilous in the extreme, and the alchemical refinements necessary wouldst take some great time to distil from the raw state of the *prima materia* of thy blood-soil… Of course, the precise place is largely forgotten except in the 'Book' and there are given only clues and not directions for its location."

Lilith smiled her Mona-Lisa smile: "Ah yes…and in the book of Genesis too… Tis written in many faiths now, and in languages from Aramaic, Arabic, Hebrew, Greek, Latin and those all of cultured Europe… yet, none hath found it in its physical form… within the *true* and 'first' Garden of Eden!"

Von-Hesse sighed. He did not want things to go wrong a second time. He valued his long and indefinitely extended life, received in grace and favour from *Lilith* in her last incarnation; but his ambition craved a far greater prize: that to be the new Adam: *Adam Kadmon* the father of the future race of humankind and immortal consort of his mistress.

However, if there were to be a similar problem; to that which had occurred in Genoa in Italy, during the year of 1348, then he may be left wandering the wide-world yet again for centuries more until he could recover her and revive her…

Worse still, he may even perish. His natural life had been artificially extended, but he was still – for now, flesh and blood and as vulnerable to trauma and to infectious disease as any other man. The long years had seen his life imperilled many times. For the sake of patience now he did not want to have to wait so long again.

Lilith read him easily: "Maximilian… thy 'adopted' family of Von-Hesse knoweth not thy true origination. Other than me: there art none alive that know of it properly: not even Reich and Scheer. They follow you on condition that they gain much wealth and great occult powers.

Thou hath sworn faithfully unto me to serve me all thine life howsoever long, or short, shall be thy years. Tis *you* who must be patient! If I have a care to, I couldst destroy even thy very soul for such kind as *you* canst I find again: and with ease!

Thy crave much Maximilian! Serve me, and thou shalt be rewarded, as my promise unto thee… But darest thou to question upon me and I shalt smite thee utterly unto oblivion!"

Von-Hesse's heart chilled. He knew that she would do just that if the fancy took her – and all with that Mona-Lisa smile…

Liverpool: Monday 23rd July 1665, 10.30 am

On this fateful day the Great Bubonic Plague arrived in Liverpool. A man had travelled from the south of Wirral to escape the boarding-up of his already infected family and had reached the old ferry at Birkenhead. Unchecked, he was carried across to the quay-side at Water Street – his clothing infested with plague carrying fleas. He got as far as Juggler Street before he collapsed. John Heron, a parish constable of Walton and Liverpool attended to him and became the town's first victim of 'natural' Great Plague.

4

The Witchfinder

anic set in. Poor John Heron was shut-up in his home with his family and himself died of the plague five days later. It was of course too late to save Liverpool. By the time that the cause of the travellers collapse had been understood, the contagion had leapt via the flea infested clothing onto several other townsfolk.

Von-Hesse was called upon to help by a desperate Robert Pym. He made a cursory effort at assistance, but did nothing that would have actually helped. He wanted the contagion to set in, for then *Lilith* could begin her proper work of extermination without suspicion.

For herself, *Lilith* was breezy and carefree, even elated in mood. This chilled her father; Matthew as for the first time his eyes beheld in her something malevolently unnatural.

In her excitement *Lilith's* nocturnal adventures intensified. Her Succubus form drained energy from its victims, energy she needed to maintain her life in this host body. This combined with her uncanny enchantment and the presence in the town of the plague conspired men to move against her.

Nathaniel Lattimer was a Lancashire man by birth. His father had been involved in the persecution of the Pendle Witches fifty years before. Under such influence he had developed a most zealous reformed fundamentalism and found his way to become apprenticed to the notorious Matthew Hopkins – the last *Witchfinder General.*

Hopkins had been given rein in the south and east of England during the Commonwealth period and his systematic approach had seen the end of many accused of sorcery, necromancy, devil worship and witchcraft. With the Restoration, such extremes had generally fallen from favour but now amongst predominately Puritan communities faced with plague – the old-superstitions and fears found fresh fuel.

So it was that Nathaniel Lattimer, the new Witchfinder General, received urgent notification and summons to return with his associates from Ireland to Liverpool town: from where one Henry Teal, Town burgess; and devout reformed protestant dissenter; had reported the presence and activity of an enchantress and demon: called *Lilith…*

Liverpool Town Hall: Friday 3rd August 1665, Noon.

Lattimer struck an impressive figure. Stern and bristled, his face wore the burden of experience dug deep into its very folds. His plain Puritan dress was accompanied only by two books: his Bible and his treasured copy of the *Malleus Maleficarum* the 'Hammer of Witches' given personally to him by the great Matthew Hopkins himself.

"Thou sayeth Henry Teal… that this woman be called *Lilith?*"

"Aye, that she be: twenty one years in age and daughter of our good reformed townsman and Burgess Matthew Hopgood…

MALLEVS
MALEFICARVM,
MALEFICAS ET EARVM
hæresim frameâ conterens,

EX VARIIS AVCTORIBVS COMPILATVS,
& in quatuor Tomos iustè distributus,

QVORVM DVO PRIORES VANAS DÆMONVM versutias, præstigiosas eorum delusiones, superstitiosas Strigimagarum cæremonias, horrendos etiam cum illis congressus; exactam denique tam pestiferæ sectæ disquisitionem, & punitionem complectuntur. Tertius praxim Exorcistarum ad Dæmonum, & Strigimagarum maleficia de Christi fidelibus pellenda; Quartus verò Artem Doctrinalem, Benedictionalem, & Exorcismalem continent.

TOMVS PRIMVS.
Indices Auctorum, capitum, rerúmque non desunt,

Editio novissima, infinitis penè mendis expurgata; cuique accessit Fuga Dæmonum & Complementum artis exorcisticæ.

Vir siue mulier, in quibus Pythonicus, vel diuinationis fuerit spiritus, morte moriatur;
Leuitici cap. 20.

LVGDVNI,
Sumptibus CLAVDII BOVRGEAT, sub signo Mercurij Galli.

Twenty one and *very* young and fair of face... and yet... still unmarried and pure in her chastity."

Lattimer let out a low sniggering laugh: "And ye recognize not her name?"

"Nay? Except that tis *Lilith*. But by what other fashion should I knowe her name to be?"

"Her family be respectable... albeit that she herself doth excite and enchant men as easily as Salome, or the Queen of Sheba!" interjected Mayor Michael Tarleton.

Lattimer exchanged knowing and excluding smiles with his associates: "Yer shouldst be educated unto such things Mayor Tarleton: that name *Lilith* be that of an accursed demon: and *mother* of witches!"

Teal searched his memory: "I hath no knowledge of it in learned books or in scripture..."

"Oh tis in scripture, but the mention is but slight and circumstantial. Yet, in other works of the Jewish faith contemporaneous with the Old Testament is she known... as Adam's *first* wife before Eve..."

"First wife ye say?!"

"Indeed, and created in womanly form out from the very earth itself. She wouldst not humble herself unto her husband's authority, and was wilful and carefree. She was cast out from Eden, and the Lord created Eve as Adam's true wife made thus from his rib, to be the mother of mankind. In wrath *Lilith* afterwards sought vengeance gainst all descended from Eve!

She bringeth pestilence and maketh herself into a *succubus* – a demon that feedeth upon the semen of men and then useth it for her devilish maintenance. She may also transform herself into an *incubus* and so taketh the shape and form of a man to impregnate women with magically transformed seed so that she mayest thereby procreate more demons and witches!"

Henry's jaw dropped as the pieces fell together into place: "She doth enchant the men of the town… *and* women too… and plague is here!"

"She shalt also kill the unborn, or replace them in the womb with her foul creations!"

"Then we must take her now!"

At the Blacksmith's Forge

"Ahem…"

Williams glanced up from his anvil, his eerie, green left eye taking the lead, with his blue right eye following. He knew anyway of course, without looking: and well before The Witchfinder had cleared his throat.

Lattimer composed himself: "Ahem… I am returned!"

The Blacksmith nodded slowly and smiled, his eyes unblinking, but full of a barely hidden power.

"I have need of your services. Your best, and strongest chains. To bind a *witch!*"

The Blacksmith turned and lifted some bright silver coloured chains from behind him. They were are small, and in their size, unimposing… Lattimer's head jolted as the Blacksmith turned to show them: "So slight?!" he queried with exclamation.

"Slight to the *ordinary* eye, yet stronger by far than the purest Toledo or Damascus steel. Only, the God of *love*, may break *these* bonds..."

Lattimer repeated the Blacksmiths' words as a whisper: "The God of Love…"

"Jesus!" declared Partington, from behind his master "He means our Lord Jesus Christ!"

"Then he be *Christian* after-all!" said his companion Amos Cain.

The Witchfinder reached out and took hold of the chains: his face ticking under the scrutiny of the uncanny Blacksmith's supernatural gaze. Lattimer licked his dry lips, nodded slightly and then turned to depart. Pausing at the door, he looked up once again at the wrought-iron leaf-head image and with a final, defiant glance at The Blacksmith, he was gone.

Then, did Williams, the Blacksmith of old Liverpool town become as still as a great oak tree: his skin all green and tawny brown, with thickened sinews of bark – vines and living green leaves covering his body. Connor came and stood close by him – master and apprentice: a protective arm from the God-In-The-Green held softly around the youth's shoulder.

Von Hesse's work rate had increased greatly. He now had the demands of the town upon him for his medicines and treatments as well as pressure from *Lilith* to complete the complex alchemical work on the soil from Eden. He still urged her to restrain herself from her *succubus* activities, but *Lilith* could not, even if she had wanted to. Without the sexual energy drawn from human beings, she couldn't maintain her control over her host body, nor could she transmit her psychic contagion. Both required energy, and like a vampire, she must take that energy from her beguiled victims…

Feeling exhausted by his labours and his responsibilities, Von Hesse paused

This Friday afternoon *Lilith* was at the Juggler Street market – which was still functioning, as despite the plague already having taken more than two hundred of the towns citizens – people still had to eat, and still had to earn a living. Her air was as breezy and unconcerned as ever as her almond shaped green-eyes sought out prey for her amusement.

"*Lilith!*"

It was the lovelorn Adam.

"*Lilith!* Oh by God's grace to see thee is the light of mine heart!"

"Have a care Adam Teal, lest thou contracteth the miasma!"

Adam was concerned… but not enough

"*Lilith*, if it means that to be by thy side then I carest not, let the plague taketh me!"

The demon eyes sparkled as the Mona-Lisa smile granted his wish.

At The Town Hall

Henry Teal was with Robert Pym – his most rational of opponents. It would be convenient, if not exactly necessary, to convince him before action was taken:

"Robert, thy mind is too narrow and without the light of scripture on these matters! Ye must see that all the facts fit! *Lilith* is a witch!" Henry's urgency didn't persuade: "I wilt nay be party to such superstition! What of poor Matthew Hopgood? Wilt thou accuse him too, and his wife and son?"

"Nay! He hath been beguiled... He shalt understand... tis through scripture and the learned explanations of Nathaniel Lattimer that he shalt be persuaded!"

"Nathaniel Lattimer, student and compatriot of Matthew Hopkins, that self-styled 'Witchfinder General' and a man whose own zeal was called into rational questioning as but a cover for his very own Satanic practices!"

"Such things were said, aye, but by those in darkness or beguilement of witches! Matthew Hopkins had lawful authority to dispense justice 'gainst witchcraft... Nathaniel is his natural successor – his father didst prosecute and punish those of Pendle who practiced necromancy, magic and fortune telling with spells and familiars!"

"Aye, so it is renowned. But hath *Lilith* done any such of those things? Nay, she hath not! How sayeth thee that she be a witch?"

Henry's frustration was breaking his concentration. He struggled to reply as Jacob Morris came in to seek him out: Henry... thy son is taken... it seemeth with Plague!"

Henry Teal blanched. And with good reason: his son would almost certainly die, but more than that – he and the rest of his family may be boarded-up until the plague had passed.

"Oh God in heaven let it not be so!"

He rushed out with Jacob to find his son already swollen with the bubo's. Jacob offered a potential way out: "Henry, shall I obtain upon doctor Von-Hesse? It may be the poor lads only hope..."

"Nay!"

"Then thinketh thee of thy family, for otherwise ye shalt all be boarded up – tis the law..."

Von-Hesse had at last obtained the correct purity in his distillations and mixed the living soil with mercury and sulphur. He only needed a few hours now and the preparations would be complete. An urgent knock sounded from above.

"Scheer... go sayeth that I am busy at my labours, sayeth that I make medicines and cannot be excused!"

"Sir!"

He became irritated at the sound of argument and shuffling steps from above: "Scheer! Hath away with them, I am occupied busily at mine work!"

The unfamiliar footfall on the steps to the basement laboratory alerted the soldier in Von-Hesse. Two cocked pistols were in his hands and concealed below the height of the table. At last the booted legs of his unannounced visitor lengthened out into the now recognisable figure of Henry Teal. Teal's eyes were full of fear as he gazed around this the most secretive of hidden depths – at last he spoke to the shadowy figure at the workshop table: "Sir… I begeth thee… for thine help, tis my son…"

Von-Hesse was annoyed at his disturbance but realized that Teal was too important to ignore. To make an enemy of him at this late stage just before all was in place would be foolish. He went to poor Adam, and saw that the miasmic contagion had progressed rapidly – he had perhaps one hour of life left if he was lucky – he also realized that it was the work of his mistress: "I must… back to my apothecary… I cannot promise nought, but I may be able to help…" so saying he departed.

Cussing against *Lilith's* name for her adventurousness, he walked back along the Old Hall Street to Water Street. Thus preoccupied, his soldier's instincts failed him and he did not see Nathaniel Lattimer's men follow him closely from behind.

"*Lilith*! Mistress! Thy must release the youth, otherwise we may be discovered afore we are ready!"

Von-Hesse had bumped into *Lilith* as she breezed her way along: "Maximilian… fear not. When shalt the elixir be refined properly?"

"Mistress… if I can have but one full day and night of uninterrupted labour: it will be complete, and dried sufficiently for our purposes."

The Mona Lisa smile smiled… "Then, go release the youth – apparently by thy actions. I will lift the contagion from him at this distance. But Maximilian… note that mine power grows weak, all that I hath gained from semen and womb hast nearly passed – I am vulnerable… make thou sure that the work is finished on time!"

"Mistress!" Von Hesse bowed and wafted his cloak about him, turning away for the return journey to the Teal household.

Unseen a figure concealed himself close by. Every word had been heard...

Von-Hesse administered powders and herbs directly to the bubo's on Adam's neck, armpits and groin. Miraculously... they began to instantly subside, and then fade like the after image of a window on a sunny day."

Henry Teal was overcome with joy and relief: "Thy hath worked a miracle in God's name I sayeth tis a miracle!"

Von-Hesse smiled as he gave an explanation: "We are fortunate... in the greater part of cases such treatment will not work... it must indeed be by the hand of God!"

Unknown to him, the facts were already being reported to Nathaniel Lattimer – who took particular interest in *Lilith's* self-professed weakened condition: "We must act now afore she regains her strength! Take a full party of men – arrest her at once. If there be any resistance – use all force that may be required!"

"What of the Bavarians sir?" asked his hefty assistant Abraham Edge.

"We must take the girl first... secure her and then we move against the Bavarians, aye and their laboratory – we shalt seize all therein and make justice of them!"

Lilith had returned home. Despite her usual demeanour she was weakened. She now desperately needed the refined elixir – otherwise she may even expire – as the hosted body of *Lilith* Hopgood. It came as a great shock to her that even as she opened the door, she was physically seized, from behind...

Von-Hesse was returning back to the apothecary and by chance glanced down the hill and to the left. His eyes bulged and then narrowed with rage as he saw *Lilith* being manhandled by a crowd of armed men shouting 'Witch' and 'Demon' at her.

His instinct was to rush to her rescue, but reason called him to go faster back to the apothecary. Reich and Scheer would be there and they must arm themselves. It would be essential to preserve the soil and its drying elixir – a lead box would suffice… also the bath, which must be removed to safety. Whatever harm was done to *Lilith*, she could not be killed by these people, only forestalled… If they tried to hang or burn her, then he could recover her body at a later date and continue with the process. That or the soil could be used to pass her into another human host – but for that at the very least the bones of her last human incarnation would be required to add to the mixture.

There was much commotion in the town.

Matthew Hopgood had to be forcibly restrained such was his anger at the allegations against his daughter. Henry Teal had been informed of Von-Hesse's overheard conversation with *Lilith* and was outraged to think that she should cast a 'spell' of contagion against his son. Mistress Penny's words were re-called as was the manner of her death. In the feverish atmosphere, many now came forth and shouted their denunciation of *Lilith* for demonic enchantment.

The plague still ravaged the town and people wanted to believe that *Lilith* was responsible for it all. There was no chance of a lawful trial, despite Robert Pym's pleas.

It was to be a lynching.

Henry Teal and the town Mayor Michael Tarleton, wanted her to be hung from St James's Mount, the future site of Liverpool Anglican cathedral; but Nathaniel Lattimer – in reference to the authority of the *Malleus Maleficarum* sanctioned the old ways: she was to be consigned to water – if she drowned she was innocent, if she floated – then she was a witch and must be summarily hanged.

A party of armed townsmen and troopers went to Von-Hesse's apothecary to arrest him and his associates – but they were already gone: gone too was the stone bath and… unbeknown to their pursuers the blood-soil from Eden.

Search parties were dispatched to find the Bavarians and bring them back to Liverpool for justice. But Von-Hesse's decades of experience as a professional mercenary soldier allowed their crafty escape and the safe hiding of the stone bath over on the common heath. He, Reich and Scheer would return…

It was still light that summers evening when Lilith was taken by cart: bound in the Blacksmith's chains; to the widest and deepest part of the Pool. Matthew and Martha with their son Henry - brother to Lilith; were brought to witness the coming 'test'. Martha was distraught beyond consolation at her daughter's seizure and now, imminent lynching.

Matthew was enraged – yet even in that state, a part of him *knew* that *Lilith* was as charged. His soul began to wretch as he contemplated the twenty one years since he had seen her born that fateful night in June 1644.

A crowd of braying townsfolk had gathered including the Mayor, Burgesses and the Witchfinder Nathaniel Lattimer; with his four henchmen: Abraham Edge, Jonathan Bradley, Thomas Partington and Amos Cain. Puritans, both men and women; were chanting: "witch, witch!" repeatedly, in condemning refrain.

Lilith was defiant and proud. Looking around at her tormentors she noted each and spoke their name: "Thou shalt be accursed for thine actions this day, even unto those of you who hath children that liveth beyond the contagion… down the generations my curse shalt smite until all of your lines of descent are extinct!"

The Witchfinder's rhetoric waxed, now that he had her firmly in his power: "Silence witch! Tis to hell that ye be bound for – eternal damnation and no grave on consecrated ground awaits thee!"

Lilith managed a Mona-Lisa smile, and then with a chilling calm, pronounced: "Nathaniel Lattimer… who calls himself Witchfinder… hear my *curse*: for thy family and descendants shalt I save my most special vengeance: and when the last of your blood-line is destroyed then shalt follow *all* of humankind descended from Eve!"

As she uttered her curse, Robert Pym arrived by cart with an exhausted and yet miraculously recovering Adam Teal. Henry was roused to anger by his sons' elation at seeing his

beloved, even in such dire of circumstances: "Boy! Art thou *still* enchanted?"

"Father! Do not hurt her, ye put words unto her mouth by terror of thy actions! Leave her, I pray thee, leave her!"

Lattimer gestured to his men to throw manacled *Lilith* into the pool. To their shock and surprise, they could not move her. With what strength that remained, she rooted herself to her Earth; casting a glance over her shoulder to make eye contact with young Adam – who immediately rushed out from the retraining crowd towards his love: "No! No, release her! She is my *beloved!*" he cried in the anguish of his life.

The Witchfinder denied him with a shake of his head: "She is a *witch* and hath brought *plague* against us! A *demon* she is who *lusts* for men's *souls!* She must die: *cast* her into the pool!"

His henchmen renewed their efforts, but still, *Lilith* was unmoveable.

Her Mona-Lisa smile broadened: "I granted thee mercy Adam Teal: thy love for me was as pure and genuine as any man or boy couldst have been.

Hearken now unto me, for I prophesize we shalt meet again… in future life times, and thou shalt remember me and thy love for me…with your *every* single heartbeat..."

Crying with love Adam despaired: "Nay, nay yer cannot die - my love for thee is *too* strong - *too* true!"

Lattimer himself was now forcibly restraining Adam: "Yer are bewitched lad - hath a care lest yer also suffer the same fate! Silence the witch, cast her hence into the water, *now!*"

Lilith made no effort to struggle, and showed no fear or alarm as she was hurled backwards into the abyss.

Martha fainted as her daughter's body disappeared from view beneath the liver-brown waters of the pool...

Over on the heath, the Bavarians were concealed on high ground. Von-Hesse had his spyglass trained on the spectacle and kept close observation on the movements of the townsfolk.

Lilith's body did not resurface – but contrary to the instructions of the *Malleus Maleficarum* she was not pronounced innocent on her presumed drowning. The evidence against her was considered overwhelming. No effort was made to recover her body from the waters. Robert Pym consoled the Hopgood family as best he could, whilst Nathaniel Lattimer and his associates wasted no time in claiming due payment for executing a witch from Mayor Michael Tarleton, Henry Teal and his fellow burgesses at the Town Hall.

The rest of the townsfolk – excluding of course, poor Adam Teal, rejoiced in the superstitious belief that the Great Plague would now be lifted from them.

How wrong they were…

Von-Hesse's military skills came into play as the night drew in. He had set his bearings by progressive land-marks whilst it was still light, and then calculated the proper course and distances he should take under the cover of dark. When he and his men were satisfied, they closed to the poolside to recover *Lilith*…

Abraham Edge was an experienced soldier too. He figured that the Bavarians would do the apparently unexpected and return to the town – either to attempt to recover their property, or, to try to retrieve *Lilith's* body. Having secured his initial payment from Henry Teal – he took his associates – four in number, with him; and waited in a narrow street passage near to the apothecary. When no one had shown up late past nightfall – he decided to see if there was any activity down at the pool.

Reich and Scheer were working hard at their labours. The stone bath and its lid were very heavy – even with the advantage of the incline downwards to the poolside. Having brought it near to the water's edge, on the opposite bank to the town they assisted Von-Hesse in digging it in to the bank-side, near to a marker so that it could be recovered again in due course, when it was safe.

Von-Hesse was concerned about the possibility of being taken by surprise and paused to take watch at regular intervals. They had a stock of loaded pistols at the ready, but if it came to a fight at close quarters then he'd prefer using the cold steel of his Pappenheimer Bavarian-style rapier sword. It was quiet, and didn't require re-loading...

Atop the bank concealed in some trees, they had their three horses and the apothecary's cart they'd used to transport the bath from the rear basement door into the courtyard and thence out from the town to the common heath.

Von-Hesse was never better adapted than when soldiering... but he didn't see, and he didn't hear Abraham Edge and his men's stealthy approach. His heart, at last overcame him...

By moonlight, he found her, his hands following the perfect form of her body. Nestling her head against his chest he lifted her from the waters. Grief, soaked his heart, as surely as the dark waters, his vestments. Pausing on the edge, he touched the chains that bound her: as if by some uncanny power, they broke, separating each, one from the other to fall away: cascading like a waterfall – back into the depths of the fatal pool.

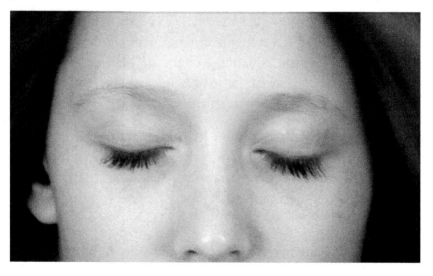

Her arms, now free, fell down limp and lifeless. He bit at his lip in anguish, as he gazed at her serene and beautiful face: licked by moonlit shadows...

Tenderly, he lay her body in the sarcophagus: a pit had been dug close-by, ready to conceal her from her enemies. Gently he caressed her face: "My mistress… my love…" he whispered in breaking voice. A single tear fell down from his cheek, moistening her half-open lips. Pained by centuries of unrequited love, he bid her farewell, softly and tenderly, with their only kiss.

"*Hold* or we *fire!*"

Von Hesse leapt immediately into the low-ground and closed to outflank his attackers: Lattimer's four henchmen led by the brutal Abraham Edge, plus a local townsman. Reich bent down to pick up his pistol, but was shot and wounded outright by Amos Cain. Von Hesse's rapier found it's mark penetrating Cain's neck on the left side, exiting through his Adams' apple. Not even pausing to check its effect - he withdrew the perfectly balanced blade and ran through the townsman. Scheer emptied two pistol volleys into Partington - killing him instantly.

A desperate life or death struggle ensued between Von Hesse and Abraham Edge, the advantage changing between the two with each successive play of sword blades, until at last, Von Hesse, ran the cruel henchman through his black heart.

The last of Lattimer's henchmen: Jonathan Bradley ran for his life with Von Hesse in hot pursuit - he could not be allowed to escape and inform on the whereabouts of *Lilith's* internment. Methodically, with Germanic efficiency, he was caught, cut down and killed...

Von-Hesse and Scheer weighted the bodies down and rolled them into Mersey – hopefully they'd stay submerged long enough to give nothing away about their exact place of death.

Reich was bleeding badly and needed his wound attending to. It was obvious that he would slow them down: so Von-Hesse coldly decided that he must be disposed of…

At last there was nothing left to do, but close the lid on *Lilith's* sarcophagus and consign her to the Earth.

Von Hesse *would* return, surely it would only be a matter of time: but for now he and Scheer must flee, before the townsfolk, supported by the local Lancashire Militia, hunted them down.

By the early dawn the following summer's morning the town was several souls less in its population. Five men including Abraham Edge were missing, *Lilith* of course gone – consigned to the waters, The three Bavarians – gone as fugitives, and… another twelve citizens dead of plague.

Nathaniel Lattimer continued on in his business and grew wealthy out of the superstition of the common folk. He followed the plague around the country – murdering innocent women and occasionally children too as sacrificial lambs: apparently to appease God for the people's sins, and of course, for their most infamous and certain practice of witchcraft.

Matthew and Martha Hopgood were both to die of plague – their resistance not helped by the shame and tragedy of their daughter's loss. Their Son Henry survived.

Henry Teal lived to a ripe old age but he didn't prosper from his planned business with the Strongbow family. Their circumstances had been changed by the plague and gradually they lost their fortune, only to fall into an anonymity - their star not rising again for nearly two hundred years, after which, through Victoria Strongbow, their secret inheritance had quietly passed over into the now Liverpool Irish family of Connor O'Riley…

Robert Pym survived… a decent man he did his best to help the town recover – only to fall victim to smallpox three years later.

Adam Teal was to survive the Great Plague, and although he did eventually marry he would never forget *Lilith*, and despite her casual evil towards his life, he never stopped loving her.

He remembered her words to him even unto his deathbed and looked forward, with his every single heartbeat, to that future promised lifetime when they would meet and be together again…

Book II

Of Adam's first wife, *Lilith*, it is told
(The witch he loved before the gift of Eve,)
That, ere the snake's, her sweet tongue could deceive,
And her enchanted hair was the first gold.
And still she sits, young while the earth is old,
And, subtly of herself contemplative,
Draws men to watch the bright web she can weave,
Till heart and body and life are in its hold.
The rose and poppy are her flowers; for where
Is he not found, O *Lilith*, whom shed scent
And soft-shed kisses and soft sleep shall snare?
Lo! as that youth's eyes burned at thine, so went
Thy spell through him, and left his straight neck bent
And round his heart one strangling golden hair...

Dante Gabriel Rossetti *Lilith* 186

Resurrectio Animus

5

Liverpool Museum:

Wednesday 18th October 2006, 9.45am

dam Mitchell was having another good look at the stone sarcophagus: "There's a residue of some kind here…" he was scrapping away at the internal face of the presumed 'head' end, where they'd found the skull.

Claudia had a look-see, she'd not noticed it before: "Might be biological – you know from decomposition? A film forming and then being preserved by some compound in the infill or even by the remains of that thin lead lining…"

"Yuk! Shouldn't we put on bio-hazard suits!?"

"Oh don't be so bluddy squeamish Adam!"

But Adam was squeamish: he was also superstitious when he felt low enough in mood. Von-Hesse had spooked him over his Laurence Olivier Hamlet act with the skull: it'd depressed his psychological defences enough for some arcane and long repressed fears to seep through into his consciousness.

What he found next under the residue didn't help his state of mind at all…

"Shit look at this!

Claudia tutted and then peered past him into the sarcophagus:

"They look like symbols, and writing – etched into the stone. It's… in Latin I think."

"Seems we might need dear old Dr Alan Flynn again eh Claudia?"

Claudia pursed her lips: "Well… he *is* the ancient languages expert, and I suppose Latin is technically one of those."

"Dead language for dead people as my dad used to say!"

"Your dad?"

"Yeah… he should know… he's dead…"

Adam's grin brought a smile to her face: "OK, crusty old git or not, I'll get in touch with him. See if you can scrape the rest of that residue away. The markings aren't deep, so be careful you don't damage them."

Adam's humour was distracting – more for him than for Claudia. His stomach didn't agree with the notion of cleaning more of that film away, but… "OK, except I'll get a mask if you don't mind, yer never know what's lurking in there…"

The Crusty-One peered through his spectacles and then his Sherlock Holmes sized magnifying glass: "It is Latin… you know you can date Latin just like you can English. It's pretty good, so its' not your common or garden variety picked up in Church or whatever."

"Woz it say?"

"Woz! I take it by that you mean 'What' does it translate into in modern English?"

"Yeah…" said Adam "Like I said: woz it translate as?"

"Not my field I'm afraid!" replied the Crusty-One curtly.

Claudia had been patient with the clash of personalities between Flynn and young Adam but now she wanted answers:

"You mean that you can't read it?"

The Crusty-One became crustier still: "No madam I do not! Of course I can read it! When will you archaeologists learn that what something *says* and what it *means* aren't always the same thing!"

"OK… so what does it 'say'?" asked Dr Moore.

The Crusty-One shook his head: "It's an incantation, a spell if you like to raise the spirit of the presumed occupant: *Resurrectio Animus!* But you inferred that you wanted me to 'translate' it – and that is impossible without an understanding of the accompanying symbols."

"Wait a min, yer said that it meant to raise the dead like? So that's it, that's all we wanted ter know…" interjected Adam.

Flynn shook his head yet again and lowered his eyes to stare at Claudia: "Stupid isn't he" he said flatly.

"Sometimes yes."

"Eh, dat's not fair!"

"Shut up Adam! Sorry Dr Flynn, you were saying?"

"I was *about* to say that this is obviously an occult burial of some kind. It isn't Christian, and yet it's from seventeenth century Liverpool. The outside of the sarcophagus has ancient Aramaic inscribed upon it: and it has soil, you tell me, in a lead box that apparently comes from Eastern Turkey or the border with Georgia and Armenia… and now we find that inside; the sarcophagus has magical symbols and some rather good quality

Latin! So… from all of that I'd have thought your next move is *more* than obvious!"

Claudia scratched her head. Adam decided that he'd crack another funny: "Hey Doc, yer crustier than an un-sliced loaf!"

"Doc?!" Dr Flynn exclaimed disgustedly.

Claudia made a suggestion: "Shall I speak to the universities anthropology department?"

"Oh good-grief no!"

"What then?"

"Anthropologists are academics in that traditional sense – just as you and I are Dr Moore" then with a sideways glance at Adam: "Other present company excluded… What you need are specialists in the occult – people who can translate the meaning of the *symbols* for you – then, you have the context for the Latin, and then… Mr Mitchell… you will have your proper 'translation'."

Claudia misunderstood: "Occultists! Surely not!"

"I didn't say 'occultists' Dr Moore, but *specialists* in the occult – *parapsychologists* for example!" came the tetchy reply.

Adam had another one of his good ideas: "I know! How's bout that Bavarian, Dr Von-Hesse, he's fluent in ancient Aramaic an all that jazz, maybe he knows!"

"Dr who did you say?" Flynn wasn't aware of any other ancient language specialists being involved.

Adam was on a roll: "Nah I don't like the new series me-self, I still watch the re-runs on Cable TV with Tom Baker!"

"Ignore him Dr Flynn he's being incorrigibly frivolous – we had a visit from a Dr Maximilian Von-Hesse from Bavaria, he's an archaeologist – but he also specialises in ancient Aramaic."

The Crusty-One was put out: "Oh does he indeed… well there's an example for you of straying out-of-your-field! Archaeologists should do what they do best… grub around in the dirt and leave the cerebral study of language to proper linguists. Which… as far as the occult goes… is why I suggest you contact Professor of parapsychology Dr Claire Lattimer at the university, or over at the ESP Institute in Rodney Street!"

In her early forties, Professor Claire Lattimer was still a very attractive and youthful looking woman. She'd had an eventful life – joining Merseyside Police at eighteen and in her but brief two years of street service she'd already seen more of everyday human suffering than most people could expect to see in a lifetime.

It was as a police-officer that she was first exposed to the 'supernatural', events so strange and overwhelming that they had decided her upon a complete change of direction in life. Leaving the police she became a first class honours graduate in psychology at Liverpool University, and then went on to read for a Ph.D. in parapsychology – joining 'ESP' the world renowned paranormal research institute in the city's Rodney Street.

At 38 she took over as director of ESP, and at 40, she was appointed as an honorary professor in parapsychology at Liverpool; a post that involved lecturing in general psychology to the universities students as well as promoting scientific research and collaboration between ESP and the university.

Twenty years ago she'd married Kevin O'Riley, then a young police constable– who went on to follow in his father's footsteps and become a Superintendent at Birkenhead over on the Wirral. They had two children: Sean, who at eighteen was about to join the police himself, and Elizabeth, who at sixteen was still at school.

With her at ESP, was her closest colleague: Dr John Sutton. At fifty-five he'd known Claire since they were both police-officers together at Birkenhead. John too had experienced the same paranormal events as Claire – and as a result, he'd given up on his own promising career in the police and followed her to read psychology at Liverpool University.

Over the years they'd worked extremely well as a team and had built an international reputation both as academics and as practical field researchers in such diverse areas as clairvoyance, medium-ship, remote-viewing, hauntings' near-death experiences and of course – claims of black magic, witchcraft and the occult.

Despite their professional standing – they were still treated as outsiders by the run of academia at the university – there was something not quite right about their messing about with things 'occult' and claims of the supernatural – not quite respectable pursuits for serious academics…

It came as a surprise then when Dr Claudia Moore called to see Claire this Friday morning in late October – a time when more run-of-the-mill academics like 'respectable' archaeologists should be busy with the new lecturing term.

Claire greeted her warmly: "Come in; lovely to see you!"

The voluptuous Claudia had never met Claire before. She quickly scanned her look as women often do to one another: Claire had blond hair, smart dress, a slim svelte figure – good skin; she was indeed stunningly attractive and very well preserved especially for her 'apparent' age: "Thanks and you too… er bit of an unusual request this!" Claudia smiled trying to suggest that there was something intriguing about the subject of her visit. For her part Claire was well used to the 'unusual' it was the stuff of her everyday life: "I'm afraid everything I do falls into that category!" she smiled.

Claudia realized that she'd better narrow things down to her precise request, otherwise Claire might embarrass her by talking about things she couldn't understand: "Well… Alan Flynn…"

"The linguist?"

"Yeah, that's him… he suggested that my department contact you about some expertise you may have on arcane 'occult; inscriptions…"

"OK… I *may* be able to help" qualified Claire "Have you made a find of some kind?"

"We have… you may have heard about it in the papers: a stone sarcophagus, just off Paradise Street."

"Oh, yes, I read about that some months back!"

"Yeah… well… its seventeenth century, and contained a skeleton of a woman of around twenty years of age: and, a lead box with some soil that's been identified as being from Eastern Turkey – near to the border with Armenia and the Georgian Republic. The sarcophagus had an outer inscription in ancient Aramaic, that's where Alan came in… he translated that, and then there was some other stuff in Latin scratched into the stone work on the inside – with a bunch of strange geometric patterns. Alan reckons they're occult; he said that you'd be able to identify them." Claudia blushed; despite herself her true subconscious opinion about parapsychology and its subject matter was displaying itself through her colour. Claire, of course read the involuntary signal easily:

"You know what we do has a lot to do with archaeology."

"It does?"

"Yep… we trawl the depths of the human psyche – you trawl the depths of the land. The main difference is that our 'old' stuff is living…"

Claudia's spine tingled and her body jerked in an involuntary nervous spasm: "Sorry! I must have a chill or something."

Kindly Claire declined to penetrate further; but she did offer to help: "I can have a look if you like? If I can't help, then I'm bound to have a contact who can."

"Thanks, that'd be lovely. The main thing is to keep this between us. Not that I mind, you understand, it's just… well, archaeologists can be a bit conservative, and er, they'd think it a bit odd that we'd gone to a parapsychologist… probably think we were spooked and wanted an exorcism or something!"

Claire smiled: "That would never do would it."

Claudia shifted around in her chair – embarrassed.

"When would you like me to call over?" asked Claire.

"Er… whenever you're free."

"I can come now if you want?"

Claudia was relieved. The sooner it was over and out of the way the better: "Sure, that'd be great" came the empty smiling response.

"Right then, let's go!"

Adam had cleaned most of the offensive precipitation away from the inner surface of the sarcophagus. There was more Latin, and a whole series of patterns and designs as well as some relatively clear engravings of men in seventeenth century dress working with what appeared to be furnaces and glass containers – oddly juxtapositioned with what looked like a strange tree, a walled garden, some mountains and a huge serpent.

He was feeling quite pleased with himself as the fascination of uncovering the ever more elaborate material overrode his subconscious fears – which by now were vainly warning of the consequences of his discovery.

He was so engrossed that he didn't notice the arrival of Claudia and Claire.

"Adam!"

"Eh? Argh!" Poor Adam dropped his tools and sat back on his ass: "Crikey yer scared me then!"

In his fright he'd forgotten his manners.

"Adam, this is Professor Claire Lattimer – a parapsychologist, she's kindly agreed to help identify the engravings."

Adam took off his goggles and stared as if mesmerized at Claire's attractive face.

"Adam!" Claudia tried to get his attention.

Adam shook himself: "Oh… yeah… sorry. Hello Professor, you don't *look* like a professor; an' that put me off me stroke a bit…"

Claire smiled as she shook his hand: she'd long gotten used to her effect on younger men. Her good looks had improved with her maturing years so that 'age-adjusted' they stood out even more now than when she'd been in her early twenties.

"Is this the sarcophagus?"

"It is" confirmed Claudia.

Claire didn't need to look too closely. Her expert eye identified the gross details immediately: "It's alchemical…"

"Al wha?!" interjected Adam.

"Professor Lattimer said 'alchemical.' Don't put on yer 'stupid act' Adam, you know what alchemy is!"

Claire decided to rescue the poor young man: "Actually, most people *don't* know what it was, or… is…"

Adam offered his wisdom: "It was ah bunch ah nutters who blew themselves up tryin' ter turn lead inter gold… Maybe that's why this coffin has a lead lining?"

Claudia didn't appreciate his direct use of the terms, but she did agree with his basic grasp of things: "That's about it…"

Claire sighed. She was used to the task of having to explain things to academics, but it was usually an effort. 'Trained' people always have the inertia of their indoctrination to overcome, that's why she preferred 'ordinary' people to work with; they generally accepted the reality of an experience for what it was.

"There were two kinds of alchemists" she explained "the first lot were called 'puffers' because they used furnaces to try – as you say – to create real physical gold out from a base metal such as lead. The second group were called variously 'philosophical' or Hermetic alchemists. The puffers as you probably know where the lineage ancestors of modern scientific chemists. However, what a lot of people don't know is that the Hermetic alchemists were the original 'depth-psychologists' people who understood the psychology of the unconscious."

"Occultists in other words?"

"Yes, to an extent: but, they were also wise and experienced beyond many of our modern day psychologists and psychotherapists when it came to understanding the mind. From a quick look at what you have here in the engravings... I'd say that they relate to Hermetic alchemy, the kind of stuff you see in old woodcuts of *Christian Rosenkreuz's* work. Some of the other stuff... is more frankly occult."

Claudia decided to stir the mix: "The soil found in the lead box: it wasn't just 'foreign' it was chemically altered at a molecular and isotopic level – apparently by some unknown physical process. That seems to me to be something the 'puffers' as you've called them might have gotten themselves involved in: maybe something they did accidentally, out of ignorance when they messed about with the soil."

Claire correctly sensed that Claudia didn't want to go the occult or psychological route to reach an explanation: "Could be... however, and you may find this hard to accept, but sometimes 'physical' changes in matter can be brought about by non-material processes."

Claudia gave out a somewhat mocking expression. It was left to Adam to reply: "Yer mean mind over matter?"

"In everyday terms... yes."

"Oh come on Professor Lattimer! We're *supposed* to be scientists!" Claudia had reached the impenetrable envelope of her understanding.

"Yes... gets in the way sometimes doesn't it - what we're 'supposed' to be... I was fortunate: I'd learned my lesson before I went to university, from some time I'd spent as a front-line police-officer. Difficult to get more 'real' and fact based than that. What it taught me though was that the truth of life goes beyond any opinion we may have about it – even 'trained' opinion. The facts are 'simply so' and it's up to us to understand them rather than allow our entrained prejudices to prevent us from even seeing them."

Adam's jaw dropped at Claire's expert put-down of his boss: his mind raced as a fantasy about a change of career into parapsychology forced itself into his mind - a fantasy where Claire had replaced Claudia…

Claudia tried to stick to her familiar turf: "The only issue here is the identification of the engravings and symbols: *if* you *can* help with that; then it'd be greatly appreciated!"

Claire smiled: "The Latin is a kind of 're-animation spell' to raise the corpse or just the spirit, of whomsoever was contained within the sarcophagus."

"That's what Dr Flynn said too…" responded Claudia.

Adam grinned: "Well it didn't work!"

"The skeleton you mean?" queried Claire.

"Well yeah…"

"Oh, right… well, this isn't quite a *Christian* resurrection of the body: it's a *resurrectio animus* a resurrection of a spirit. Strictly speaking you don't need a body for that – she, if the corpse was indeed female, could be re-animated into the reconstituted body of which all that remains is the skeleton, or, only in spirit – so that a new host body could be found at a later date. The soil, if it is alchemical, and the inscription does identify it as being so; is a kind of *prima materia* an original pure substance; out from which the first host body was formed."

Claudia had recovered her composure and was musing on the translation of the ancient Aramaic: "Alan Flynn said that the Aramaic inscription gave a Biblical personal name; *Lilith*."

"*Lilith*?" Claire shook her head. "No, sorry I'd have to look it up. What I can say is that the engravings are alchemical, and of a Hermetic nature – and that they include some pure occultism, and have to do with re-animation. Whoever put the corpse into the sarcophagus expected to come back for it. The soil is there for that purpose. It'll contain the essence of the supernatural spirit."

Adam was fascinated: "So, that soil stuff is like a black-magic who-do-voodoo kinda thing?"

"That's what it was intended for yes. Where's the skull by the way, was it missing?"

Claudia, was at last, being inducted into an inwardly reflective trance as the latent psychological fascination of the find finally took hold: "No… it's been taken… taken with some of the soil."

The moment was exactly right. All three felt a chill as their spines tingled. However only Claire's experienced psyche really grasped what may be going on: "Taken, by someone who knows what this stuff is?"

Dr Maximilian Von-Hesse was at the great-hall in Oxton with his Bavarian assistants: Hans Meier and Gustav Adler. Von-Hesse was aware that he'd kept the skull and the soil sample for five days now, and hadn't even so much as bothered to keep in contact with Dr Moore at the Museum. Nevertheless his hi-tech approach to 'alchemy' had clarified one important detail – just to be sure, they'd need more of the soil. The centuries it had been locked away in the sarcophagus may have reduced its potency, by mass. This would mean a further visit to the tiresome Claudia and her buffoon of an assistant; Adam Mitchell:

"I would expect some questioning from them about my request – but… they will find themselves agreeing with me." The confident statement drew knowing smiles from Meier and Adler. Over the intervening years, Von Hesse had acquired many new skills, including that of a potent, almost irresistible Mesmerism.

"I'll get it over with now, and pay them an unexpected visit. Keep the analysis going with the mass-spectrometers, I want everything to be just right, for *Lilith's* return…"

"Adam!"

"Argh! Shit!"

For the second time that day, Adam Mitchell was startled as he worked on the sarcophagus: "Crikey, must everyone creep up on me! Oh… it's you Dr Von Hesse."

Von-Hesse joked to make him relax, and become even more 'suggestible': "You were expecting Christopher Lee perhaps?"

"Ha!   Er… he's a bit before my time… Hammer-Horror actor wasn't he?"

"Yes... but isn't he the kind of stereotype you Britishers' expect from a 'Central-European' scientist with an interest in the occult?"

Adam's eyes shifted leftwards as his mind processed the suggestion.

Von-Hesse let it do its work: "Is Dr Moore in?" he continued.

"Er... yeah... should be, she was in her office just a while back."

"Good, I need some more of the soil."

"The soil?"

"Indeed." Von-Hesse wheeled about and strode purposefully towards Claudia's office.

"Crikey!" mused Adam "Christopher Lee... Come to think of it I hadn't noticed before but yeah... he does look a *bit* like him..."

Claudia's office door was open – which meant that Von-Hesse could look in without the tiresome preclude of having to knock: "Dr Moore!"

The richly deep and authoritive voice jarred at Claudia's nerves shocking her out of her concentration: "Oh! You startled me Dr Von-Hesse... Have you come to return the skull and soil sample?"

"Not... yet... in fact I require a little *more*... of the soil."

"More?" Claudia shifted about in her chair. Her authority had taken a few knocks already today during Claire Lattimer's visit. She felt the need to dig her heels in and recover some of it back: "I'm afraid that the Museum wouldn't allow that Dr Von-Hesse. The total sample is limited, and we don't want what's left of it to go missing. You would be welcome to do some non-destructive analysis here, but we can't allow it to be taken from the Museum."

Von-Hesse read Claudia's use of 'the Museum' and 'we' as substitutes for 'I': "Dr Moore; I have some sophisticated equipment at my disposal, I have also had experience with... identical samples in the past... I could be of assistance to the 'Museum' in identifying the unknown compounds and the chemical processes used in their creation and synthesis."

Claudia shifted about again in her chair: "Thank you but I doubt that whatever portable equipment you may have at your... disposal...could be as effective as the soil science laboratory at Liverpool University!" Claudia's voice betrayed a nervous tremor.

Von-Hesse's black-brown eyes darkened as his own voice became soft and slowly articulated: "You... seem... anxious, Dr Moore, perhaps you are feeling very... tired..." Claudia's eyes blinked slowly indicating a receptivity to hypnotic induction.

"No... I'm fine..." she murmured.

Von-Hesse continued: "You must.... *allow* yourself... to relax..."

The 'permissive' suggestion that she allow herself to relax immediately undercut her resistance – it gave her the illusion that she had her authority back; that she was in control... her eyes blinked slowly again, twice, indicating a deepening state of receptivity to Von-Hesse's skilled Mesmeric mind.

"I…" Claudia felt herself floating "I…"

"Want to close your eyes" he commanded, softly.

Claudia's eyes did close – and Von-Hesse continued: "Listen to my voice… only my voice… no other sound you hear will have *any* significance at all…"

Claudia took an involuntary long, slow and deep breath. Von-Hesse smiled to himself in satisfaction. Claudia was an easy hypnotic subject. Her rational-minded persona hid a deeply ingrained superstition. She was in effect, hypnotizing herself:

"Now, Dr Moore… you will *allow* yourself to release more soil to me… this will be *agreeable* to you… it is, after all, your *own* decision… it will make you feel *contented* and relaxed to assist me in *any* way that I ask. Now… your subconscious mind can signal to you that it agrees with my words by *allowing* your left hand to float, and rise, as if *all by itself*…"

Claudia felt her left arm jerk as the muscles came to life. A deep relaxation in the limb followed, accompanied by a tingling sensation as her arm floated higher and higher into the air. Any last vestige of resistance she may have felt floated away with it – she now felt as two people, one her conscious everyday self – who was a relaxed observer, and the other, her true albeit 'subconscious' self who simply complied with every word Von-Hesse uttered…

"Your subconscious mind has agreed to release the soil sample to me, in whatever amount I should require… In just a moment, you will find yourself able to speak with me, and answer my questions directly. Your voice will be calm and relaxed…

Dr Moore… you have heard and will act upon each word that I have said"

Von-Hesse's voice was authoritive as he directed her.

"Yes…" Claudia heard her voice reply.

"Good… now… you *must* inform me of any matters arising concerning the sarcophagus, the skeleton or the soil, you *will* make this your overriding responsibility… I am to be informed of *anything* the museum, the university, or any other third parties do, or wish to do, in *any* way concerning the finds…"

Von-Hesse had included this command as a prompt for him to be kept updated on any developments – he didn't however expect Claudia's response:

"Claire… Alchemy… Occult symbolism…"

Von-Hesse restrained himself from making an audible exclamation, but he was surprised: "Dr Moore, explain what you have just said…"

"Claire Lattimer…"

"Lattimer!" This time Von-Hesse couldn't stop himself, his voice was raised and urgent: Lattimer was the family name of *Lilith's* executioner… "Continue Dr Moore…"

"Professor Claire Lattimer... parapsychologist... saw the finds, said that the inscription is occult, alchemical..."

"Did she indeed..." mused Von-Hesse "When did this happen?"

Claudia took another deep breath as the memory of Claire's visit stimulated her complex about losing her authority: "Today, this morning..."

"I see... continue..."

"She... undermined my authority with Adam."

Von-Hesse thought the detail trivial: "What were her comments about the find?"

"I..." The strength of her authority-complex was showing. Von-Hesse, now had to placate it:

"You authority is secure Dr Moore... you can *allow* yourself to be *relaxed* with it. Now, continue about the woman Claire Lattimer."

"She's... an honorary professor at the university... and director of the ESP Institute in Rodney Street."

Von-Hesse's eyes narrowed. It could just be coincidence, or, it could be that this Professor Lattimer was indeed a direct descendent of the Witchfinder Nathaniel Lattimer: "Dr Moore, you will... engineer a meeting between myself and this woman, here at the Museum. I would... assess her, as a threat... to your authority. You *must* understand that I am here to help you... and that you must *obey* my every instruction.

Whenever you and I meet subsequently, if I should nod my head slightly you will immediately enter trance... and *allow* yourself to follow my every suggestion..."

"I... will allow myself... to follow your every... suggestion."

"Good, now in a moment you will hear my fingers snap, and when you do, you will return to full consciousness and be happy, calm and contented, understanding that my every request must be met with on demand… you will have no conscious memory of your trance, but your *sub*-conscious mind will remember… and will obey…"

Von-Hesse waited a few moments for his suggestions to percolate deeply into Claudia's psyche – then… his fingers snapped.

Claudia opened her eyes: "Dr Von-Hesse! What a pleasant surprise!" she said smiling…

Claire had gone straight back to ESP in Rodney Street. Her work for the day at the university was done. She was met by Dr John Sutton, her older but junior colleague at the Institute: "Hello Claire, how did the visit to the Museum go?"

"Hi John, it was interesting… as far as the finds go anyway. The archaeological staff there were just as you'd expect."

John smiled: "Academic?"

Claire smiled in return: "That about sums it up! The sarcophagus had a whole series of alchemical and occult symbols etched into its inner surface. The Latin clearly identified it as an incantive spell to resurrect the spirit of the corpse lain inside. There was a well preserved skeleton, but someone had buggered off with the cranium, and some of the strange soil that had been found with it, a German archaeologist apparently."

"Professional competition eh… just the same as in our field!"

Their laughter was interrupted by the telephone ringing. Claire answered: "Professor Lattimer… Oh hello Claudia, what can I do for you? Oh… OK, Monday? Right… I may bring a colleague with me if that's OK? It is? Good, see you at 11.00 then, bye" Putting down the receiver she grinned at John "Looks like your gonna get to see the stuff for yourself – I've er… invited you to come along to the Museum with me. Apparently, the German wants to ask me some questions…"

John grinned as he formed a pyramid shape with his hands, Claire was always at her best when 'summonsed' by curious academics - she was a first class advocate for her discipline of parapsychology - the scientific investigation of the paranormal.

That evening, Von-Hesse returned to Lake Hall with the extra soil samples. He calculated that he now had enough to bring the re-animation process to a successful conclusion. He was nervous… what would *Lilith's* response be to the passage yet again of so much time; would she blame him for what had happened all those years ago in Liverpool?

Deep in contemplation he stared at the skull. This alchemical *operatio* would be an unparalleled synthesis of arcane magic and twenty first century high technology. It would be a very different world that *Lilith* was re-animated into. Could he perhaps find some way to placate any anger she may have… maybe by tracking down all living descendants of her tormentors? *Is* Claire Lattimer in the blood-line of the accursed Nathaniel Lattimer, Witchfinder?

For the sake of a weekend's patience, he decided to postpone *Lilith's* reanimation, until after he had met with Claire face-to-face…

Liverpool Museum: Monday 23rd October 2006, 10.45am

Von-Hesse arrived at Claudia's office some fifteen minutes early. He fully expected that she'd have to be prepared in advance so that her authority-complex didn't create any unnecessary problems. However, he needn't have worried, he only had to bow his head slightly and poor Claudia immediately entered the predetermined trance state: "Now, Dr Moore… you will be facilitating to our guests and feel no anxiety or tension… simply *allow* yourself to be led by me."

"I will allow myself to be led by you…" she murmured through half closed eyes.

"Good! Now, accompany me to the examination room, and be as 'normal' in front of your student, Adam."

Adam had laid everything out as before. He wished the skull had been returned though, just in case… just in case it somehow took on a life of its own like in that damned Christopher Lee movie *The Skull*. Von-Hesse did look a *little* bit like him after all…or maybe that footballer, Eric Cantona…

"Ah Adam… would you go upstairs and wait for Professor Lattimer and her colleague?"

"Sure… why not: come here, go there, do this do that…" Adam muttered to himself as he walked off – chilling suddenly as the tall figure of Von-Hesse passed him in the narrow corridor.

The Bavarian didn't give him a first glance – he wasn't even that important.

"Haven't been here for years, since I was a kid in fact" said John.

"Changed a lot hasn't it" replied Claire.

"Yeah, I can still remember it, the dinosaur skeletons, the mummies. Why are we here anyway Claire? I mean it's not like it's our turf or anything. There have been no paranormal events, just dry bones and old stone."

Claire furrowed her brow as she stared out across the cavernous museum foyer: "I don't know; an intuition or a hunch maybe. It just felt right to ask you along somehow. I'm not even that sure what they want from me, except to speak to this curious Bavarian archaeologist."

"Professor Lattimer" Adam had found his way to them at last.

"Hello again Adam, this is my colleague Dr John Sutton!"

"Hi doc. Best come on down, they're both waiting!"

John and Claire exchanged an amused look and then followed the comedic Ph.D student down the stairs.

Claire was all smiles as she acknowledged Claudia. She hadn't had any personal issues over their last meeting and didn't feel any of her own authority was under threat. She was aware that Claudia hadn't taken to her asserting her opinions, so she was making an effort to build bridges and keep her at her ease.

Claudia too was all smiles. Claire was so taken up with the niceties of the exchange that she didn't notice the dark-eyed Bavarian scanning her intently.

"Claire, this is Dr Maximilian Von-Hesse of the Otto-Friedrich University of Bamberg in Bavaria, Dr Von-Hesse, Professor Claire Lattimer."

John Sutton patiently waited his turn to be introduced, but the experienced parapsychologist and former police-officer noted an immediate reaction in himself as his spine tingled and the hair of the back of his neck rose up.

Claire faltered slightly as the black-brown eyes penetrated her – there was something uncannily familiar about them. Von-Hesse's large, powerful hand enveloped hers softly – the energy in his body sending a surge of static electricity into her.

She gasped: "Oh!"

"I'm sorry, Professor – I seem to have a surplus of energy this morning."

"That's OK… er this is Dr John Sutton, my colleague at ESP." She tried to loosen her grip from his hand. Although firm it wasn't tight – yet her hand seemed to have adhered to his. Laughing in some embarrassment she looked to John for help."

"I seem to be stuck!"

The Bavarian smiled faintly and Claire's hand withdrew as if repelled by a magnetic energy. She looked into his eyes – her incredulity matched oppositely by the dark-presence looking out from behind the black-brown eyes.

John read the situation as clearly as he could. It was obvious that Von-Hesse was signalling something about himself that extended way beyond his persona as a visiting archaeologist.

The Bavarian turned to shake his hand.

"Er… no thanks Dr Von-Hesse, and no offence, but I gave up on hand-buzzer jokes in my teens."

The Bavarian's darkly handsome features broadened out into a smile: "You parapsychologists are as prone to superstition as anyone else, perhaps… even more so."

"Well, it's the company we keep" replied John "They tend to be unusual people… or things…"

"Quite so" then turning back to Claire: "You made some very interesting observations professor."

"Call me Claire… Thanks, er… if its archaeology you want to talk to me about then it's not my area of expertise – that's Claudia's."

The Bavarian's head tilted back as his dark hooded eyes regarded her: "It is not… about archaeology, as such, more about your antiquarian knowledge of alchemy, and the occult."

Claire nodded slowly, glad that had been cleared up in front of Claudia. She had no wish to rub her face in anything: "Well, my knowledge of it is specific to my field. We routinely investigate the occult, and this kind of symbolism turns up all the time."

Von-Hesse questioned her further: "Is it perhaps, a *family* tradition of yours?"

"Family?!" Claire was genuinely taken aback by the question, and for a moment wondered if it was a language issue – as excellent though Von-Hesse's English was, it wasn't his native tongue: "No… but my immediate family have experience of such things, my husband and father-in-law in particular."

"You're married? I see… so the name 'Lattimer' is your married name?"

Claire paused before answering. This Bavarian was taking quite an interest in the minutiae of her background: "No my married name is O'Riley, but I've always used Lattimer for my professional work."

"Ah! Good!" exclaimed the Bavarian. Claire looked at John and exchanged a quizzical look with him – 'what was all this about?' she thought: "Good? I'm sorry Dr Von-Hesse, I don't follow you."

Von-Hesse smiled at Claire's unintentional joke: "Of course you don't… It's just that I have known many people by the Lattimer 'clan' name, and… I wondered if you were a part of that extended family. Are you from the local area?"

"Yes…"

"Have you by chance traced your family tree?"

Claire's incredulity at the line of questioning showed on her face – but it didn't stop her own curiosity from answering: "No, but my husband has. A branch of his family have been around here in Liverpool and over on the Wirral for centuries. The Strongbows'… one line of them descends from a Norman Earl of Pembroke, in Wales."

The Bavarian smiled a wry smile: "Yes, I recall the family being prominent in old Liverpool town… So, professor, you're a parapsychologist. In centuries past you'd probably have been a Witchfinder."

Claire laughed: "Ha! Yes, probably. Good job we've moved on a lot since then. Although… I have had more than my fair share of run-ins with witches of one kind or another. You'd be surprised…"

Adam decided to butt his butt in: "Wha? like 'real' witches and stuff like tha'?"

"That's right Adam, beneath the surface of this city and the surrounding areas are things most people only see in horror movies or in nightmares…"

"Bollocks!" Adam couldn't help himself "Shit, sorry!"

"Don't worry Adam; we're used to that kind of reaction."

Adam put his foot in it again: "That's probably because parapsychology ain't generally recognised or respected by mainstream science."

John came to Claire's aid: "That's the fault of so-called mainstream science. You see we *are* scientists. It's just that the phenomena we investigate are far too complex to reduce down to controlled and repeatable experimentation in a laboratory. The stuff we work with has two faces – one it shows to the world and one it does not. It's like looking at a coin; it has a head, and a tail. The head-side can be addressed by science – but it's not the whole coin. The tail-side by the so-called occult, but that's not the whole coin either. So, if you see the whole of one side then you don't see *any* of the reverse side.

In parapsychology we approach the coin from the rim, and tilt it so that we can view *either* side. That means sometimes using the language and skills of science and sometimes… of the occult."

"Very well stated Dr Sutton!" The Bavarian seemed truly impressed: "That's probably the most balanced and eloquent explanation I have yet heard of the problems in your field."

John smiled slightly in acknowledgement, but didn't allow himself to be flattered.

Claire re-joined the conversation: "But that's not why we are here is it Dr Von-Hesse?"

The Bavarian tilted his head back once more, narrowing his hooded black-brown eyes: "Partly professor, partly… I am also interested in your knowledge of alchemy, and what you may have gleaned from your viewing of the etchings in the sarcophagus."

"I've become interested in alchemy since some very early experiences in my career, twenty to twenty-five years ago in fact. But, most of what I know I've learned from my father-in-law. He's a Jungian psychotherapist, over in Rodney Street at the Eden Institute."

"Eden? What a quaint… and appropriate name…" mused The Bavarian "So you really have no idea what all of this means?"

"What, the finds or your line of questioning?" John interjected.

Von-Hesse squinted as he looked at John: "You have a military… no, a *police* background don't you!"

John raised an eyebrow in mock surprise and continued sarcastically "Police, yes, that's psychic of you isn't it?"

The Bavarian scanned his face: "No, you really don't have any idea. Well… it was charming to make your acquaintance and my thanks for your time. Now I really must get back to my labours… Oh and professor Lattimer, I should very much like to meet with you again, perhaps at your 'ESP' Institute?"

"Yes, of course, come-along whenever you have the time. If we're in, you'll be made very welcome."

Von-Hesse wheeled about and strode purposively away snapping his fingers as he did so. Claudia let out a start: "Argh! Where's Dr Von-Hesse?"

"Wha!" exclaimed Adam "He's just walked out, right past you!"

"Eh, I… I don't remember: was he here; what happened?"

John turned to Claire: "I think that Bavarian fellow has just left us his business card…"

Claudia was genuinely distressed. She had no recall of what had happened, not even of introducing Claire to Von-Hesse. Adam thoughtfully sat her down in her office and made some black coffee. Meanwhile John and Claire had a confab: "You think that's what he was doing John, letting us know something?"

"Oh fer sure. Even if I wasn't into parapsychology, my police experience would have sniffed it out – hence his inquisitive remark about me having been in either the military or the police. He tried to suggest that he'd read my mind. More likely he'd just worked it out logically – although the snapping of his fingers and then Dr Moore apparently coming out of a trance – well that was a real enough demonstration. But he didn't suss you out on your police background, so he wasn't being 'psychic'."

Claire wasn't so sure: "Or maybe he just wanted to keep us guessing? He took a bit of a broader interest in my background though. It is worrying… I wonder what he wants from Claudia?"

John just shook his head: "At this stage… who knows."

"I got a feeling from him John… one I've felt before, it wasn't just my hand being shocked and then stuck and repelled, it was something in his eyes."

John looked at his old friend. He'd known and worked with her for so long now that the understanding between them was very deep: "No… you don't mean…"

"It was very similar: but they are all a bit different aren't they; I mean they're never *exactly* the same?"

John breathed in hard: To be honest the hair did stand up on the back of my neck."

"I think that it was his eyes John. They were… like *his* were, like Dominic's…"

"If yer ask me he ain't from Bavaria, he's from downtown Freaksville USA, one of those perverted Bible belt types: so 'down'-town he's hangin' upside-down in ah cave!" Adam had returned with some coffee for the parapsychologists.

"How's Claudia?"

"Oh confused, but then she bollocked me an' made me feel like a naughty schoolboy – so… she's normal."

"Well that's something" murmured Claire.

"He's still got the skull yer know, and most of the soil."

John put his police helmet back on: "That's a matter for the museum, not us; they'd have to make an official complaint."

Claire burst into laughter: "See, he has got to you John! You'd gone back in time over twenty years!"

"Ha! So I had! Next thing, you'll have me calling in at the Eden Institute to confer with your dad-in-law."

"And you'll be bringing Carla back into the team."

"And Crazy-Horse!"

Adam's eyes were crossing: "Crazy-Horse! Crikey… an' I thought it was psychiatrists who were trees hidden in forests!"

Back at Oxton, Von-Hesse was unconcerned at any reaction he may have kindled in the ESP team. He was concentrating on a side-line to his final preparations: "Adler… here are the details on Claire Lattimer's date and place of birth – taken from professional journals. Go onto the internet and do a genealogical search. Start with ancestry.co.uk – identify her parents, and then trace birth, marriage and death certificates for her 'Lattimer' ancestors. Work through census returns as far back as you can, and then check any leads on the Mormon Family Search website. Let's see if we can link her to Nathaniel Lattimer… what a resurrection gift for *Lilith* that would be!"

That night Claire was having disturbing dreams. She'd gone to bed feeling more tired than usual, but hadn't had any undue conscious concerns or worries about the events of the day. Her husband Kevin, who was a little over five years younger than her, was curled up around her in the spoon position.

She'd felt safe, comfortable, loved and secure as she'd past through a mentation phase of sleep and into true dreaming…

The shrill androgynous laugh was familiar. Fear gripped Claire as she felt her arms and legs shackled in chains. Opening her eyes she saw herself naked and laid out on a satin-backed black-velvet cloth atop an ancient stone alter: "Claire! Welcome back, you didn't think that you could have escaped me so easily did you? Ha ha ha!"

"No!" Claire's fear tore into her stomach as she turned in terror to see the Harlequin's grinning face.

"Oh bothersome isn't it? There you were, being oh sooo successful with your life and then, suddenly twenty two years later, along comes your death! Ah well… you see Claire, we have a covenant to keep, your earthly life in exchange for… *two* others…Mine… and Rowena's!

That's why I'm here, in your dreams… your time of death approaches… and *our* time of liberation! Ha ha ha!"

"Oh God no! You're gone, you were destroyed!"

"Who me? Destroyed? Oh tut tut… have you learned *nothing* on your borrowed time? I cannot be 'destroyed' dear-thing, merely… forestalled… We made an agreement don't you remember?"

"I agreed to nothing!"

"Oh but you did… You see you did *die*, you were sacrificed… So, your soul should have been exchanged… for Rowena's. But that bungling buffoon of a former lover of yours went and spoilt it… temporarily anyway. And how's that husband of yours, young Kevin? All grown up is he? Such a shame that he'll *still* have to pay for his treachery… Oh, I nearly forgot! You have children now don't you? Ha ha! Not for long…"

Claire writhed around struggling against her chains as The Harlequins shrill androgynous laughter pained at her ears.

"Soon Claire soon Ha ha ha!"

She woke up with a gasp. Kevin was fast asleep besides her. The night was still and calm…

By 2.30am Gustav Adler had completed his internet search. The ancestry.co.uk site had given him everything he needed including census returns to get him back to the early 1800's. From there, the Mormon Church of Latter-Day Saint's website 'Family Search' had taken up the slack and very quickly he was able to establish the link: "Master… Claire Lattimer, born Birkenhead on June 12th 1961 – is… the tenth generation in direct paternal descent from Nathaniel Lattimer born 1616 in Cambridgeshire died 1702 in Hale, near Liverpool."

"So he is her seventh generation great-grandfather, excellent! He lived to a generous age for his times… that will not be so for his descendent!

You have done well Adler, now… we can bring *her* back!"

Claire couldn't get back to sleep; at last her tossing and turning woke her husband: "What is it love, can't you get to sleep?"

Claire sighed: "I got to sleep Kevin… it's what happened when I did."

"What, you mean dreams or somethin'?"

"Yeah…or something; a nightmare. It was *him* he'd come back to take me again… The Harlequin, Dominic Magister!"

Adler and Meier had prepared the basement laboratory room well in advance. Von-Hesse had instructed that it be kept ready on immediate notice. The two Bavarian assistants – the lineage descendants of Reich and Scheer, had followed their master in all matters scientific and occult for ten years now. Adler was an information technology specialist – a top drawer internet hacker who prided himself in being able to access any data-base stored in any retrieval system anywhere in the world. Meier was the 'heavy' of the two – the physical enforcer, as well as being the specialist in such diverse fields as psychology and archaeology.

Both would have been classified as criminal psychopaths – except that they were more than that, far more and far worse. Under their master's instruction they had become inducted into the Cult of *Lilith* –and had sold whatever remained of their human soul for the price of promised magical powers.

As Von-Hesse prepared himself Meier had a question: "Master, when she is returned to us, how will she understand the modern world... even the language has changed?"

The black-brown eyes narrowed. The timing of the question was not appreciated, but, he would answer it: "It is like the Earth itself. *Lilith* is *made* of the elements of the Earth. Think of volcanic rock – not the explosive kind, but the kind that seeps slowly out from the ground. When it cools and solidifies, it takes into itself the direction of the Earth's magnetic field – the rock itself becomes magnetised – but by the field that exists around it at that time! So, it is with *Lilith*, when she is reanimated through the alchemical fires – her blood-soil will absorb the times in which she lives – the psyche, the culture – the language, the history – the knowledge. She will be of *this* time, this twenty-first century of the Common Era. You need have no concerns about her fitting in... she will be created as an adult, and not as before within the host body of a new born child; but from the bones of her past incarnation – and in so doing, absorbing these present times, in which we now flourish.

We must though have a care. Her memory will include *all* of her past incarnations and all that has happened to her within each. I cannot be sure of her temper... but I have faith that she will forgive the long passage of time since I buried her on the shore, not of the 'wasteland' as it says of her in the Jewish book of Isaiah: but of old Liverpool's common heath and pool-side... She *will* require vengeance against all living descendants of those who formerly tormented her, so you will work on tracking down the descendants of the individuals on the prescribed list of names – for their torture and elimination.

So... it will be different this time – there is no living host. She will need some time to gain her strength. She will do this in adult human form and move about freely within society – taking her strength – her vital energy from the Libido of living humans – both men and women alike.

Gustav... you will also be required to create an identity for her, a perfect record – birth certificate, passport, electoral roll, educational certificates and school records, employment, national insurance number, tax records, driving licence – everything she would need to take up an 'instant' identity.

For myself, I... must adjust to her... it has been some centuries since I was last graced by her presence and her immortal beauty. In that time, I have travelled wide, learned many, many things and made accomplishments greater than any I had before. Thus I have no *need* of her... I can continue on indefinitely, acquiring more and greater wisdom with each passing century... yet, I made a covenant with her, and one that I am sworn to keep. When the time was right, and we could recover her bones and her blood soil – then I was to re-animate her, and just as you may claim your reward from me, so I from her – to be her consort and new Adam!"

4.00am and Von-Hesse was trembling. Seated in the centre of the Magic Circle he was surrounded by arcane instruments of demonology and black magic. Ancient scripts that told the story of Lilith from Sumer in 3,000 BC, from Hebrew lore, from Babylonian texts, from the Jewish Bible… her long history written into the collective psyche of humankind as death demon, succubus, bringer of pestilence and… as Adam's first wife in Eden before Eve.

In the 'Western' occult tradition – the magus or alchemist stays within the magic circle, protected from the activated psychic and supernatural forces. In the Eastern tradition, the circle or mandala is used to contain these forces whilst the magus remains outside. Von-Hesse was very much in the Western and Near-Eastern tradition. The skull was outside of the magic circle and placed on an altar – within easy reach of the circle's centre. With Von-Hesse were his Bavarian students, Adler and Meier. It would be necessary for them to remain within the protective boundary; otherwise they would certainly be at mortal risk.

The passage of the years had made Von-Hesse a curious mix of the arcane and the scientific. As well as the darkened room, black velvet cloths, black candles, and magic circle – he also had a battery of scientific recording and measuring equipment trained on the altar: an infrared thermal imaging digital video camera – to record the resurrection for posterity; an electro-magnetic field meter to detect disturbances in the ambient electromagnetic field of the house; freestanding infra-red temperature sensors and motion detectors; a Geiger counter to detect changes in background radiation levels and an ion detector, to measure changes in negative ion ratio's. All were linked to a network of computers each capable of independently controlling the detector and recoding arrays.

Within the circle itself – he allowed only the traditional alchemical artefacts and occult texts. He had to get this right…

Entering a trance, his hooded black-brown eyes closed and his breath deepened. His heart gradually slowed, though its beat throbbed and pulsed through his fingertips and ears. A gradual tingling in his arms changed to pins and needles as mind and breath conjoined as if to leave his body.

"*Lilith…*" his mouth uttered.

His energized body ducted its power into his warming left hand until he knew with certainty that the moment had come.

The infra-red detectors picked up a massive heat signature emitting from his left hand and projecting towards the alchemist's phial at his side – containing the refined blood-soil, mercury and sulphur mixture. The ion detector picked up an anomalous surge in negative ion concentration around the altar, at last resolving into a dynamic field fluctuation.

Adler and Meier were frozen like petrified statues as surges of static electricity sparked off the shielded electronic equipment. Despite their psychological preparation the hair on the back of their necks stood up and involuntary fear gripped at their guts.

Von-Hesse began the arcane incantation, spoken in fluent ancient Aramaic with his rich bass-tone voice. As he spoke his right hand took the alchemical compound container and emptied a proportion of its contents into his left hand. Immediately the ion detector registered an extension of the field from around the altar; now connecting Von-Hesse's hand with the skull. Further incantation and he cast some of the mixture across the skull – guided by the charged ion particle field – the powders passed through the eye sockets and nasal cavity- at which point the Geiger counter detected a sudden surge in radiation focused on the skulls dark interior.

More incantations, more casting of powders, still greater surges of energy until at last the motion detectors registered an unseen presence emerging from the skull.

Lilith had returned…

Claire's dreams had let her down. The terror of old memories had awoken her, and unable to get back to sleep her psyche had missed its chance of warning.

Her husband Kevin was concerned enough to sit-up with her. It was very unusual for Claire to be so troubled. Years of experience had strengthened her mind, so when something did break-through then it had to be significant. Kevin had spent his whole adult life with Claire – literally grown up in relationship to her. For a police-officer, his own knowledge of the psyche was exceptionally well-developed. He'd had life-changing experiences too – mostly shared directly with Claire, from the very start of their relationship.

"You think that this was kicked-off by your meeting with this Von-Hesse character?"

"I can't be sure… he *did* remind me of him, around the eyes… You remember Dominic's eyes? Incredible power in them."

"Maybe it was just that, a faint resemblance, and that was enough to bring up those old memories. If your psyche really was warning you about Von-Hesse, then why didn't the dream simply portray him? Seems it just mirrored fears. Anyway, Dominic had his Sister and Rowena…"

Claire shuddered: "God don't I know!"

"But there's no woman associated with Von-Hesse is there?"

"No, only an old skeleton… Maybe I'm just being a bit superstitious and vulnerable. I can't see how they're connected. The sarcophagus has been buried for centuries and can't have anything to do with Dominic Magister."

"Well… there you go, just an ordinary dream, doing its ordinary job – shaking up your ordinary emotions a bit. You'll be fine… there's absolutely nothing to worry about…"

Convinced, Claire relaxed.

The shimmering shape gradually took form like a developing photograph. Naked and perfect, its' windswept glowing russet honey- blond, hair seemed independently alive: each lengthy strand swirling as if submerged under clear water.

Her face a perfect angelic symmetry revealed a Mona-Lisa smile, set off by almond shaped eyes of the deepest green. Her white alabaster complexion suggesting an untouchable purity.

Adler and Meier gaped at the beauty of the vision unfolding before them, but Von-Hesse scanned her for the slightest hint of capricious malice – he knew that the Mesmerising form before him was capable of dealing cursory death on the merest of whims.

Gradually the glow of ionised particles subsided, the Geiger counter dropped from red to a normal background level, and the infra-red detectors showed only an ambient body temperature.

The coquettish tilt of the head and the broadening dimpled smile induced Von-Hesse to prostration. Flinging himself down to the ground he exclaimed: "Mistress!"

"Maximilian... it's been some time hasn't it?"

  "Mistress... forgive me!"

"Forgive Maximilian? Before you've given your account of yourself?

Von-Hesse relaxed – just a little; it looked as if she would at least give him a chance to explain: "Mistress, Reich was wounded; we had to... set him aside. Then they pursued us all across England, out of the country and overseas. I barely escaped with my life!"

"As before in Genoa?"

"But this was worse... by the time I came back; the markers of your resting place had gone. The town had been built over the site – the pool was filled-in, I had to wait... to be patient..."

Lilith smiled the smile that normally presaged someone's destruction.

"Mistress, I am loyal! I could not have returned sooner, you were discovered by archaeologists... and for your vengeance; I have found a descendent of Nathaniel Lattimer!"

Lilith's smile softened: "Ah yes, my curse upon him and all those who tormented me: all their descendants to their utter extinction... Good... very well Maximilian, we shall resume our covenant."

"Mistress... you will need time to stabilize your form... to gather your strength if you are to release your plague upon humankind. My assistants and I are working on tracking down the descendants of *all* of your enemies... also; we are creating an identity for you, so that you may walk amongst the people of this century without drawing attention to yourself."

"Maximilian, really! I *always* draw attention, how could I do otherwise? Nevertheless, despite your lateness in recovering me, you have done well...

I'll attend to my *personal* vengeance first... it would be a pity for them to die quickly from plague when I could have my entertainment with them first.

Who is this descendent of the cursed Witchfinder?"

"A woman Mistress... Professor Claire Lattimer, a parapsychologist at Liverpool University, and director of the ESP Institute in the city's Rodney Street."

"Does she have family?"

"She does, a husband, although she uses her maiden name; which is Lattimer. She has a son called Sean who is eighteen, and a daughter Elizabeth, who is sixteen."

"Good... they must suffer too. I'll save their ultimate destruction until nearly the end – their torment will be prolonged, deep and all encompassing..."

6

Lillian

Tuesday 24ᵗʰ October 2006: ESP
Rodney Street Liverpool 1.00pm

 laire had come into work late. Making her excuses by phone to the university – she eventually found her way into ESP by One O'Clock in the afternoon: "Hello stranger… you look *awful*" grinned John.

"I *am* awful… had a bloody awful night – full of bad dreams after meeting that Von-Hesse character!"

"Young Adam Mitchell reckons he's really Christopher Lee in disguise. Does look like him…or maybe Eric Cantona!"

"Maybe… but in my nightmare, Dominic Magister was back."

"The Harlequin!?"

"Yep… you bet, the very same. Kevin tried to say that it didn't mean anything, it was just me seeing some similarity between them in Von Hesse's eyes."

"Well, you did say that to me yesterday, so maybe he's right and you've just been a bit spooked by an old memory. What happened in the dream?"

"Oh nothing much, Magister just prophesized my imminent death and said that my soul would be exchanged, this time for *both* his and Rowena's. He said that I'd actually died on that Church altar, and that I'd been living the last twenty two years on borrowed time."

"Not a nice experience for you, that dream… but was Von-Hesse in it?"

"No…"

"Rowena or Dominique?"

"No."

"Then it's probably like Kevin said."

"Men!"

"Hey!" grinned John "What happened to all that post-feminist stuff you're into?"

"Got carried away on a dream…. Seriously, John, I think something's going to happen… don't know what yet, but something. If someone we worked with professionally came up with a dream like that – someone who'd had the kinds of experiences we've been through – then we'd sit up and take notice wouldn't we?"

"Well… yeah"

"Well yeah *and* I think we should now too!"

John drifted off in his thoughts for a while and then said: "We could always test him."

"An ESP test?"

"Sure, he was playing the 'mind-reader' game with me, and he had that strange effect on you through his handshake – some kind of energetic transference. Why not? If he is a problem then we should take the initiative and get to him first."

Claire smiled: "Same old John, you were always first up an' at 'em in the police too weren't you!"

"I was, but that was a couple of decades ago and I was a young man then. Still, not as old as Kevin senior – he's what, must be sixty-seven now?"

"Sixty eight, and he's still working."

"Well there yer go – he's got years on me!."

"You know that you're talking yourself into being *the* 'Action Man' all over again?"

"Perhaps… but then Von-Hesse is probably just some innocent eccentric who just happens to look a *tiny* bit like Eric Cantona..."

The 'innocent eccentric' had gone without sleep too. However unlike Claire he was untroubled. Not just because he was elated at *Lilith's* re-animation, and the resumption of his covenant with her, but also because he no longer needed sleep like ordinary people did. The centuries of alchemical practice and administration of elixirs had transformed him at a cellular – even genetic level. In effect, he was no longer 'human' in the strictest sense. He was a highly evolved being with an indefinite lifespan, and, an increasing bandwidth of occult powers.

Since he'd last met *Lilith* he had developed to such a point that a total transformation was within his potential reach. As he had said to his associates Adler and Meier– he didn't *need* to re-animate *Lilith*, she could have been left buried until the city of

Liverpool itself passed into the dust of time. No… he *wanted* her, which was something altogether different, and was his greatest vulnerability.

Claire had indeed seen something in his eyes. He was still some way behind The Harlequin in his occult powers and supernatural development, but the foreshadow of such attainment cast itself in his black-brown eyes.

If he could become *Lilith's* consort – then he would equal – perhaps even exceed The Harlequin's power – albeit in a different way. Von-Hesse would become the father of the new demonic race of humankind – sprung from *Lilith's* womb. *Lilith*, who could not mother human children… *Lilith* who cursed all who descended from Eve would be the vengeful destroyer of her lineage and mother of demon-kind.

"Adler… we must create this identity profile as quickly as possible. It must be seamless, and contain a complete and verifiable antecedent history – including medical records.

Meier… *Lilith* will need clothes; you will have to shop for her. I suggest 'House of Fraser' in Grange Road, Birkenhead, for convenience, and for style. She can add to her wardrobe after the basics have been acquired. Make sure that you choose something that is commensurate with her new persona…"

"Master?" Gustav Adler wanted a decision on a major point of detail "I can do as you ask, easily, but I need to have an agreed name, an age, and date and place of birth to build the identity around."

A soft feminine voice answered from the shadows: "I shall be known as Lillian… from the Lily flower, symbol of my purity. Lillian Hopgood, yes, why not – the same family name as last time. My age? Nineteen, my date of birth… make me a *Scorpio* for it is written that my vulva is as the scorpion's sting…"

Adler shuddered involuntarily at her words: "Yes Mistress."

Von-Hesse turned to face her. She was wrapped temporarily in a black velvet and satin cloth – which contrasted in striking manner with her pearlescent skin and lustrous russet honey blond hair: "Mistress…" he said quietly "Your beauty seems even greater than before…"

"True beauty increases with age and experience Maximilian, but remember… men… *and* women… each will see me as a reflection of their own soul-image…and who can resist that? Now, hurry with your preparations, for I am… impatient to explore this new world. I think, I'll call at the Museum first…"

Thursday 26th October 2006: Liverpool Museum 10.00am

Adam was in a daydream as he passed through the Egyptology Exhibition at the museum. On an intuition – Adam was always being led by random intuitions; he'd detoured from his proper route on his way back to the basement and Claudia's office. His eyes happened to fall on the back of a tall long wavy blond haired woman who was viewing some of the ancient stone sarcophagi.

Feeling strangely compelled, he approached her from behind. He thought himself important in his museum white coat and staff-badge: maybe he'd pass some time in conversation with her: "We've just found one of those under the foundations of a building in Paradise Street – not Egyptian, but it is a bit of a mystery. I'm an important part of the team working on the find!" he announced proudly.

The girl's extensively long russet honey-blond hair covered her face. He'd just noticed a reaction to her natural ascent, stirring in his loins, when she turned around and slowly parted her hair – like golden curtains revealing a beautiful pre-Raphaelite painting.

With a coquettish tilt of her head; her heart shaped porcelain face and deep green eyes stunned him. His mind clouded and struggled to clear as his heard his voice say: "I know you…"

"Yes…" said her soft voice "You do…"

A flickering screen of indistinct images ran through his mind.

A Mona-Lisa smile passed across her face as she slowly walked on.

"Wait!" feeling drawn as if by a magnetic force he ran ahead of her: "wait… don't go again! Whatever that means…" he said feeling puzzled at his own words.

"Wait? Oh I've been waiting for… let me see… seems like centuries: how about you?"

"Centuries…" his voice trailed in echo "I… I…"

"I know" she said with a broadening dimpled smile." She went past him and headed for the exit stairwell.

"No! Please! Come back!"

She flashed her green-eyes at him, framed in the doorway like a pre-Raphaelite oil painting.

"I love you…" he heard himself say.

Claudia was impatiently waiting for Adam to return. An attractive woman in her early thirties, she'd developed a hard outer cusp – largely as a result of being hurt in relationships, but also as a career move in a competitive environment. She was unmarried, but had a long-term live-in partner, a fellow archaeologist who worked at Liverpool John Moores' University. At last the familiar erratic footsteps of her student could be heard in the corridor.

"Where did you wander off to this time? Was it Greece, Rome… no, don't tell me, it was Egypt wasn't it!"

Adam was all smiles: "Almost heaven!"

"West Virginia?" Claudia was old enough to remember John Denver lyrics, but even if he did, Adam was as far away from the Blue-Ridge Mountains of West Virginia as old Liverpool Town was from the twenty-first century: "I'm in love!" he exclaimed.

"In love? Who with this time, some Brazilian model? Or maybe one of the 'Yummy Mummy' teachers on a school visit?"

Adam didn't read Claudia's remarks either as friendly banter or sarcasm – he was far too engrossed with his memories: "It was love at first sight! Or is that second sight? I feel like I've known her for ever…"

Lilith made her way over to Rodney Street. She wanted to have a good look around – see this 'ESP' Institute where the female descendent of Nathaniel Lattimer worked. Walking along past the impressive Georgian terraces she noted the concentration of medical clinics that had long-ago earned the street its nickname of being 'The Harley Street of the North.'

"Ah… here we are 'ESP' Paranormal Research Institute."
The Mona-Lisa smile took in the building's façade as the almond shaped green-eyes penetrated deeply within.

In her office Claire suddenly shuddered and gasped loudly. John was passing and heard her: "Claire? You OK?"

Clutching at her chest, she managed to call out: "John help me!"

Sensing her urgency he rushed in: "What's wrong, are you ill?"

Hyperventilating, Claire's eyes were wide and staring: "Something was in here, I felt it! It looked right *through* me!"

For just a second, John had a 'rational' reaction and dismissed Claire's state as a panic attack – but then he remembered how experienced she was: "In here? Is it still in the room?"

Calming her breathing she replied: "No… no it's gone. My God it was strong… malevolent, *really* malevolent!"

"Did you 'see' anything, or was it more of an inner vision, an apperception?"

"Both… a bit like one of those experiences people have when they are just falling asleep or waking up."

"Hypnogogia?"

"Yeah… it was as if I was being scanned or something, it 'read' me really fast and then was gone. It was like having one of those laser gun-sights trained on me!"

John thought that he'd better lighten things up – to help her come down off the anxiety: "Hmm we'll have to think about who we've upset recently in the spirit world…"

Claire laughed: "Oh there's plenty of those! Why can't we have 'ordinary' enemies like everyone else!"

"Seriously though Claire, we know that things like that don't 'just' happen, they're intelligently directed."

"Thanks for the cheery thought!" then sighing she said "I know John, you are right… we do need to get to grips with it rationally and work out who, or what was behind it." then she remembered her dream: "Maybe it's the Harlequin?!"

John shook his head: "He's gone Claire. If it is connected to your dream, then it's more likely to be your psyche trying to warn you about something that's a real and present danger, by comparing it with an experience from the past."

Claire was in 'professional mode' now and relaxed back into her chair. Breathing out slowly she said: "Who's on the radar at the moment?"

"Well… there's a couple of mediums who may have channelled something. The Remote Viewing studies are on-going. It could've been a Remote Viewer from a foreign government funded lab using a *bio-PK* attack. We have drawn attention to ourselves Claire, with our Ministry of Defence and Secret Service work."

"It didn't feel like Bio-PK John, that's usually discrete, an attempt to alter a target person's physical or mental state at a distance… for health or for harm. This… this was blatant, extravagant almost, as if whoever or whatever was behind it simply didn't care if I knew about it or not."

"An extraverted spirit then perhaps?"

"You could say that… It certainly wasn't shy about coming forwards!"

Lilith was strolling along reading the brass name plates when at last her eyes settled on a large sign announcing the name of a psychotherapy and personal development centre: "The *Eden* Institute… well, well, well… how… quaint."

Smiling an extra-broad Mon-Lisa smile she climbed the short flight of steps and entered through the heavy, green painted, Georgian door.

In the reception area she saw a smartly dressed woman of about fifty: "Hello, I was just passing and wondered what it was that you did here?"

The receptionist was used to inquiries from unusual people, and *Lilith* not only looked unusual, she was of course un-human: "We offer psychological services… including therapy and personal development. We have a full range of therapists here from all the major schools. We also run professional courses to train psychotherapists."

Lilith's Mona-Lisa perma-smile fixed the middle-aged woman causing her spine to tingle uncomfortably: "Er… would you be interested in any of our services?"

"I'm interested in everything… life itself is so very interesting don't you think?"

The receptionist was too experienced to be distracted by the word play of the often surreal and unorthodox people who walked in through the reception door: "Dr O'Riley is available: our initial consultations are free of charge."

"Dr O'Riley? That's a familiar name…"

"He's our senior practice-partner, been here over twenty years now."

"That's nice… OK, I have plenty of time to *kill*."

"What name is it please?"

"My name? Lillian, Lillian Hopgood."

At sixty eight years of age, Dr O'Riley was still an impressively handsome man. His face wore concern and care as easily as a glove – yet his deeply compassionate heart softened his lines into a face that extruded trust and confidence. This was a man who had seen much in his life. In fact he was Claire Lattimer's father-in-law and had guided both her and John Sutton through their initial encounters with the paranormal some twenty five years previously. Like them a former police-officer, he had walked away from the pinnacle of his career to follow his true calling working with the suffering human soul. But what walked into his office now… had no human soul…

"Miss Hopgood?"

"Lillian."

"Welcome Lillian! Please sit down, would you like a coffee?"

"Black please… and no sugar."

As O'Riley turned to pour the coffee he felt his spine tingle in a way it hadn't done in years. He'd hardly looked at the young girl when she came in; he preferred to make a gradual eye-contact with people – creating an increasing gradient of communication rather than a falsely crafted persona.

However he certainly felt her penetrating eyes as they scanned his form from behind.

Sitting down with a smile he at last made full eye contact immediately registering her unusual beauty – quite breath-taking in its pre-Raphaelite perfection: "What can I do for you Lillian?"

"Well… I was just passing by, and my attention was caught by the sign outside… and its name: *Eden.* Such an unusual choice I thought."

"Eden? Oh… the name goes back years – back to the late nineteen seventies in fact. The original founder, Dr Oliver Blackmore was a rather unorthodox Jungian therapist; he thought that it was somehow very appropriate. You see for him… depth psychology was a process of self-discovery, and he believed that in our culture self-inquiry was a forbidden fruit – like taking an apple from the Tree of Knowledge in the Garden of Eden."

"Oh yes… The Tree… It was supposed to be a Serpent, or as some say, another woman... wasn't it, who gave the apple to Eve and then persuaded her to tempt Adam with it."

"Yes, and for that sin of gaining self-knowledge they were cast out of the Garden. That's what can happen here. Your whole life can change, nothing is ever the same afterwards, and you may even be rejected and shunned by family and friends who have never felt the urge to develop beyond themselves.

But I haven't been happy with the Eden analogy, I prefer Plato's allegory of The Cave. You see, people can't opt out of life, they have to live in this world, and that means that even after self-discovery and transformation you have a responsibility to go back - despite its limitations - and to help others."

"Then you should call this place Plato's Cave" smiled *Lilith*.

"Maybe… but then it'd sound like a night-club wouldn't it?" smiled O'Riley in return.

"Speaking of night-club's the Cavern Club in Mathew Street…"

"Ah yes, The Beatles!" interrupted O'Riley

"No…not them: but *nearby* the Cavern Club, in Mathew Street, there's a statue – more of a bust really, of your 'spiritual' mentor… Carl Gustav Jung… isn't there?"

"You know about that?" O'Riley answered, somewhat intrigued.

"Of course… and the inscription beneath it says: "Liverpool is the Pool of Life"

"That quote comes from a dream Jung had."

"Yes, dreams are very important Dr O'Riley… I should know: lots of people dream about me… both men *and* women."

O'Riley raised a curious eyebrow "And they tell you about them, do they?"

Lilith smiled appealingly: "It's a bit like a drug for them, poor things… like their very lives depended upon me."

"That must get tiresome for you" he replied.

"Oh not at all, in fact it's the perfect buzz: you could even say that I get high on it…"

"I see…" He didn't, of course.

"Funny, about the old Liverpool Pool, being the 'Pool of Life'… It's been the 'Pool of Death' for some too."

O'Riley's eyes half closed and then fixed on her as he tried to make sense of her words: "Perhaps once, but much of its' been built over for nearly three hundred years now... It was believed in ancient times that the liver, in the body, was the seat of the soul – that's the true meaning of Jung's dream."

"Then from now on, this city of 'Liver-Pool' will have to be the 'Pool of Rebirth' instead, won't it?" *Lilith's* Mona-Lisa smile broadened to show her lovely dimples: "That's an unusual charm you're wearing on your neck chain."

O'Riley was surprised: "You can see it?"

Lilith didn't reply, thereby inviting an explanation from him.

Off guard, O'Riley failed to follow his intuition. Instead he lifted the chain from behind his tie.

"May I see?" she enquired.

He paused momentarily. In the past, some had been burned by its touch. The charm had been given to him by his late mentor as protection against maledictive forces. *Lilith* saw him falter:

" I see it's a device against the devil."

"You know what it is?"

"Of course."

At last O'Riley's intuition broke through from the back of his mind. He looked deeper into the almond shaped autumnal green eyes – looking for any sign he could recognize.

Reading his mind: "We haven't met before…" she said.

O'Riley's body involuntarily relaxed but his deepest sense of curiosity was aroused: "How did you know what it was?"

Lilith had no desire to take hold of the charm. Waving her elegant hand dismissively she said: "It's OK I don't need to look any closer: its Gawain's shield isn't it, with Celtic Ogham script writ onto the pentacle points."

O'Riley sat back deeper into his chair. He was *very* curious now, fascinated even: "His shield is a common enough symbol, you see it around a lot on occult websites, but the Ogham… that is a rare knowledge, very rare…"

Lilith didn't answer directly, instead she responded with a question: "You know his story do you… his *real* story?"

O'Riley's smile widened: he was beginning to lose his capacity for critical awareness: "Better than most" he all but boasted.

Lilith changed tack again, sensing that O'Riley was still off-guard: "I live on the Wirral."

"Me too, I'm from Liverpool originally, but I've lived over there for oh… thirty years now."

"I'm from Oxton, near to Mere Hall."

"I know it, it's a beautiful area." His mind flashed back to someone else he had known who had 'lived' in the shadow of the old hall: "I'm in Prenton" he disclosed.

"Pine Walks?" she asked.

"No… not Pine Walks, why did you think that?"

Lilith was trawling memories and associations from him. They were leaking out from his brain like microwaves from an old oven: "Oh it's just a long-standing Prenton joke isn't it – if you don't live in Pine Walks then you must live at the bottom of their gardens."

O'Riley was being inducted. The 'joke' was in reality a private one between his wife Maggie and her friend Davina Wallace-Jones. He hadn't heard it in years…

He rallied himself: "So… are you considering some personal development or psychotherapy?"

Lilith tilted her head in her inimitable coquette style: "Is it fun?"

"Fun?"

"Yes… is it fun? Perhaps… if it is, and if it amuses me."

O'Riley pondered her question: "It's hard work, but yeah, it can be fun, it's certainly an achievement to work on yourself in depth."

"Oh good. You'll find that I'm *very* deep Dr Kevin O'Riley, as deep as the deepest of pools…"

"Mistress!" Von-Hesse was relieved to see her back. *Lilith* could be wilful and as in her past incarnations she'd had a tendency to wander and stray where-so-ever she pleased.

"Don't fuss so, Maximilian. I have walked abroad amongst my enemies – even though they did not know me."

"Your enemies! Have you been to the ESP Institute?"

"I passed-by, and took a 'look' inside. I saw into the Lattimer woman… I also met an old friend at the museum, and then later on I called in to see the only man alive who has the power to stop me…"

7

Past-Life Regression

oung Adam Mitchell was troubled. Since he'd met the stunning pre-Raphaelite vision in the Egyptology exhibition some twelve days ago he'd not been able to get her out of his mind. So intrusive had her memory been that his nocturnal dreams were full of her: strange dreams that seemed set in some past historical time. His day-dreams too were crowded by her face. He was the 'dreamy' type anyway, always disappearing off in his own mind somewhere but this was different. It had a compulsive feeling to it. Never one to be fully focused on his work his mental absences now exceeded Claudia's capacity to be patient with him:

"Adam… you'll have to get your head sorted out on this one. It's like you've got some kind of… I don't know… 'obsessional thought disorder' or something!"

"I'm not bonkers yer know!"

"Frankly, Adam, I don't 'know'… maybe you are?"

Adam's intuition came up with a scenario for his salvation: "Look, Claudia, I know this does sound a bit sorta bonkers... but, I've been havin' weird dreams with her in..."

"It's adolescence Adam."

"I'm in me twenties!"

"Exactly... you should have moved on from this kind of thing years ago!"

"No, let me explain: the dreams are... set in some time in the past – like yer know, in history like."

"A knight in shining armour rescuing your fair maiden: are you?"

"Please... Claudia... I know this is really gonna sound weird but it's here in Liverpool, about three hundred and fifty years ago: I seem to be a young lad..."

"That's accurate."

"Part of a Puritan family, and this girl is some kind of bewitching local beauty, and I'm following her everywhere, desperately in love with her, but all she does is lead me on, teasing me!"

"Apart from the time period it doesn't sound any different to how you live your life any weekend night."

Adam was getting pissed-off with Claudia's dismissive attitude: "So, I'm gonna ask professor Lattimer to hypnotize me!" he declared.

"What?"

"I'm serious, I'm gonna ask her to hypnotize me an' see if I've had a past-life in Liverpool in the seventeenth century. She must do that stuff is she's into parapsychology."

"Oh my God you really have flipped!"

Adam decided to go on the offensive: "That's not fair Claudia, you may be my Ph.D. supervisor, and you may hold my future career in your hands… but remember the effect that Bavarian archaeologist had on you? How your mind went blank? I didn't judge you then, I just helped you get your head straight!

Anyway, think about it… my dreams are here in Liverpool in the seventeenth century – the period of the sarcophagus!"

Friday 10th November 2006: Liverpool Museum 9.45am

"John's the hypnotist at ESP. What do you think John?" queried Claire.

Dr John Sutton looked at Dr Claudia Moore, and then at Adam Mitchell: "Well Claire… it's one of those things: almost everyone wants to *believe* that they've had a past-life. I guess that Adam's dreams give us an indication that we're likely to get material from his regression… *but* it's absolutely no guarantee that what we get is in any way anything other than fantasy."

"He's convinced me that it's worth a shot. That's why I agreed for him to invite you over today. I'm his supervisor and I'm happy for you to use the museum premises if you want."

John now turned to Adam: "You realize that there are risks?"

"Yeah… like what?"

"False memory syndrome, cryptomnesia, severe abreaction, even mental illness."

"Er, can yer explain them things?"

"False memory syndrome is where someone who undergoes hypnosis apparently recalls events as being true that didn't actually happen. The belief in the veracity of the events continues on after the termination of the trance state – and can cause all sorts of psychological, social and even physical problems.

Cryptomnesia in hypnosis is where something a person had read, seen or heard in the past, but has forgotten, gets woven into a fantasy experience under trance-state conditions, and is then consciously 'remembered' as being a real event that's actually happened to them. It's a kind of false-memory; technically separate from that specific category of induced mental artefact I suppose, but it is related.

Severe abreaction under hypnosis comes about through the increased suggestibility induced by trance – hypnosis relaxes a person's normal psychological defences and can allow repressed emotions to burst through into the mind and body, it can be a shocking trauma. Abreaction is a valid therapeutic technique of course, but the severe uncalled for and unexpected variants must be avoided."

"Crikey!"

"Still wanna do it?"

Adam grinned: "Yeah you bet!"

"OK… but on condition that you get checked out physically first by a medic, probably your own doctor. We also need to agree just *why* you want to do this, what's its purpose and its justification?"

Claudia intervened again: "Its purpose is to find out if his daytime fantasies and night-time dreams really are trying to communicate some useful information to him. The justification… well in archaeological terms, is that the content of his dreams seem to be related to the precise location and time period for the sarcophagus find."

Claire responded: "That would normally be considered a good enough reason John."

John nodded: "It would… OK, so long as he's pronounced fit by his medical practitioner *and* so long as he understands and accepts the risks. Also, given that this would in effect be an inter-disciplinary inquiry – I think that it should be recorded on audio and filmed separately on digital video."

"OK, all that remains is to set a time and venue" said Claudia.

"Next Monday day; say 11.00 here at the museum?"

"Right… we're all agreed then!"

A twinge of fear bit hard in Adam's stomach…

Von-Hesse had been unhappy at *Lilith*'s pronouncement of finding the only man alive who could stop her. He'd pressed her for his identity but *Lilith* had breezily refused to tell him. The Bavarian felt that he'd waited long enough: "Mistress, this enemy of yours, the one you haven't yet identified to me. Surely, I could just kill him and be done with him as a threat?"

"That particular pleasure will be mine Maximilian, no one else's. Anyway, soon, I will have to strengthen myself, and that will mean… some nocturnal visitations…"

Von-Hesse knew that she spoke the truth, but he also understood the risks: "That's what caused our difficulties last time!" he cautioned.

"But this isn't *last* time is it Maximilian? This is a very different world, so many… victims for the taking, and such a licentious society. If I do not maintain, and then increase my strength, I will not have the resources to release my plague as a globally fatal pandemic. The medicine of this century is very advanced, the contagion will have to be… intelligent, and capable of a rapid evolution.

I also require *you* Maximilian, to complete the list of proscribed names – they shall be the first to die of plague, for their ancestor's torment of me. Although I'll save my most personal vengeance for a very special reserve-list of individuals. Their torture will be exquisite…

Have you obtained personal transport for me?"

 "Your car, yes, I thought a 'Mini Cooper S' convertible would be suitable. It's fashionable but unobtrusive. It suits the 18-24 year age-group that your appearance will suggest to people. It's a British built vehicle but the manufacture is owned by BMW, a German company, from Bavaria…"

"How very *apropos*… Very well: its colour is?"

 "Why black Mistress, what else?"

Adam's dreams had intensified over the weekend, as if they were impatient to be expressed through his coming encounter with hypnosis. For himself, he was feeling very agitated. John Sutton's words of warning had eaten into him, and it was in this divided state between elation and anxiety that he brought himself into work, as ready as he'd ever be for what may prove an overwhelming ordeal.

"Did you get your GP's go-ahead to do this Adam?" asked Claudia.

"Er..."

"He said no?"

"He didn't say no... he didn't say anything."

"You mean you didn't ask him?"

"No! It's just that you have to make an appointment... and I couldn't get one until tomorrow..."

"So, like I said, you *didn't* ask him! Let's hope that the ESP lot still agree to go ahead with it."

"I've given my own informed consent that should be enough!"

"Let's hope so. I've arranged separate digital audio and video recording equipment to be set up. If this works it could be a fantastic new dimension to archaeology, it'd put us on the word archaeological map!"

Adam began to realize that Claudia had other interest at heart than *just* his own: "And there I was thinking you cared!"

"I do Adam, I do.... About you *and* the department. Anyway, I can hear some footsteps in the corridor now, it must be them."

Adam swallowed hard. This was it…

Claire spent some time with Claudia whilst John made his preparations with Adam: "The proof will be in what *new* and subsequently verifiable information comes up from this Claudia. Many people produce 'material' but for scientific purposes it would have to be entirely new, and, something that leads to discoveries in the field, in this case: the archaeological field. We'd have to be able to rule out cryptomnesia for a start."

"I agree. As far as I'm aware, there isn't any precedent for using past-life regression hypnosis in archaeology."

"Actually, there *is* some, but it probably never made the mainstream in your field. Thirty years ago, back in 1976, the BBC televised a documentary called: 'The Bloxham Tapes' about an amateur hypnotist: Arnall Bloxham. He was filmed using regression-hypnosis and some previously unknown information came up which did lead to some new discoveries.

Parapsychology is still seen as a pariah discipline by many academics. I guess even science has its superstitions, just like the Reformed Christians of the seventeenth century!"

Claire smiled as she made her point.

Claudia smiled back in acknowledgement: "And I guess that Adam is a dreamer… and prone to fantasy… So, what's your instinct on all of this?"

"My instinct? That's a difficult one. You see, I *know* the reality of the supernatural… it's been a cornerstone of my life for twenty-five years: but… I also 'know' that ninety-nine percent of claimed paranormal phenomena are just over-excited intuitions or even down-right fraud. It'll be interesting anyway.

Hey! I've just realized, we forgot to invite someone!"

"Oh, who?"

"Dr Von-Hesse! Freud would have called that 'intentional' forgetting!" The two women shared a knowing smile…

Claudia had managed to procure a reclining chair for the session, which Adam gratefully took to. Anything that increased his comfort and convenience was always welcome.

John insisted that the audio and video be switched on ahead on the hypnotic induction. He wanted as full a record as possible to be made. A skilled hypnotist, he understood that the formal induction phase is preceded by a preparatory period – wherein the hypnotic-subject already begins to slip into an altered state of consciousness.

"Now… Adam… just for the record… have you ever experienced hypnosis before?"

"No."

"Do you have any worries or concerns about what's going to happen?"

"Only that I might lose my mind, but you've reassured me that ain't gonna happen."

"There are risks, Adam, and we *have* discussed those with your supervisor. Can you confirm that you still want to go ahead?"

"I do, Dr Sutton, yes…"

"OK… as well as you Adam, I, Dr John Sutton will be present of course; and by your agreement: Dr Claudia Moore and Professor Claire Lattimer. The session will be synchronously recorded on digital audio and video. Dr Moore and Professor Lattimer have been made aware that they may feel the effects of the induction process on themselves, and have acknowledged their consent on the recording media."

Adam relaxed back into the chair.

"Just make any adjustments you need to in order to *allow* yourself to relax."

Unwittingly, John's use of the 'permissive' style of hypnotic language patterning was indeed affecting one other person in the room – Claudia had been covertly hypnotized by Von-Hesse using the same verbal method. As she sat in the shadows of the darkened room, her eyes slowly blinked as the trigger-word 'allow' reconstituted her former trance state as instigated by Von-Hesse; she was now more open that she had bargained for, to the coming experience…

John knew that Adam was an 'intuitive' type, someone who rapidly processed simultaneous channels of information – some of which were based on his immediate sensory experience of the 'real' here-an-now world, others, a more internal and imaginary world – the world inside his own head. It was this that made him appear scatty. Accordingly, John calculated that the best way to induce a successful hypnotic state was to give him paradoxical instructions: some would ask him to focus on his awareness of his body – a place his mind never usually bothered with, and others on the background stream of consciousness that would produce a narrative of his 'past' life…

The paradox part would be him being instructed *not* to follow the instructions given to him. Then, as the induction continued, John would introduce confusion techniques – designed to overload Adam's capacity to resist hypnosis, so that eventually, his mind would simply go into a neutral state – allowing his subconscious to communicate freely.

In effect, at that point, Adam would be an 'observer' of himself, as separate to the experience as either John or Claire.

"Now… Adam, you don't *have* to listen to my voice… *only* my *voice*, you can… *choose* instead to listen to the background of your mind, but… no other sound you hear will have any significance at all… *only* my *voice*."

Adam's mind was given an apparently permissive choice, as he relaxed, would he listen to the internal chaos of his psyche, or to the certainty of the hypnotists' outer voice?

"When you are ready... and not before, you can *allow* yourself to enter a state of inner contemplation, you will *know* when you are ready, as your subconscious mind, will cause your eyelids to begin... to feel drowsy... and *very* tired... This will be the *signal* from within yourself, that your subconscious mind is *ready* is *willing* to..... *help* you... to relax... when you can feel this, it would be... polite to yourself, to allow your eyes to *close.*"

Adam's eyelids were fluttering

"And... enter *trance*"

He was of course already in trance state; it was now just a question of its depth. John began to pace Adam's breathing with verbal statements, so that the said *lighter* with a raised but gentle tone as Adam breathed in and *deeper* with a deepening tone as he breathed out...

"*Lighter*.... allowing your body to feel as if it weighed no more than your breath... and how much does your *airway* clear, light and relaxed" Here John introduced a confusing connection between the 'weight' of air, and Adam's 'air-way' – being light and relaxed, with the suggestion that he felt as if he weighed as light as air. Adam's conscious mind would look for more confusing word-meanings and as it did so, become ever more tired with the effort as his body became ever more deeply relaxed.

"*Deeper*... allowing yourself to become... more deeply *relaxed.*"

The sensation of his body relaxing as he breathed out was being reinforced by John's words with each natural breath cycle. Already Adam's mind was becoming divided – his conscious mind struggled to make sense of John's words and, in the background the stream of subconscious thoughts and images were encroaching ever more forwards – the thoughts and images of the vision of pre-Raphaelite beauty and the mysterious dream world she brought with her, were becoming his *only* focus of attention.

Her smile in itself was hypnotic. Its power was drawing him away from John's voice, away from the reclining chair, away from the museum… and away from the twenty first century.

Over in Oxton on the Wirral, *Lilith*'s eyes suddenly widened.

"What is it Mistress?" Von-Hesse sensed a change in her demeanour. She smiled faintly as she replied: "They're looking for me Maximilian…"

"*They*, who?!"

"Oh…inquisitive humans… they should be careful, for once opened, Pandora's Box cannot be closed …"

Von-Hesse didn't like to be perplexed: "Your enemies are seeking you out: now?!"

"Not quite now… more, 'then'… How very resourceful of them!

Maximilian, I'm driving over to Liverpool, to the Museum…"

Although he couldn't directly experience Adam's internal mental state, John was carefully monitoring his external signs, and had established an accepted system of communication with Adam's subconscious mind called 'ideo-motor signalling' which meant *idea* or thought communicated through *movement*. An ideo-motor signal feels 'involuntary' to the person experiencing it, it's as if something outside of yourself takes control of a part of your body, usually a finger, but sometimes a whole limb or even your head – so that simple yes-no signals and confirmations can be communicated outside of conscious will and intention. This way, direct cooperation can be obtained with a person's subconscious.

John had already established the link through the index finger of Adam's left hand. Adam's subconscious mind had signalled that it was safe for him to follow direct instruction and go back in time…

"Now Adam… your subconscious mind has agreed to *allow* you to safely go back, in time, back before your present identity was formed. I'm not going to suggest *when* or *where*, rather, I'll ask the subconscious mind to choose a time and place that is most relevant to it, and, to you. When your subconscious mind is ready, it *will* take you back, Adam, back to a time before you were born… when you have arrived, safely, then your index finger, on your left hand will raise, all by itself, just as it has already many times this morning, as a direct signal to me, and to you, from your *subconscious* mind that you are indeed safe, calm, relaxed and confident in this past-time, and past-place…"

Adam's body convulsed slightly, and then let out a gross muscular jerk as internally, his identity as 'Adam Mitchell' was replaced by that of someone else… 'Adam' was now truly an observer; although he could think, feel and experience as this 'other' identity. John's trained eye recognised the gross motor response in Adam's body, and waited patiently for the agreed signal. At last – the index finger quivered, trembled and floated – a clear and unambiguous signal – as mysterious in its way as receiving a message from an alien civilization from another galaxy.

"Thank you" John had long-ago learned that the subconscious mind appreciated polite requests and mannered responses.

"I'm going to ask the subconscious mind now, to allow the voice of this other part of Adam, this past-identity, to speak with me, directly, clearly and without distress – using Adam's voice, and responding *only* to my voice…"

The index finger trembled, quivered and floated once again.

"Thank you… I'm now speaking directly to Adam's past self… can you hear me?"

A long pause… then Adam's mouth silently mouthed a reply.

"Thank you, but I didn't quite catch that, could you repeat it please?"

Then the voice from the past spoke: "Yes, I hear you…"

John thanked him again: "Do you know who I am?"

"I do…"

"Good, I'm here to help Adam, and to be interested in you. Can you tell me your name?"

"Adam, I'm Adam…."

"Adam Mitchell?"

"Adam Teal…Adam Teal of Liverpool Town…."

"Thank you 'Adam Teal…' I'm a visitor to your town, and… to your time… can you please tell me what the year is?"

"The year, knowest thou not?!"

Despite his experience – the sudden and assertive use of a seventeenth century Lancashire accent caused John's spine to tingle.

"If… you could just remind me, please… Adam?"

Adam Mitchell's head shook from side to side, his face grimacing, as if 'Adam Teal' thought the request amusing: "'Tis 1665: the fifth year since the Restoration!"

"Thank you Adam, can you tell me about yourself?"

"Thou speaketh strangely… I canst tell thee, but thy words are, not familiar unto me… I am Adam, son of Henry, a Burgess and Reformed Christian of this Liverpool Town."

"Thank you, and how old are you?"

"Eighteen since my birth, but in the summer of my nineteenth year."

"Thank you…" John decided to do an 'identity test' "You know who Adam Mitchell is?"

Adam's face furrowed into a deep frown: Adam… Mitchell… only… in dreams, he hast scareth me, with his questioning."

"Questioning?"

"Aye, verily, he is in mine dreams and makes rough question with me 'bout my sweet love, *Lilith*!"

John cast a quick glance over to Claire who was perched forwards in her chair following developments intently. They exchanged a look over Adam's mention of the name '*Lilith*'. John then glanced at Claudia, and saw that she was slumped in her chair with her eyes closed – obviously the induction had taken her too. Inconvenient that, as for safety reasons he must concentrate of the Adam Mitchell –Adam Teal 'dissociation' for now.

"Can you tell me about *Lilith*?"

"Oh *Lilith*! Fairest of all of Eve's kind, her hair is as the deepest honey-red blond, with skin of porcelain, and eyes greener than summer's grass: she enchanteth me with her smile, which I doth live to see with each new dawn!"

"You're in love?"

The question caused a convulsion in Adam's body. His face contorted in anguish and tears streamed from his eyes: "I doth! Verily I do, but she… teaseth me, and maketh a joke of mine affections… Oh *Lilith*!"

"Thank you Adam Teal, can you tell me more about her, how old she is, about her family, where she lives?"

"How old?" Adam Teal's tears subsided and 'Adam Mitchell's face relaxed: "twenty one, for she was born upon the night of the great investment."

"Investment?"

"Aye, knowest thou nought!? The investment of the town by Prince Rupert! My uncle Benjamin wast cruelly slain there by Bavarian mercenaries in employment of the Prince – whilst giving his protection to her sweet mother Martha as she layeth abed confined in her labours that very night!"

John shared another glance with Claire over the 'Bavarian' reference.

"I see… you say her mother is called Martha. What about her father and the family name?"

"Oh he be Matthew, and the family be called Hopgood. Matthew Hopgood is a good man, honest and God fearin' a great friend of mine own father…"

John thought that the information so far was potentially good, even perhaps verifiable; so he pressed him further: "Where is the family home?"

"Why, in Water Street of course, close by the Custom House; on the foreshore. Knoweth ye not the town?"

"Thank you Adam Teal… you said it was the summer, of 1665, I'd like you to move forwards in time a while now…"

"Nay!"

"I'm sorry?"

"Nay! *Lilith* be innocent! She hath been beguiled by the Bavarian!"

Adam's body writhed violently in the recliner.

John noted the highly charged emotional reaction, but decided *not* to calm Adam Mitchell's body down – if he did, he may lose the connection to Adam Teal, and to potentially important information. It was a calculated decision: "Adam… tell me of the Bavarian…"

"He be the Alchemist: Maximilian Von-Hesse!"

Von-Hesse's black-brown hooded eyes watched as *Lilith* drove breezily away in her new black Mini convertible. Her 'absorption' of the times when she had reanimated – included that of the skill of driving. She was determined to call over at Liverpool Museum – but for precisely what, she wouldn't say.

However it wasn't only the times that'd changed since 1665, Von-Hesse had too. Inside, he bore the seed of resentment against *Lilith* for – in his eyes – throwing away her last incarnation by her frivolous indulgences. Now, he suspected, she was at it again.

This time though he was a much more formidable figure in his own right. If need be, he thought, he may just have to do without *Lilith*, once again…

Nodding silently to himself he decided to take action – against a possible threat... and in so doing, to signal clearly to *Lilith* that he would if necessary, act independently of her: "Meier!"

"Master?"

"Meier, the Mistress is being… incautious… she is going over to the Museum. She has detected a 'threat' – a human threat against her, and therefore against us. She will not say who this person is, just that it's a male. I am determined that no potential enemy shall be suffered to live... therefore…"

"Therefore, I am to terminate this threat?"

"You are... but be discrete. There must be no corpse, you understand?"

Meier smiled: "Who is this man?"

"I suspect... that he is someone who knows the old language... who reads it fluently, and could conceivably therefore use an ancient incantation in attempt to 'forestall' our Mistress. His name, is Dr Allan Flynn, and he's an ancient languages expert at Liverpool University... Adler will obtain his home address from online data-bases."

Meier's smile suddenly evaporated: "But the Mistress?!"

"She will see our reasoning, Meier" soothed The Bavarian "his 'disappearance' will not draw undue attention from the authorities, but it will notify our enemies that we mean business with them.

"When, Master?"

"Tonight!"

"Von-Hesse!" John spoke in almost frank disbelief. This was too much of a coincidence. Maybe young Adam Mitchell was just fantasizing and using cryptomnesia after all?

"Tell me about Von-Hesse, Adam."

"He be an ungodly practitioner of the black arts, of alchemy and such, at the apothecary in the Chapel Street. He wast overheard making plans with *Lilith*, to release a great contagion upon the town!"

"Contagion in 1665, you mean plague?"

"Verily! Yet my *Lilith* be innocent, they accuse her of being a demon, a *succubus*, and now the Witchfinder hath taken her to the pool."

"And who is this Witchfinder?"

"He be… Nathaniel… Nathaniel Lattimer…"

"Lattimer?!" John's face broadened into a grin as he looked over at Claire. He now felt certain that Adam was just including people around him in his cryptomnesiac fantasy.

But 'Adam Teal' wasn't finished:

"*Lilith* hath cursed them: all of them unto their descendants hence forward's and for all time! She sayeth that she knowest my love for her is true, and promises that we shalt meet again in future life-times!

Lilith! *Lilith*! They hath cast her into the pool! *Lilith*!!!"

Adam's writhing turned to a screaming agony, forcing both John and Claire to intervene to terminate his trance.

Claire soothed him by holding his hand and stroking his forehead whilst John re-commenced his direct contact with Adam's subconscious mind gradually establishing ideo-motor signalling responses: "Listening *only* to my voice... Adam Mitchell, your subconscious mind has agreed to *allow* you to return to your *normal* state of conscious awareness – becoming... calm... relaxed... and confident: *allowing* 'Adam Teal' to peacefully and safely return to *his* time... Coming back *now* Adam Mitchell, back to the twenty first century, back to 2006, here at the Museum... calm, relaxed and confident. When your subconscious mind is ready, you'll want to open your eyes, being able to remember all that has happened, but being *very, very* relaxed...."

Adam's body had ceased its convulsions and his breathing had returned to a relaxed and deep state. Claire gently took her hands away, and returned to her chair, smiling at the sight of an unconscious Claudia as she did so.

"Oh God..." Adam was coming back...

A moan signalled Claudia's return too.

Adam's eyes opened and squinted heavily. Putting his head in his hands he gasped: "It was *her*, the same girl… she was the one I saw upstairs, in the Egyptology section!"

John didn't want to pop his fantasy – just yet. It was more important to get him to return safely to normal consciousness: "You feeling OK?"

Adam felt patronized: "OK! How in hell can I feel OK? I've just seen the love of my life murdered by drowning and you ask if I'm OK!"

Claudia had escaped the attention of the parapsychologists and was shaking badly.

"Claudia?" asked Claire "How are you? It must have been a surprise to find yourself drifting off?"

"Wha? I don't know what happened. How'd it go?"

"Best watch the film: it was quite dramatic in parts."

Claudia had simply gone into a state of unconsciousness. She had not however been unreceptive… at a deep subconscious level; her already prepared mind had heard the name 'Von-Hesse' and had assimilated the essence of Adam's account. The Bavarian's power over her was now even more enhanced than before. Only her recollection at the conscious level of awareness had been abated.

John decided that Adam was too disturbed by his ordeal to be debriefed at that time: "Look, I think we'd better call it a day for now Claudia. We can study the film together next time, perhaps tomorrow if you are both free?"

Claudia nodded, as did Adam from behind his hands.

"OK, we'll take the film back to ESP, and return with it in the morning."

They said their goodbyes, and left Claudia – who now appeared fully *compos mentis* to take care of any after-needs in Adam.

"Adam… I need to get some fresh air and then maybe have a coffee. Will you be OK for ten minutes?"

"Sure…" he nodded. He preferred to let his experiences percolate a while "I'll stay here then, I want to think about what's happened."

In John's Lexus heading back to Rodney Street: "What do you *really* think of all that?" asked Claire.

John sighed: "I suppose it was to be expected. I did hope for a while that we may get some interesting stuff – but he abreacted very strongly. And then keeping his own first name: 'Adam' and then again when Von-Hesse was mentioned, and your name as the name of a Witchfinder!

Well, that stretched credulity just that bit *too* far. Sadly, it all seems like a case of straightforward fantasy and cryptomnesia."

Claire wasn't so sure: "We may be throwing out the baby with the bathwater John. What if there's some accurate detail in there with the fantasy – all woven together?"

"Could be… could be… Let's watch the film and do an analysis of what *can* be checked out.

We may find records somewhere of that 'Hopgood' family: but '*Lilith*' as the name of his 17th century girlfriend… I mean, come on, how likely is that!"

Adam eventually tired of the darkness in the room. The ambiance now spooked him. Feeling a sudden urge to escape he ran out into the corridor.

"Crikey!"

The soft feminine voice stunned him: "Hello again… I seem to have lost my way somehow."

"It's you!"

The Mona-Lisa smile seemed to catch a halo of light around her lustrous golden-blond hair: "Yes…Adam Teal… I've come back…"

Adam's legs buckled as he grasped at the wall for support.

Her porcelain perfect hand reached out and touched his face. A penetrating warmth pulsed through his body as he stared into the lovely green almond shaped eyes.

Then… all went black.

11.30 pm Monday 13th November 2006: the home of Dr Allan Flynn, in Formby, near Liverpool.

The grey, super-charged Range Rover SUV rolled to a halt as silently as a ghost – its headlights unlit. Meier had already reconnoitred the property – although set back from the main road, there was no security – no CCTV, not even an alarm. A line of mature trees bordering the house symbolised the privacy of its owner's life – for he was a reserved and insular man – prone only to animation upon the subject of his lifetime's single passion: ancient near-Eastern languages.

And yet something had been troubling him… Since his visit to the Museum to inspect the Aramaic inscriptions on the '*Lilith*' sarcophagus – his sleep had been restless – his waking hours filled with a most persistent foreboding. At first he'd dismissed this as a mere superstition, arising unbidden from his subconscious – something to be trivialised and set aside.

But it would *not* be set-aside and by now, on this mid-November evening, it had taken on an obsessional strength.

Sensing the encroachment of an unknown, but mortal peril, he picked up his land-line telephone and with shaking hand, dialled Professor Claire Lattimer's home phone number...

St Stephens Road Prenton

"Sean, will you get that please!" Claire called down to her teenage son who was thoroughly preoccupied, watching an adult, cable TV channel, in the family living room.

"In a minute!" he called back, irritated at being interrupted.

"It'll ring off before then!" she shouted down.

"OK, ok, coming now... er, I mean, *she's*... just... ahem..."

"Too late!" called Claire as the phone rang off, silent.

"Can't be important, Mum, if it was family or anything, then they'd have rung on yer mobile!" retorted a still irritated Sean.

Dr Flynn's hand was enveloped in a crushing pressure as Meier's fingers dug claw-like into it. The irresistible force obliged Flynn to let go of the handset, which the German placed slowly back onto the receiver. Now terrified, Flynn's eyes widened to take in the huge form before him. Tall, blond and powerfully built with piercingly cold and merciless blue eyes, Hans Meier's massively spanned right hand now closed like a vice around the academics throat – his immense strength lifting him clear from the floor, dangling him there like a writhing marionette as the very breath of life was choked out from him.

"Unconscious!"

"Yep, I came back after taking a break and there he was flat out in the corridor. He came round pretty-quick, but for health and safety reasons we had to call an ambulance. He was muttering about the '*Lilith*' girl again, saying that she'd been in the corridor, and had recognised him; calling him 'Adam Teal.' Then he said that she reached out and touched him and he fainted... which I guess you would do if a hallucination you'd last seen under hypnosis in 1665 did something like that."

John picked up the sarcasm and even hostility in Claudia's words: "Wait a minute Claudia; he 'met' this girl, so he says, up in the Egyptology exhibition about two weeks ago. *That* was why we did the regression-hypnosis, he was already convinced that he'd known her in some past life from the intrusive dreams he'd been having!"

"It's alright Dr Sutton, you can calm down: no one's blaming you or anything."

Claire decided to interject: "We have a copy of the digital video here, transcribed onto DVD. It makes interesting viewing. We also have a list of testable references he made to people in the town of Liverpool in 1665. Before we get lost in the 'subconscious' effects of what we all witnessed, well, all except you Claudia as er... you'd slipped into trance too, let's be like the scientists we're supposed to be and deal with the observable data."

Claudia bit on her lip. Part of her motive for sarcasm was sour-grapes over the fact that she'd embarrassingly zonked-out and missed virtually everything - the other part... was more sinister.

John was still thinking about Adam: "He's obviously off-work... when is he due back?"

"Tomorrow: he's had tests of various kinds and they're all negative. He's still convinced though – about this girl. Maybe he needs some kind of therapy or something.

Claire and John exchanged looks: "Perhaps" she said "But... however improbable his account may seem, we should exclude it on *evidential* grounds rather than outright, uninformed dismissal."

Claudia added a frown to her lip-chewing behaviour: "You mean that you're prepared to take it seriously?"

"It's a hypothesis: scientists are supposed to *test* hypotheses."

"Well no wonder you guys get treated the way you do!"

"You know Claudia" added John "If I remember rightly *you* supported Adam on this: until now that is; after the actual event itself is over. You were clearly in favour of it, and wondered if it could add anything to your own discipline of archaeology!"

Boxed-in Claudia issued a challenge: "OK, tell you what, you produce some verifiable facts that he couldn't have known about before hand – from some other source – and I'll think about taking your 'data' seriously."

Claire smiled: "There's a 'Catch 22' in all of this, and you must know that Claudia: *any* verification for historical events must come from existing records. So, they're easy to dismiss as being cryptomnesia or otherwise falsely claimed. There are only two ways to get objective data."

"Yeah, and what are they?"

"Either through previously undiscovered archaeology – which he leads us to under hypnosis: or... we find this girl and he shows us that he's been right to believe what he's believed all along."

Claudia's frown now turned into a smirk: "Well, don't hold yer breath on *either* of those!"

Back at ESP later that morning: "Where do we start then Claire?" John's tone was surprisingly uplifted.

"You think we actually have a chance with this one?"

"Yes" he said confidently "I do. We both acknowledge synchronicity don't we?"

"The notion that 'meaningful' coincidences of events cluster around one-another, or around people, and that their significance only emerges when the linking pattern is understood?"

"As we take synchronicity to mean in modern parapsychology… yes. I've been er… thinking."

"Oops, that can be dangerous John, remember last time you did that?"

"Oh yeah… took six months to get rid of the haunting… Anyway, I've been thinking about how events have 'clustered' around us these past weeks – including that strange event here when you felt that presence 'scanning' you."

Claire shuddered as she remembered: "How could I forget!"

"Then, there's what's been happening at the Museum, how we got called-in originally, how we met Dr Von-Hesse – his odd effect on you – with the energy transference – then all the various stuff with young Adam."

"And your conclusion is?"

"That there's more to come. More 'coincidences' of events, and that they'll all start to converge, either on a place, and/or on a person…"

Claire's head was unconsciously nodding: "On who?"

John's grin nearly cracked his face: "There's only two possibilities so far... it's either Adam or..."

"Or me..." said Claire...

Lake Hall, Oxton, at Midday.

"Well Meier?"

"It is done Master."

"And the body?"

"Taken to the warehouse at the West Float dock in Birkenhead – where it was reduced in a bath of sulphuric acid. The remaining waste was drained into the dock. His teeth proved durable, but they have been pulverised into powder and likewise dispersed."

Von Hesse nodded with approval "Good... Flynn was of a nervous disposition, and likely to take fright prematurely. The Mistress would have struck him down with her contagion, but not until her strength was near its maximum. He would have had time, in his fear, to raise the suspicions of Lattimer and her team... and so given his specialist knowledge of ancient Aramaic – he may just have found a curse or incantation to forestall *Lilith*...."

Meier believed him, even though The Bavarian had exaggerated his case. In truth Von Hesse was simply impatient to kill, and to signal his resolve... and mostly of all... to *Lilith*...

Next morning Claudia had started her own kind of 'head-work' on the hapless Adam: "Look Adam, I accept that you wanted to do that regression-hypnosis stuff, and I accept that you still believe in this girl you say you've seen here twice now, but, think about how it looks… how it'll look to the museum and to the university?"

"Wha' are yer sayin?"

"I'm saying… think of your Ph.D. and then your post-doctoral prospects! If you get a name… for being…. yer know…"

"A nutter?"

"Your words Adam."

Adam felt his shoulders droop and his heart sink. Claudia had immense influence over the future course of his life: "What do you recommend…"

Finally she showed some compassion: "I can see that you're suffering Adam… I'm not going to suggest that you just stop thinking about this girl, and what you believe you experienced under hypnosis… but, you should get some help with your feelings, some professional help…"

"I'm not seeing a counsellor if that's what yer sayin!"

"No Adam, not a counsellor. Ventilating isn't going to help you much I know. I was thinking about therapy."

"Therapy, crikey, people will think I'm barmy!"

"Personal development therapy, Adam… it's… different."

"It is?"

"Yes. Lots of people have it, lots of *intelligent* people."

"They do?"

"Yeah, you could go and talk through your experiences with someone who'll take great interest in you, and how you can develop. There's a place in Rodney Street: the Eden Institute."

Claudia agreed to give Adam some time off. However, as with all things of a 'personal' nature her motives were never quite what they seemed. Yes, she had a modicum of genuine compassion for Adam's state of mind, but, she also wanted to prevent any potential for criticism against her for getting museum staff involved in the first place, and… she wanted to snooker the ESP parapsychologists by involving another kind of psychological professional.

Walking down Rodney Street, Adam eventually found the right building: "Hah! next door but one to the ESP Institute. I might call in there afterwards…"

Finally, after licking his dry mouth a few times, he plucked up enough courage to walk in.

Dr O'Riley's phone rang: "Hello? Yes Susan… OK, I've got thirty minutes, I could fit him in… he knows initials are free of charge doesn't he? He does, good, OK send him up."

"I don't know why I'm here…"

O'Riley had scanned the young academic and read him correctly as an intuitive type, prone to spontaneous absences of thought and sudden inspirations. He also identified a quirky humour in him: "Ah, the deep philosophical questions first!"

Adam grinned. Maybe the old guy wouldn't be as stuffy as his age suggested: "I've been sent here…"

O'Riley hid his reaction. Whenever someone had been 'sent' – often by a spouse or live-in friend, then the real issue usually wasn't to be found in the person of the presenting individual, but rather in whoever had done the sending: "I see, by whom?"

"My boss at the museum… Dr Claudia Moore, she's my Ph.D. supervisor."

O'Riley's eyes narrowed, but his face gave off an accepting warmth: "I'd be very interested to hear your story."

"My story?"

"Yes…" he said with genuine humanity "your *untold* story."

Adam suddenly felt a surge of emotion rising up within him. The old guy's experience must be telling: he'd somehow cut right through the superficial niceties and sand-waving and reached right into his soul.

Adam's eyes filled up as inwardly he separated a little from himself and made room for his true heart to speak freely and without fear of rejection or of misunderstanding. In this natural trance-state he said: "My life… reaches back into the centuries, this life; this here-and-now, I understand is just a dream – and I'm waking up to who I really am, who I've always been…"

O'Riley recognized the ambiance of Adam's soul. He was not, as some therapists of lesser experience might believe, someone on the brink of a psychotic dissociation – a separation from reality and flight into fantasy – there was something *else* coming through: "I'd really like to learn about who you've always been Adam…"

"Not *just* Adam… I mean, my name *was* Adam then too, but names are just labels, aren't they… My existence only has meaning in relationship to *her*…"

ESP Institute

"I've started on the record checks Claire: thought I'd do a broadly bandwidthed approach first."

"Oh yes?" Claire was used to John's little ways. He often spoke about his own ideas and names for things as if everyone else knew what was going on in his head and what he meant by them.

"Yeah…" he asserted with a grin "we should start with *you*!"

"Me?"

"Absolutely: my hypothesis is that you are the focus of all of these synchronistic events, so it makes sense that we should put you at the centre of the information!"

Claire smiled broadly. Usually John was very rational and sequential about how he approached things, but when something passed below the surface of his mind and activated him deeply he could come over all 'strange' and apparently disconnected.

Her father-in-law, the Jungian psychotherapist reckoned John was an Intuitive-Thinking 'type' who was normally thinking dominant, but whenever he had to draw on his deeper resources, then his intuition took over and turned him into a 'nutty-professor'.

"This idea of yours that somehow I'm the focus has really gripped you hasn't it John?"

"Well of course, it's obvious! Thing is… what does it mean?"

Claire thought she'd better anchor him with some direct questions: "What exactly have you been doing?"

"I've started your family tree in this computer program, using on-line data bases."

"Eh?"

John looked exasperatedly at her: "Claire *if* there really is something in Adam's regression-hypnosis – and – *if* it is related to your reaction to Von-Hesse, and, *if* your sensation of being remotely 'scanned' here in the office *are* all connected – then, we have to put you into a context.

"OK…"

"Well obviously, in a past-life regression, the context is in the past! Adam mentioned a Witchfinder called Lattimer – which of course is your name."

"Yeah… but you were quick to write-off Adam's use of my name as cryptomnesia."

"I was… and then I did some thinking, and then I *stopped* thinking and let my psyche 'tell' me what I was missing."

"And that was?"

"The bleedin' obvious!"

"Go on."

"Remember when we met Von-Hesse?"

"Of course, he zapped me with that strange energy when we shook hands!"

"And remember what he said about parapsychologists and in particular about *you* as a parapsychologist? He said that in centuries past you'd have been a Witchfinder!"

The hair on the back of Claire's neck leapt up: "Shit!" she breathed.

"We wanted to see if we could trace historical records for the 'characters' in Adam's regression – well, how about tracing certain people's *ancestry* back, and look see if we have a match-up!"

"Between me and this Nathaniel Lattimer…"

"If we were back in our 'other' job Claire, and if this were a routine day-to-day investigation, then it's exactly what we'd do. But we've also had other experiences haven't we… We know how the psyche works, we know about the occult and the supernatural. If we'd overlooked this 'obvious' line of inquiry then we'd have been letting ourselves down both as former crime investigators *and* as parapsychologists. It's what makes us unique Claire, that special combination of training and real-life experience."

It sank in. Claire's widening light-blue eyes at last saw what John's intuition had been telling him.

The Eden Institute

"Adam... you should know that Claire Lattimer is my daughter-in-law."

"That's OK, I trust you to keep it confidential, but I wouldn't mind her knowing about me coming here at some point."

"Thank you... but, I'll leave that up to you. If you choose to tell her, or indeed anyone else, then that's your own decision."

"So, you *believe* what I've told you?"

"My mentor, the late Dr Bruce Irving once said to me that 'belief' and 'knowing' were two different things. He said you only had to believe something if you didn't know if it was true, and, that if you did know, then you didn't need to believe it. I *know* that you're telling me your personal-truth Adam: so, regardless of how anyone else may judge just what 'truth' is; for myself, I 'know' the value of the truth of the soul..."

Adam left Dr O'Riley's consulting room, content that he'd met someone who really understood what he was going through.

Outside, in Rodney Street, he stared up at the ESP building, next door but one, and... went home.

Succubus

Friday 17ʰ November 2006:
Oxton, Wirral 2.30pm

 on Hesse had been carefully monitoring *Lilith*'s energy levels. Soon she would have to draw strength from unwitting victims to maintain herself. This could be achieved by entering a man's dream-world and draining energy from him through orgasm – a 'wet-dream' or nocturnal-emission. This was one facet of *Lilith* known to mystics and occultists in all cultures down the centuries – where her name as *Lilith, Lilitu, Lilu, Lamia* and *Lili* brought fear of sterility, or death – even the harvesting of semen by *Lilith* to then transform magically into demon-seed so that in her *incubus* form, she could impregnate women with her demonic children.

In the modern West, this old knowledge had largely been lost and now remained the province of specialists in arcane occultism or of ancient near-Eastern religions. Even her appearance in the Bible went largely unnoticed.

Now that she'd settled-in to the twenty-first century, *Lilith* was becoming hungry: "Mistress, you must be careful. If you wait

too long, then you will have to kill to obtain your energy. If you don't, then perhaps just a simple harvest would be enough?"

"Maximilian… my purpose is to kill, you should know that."

"Of course: but not *too* soon! In this technological century, every unexplained cause of death is investigated scientifically. Eventually, someone would realize what was going on!"

Lilith's Mona-Lisa smile cast a dark shadow across her beautiful face: "You're thinking of my 'enemies' aren't you Maximilian. You actually *fear* them!"

"No! I'm just… concerned that they should be allowed to gather information on you."

"You needn't worry; they're looking in the wrong century."

Von-Hesse's hooded eyes took their turn to darken: "The Lattimer woman!"

"Oh it's not just her… there are others, but, they are disunited and cannot see the bigger picture. It amuses me that they scurry around like rats tasting morsels and miss the full plate of food right there before them."

"The Museum: the woman Moore and her idiot assistant?!"

Lilith bridled a touch: "She's not a threat; she is after all under your latent control is she not?"

"Yes, she's an easy Mesmeric subject: I can activate her at will. As for that fool Mitchell…"

"You will *not* concern yourself with him, Maximilian! He is… mine, for my personal entertainment. Do you understand?" *Lilith*'s tone was suggestive of a threat. Von-Hesse noted the embedded command to keep away from Adam – even if he did resent it: "As you instruct… Mistress."

Lilith's smile took on its honey-golden hue again: "I know all about what you got Meier to do… Maximilian. That linguist…

was no threat to me. Of course, killing the innocent is a pleasure in itself, but I have no need of any demonstration of your... 'resolve' to protect me.

 So, now it's time for me to look for my… refreshment.
I'll start here I think on the Wirral: over in Prenton in fact, I have an inclination to dine there…in St Stephens Road…

Claire Lattimer's home in St Stephens Road Prenton

Claire was deep in thought as she drove home to Prenton. She and her husband had settled their family just around the corner from her father-in-law – Kevin O'Riley senior – who'd lived in nearby Prenton Lane for thirty years.

Despite being a post-feminist academic and professional, Claire was still the home-maker to her family. Her daughter; Lizzie, sixteen, was at Wirral Grammar school, and her son; Sean at eighteen was at Wirral Metropolitan College – finishing off his studies before he followed his father, grandfather, and even in her early adult years – his mother, into the police.

Sean was making his way home too, by bus from college and had just alighted at the stop on Woodchurch Road near to Bryanston Road. From here he was to take a short walk along Bryanston and then left across Waterpark Road and finally into St Stephens Road and home.

Like his dad and granddad Sean was lively minded, and often entertained himself with a never ending stream of inner images as he wafted haphazardly along on his way. It relieved boredom; and was better than his MP3 player, but almost never offered any reality orientation or early warning of an imminent accident. So it was that he didn't see her until after the impact…

Sean sat down on his ass – and, between the girls spreading tight-jeaned legs. He couldn't see her face at first, the light was fading, and her heavy long hair fell forwards and over him like lustrous curtains. His response was muted by her incredible natural scent. So lovely was it that it acted as an anaesthetic. He no longer felt any discomfort just a relaxed and comfortable resignation. Gently she sat back onto his lap and parted her hair. The headlights of a passing car revealed her stunning features. He couldn't help himself: "Wow!"

Lilith's head tilted in her signature coquette fashion.

"Wow!" he said again, now enjoying the sensation of her buttocks resting on his crotch: "Botticelli's Venus!"

At last she stood up and held her hand out to assist him. warmth passed through her porcelain perfect fingers, causing his spine to tingle.

"Dear Sandro…" said her honey-soft voice "He didn't quite get my eye colour right did he?" She smiled a Mona Lisa smile…

 "Sandro?" queried the mesmerised youth.

"Botticelli: he saw me in his dreams" she breezed airily "but I was otherwise engaged at the time and couldn't visit him in person."

His quizzical look softened into a broad smile: "I'm Sean!"

 "I'm called Lillian… for now…" she said with a single raised eyebrow and flirtatious tilt of her head.

"Lillian! Sorry for bumping into you… I was miles away."

 "It must have been the twilight – strange things pass in and out of this world at twilight." *Lilith* smiled again showing her lovely dimples, and then went to go on her way.

"Wait!" Sean hyperventilated "don't go… er, can I bump into you… again?"

"It's a certainty, the way you go about your life; so *off*-guard" she breathed with her honey scented voice.

Sean watched as *Lilith*'s curvaceous form walked on down the road, her shape shimmering as it passed beneath the street lights and at last seeming to glide away like fairy lights into the gathering darkness.

"Wow, I'm in love!"

Claire was all smiles listening to Sean's account of his meeting with the unearthly beauty in Bryanston Road: "Like a living Botticelli painting you said?"

"Christ I'll say!"

"Always spooked me that picture" his dad muttered as he watched the evening news.

"Venus?"

"Yep... look at her eyes: they're *inhuman*."

"That's coz she's supposed to be a goddess."

"As this young lady was?"

"Too right, I've gotta find her again!"

Kevin smirked at his idealistic young son: "If it's meant-to-be, Sean, then *she'll* find *you!*"

All that evening, the memory of 'Lillian' intruded into Sean's every thought and every quiet moment. At last retiring to bed, he wistfully hoped to see her in his dreams. But of course, as with all things uncanny, one must be careful what one wishes for...

He became aware of a rushing noise in his ears: It was like the sound he'd heard for days after he'd seen the heavy-metal band *Motorhead* live in concert. Half-conscious he tried to move but was paralysed: feeling a sensation like he was being ventilated by a machine – his shallow breath completely outside of his voluntary control. Panicking he tried to open his half-closed eyes, to find that an eerie grey light bathed the bedroom.

Then from the direction of the window he could just make-out a shimmering silver form. Convinced now that he was hallucinating he struggled in vain to wake-up. The shimmering shape at last began to resolve – the outline of long waist length hair, then the unmistakable womanly hour-glass figure. The uncanny light caught her features, just as the car headlights had in Bryanston Road, it was her… it was Lillian.

Ghost-like she floated through his bed until he could look directly into her spectral eyes. Just as his father had said – they appeared inhuman… inhuman and yet terrifyingly seductive. Her naked body seemed to join with his breath until its weight became tangible, her flesh soft yet solid, and 'real' in its proximity.

His body began to feel aroused, a warm glowing feeling at first and then a deep sexual urgency. The spectral shape settled her vulva over his fully aroused penis enveloping it in an energy that seemed to draw and pull on him like a powerful vacuum.

Desperately he wanted to move, to enjoy what he still believed was some kind of dream or hallucination – but his paralysis held him so that all voluntary movement was impossible. Only the involuntary actions of respiration and sexual arousal – and these were experienced as if he were a mere observer.

At last the stunning vision of her beautiful face and body was coupled with his intense and draining orgasm – he felt his heart rate and breathing match as he gushed in ejaculation and passed into dreamless unconsciousness.

"You seem… refreshed, Mistress" remarked Von-Hesse.

"I am Maximilian, I am… temporarily. It's been a long time. I didn't kill him; I left him some life-energy, at least for now.

Von-Hesse was curious: "Was he a random target?"

"Random? Oh no… he's in the blood-line of Nathaniel Lattimer. It pleased me to make such a one as he my first. But it isn't enough. I must increase my strength."

"I agree. We have nearly completed the data collection. The living descendants of Henry Teal have been identified too."

"Good!"

"There is some irony."

"Yes?"

"The direct descendants in Liverpool include an academic who works in a certain scientific field."

Lilith's smile broadened: "Oh I do like irony – that condition wherein one's enemies are mocked by fate…"

Monday 20ᵗʰ November 2006: ESP Rodney Street, 9.40am

"Good weekend Claire?" enquired John. He was smiling to himself. He had some interesting news for her.

"Yes thanks, Sean had a 'love-at-first-sight' experience Friday, coming home from college – literally bumped into her, Lillian her name was apparently. She said a few mystical things to him and then walked away into the night. He was all enchanted! Then we couldn't get him out of bed the next day, he was spaced out and exhausted."

John stopped what he was doing and looked concerned: "Not 'on' anything is he?"

"No! I've no reason to suspect that… he was probably 'thinking' about his new love all night – if you know what I mean?"

John grinned: "Yes… oh to be young again!"

"Any more results on your genealogy search?"

"Indeed there are! That name: 'Henry Teal' guess what?"

"What?" complied Claire.

"I've found him: he really did exist!"

"In Liverpool?"

"Yep. And… he was around at the material time."

"Any family?"

"John's face gave it away.

"You're kidding, not a son called Adam?"

John nodded.

"Ha! But I suppose Claudia will just say that Adam must have come across it on the internet and then 'forgot' only to incorporate it later into his regression-hypnosis fantasy."

"Probably, but I wonder how she'd explain the 'other' fact I've uncovered?"

"Other fact? Come on John spill the beans!"

"You've heard of Dr Jonathan Teal?"

"Er… no…"

"He's at the Liverpool School of Tropical Medicine specialising in infectious diseases, including bubonic plague. He's a direct descendent of Henry Teal, through Adam!"

"Well I never! I wonder if he knows about his family tree?"

"Well he won't know about what's going on at the Museum… Interesting though isn't it?"

"When did you find that out?"

"Oh over the weekend, it's addictive this genealogy stuff!"

"Did you find anything on me?"

"Ah… sorry, I haven't got back very far with your line yet. But I'll get on to it right away."

"So much for me being the centre of the investigation eh John!"

"Sorry Claire, I got distracted."

Claire wasn't too surprised. When John got into detailed investigations he often wandered off on a side-trail: "Let's get what we can and then call back and speak to Adam and Claudia."

Midday and *Lilith* was back in Rodney Street. She was still very curious about this elderly psychotherapist who just happened to be Claire Lattimer's father-in-law, and, who carried a powerful protective charm around his neck. He was of course, also Sean O'Riley's grandfather: "He is in…it's Miss Hopgood isn't it?"

"Last time I called it was" smiled *Lilith*.

Susan the middle-aged receptionist didn't like the vibes she felt emanating from the stunning young woman. As the gatekeeper to the psychoanalytic mysteries, she always felt protective of the therapists at Eden, especially old Dr O'Riley, who was such a caring compassionate and deeply wise man.

A quick call and he confirmed that he would see her. Susan frowned as she gave his reply: "He is available, you can go up."

Lilith tilted her head: "You really should get your health checked out you know… time is short." Callously, and casually, *Lilith* had marked Susan out for death.

"What do you mean?"

"Oh… winters coming, all sorts of infections will arrive with it."

"I'm due to have my seasonal flu jab."

"Then you've nothing to worry about have you!" *Lilith* breezed up the stairs leaving Susan chilled. Staring up to O'Riley's office the middle-aged widow felt a deep concern for him.

O'Riley, ever the old fashioned gentleman greeted *Lilith* warmly, held the door open for her, and took her coat: "So, you've decided to come back and do some work!"

Lilith's Mona-Lisa smile was her only reply. She caught O'Riley taking a second look at her: "Yes, I am like her aren't I?"

"Her?"

Lilith sat back and crossed her legs: "Yes… you were thinking of a young girl… no, *how* someone used to look at my age."

It was O'Riley's turn to smile: "That's either a very good guess or, you've read my mind."

Lilith raised an eyebrow as her smile broadened. What was your daughter's name? It was her I saw in your mind's eye."

O'Riley – in turn – sat back in his chair, and likewise his own smile broadened: "As I said, that's either a very good guess or… you *are* some kind of psychic."

"Mary, her name's Mary."

O'Riley nodded: "But, you could conceivably have found that out somewhere."

"Oh I did… it's written on your heart, and you are so very open with it aren't you?" she smiled her Mona Lisa smile.

O'Riley's psyche now triggered an involuntary chain of associations – associations going back thirty years.

"My… there have been some very special women in your life haven't there… *very* special. I really had no idea… how interesting" *Lilith* was on a roll.

O'Riley's mind began to divide in two. One part was the caring therapist who only wanted to practice compassionate humanism – the other, was a curious amalgam of alarm and curiosity about just who the mysterious Lillian Hopgood really was.

"What precisely is your purpose in coming back Lillian?" O'Riley was trying to get *Lilith* to open up, rather than perhaps… play games.

"You didn't answer my question about your daughter Mary. She was very pretty; at least her image in your heart suggests that."

O'Riley decided to pass on that, and instead he gave a response to the 'very special women' comment.

If you really can see into me: Lillian, then you'll know who, and what, those people were."

As statements go, it was an obvious challenge. O'Riley wanted to test out her apparent ability to read into his soul.

Lilith, of course, smiled her Mona-Lisa smile: "It may be too indiscrete of me to say…."

O'Riley, once again smiled back, and gave a facial expression that suggested that perhaps, she couldn't see deeply into him."

"Too indiscrete, or perhaps, as yet somewhat premature" she continued.

"Or perhaps your psychic ability is nothing more than a rather generous helping of intuition. It often passes for… extra-sensory perception." Despite himself, O'Riley was being unwittingly seduced and led by *Lilith* wherever she wanted him to go.

"Extra Sensory Perception… ESP… that's a name I've seen…. Oh yes, on a building next door but one!"

"It's a paranormal research institute."

"How silly!" *Lilith* laughed.

"Silly?"

"Yes, how can anything be paranormal… or supernatural? Something that actually *happens* must be 'normal' mustn't it, and as for super-natural, what can possibly happen that actually occurs outside of, or beyond, nature herself?"

"Ha! I'll have to introduce you to my daughter-in-law."

"Oh… is she an analyst like you?"

"No, she's a parapsychologist, and the director of that ESP institute you've just been deriding the raison-d'être of!"

"Thank you, that'd be lovely. Can you make a formal introduction?"

"I could… but she's very busy: she'd be interested if you had any demonstrable ESP abilities though."

"I'm sure if I have, then she'll be the first to find out."

O'Riley's eyes narrowed, but he still smiled: "I don't really know anything about you. Obviously, if you want to keep that information to yourself you're welcome to, we can still work together."

Lilith mirrored his facial expression: "I have a problem with men."

"Oh yes?"

"They keep falling in love with me."

"Are you surprised by that?"

"It never does them any good."

O'Riley paused, as therapists do, when they are unsure about which direction to take things: "Nevertheless, are you surprised?"

"Oh no: not at all."

"Then, in what way is it a problem, are you perhaps bored with it, with the attention you get?"

"You see, I have to find a special one, and *only* one amongst them all: one to father my children."

"Yes, in itself a common enough problem for women, always has been, always will be: who does a woman choose to raise a family with?"

"There is one fellow; he's been following me around for centuries! He thinks that he's the *One*."

"But you're not sure?"

"Not any longer… There are one or two others… This first fellow has been useful… but… he may be becoming too self-important, and you know what happens to people who think that they're important, but really… they're nothing…"

That got through. It was a reprise from way back in O'Riley's past – the catchphrase of perhaps the oddest individual he had ever met and the person responsible for the change in direction in his life that had taken him out of the police, through the occult, and into psychotherapy.

"I'm sorry did I say something to trouble you?" *Lilith's* pseudo-concern was transparent. O'Riley's spine tingled as the hair stood up on his neck.

"What did you say?" All he could do was bring himself to ask for clarification.

Lilith was enjoying her little game and moved on as if she'd not said anything of particular importance: "I was living with this first guy Adam for a while… but he was too, male-chauvinist about things, so, I left. That's when Evelyn moved in with him, and they started a family. I hated those children: you know, I used to fantasise about killing them and all of their future descendants?"

Pointedly, O'Riley missed *Lilith*'s immediate words: "You said something about what happens to people who think that they're important, but really they're nothing?" His throat went into spasm as he spoke.

"Yes… his names Max, such a dear friend, but getting a bit beyond himself with his exaggerated sense of entitlement… I live-in at his place now, but he's got two of his male friends there too. Oxton's so full of bed-sits isn't it? But I'm in a big old house now. You know, technically, I'm still a virgin. Adam couldn't wait… he kept making demands: that's why I left him!"

O'Riley had reached into his shirt – subconsciously checking his talisman – sure enough it was hot.

"Is that your little shield thing again?" she asked in silky tones.

"Yes… you seem to know a lot about it, and about me: too much to be a coincidence in fact!" O'Riley's trip down memory lane had brought the latent suspicious policeman out in him.

"Do you wear that thing all the time? How superstitious of you! Never mind, like you said I'm just an intuitive; I seem to be able to guess things about people…"

"Those words of yours… when you said about someone thinking they were important… Do you know who used to say that to me, someone important in my past?"

"How should I know that? Did he stand out like he had funny odd-coloured eyes or something?"

O'Riley was sure now that she was playing games. His patience had run out: "Lillian, either you've done your homework on my background, or, you *are* psychic. Which is it?!"

The Mona-Lisa smile broke out again: "I think I'd better be going now... I've upset you haven't I... Never mind... I'm sure that we can still be friends. May I come back and see you again soon?"

He recognised the strategy. Thinking he had only everything to gain by understanding her and her motives he agreed: "Yes... OK. You can make an appointment with Susan, or, if you prefer, call in on the off-chance."

"How kind... I do hope Susan is alright, she looked 'ill' to me. Will you introduce me to Claire too; you did say that you would, *if* I had 'demonstrable' ESP abilities?"

O'Riley took that as her answer to his as yet unanswered question: "Very well, I'll mention you to her, and take it from there."

"Thank you!"

Lilith took her coat and then paused in the doorway: "By the way, am I as pretty as Rowena was?"

Claire's face was a picture of deep concern. O'Riley had called around to ESP immediately that 'Lillian' had left: "Are you sure? Sure that you didn't unconsciously 'add' to what she said?"

"I *am* sure Claire: she knew a great deal about my background, all cleverly hinted at or directly stated – names, relationships – significant people... she even knew about the Gawain Talisman and what it was!"

John offered a point of view: "She seems a genuine 'psychic' Kevin, if – with respect – your account is accurate: unless, you're thinking that its one of 'them' again?"

The 'them' referred to by John, were their original occult opponents – entities they had confronted together in the early and middle nineteen eighties.

O'Riley couldn't bring himself to believe it: "No… she didn't mention The Harlequin, which would be a strange omission if she really were connected to them: she's *probably* just a very good natural psychic. She also seems a very mixed up kid, with some deep personal relationship issues." Then O'Riley's professional conscience caught him out: "But… I shouldn't really discuss them, even if she was malintentional towards me; she came to me as a 'patient' not as an enemy."

Claire understood but felt she had to keep him focused: "The boundaries may be blurred already: she could present in that distressed state of mind and still be maledictive!"

O'Riley nodded: "True… anyway, would you see her and check her out? You, and John?"

Claire sighed: "We've got a hell of a lot on at the moment Kevin. The Museum job has uncovered all sorts of strange things – things that really need all of our time and energy. John's searching for a woman at the moment in the genealogy records – a young woman called *Lilith*."

1.00pm and Adam Mitchell had some more time-off courtesy of Claudia, ostensibly to go back to Rodney Street for his 'personal development'. He'd started off going in that direction, but his subconscious intervened and he'd found himself detouring and standing over in Water Street, looking down towards the Pier Head and the Mersey.

In his past-life hypnotic regression as 'Adam Teal' he had 'seen' this view as it had been in 1665. How different it was now… He looked to where the Hopgood House had been – long gone of course as the old town had grown over the centuries into a bustling city and international seaport.

Walking up the incline of Water Street he arrived at the junction of Dale Street – his mind flickering like some old-time movie as sounds and images from the past intruded, projected before his eyes as if on some great canvas .

At the Town Hall he turned right into Castle Street walking on towards Derby Square and the Queen Victoria Memorial; the site of old Liverpool Castle.

Still in a trance of kaleidoscopic memories he heard her voice: "Hello again."

"You!"

Her Mona-Lisa smile lit-up her face, as the background cacophony of city life faded from his senses.

"Does it take you back? It does me!" she said.

Adam's eyes were wide – trying to take-in every minute particle of her being: "Is it *really* you... I am I really *him*?"

"What does your beating heart tell you... Adam Teal?"

"There: you called me Adam Teal again! You must come-back with me, back to the museum and tell them!"

"Must I? You know better than that, I *never* do as demanded by anyone, not you, not even Adam in Eden himself!" She ran off laughing towards the memorial followed by an anxious Adam:

"Adam in Eden?! Wait! *Lilith*!"

Dodging the traffic she finally stopped under the gaze of the memorial statue and allowed hapless Adam to catch up.

"How? How did all of this happen? I'm like two people... me; Adam Mitchell, and *him*... Adam Teal!"

"Don't you remember my promise?" she said with a coquettish tilt of her lovely face.

Adam stared down and away to the ground as his mind searched his fragmentary recollections: "Yes... but they killed you, they cast you into the waters... by the old Pool, you drowned!"

"And you grew old and died, but you're still here aren't you!"

"This is crazy.... But how, how, did you recognise me, how did you know where to find me?!"

Her face lit up with a golden radiance as she smiled: "Oh that was easy Adam Teal, I read *hearts*... I knew yours by its beat... its rhythm of life, it was the same then, as it is now... the same as the First Adam..."

"My heart beat..."

"Every single heart beat..."

Adam closed his eyes, touching the centre of his chest and felt it pound. Then a sudden fear overcame him – his eyes opening wide in case she'd gone.

She laughed and ran away from him as if hiding behind the far side of the monument.

"You'll not get away from me again *Lilith* Hopgood!" he shouted.

He dodged back around a few times, but couldn't find her.

Once again, he was alone...

He was low in mood when at last he turned up at the Eden Institute in Rodney Street; fifty minutes late for his appointment. Susan was not amused: "This is no good Mr Mitchell: Dr O'Riley has been waiting for you for an hour!"

Adam looked at Susan with eyes that pleaded reasonable excuse: "She left me... she left me again, in Derby Square!"

"Yes, well you can discuss that with Dr O'Riley: I'm afraid I'm not here to listen to patient's troubles merely to manage the administration of the day for our therapists!"

"Have you ever loved and lost?" he mewed.

"As a matter of fact, I'm a widow" she replied.

Adam nodded: "Me too!"

Susan gave him a look that only a veteran receptionist could: "Up you go young man!"

O'Riley was still processing his encounter with the enigmatic Lillian: "Ah, Adam, did you get the time mixed-up?"

"No... sorry, I got distracted on me way here: I ended up in Water Street staring down at the Pier Head."

Dr O'Riley took a moment to allow 'Adam's World' to resolve into his focus: "What was significant about Water Street do you think?"

Adam's self-absorption led the way: "It was where 'she' lived."

"She?"

"In my past-life."

"Ah... this is from your regression-hypnosis with the ESP team."

"No! They just... helped, in a way... I'd already met her again: remember?"

"In the Museum's Egyptology exhibition?"

"Yeah, and in me dreams, and then just a while ago, today, in Castle Street."

"You met her just before you came here?"

"Yeah! That's why I'm late. I thought that you believed me?"

O'Riley nodded his confirmation that he did 'believe' him.

"I asked her about what it all meant, and she said that she'd promised me – back then – that we'd meet again in future lifetimes – and that now we had. She teased me, just like she used to, in my past life, saying that she knew me by the rhythm of my heart beat...then she vanished... again!"

O'Riley silently drummed his fingers on the arm of his chair. Either Adam was bonkers or he was telling the complete truth. There could be no middle-ground on this one. Claire hadn't told him just how far the regression hypnosis had gone, and he'd promised Adam that he'd maintain proper confidentiality. Yet, he didn't see how he could help him without seeing the bigger picture: "Adam… what do you want to come from your relationship to this girl?"

"I want *her*: she's the love of my life… *all* of my lives, all both of them!"

"Have you thought that *if* you've had *one* previous life, then, you may've also had others?"

That hadn't occurred to him: "Er… no. Are yer sayin that maybe I should do more of that regression stuff and find out?"

"That'd depend on what the ESP team suggest."

"What would *you* suggest Dr O'Riley?"

"Well, strictly speaking, I'm not supposed to suggest anything, at least not in 'normal' circumstances. However, when I was going through the trial of my own life, my mentor, and therapist – the late Dr Bruce Irving, turned that orthodoxy on its head – he believed that extraordinary circumstances require extraordinary commitment, *and* involvement."

"In my book what I'm goin' through is extraordinary enough!"

"Then we'd have to blur the edges, between what we do here, at what you're doing over at ESP."

"OK…" agreed Adam.

"It'd mean breaches of confidentiality, and, you must remember that Claire Lattimer is my daughter-in-law."

"I'm cool with that" responded Adam dismissively.

"Very well, we could start by seeing if you could find a way of introducing me to this girl *Lilith*."

"Ha, easier said than done Doc. I have no idea where and when she's gonna turn up next!"

Lake Hall, Oxton

"Well!" Von-Hesse's urgent impatience had turned to irritation.

"I had to be careful Master, you said to ensure that I wasn't seen. Her powers are great and I was in fear!"

Von-Hesse was unmoved: "The details Adler!" he snapped.

Adler's eyes betrayed him, but he continued anyway: "She went to Rodney Street at noon, and walked inside a building: The Eden Institute."

"Eden? That's a psychotherapy practice!"

"It is Master, its two doors away from ESP."

"So it is… And then?"

"She was there about forty-five minutes. Then she drove away towards the Pier Head: she parked near to the Town Hall. I lost her for a while, trying to park my own car, but I saw her again in Castle Street – with Adam Mitchell."

Von-Hesse's hooded eyes darkened as his voice lowered: "Go on…"

"She was with him but a brief while, perhaps five minutes. Somehow she shook him off. I went back to my car, and saw her drive away. I followed her… she went to the Royal

Liverpool Hospital car park, and then walked to Pembroke Place."

"Pembroke Place?"

"The Liverpool School of Tropical Medicine, I saw her go inside. I waited but she was gone ages, I thought that I'd better come back and report – you said *not* to use mobile phones."

Von-Hesse's irritation had abated – mildly: "You've done well. However, next time, do not abandon surveillance on your own initiative; keep to the brief as given."

"Yes, Master. Master... may I ask what it is that you fear from her?"

Eden Psychotherapy Institute

Susan was just winding down things in reception when she was startled by the sudden presence of a tall dark figure: "Oh! You scared me!" she exclaimed, clutching at her chest.

The angular shape moved out from the shadows – its dark hooded eyes fixed her with intensity: "An attractive young girl called here at noon today, long auburn and blond hair, and striking green eyes!" It was a statement rather than a question.

Susan faltered: "I'm sorry I cannot discuss details about anyone who may have called at Eden, it's a confidential service. Now, I'm just about to close the practice, if you don't mind!" she felt a twinge of fear in her belly as the figure closed a few steps towards her.

"Look at me!" the voice commanded.

Susan let out a fearful moan but felt compelled to obey.

The black-brown eyes penetrated her from behind their heavy hooded lids: "You will tell me who the girl was, and what her business here concerned!"

Susan's wide staring eyes and gaping mouth were as a terrified rabbit in a car's headlights: "Miss Lillian Hopgood, to see Dr Kevin O'Riley… for a follow-up appointment…"

The Mesmeric beam from Von-Hesse's eyes relaxed and Susan's mind became pre-occupied with her sudden amnesia: "What… what did you say? I can't remember…"

Von-Hesse turned to leave. Passing through the door from reception he met a tall, elderly, but still well-made figure descending the stairs. For a moment their eyes met. In that instant Von-Hesse recognised his potential enemy for who he was. O'Riley, also sensed a presence behind the Bavarian's eyes.

Von-Hesse curtly bowed with a slight nod of his head in the old-fashioned 'continental' style and then left. O'Riley watched the door close and then went in to reception.

Susan was standing by the reception desk looking perplexed.

"Who was our impressive looking visitor Susan?"

"I don't know… I can't remember."

O'Riley frowned curiously. Walking over to the window he saw The Bavarian standing ram-rod straight on the pavement by the roadside. A huge black Mercedes Limousine wafted to a halt in front of him. Turning for a last look at the building, Von-Hesse's eyes made a lingering contact with O'Riley's. Then in a moment, he was gone – climbed into the back of the limousine. Silently, the Merc wafted away down Rodney Street towards the city centre.

O'Riley guessed that the mysterious visitor had been significant, even if he couldn't know yet in just what way…

Young Sean O'Riley hoped that the beautiful young girl would be in Bryanston Road again. Since his enchantment on Friday she'd hardly escaped his thoughts for a moment – and especially since his 'wet dream' – an unusually intense experience that had left him drained; drained – but like the victim of a blood-sucking vampire – addicted…

He was it seemed to be disappointed. No golden vision floated amongst the shadows of Bryanston Road. After pausing a while, just to make sure, he at last made his way to the junction of Waterpark Road and was about cross diagonally to the left and towards home. Just then, at the junction directly opposite he saw the shape of a long haired young woman walking purposefully down Reservoir Road. Was it her?

It was.

Emboldened he changed direction and contrived a meeting.

"Hello again!" he offered "On your way home?"

The tilt of her head and raised eyebrow invited further questions.

"Are you coming from work?"

"I've just been to the Mormon Church" she replied.

The Mormon Church? Are you…"

"One of them?"

"Well… yeah"

"I'm studying at their Family History Centre; it's the official one for Birkenhead: checking out the British Vital Records Index."

"Oh… woz dat?"

"It's got copies of parish church records dating from 1538."

"Oh right, cool." He said impassively.

"Aren't you interested in your ancestors?"

"I've never met any of them."

Lilith smiled, even though it hadn't been a joke. Sean could be as literal and dense as his father and grandfather had been at the same age: "You must be an orphan then?"

"No: me parents and grandparents are still alive!"

"But, none of your ancestors?"

Sean's head hurt.

"Look, are you going home right now?"

"I was, do you have a better offer to make?"

Sean's stomach churned like a rotating cement mixer full of garden fairies: "Sugar! Er... come back to my place for a bit?"

"Your place or your parents?"

"Damn... Yeah, me parents."

"Do they mind you bringing strange girls home?"

"But you're not strange; I told them that I'd bumped into you on Friday. They're nice people, dad's a police superintendent, and Mum's a sorta psychologist kinda thingy."

Lilith's smile broadened into a huge grin: "Oh but I'm *very* strange. I doubt your parents have ever met anyone *quite* like me."

"Ha, actually, you'd be surprised: they've both encountered well-weird birds in the past! Shit! Sorry, didn't mean that!"

"That's OK; you can offer me a cup of tea if you like."

Sean was in hog's heaven, except of course that in reality he stood before the very gates of Hell itself...

"Mum!" Claire was inconveniently upstairs when the couple arrived home. Although he was eighteen, Sean still treated his mum like he was five years younger.

"Yeah!"

"I've broad a friend back for a cuppa!"

"Broad!?"

"Sorry… bird, no, no, a *girl*, kinda friend, sorta like, I meant…I've *brought* her back… for a drink!"

"OK! Can you put the kettle on yourself? I'll be down in a minute."

"Me-self! Oh… OK." Sean's idea of hospitality was his mum acting as an 'on-demand' maidservant.

"You have a lovely house Sean. What's your second name by the way?"

"O'Riley, its Liverpool Irish I'm afraid, me dad's dad was called O'Riley, that's how I came to be called it."

"That's how it usually works" smiled *Lilith*.

"What's your second name?"

Lilith only smiled her Mona-Lisa smile.

At last Claire came down-stairs and into the front living room. She'd wondered if Sean had bumped into his mysterious female friend again, but hadn't quite expected what now filled her eyes.

"Hello, you must be Mrs O'Riley, I'm Lillian…" *Lilith* held out her perfectly formed hand to shake. Claire was taken sharply back by the ethereal beauty of her houseguest. Even more so when an eerily familiar sensation passed into her from *Lilith's* hand: "Hi… Lillian?" she faltered then with some incredulity she asked: "Forgive me, but where on *Earth* did Sean find you?"

"Mum!"

"You mean tonight? Oh, that was in Reservoir Road. I was just coming back from the Mormon Church."

Sean thought he'd better explain: "No Mum, she's not, sorta, yer know…" he was gesticulating animatedly; doing his best Mr Bean impression.

"I'm researching my family history" explained *Lilith*.

Claire smiled: "Oh what a coincidence! I'm doing some genealogy at the moment too."

"Really? Have you got back very far?"

"No, a colleague of mine John Sutton is doing most of it, but he tends to get side-tracked.: how about you?"

Lilith smiled: "All the way back to the Garden of Eden."

Claire saw a seriousness in her green-eyes, and then felt a chill as something deeper betrayed its presence.

"Oh… right. I've seen some pedigree's on the internet that link up with myths and claim to go all the way back that far."

Lilith's Mona-Lisa smile was fixed: "There's a lot of truth in myths. Didn't Jung say that they were the 'dreams of cultures'?"

"Jung? That's a rather specialized field!" Claire was wondering why someone so young in years should know about his work. "I suppose… that for believing Christians… all pedigree's go back to Adam and Eve" she offered, faltering again.

Lilith's smile broadened as a trace of mockery formed across her face. Claire saw it, and although she didn't understand the reasons behind it, she nevertheless felt uncomfortable.

Switching back into 'host' mode: "Anyway… would you like that cup of tea now?

"Thank you: green if you have it, with no milk or sugar."

"Green tea? Yes, I think we have…" Claire went to the kitchen to make the drinks. It'd be a welcome pause in the conversation and allow her to weigh up her son's pre-Raphaelite friend. Young Sean had been watching the interaction and was concerned that Lillian and his mum weren't getting along: "Sorry about that, mum's a bit yer know… well, she's one of those psychologists that study the occult, me an me sister Lizzie reckon that it's made her a bit odd!"

Claire overheard him and called back: "Yes Sean; insanity *is* hereditary, you get it from your children!" Nevertheless her curiosity about 'Lillian' was bordering now on being intrigued. Coming back in with the tea she asked: "Are you from round here Lillian? Your accent doesn't seem local."

"I live in a big old house Oxton, but I've had a long association with the area" she replied evasively.

"And your parents?"

"My… father and I haven't been on speaking terms for years… seems like simply millennia. My mother's very 'earthy' you could say, but I only see a little bit of her once in every so many years."

"Oh, I'm sorry."

"Oh please don't worry; it's all made me *very* independent."

"Yes, I'm sure it has. Do you work?" Claire was trying to get as much information from the elusive Lillian as she could; especially if there was a chance that her mysterious guest was going to become a frequent visitor.

"I'm a freelance researcher. I'm doing the genealogy as part of a wider project."

"That's interesting; maybe you could help with my enquiries?"

"Yes, I expect I will… in the fullness of time."

Claire felt her body twitch in an involuntary muscular spasm. Her trained-experience told her that she must have subconsciously registered something, something perhaps untoward about her guest. *Lilith* had noted Claire's reaction too. She decided to shift the focus onto her: "So tell me, Mrs O'Riley, what does your psychological work involve?"

"Oh that's a difficult one… where to begin?"

Sean tried to fill the vacuum – as nature will, with any old nonsense: "She does stuff with freaks who think they've had past-lives or can see into the future, all dead-weird crap like that!"

"Sean! What he means, Lillian, is that I'm a parapsychologist who investigates claims of the paranormal."

"Like CSICOP – the 'committee for the scientific investigation of claims of the paranormal' do you mean?"

Claire was genuinely surprised: "You know about them?"

Sean was feeling left out: maybe Lillian was dead-weird like his mum after-all: "Arh-eh not *two* of yer!"

Lillian tilted her head in coquette style: "CSICOP haven't been very successful have they?"

"They're scientific sceptics. They'd say that they've been very successful, as they haven't – according to them – found any convincing evidence of anything paranormal being true."

"Well you see" continued the ethereal Lillian "the trouble with sceptics – these days anyway – is that they are sceptical about simply everything except scepticism itself."

Claire raised an eyebrow: "Indeed?"

"Certainly; they forget the motto of the Sceptical Philosophers of Alexandria: 'Nothing is certain, not even that!' Dear Pyrrho would have been disappointed in them."

"Pyrrho? You mean the ancient philosopher?"

"Yes, 4th century BC, or 'Before Common Era' as some archaeological types like to say these days. Isn't political correctness such a bore? Anyway, he didn't like wooden thinking: or politics masquerading as wisdom."

"You make it sound like you knew him personally!" joked Claire.

"Do I *look* that old Mrs O'Riley?" replied *Lilith,* inviting eye contact. She was enjoying herself being a tease.

The suggestion induced Claire to look more-closely: as she did so her field of vision suddenly funnelled – going black around the edges as the young girls face seemed to glow like the imago of Botticelli's Venus. Claire's body reacted viscerally, with fear causing her to gasp out aloud.

"Mum, are you alright?!"

Claire became light headed and took hold of the arms of her chair for support – still transfixed by the beautiful yet unworldly face before her. Sean looked at *Lilith* who seemed to be as motionless as an oil painting. Rousing himself he went to his mother's aid. Inside, Claire's mind was a kaleidoscope of images from the past: Dominique, Rowena, and then back before any 'personal' life experience to strange unknown places and 'memories' from unknown times.

"I'd better be going Sean; your mum seems to have become suddenly unwell…"

Torn between his mum who was by now near collapsing, and his 'love' who was about to leave, Sean dithered.

"Please give her my apologies" *Lilith* was smiling as she left the room.

"Lillian! Don't go!"

"Don't, did you say Sean? Oh I never accept demands, not from anyone, didn't you know that?"

"Will I see you again?" he asked desperately.

"Of course you will, just like last time."

"Last time…" he echoed. The last-time was in a dream, a wet-dream. Just as he was distracted inwardly, he heard the front door of the house close. Lillian was gone…

The next day it was a sombre Claire who turned up at the ESP office in Rodney Street: "You're looking tired again Claire" offered John.

"I've had a weird encounter…" she murmured.

"Oh, on the way in to work?"

"No, at home. Sean brought a girl home with him."

John smiled, misinterpreting: "Ah, a little motherly jealousy perhaps?"

"She was stunning… but it wasn't that" Claire was staring into space as she spoke slowly.

John at last took it seriously: "Go on…"

Claire just shook her head and raised her arms. I had a 'flashback' with her."

"A flashback? What, you mean to Rowena, or Dominique?"

Claire nodded: "Yes, both, but… more than that, I *saw* things, things, places, people… I can only describe them as being from the past, the *historical* past."

"How on earth did that come about, do you know?"

"The conversation got progressively more strange, and then suddenly she seemed to suggest that I look at her, closely, to see how 'old' she looked. That's when it happened; it was like being in a trance, or looking at some kind of film show. My body reacted strongly, in fear, genuine, terrified fear!"

"How old does she look?"

"Like a twenty to twenty three year old, but one of those young women who seem like they're really about fourteen and just big for their age, you know, she was just too perfect, like a kind of grown-up child. I can certainly see what Sean see's in her, she was like a living pre-Raphaelite oil painting, but... I saw *deeper* than that."

"This is the girl he bumped into last Friday is it?"

"Yeah... she's tall, porcelain skinned, long blond hair, heart or shield shaped face, and the deepest green-eyes you've ever seen."

"Hmm could be contact lenses."

"No, they're 'natural', if that word applies here... Natural in colour; but with that unmistakable 'something' behind them, that we've known before..."

"With Rowena and Dominique?"

"Yes, or even in Petra, and of course Carla – except that their light shone in a positive, healing way."

"Wait a minute... Haven't you made the obvious link yet!"

"Yeah, with Rowena and Dominique."

"No, with that girl who turned up to see Kevin at Eden!"

Later at the ESP Institute

"Her name?" O'Riley paused at the request. Claire was his daughter-in-law and very dear to his heart, but... "We did say yesterday that there was an issue of confidentiality."

"Oh don't be so lame Kevin! You called into ESP and told us about her yourself, and how she knew so much about you. It must be the same girl! She's ingratiated herself with Sean your *grandson* and, she's had a 'go' at intimidating me!

You even asked if we'd see her and check out her Psi abilities."

O'Riley nodded. "I did didn't I... *if* it really is the same person.?"

Claire's head tilted back as she spoke: "She said her name was Lillian."

O'Riley's stomach twinged: "It's the same name..." he murmured in stunned reply.

"Same name, same looks, same 'manner', it's the same girl. We *have* to wake up on this Kevin, there's a terrible threat of some kind looming!"

O'Riley nodded: "Time to join the dots and make the picture. One other thing... There was a late visitor here in reception yesterday evening. He'd spoken to Susan, but she'd blanked it out; apparently having a sudden attack of amnesia. I saw him myself as he left."

"What'd he look like?" asked John.

O'Riley breathed out hard as he recalled the details: "Like... well like... that footballer Eric Cantona or even Christopher Lee: the old horror movie actor – very tall, slim but strongly built, black hair, swarthy or olive skin, very dark-brown hooded eyes, immaculately dressed, and had an 'air; about him: a central European manner, he even bowed slightly when I bumped into him, almost as though he was about to click his heels..."

"Von-Hesse!"

"Who?"

Liverpool Museum

Claudia was insistent: "Dr Von-Hesse, we really *must* have the return of the skull, and the soil samples!" Claudia was having a bad day: news of Allan Flynn's disappearance had finally filtered over from the University. Having no family, and living alone, it had been some time before the bachelor's unexplained absence from work led to a real concern amongst his friends and colleagues.

The Bavarian had received a text message from the Museum's admin department to the effect that the sarcophagus finds should be returned immediately. Now, even Claudia's own line management had started to ask awkward questions. Von-Hesse had thought it appropriate to 'explain' to her in person. He'd allowed her some rope to show her hand: but it was time to reel her in: "Dr Moore..."

Claudia looked up at him; up until now she'd avoided making eye contact. With the signal of a slight bow of his head, the pre-conditioned Mesmeric trigger fired in her brain: at once her eyes slowly blinked, twice and then closed: "You... will

explain... Dr Moore, that it is necessary that I have possession of the... items... for a short while longer"

"Necessary..." she repeated

"*If* it becomes unavoidable, then you will *substitute* the skull with a... replacement from the museum's store of un-displayed items. The soil may be substituted from a chemically similar sample that my assistant Meier, will supply to you. You will report these instructions to no-one..."

"No one..."

"Merely, carry them out without question."

"Without question..."

"You will remain in trance until I have left, and you will have no conscious memory of our meeting."

"No conscious memory..."

Von-Hesse turned to leave and saw a DVD case on top of a filing cabinet. Curious, he picked it up. "Adam Mitchell – Past-Life Regression Hypnosis..." he read.

The Bavarian left, slipping the DVD into his overcoat pocket.

That evening Sean was disappointed to find that there was no sign of Lillian at all. He even walked up Reservoir Road crossing the junction with Prenton Lane to the Mormon Church, but still nothing. At last, giving up, he made his doleful way home. Maybe she'd been scared-off by what had happened to his mum?

Claire didn't mention the incident at all when she came in from work: she did seen preoccupied with something, but whatever it was, she wasn't saying.

Sean went on his lap-top and played a video-game, idly passing the time until he went to bed. Maybe he'd at least dream about her?

"See Mistress, they know about you!" Von-Hesse's tone was urgent and hurried. *Lilith* did not like to be hurried:

"Maximilian I already knew about this... DVD!
They do *not* 'know' about me, merely about Adam Mitchell's hypnotic fantasies, as they believe them to be."

"He *names* you mistress, and he names himself as 'Adam Teal' the stupid youth who fawned all over you in 1665!"

"Is that a note of jealousy in your voice Maximilian? What if he is 'Adam Teal' reincarnated? Haven't I already clearly warned you that you *must* refrain from hurting him in any way! I shall deal with him at my pleasure… Anyway, he doesn't name me as Lillian, he says *'Lilith'*. They won't believe that I've returned to Liverpool in 2006!"

"And O'Riley… he has the same surname as the blacksmith's apprentice from old Liverpool Town!"

"Oh yes… the boy Connor… I wonder what happened to him?"

Von-Hesse noted that *Lilith* hadn't penetrated his defences enough to know that he had Adler follow her. With some satisfaction he believed that this was a sign of his own increasing powers: "How are your energy reserves Mistress?"

"My reserves? Not yet high enough. Tonight, I must feed on my two victims again... Dr Jonathan Teal and the... boy Sean O'Riley…"

Sean was unable to sleep. He was coming off the expectant high of seeing Lillian again, and that 'high' had never actually come. Wide awake the hours passed until by 3.00am the night was as quiet as the grave. He scanned his mind trying to find something interesting to think about, but all he could think of was Lillian; imagining her coming into his room, and into his bed. He smiled to himself as he allowed the fantasy to unfold.

The noise in his ears was faint at first and then gradually increased until it was like the 'white-noise' from a portable TV set when the aerial needs adjusting. Agitated at its intrusion he covered his head with the bedclothes, but it only got louder.

There was a sudden intensity of light – a grey-white light, like that from the full moon. So strong was it that it shone through his duvet. Combined with the white-noise it was too much to bear. Now annoyed as well as agitated, he cast the duvet down over his lap and sat bolt upright.

His heart actually murmured in its palpitations as he saw her – a ghostly grey-scale form with sliver moonshine hair billowing as if in a silent breeze. Her usually deep-green eyes: now almost black – yet still with wide discernable pupils. Her Mona-Lisa smile worn like a mask – her voluptuous curves as alabaster or marble; a living renaissance statute that would have graced even Michelangelo's skilled hands.

"Lillian!?"

His gasp of disbelief was the last word he could utter. His body tingled and then glowed as an invisible pressure forced itself against him, making him lie back and paralysing his muscles. Slipping into an altered state of consciousness he felt as if he no longer controlled his own breath.

Lillian's lovely face hovered over him as her spectral form passed through his solid bed as if it were mere smoke. Suddenly he felt an intense vacuum pressure pulling at his testicles – draining him as he orgasmed and fell unconscious.

Wednesday 22nd November 2006: ESP Rodney Street, 9.30am

"I see that Dr Jonathan Teal has been admitted to hospital with a suspected heart attack., and guess what? Allan Flynn's gone missing from home!"

"Eh?" Claire was preoccupied "Sorry John, what was that?"

"Dr Allan Flynn, our linguist friend at the university, he's vanished, gone missing from work and his house was left looking like the *Marie Celeste*."

"Missing?! Well... are the police on to it?"

"They are.... consensus is that he's a loner, and maybe a suicide risk... He was a bit crusty, but I wouldn't have said that about him."

"Oh..." Claire's voice trailed as her preoccupation with her son Sean covered-over any further room in her psyche for compassion for her missing friend.

"And Dr Teal, he's that fellow from the Liverpool School of Tropical Medicine, yer know, the chap descended from 'Henry Teal' the Liverpool Burgess who turned up in Adam's past-life hypnotic regression" continued John.

"A heart attack you say?" responded Claire, trying to focus back on the immediate situation.

"Yep, an emergency admission overnight. It's gossip at the university. Some are even spreading a rumour that his gonads had burst."

"Burst!"

"Or at least he'd made a hell of a mess of himself. Perhaps he'd been... er... yer know, and had a heart attack in middle of it."

"Er yer what John, I have no idea what you mean?"

"Well... masturbating! It is a health risk for men of his age group if they've got dickie tickers... I remember a couple of sudden-deaths like that when I was a young policeman."

"You're saying his testicles had burst?"

"Well it's only rumour Claire, apparently the 'residue' was a lot greater than you'd expect, like he'd been drained to the dregs."

"Well I hope you lot who are doing all of this gossiping think about how his wife and family must be feeling!"

"It's not me Claire! I'm just telling you that's all, and then only because his name's come up on the genealogical list. Trouble with old Teal was that he was sent to the university hospital casualty department, and yer know what some nurses can be like. They saw what had happened – with his gonads, and next thing it was all over the university!"

Claire was frowning: "I'm sorry John; I'm preoccupied with Sean's health at the moment. He couldn't get out of bed again this morning, looked as white as a sheet, really washed-out and grossly fatigued."

"I'm sorry too, it's a worry when it's your own kids isn't it?"

Claire nodded. "Anyway, back to business, we need a council of war with Kevin."

O'Riley put the flip chart up on its stand and got the red marker pen out: "OK, we have this Von-Hesse character who's an archaeologist, right?"

"Yep."

"And he's connected to the Museum – with investigating that seventeenth century find. He also knows you John, and you Claire, and, it 'appears' that he turned up here on Monday evening, and was able to induce an 'amnesia' in Susan."

"He also passed some kind of energy into me, maybe even a Bio-PK force" added Claire.

"Right... a character with his name also turns up on Adam Mitchell's past-life regression tape. Let's ignore cryptomnesia for now and just look at the connections. Moving on, the name of the 'occupant' of the stone sarcophagus has been translated to be '*Lilith*.' *Lilith* is also a character in Adam's past-life regression – someone he's in love with... and whom he claims he keeps seeing here in *this* life.

"And, we traced the identity of her supposed father: Matthew Hopgood, who was a real historically verified character – also a burgess in Liverpool in the 1660's."

"But no trace of *Lilith* herself?"

John sighed: "No... not as yet. We did trace one other character from the regression hypnosis: Henry Teal. He was one of the main individuals involved in *Lilith's* supposed execution. In fact, not only did we trace him, but I found a living descendent – of all people he's Dr Jonathan Teal, a specialist in Bubonic Plague at the Liverpool School of Tropical Medicine; who by coincidence... has just last night had a non-fatal heart attack, but under some 'odd' circumstances."

"In what way?"

"Well, it's just a rumour, but it seems that his semen was violently evacuated from his testes – so much so that they've collapsed. The suggestion is that the shock of it induced his heart attack."

"These are just rumours though John" cautioned Claire.

"The heart attack is verified Claire, but, yeah, the other 'facts' are speculative, even just gossip at this stage."

"They may still be significant though, we need to consider every detail."

"We do indeed; remember that *Lilith* was accused by Henry Teal of spreading the plague – and now his descendent a plague specialist has an unusual illness!"

"Good point John... Then, we have this 'Lillian' girl – connected to you Claire, and to me. She's definitely the same girl, same appearance, same manner."

"She's also hanging around Sean, who of course is my son and your grandson – so that's another multiple connection."

"OK... can we place Lillian with Von-Hesse?"

John and Claire shook their heads: "But something else has happened too – Allan Flynn the linguist who translated the ancient Aramaic on the sarcophagus, and who advised Claudia to call ESP in – he's gone missing..."

"Missing, Claire?"

"He is a loner, Kevin" said John "and unmarried, except to his work. Middle aged loners *do* just go missing, as we all know from our law enforcement days. It could be significant though: even if only as a meaningful coincidence."

"All coincidences in the paranormal are meaningful John..." O'Riley drew a series of connecting lines on the flip chart: "If we look at how all the associations fit together then we have to conclude that those two individuals *must* be linked... and, that you Claire, seem to be the most common of the denominators!"

"I was working on that hypothesis myself. That's why I started the genealogical searches" asserted John.

"You haven't traced mine back that far yet though have you?" Claire asked.

"No, but obviously that's got to be a priority now."

O'Riley's eyes narrowed as something occurred to him: "What if... what if Lillian Hopgood as she called herself to me, *is* *Lilith*, the *Lilith* Hopgood of 1665!"

"You mean like Adam Mitchell is in some way 'Adam Teal'?" asked John.

"Perhaps, or... maybe she's actually *Lilith*, the *same* continuous personality as she who apparently lived in Liverpool in the mid-seventeenth century?"

"How?" queried Claire.

"I'm using intuition now just to brainstorm, but suppose she's not a re-incarnation, but a *re-animation*!"

"Of course! The re-animation spell: *Resurrectio Animus!* That was carved into the inner face of the sarcophagus!" Claire exclaimed.

"As translated by the now missing Dr Flynn" said O'Riley.

"And then this Von-Hesse fellow suddenly turns up again from Bavaria, takes an interest in the find and disappears with the skull and a soil sample" added John."

"Which would make him what, 400 years old? Sorry to throw that spanner in the works..." said O'Riley.

"Or, Kevin, *our* Von-Hesse is a blood-line descendent and somehow his family kept the secret of the sarcophagus all of this time, until it was rediscovered and dug-up?" offered Claire.

"Possibly... now, why the apparent focus on our family? I ask as 'Lillian' knew what my talisman was, and its background."

"Maybe, if they know who we are, then they see us as the only real threat to them?" said Claire.

"Then they'd probably be right. There's no one else with our collective experience who could stand against them. So..."

"So first they infiltrate, and then they destroy us?"

"Perhaps, but surely that's not their main motive? It's more likely that we're just 'in the way' of whatever their final goal is."

Silence fell over them as they searched for a possible answer.

"We need to finish the genealogical scan – it's becoming clear that the roots of all of this are in the past" said Claire.

"True, but there's one obvious resource we haven't turned to yet!" grinned John.

"What's that?"

"Google!"

9

The
Séance

Hold then thy heart against her shining hair,
If, by thy fate, she spread it once for thee,
For, when she nets a young man in that snare
So twines she him he never may be free

Dante Gabriel Rossetti 1867
Translation from Goethe on *Lilith*

Wednesday 22nd November 2006: ESP Rodney Street, 11.00am

ohn Sutton was dutifully following up his 'obvious resource' on his laptop. He turned up relevant information almost immediately: "Shit, look at this!"

"What is it John?"

"*Lilith!* Look what Google brings up!"

Claire came over and scanned the references, selecting the links with the most promising information: "No… this *can't* be her!"

"Better get Kevin back over ASAP, he needs to see this!"

Claire hardly heard him. She'd followed a link to Wikipedia – the online encyclopaedia, and there, in an 1892 oil painting entitled '*Lilith*' by the artist John Collier, was the unmistakable face of Lillian…

O'Riley made it back to ESP for 12.30pm. By then, John and Claire had amassed a great deal of information: "If I didn't know you better Kevin I'd say that you weren't gonna believe this!" John hardly believed it himself.

Claire reloaded the Wikipedia page with the Collier oil painting: "It certainly *looks* a 'little' like the girl who called at Eden…"said O'Riley.

"Allowing for the fact that this isn't a photograph, and that's she's naked rather than dressed in the street fashions of 2006, I'd say it *is* the 'Lillian' or at least as near as damn it…who Sean brought home with him!" asserted Claire.

"That would mean that she was active in 1892" said John "Which scuppers the idea that she's been buried under the streets of Liverpool for 341 years!"

O'Riley's brow furrowed: "Yes, *if* we forget that John Collier was an artist. Creative people of all kinds can tune into the collective unconscious psyche. It'd be more than plausible that he'd 'find' an image of *Lilith* in there that corresponded to how humankind has actually experienced her over the centuries."

"An 'archetype' you mean?" asked Claire.

"Yes… a primordial *imago* of *Lilith*."

"But wouldn't Collier have used a live model?" suggested John.

"Probably: Collier was associated loosely to the Pre-Raphaelite Brotherhood – they did use their favourite models as muses, but then you can never stop the psyche 'projecting' archetypal images onto 'real' external people, even artists models. That's the purpose the models truly served, to allow the artist to access archetypal images and give them life. So, whatever the model *really* looked like, 'Lilith' came through, as if the artist was a channelling medium. That's what we see when we look

at the painting, we see Lillian, as we have known her, but behind both the painting *and* Lillian is the real *Lilith*..."

John shuddered involuntarily: "Look, let's get a grip on ourselves here before we get carried away on a tidal wave of 'auto-suggestion' - we must be really certain... *really* certain, otherwise all we've done is allowed the *Lilith* archetype, as Kevin's described it... to... to *possess* us!"

O'Riley's head jolted as the rebuke penetrated home: "Well... you do have a point John... trouble is... what if you're wrong?"

Claire shook her head: "All well and good and academic too" said Claire, "but read just what *Lilith* is supposed to be!"

The trio sat down and browsed the references...

Von-Hesse was still agitated about *Lilith's* behaviour: "Mistress, I heard the news about Dr Jonathan Teal, about his 'heart-attack', if this is as a result of your activities..."

Lilith's carefree demeanour was unfazed: "Still worrying are you Maximilian? Teal's condition is not *yet* fatal; I am saving the contagion for him and his family."

"But should he talk... should he tell about your visitations..."

Lilith showed a trace of impatience with him: "Talk? Maximilian really! These are *not* superstitious times, people no longer believe in dreams, or even in demons – which for them... is unfortunate. Did you really think that he's likely to tell anyone? He hasn't even met me 'in-person' yet, only in his sleep."

The Bavarian wasn't satisfied: "Then what about Sean O'Riley, and his mother and her ESP institute!"

"Oh yes…" she replied "I meant to mention it, I don't mind you having Adler follow me around, but do make sure that no one else see's him!"

Von-Hesse's eyes showed alarm.

"Maximilian, really, did you think that I wouldn't know? It's you who should be careful; your visit to the Eden Institute was noted by Dr O'Riley, oh yes, I know about that too!" *Lilith's* smile was accompanied by a cruel tone to her voice *"You* are far more vulnerable than I am, Maximilian Von-Hess: it would be wise of you not to forget that fact…"

Adler who was sitting in the corner, shook with fear. *Lilith* gave him a beatifying smile: "Don't be afraid, just don't let me down" she said. "Now, I'm off to tease young Sean a bit. Make sure that you aren't seen when you follow me!"

Von-Hesse was exasperated, but he realized that he'd just received a clear and present warning. If he was to deceive *Lilith*, and he did intend to do so, then he must be far more careful…

Over at ESP the faces were becoming increasingly more glum and concerned as their research got deeper and deeper into online resources on the 'Goddess' *Lilith*: "In the Semite traditions…Adam's first wife before Eve, and ejected from Eden, created from the blood soil of Eden itself, thrives as both *succubus* and *incubus*, kills unborn children in the womb and brings pestilence, contagion and plague. She can shape-shift, appearing to her victims psyche as the embodiment of idealised and irresistible feminine beauty… She has a hatred for all who descend from Eve and wishes to repopulate the Earth with her own demonic offspring!" Claire read out the details with alarm.

"Bloody hell!" John's words said it all…

"It fits…" murmured O'Riley "It fits exactly: the sarcophagus, the past-life regression, the soil… even her appearance… we all somehow see her slightly differently…but with that mesmeric essence coming through…"

John was suddenly focused on outcomes: "Yeah, OK, *but* how in hell do we stop her? From that description she's got to be the most dangerous enemy we've ever faced!"

O'Riley stared, trance like, to the floor: "Let's hope that we do find a way… otherwise…"

Claire sighed: "Well, as it isn't 1665 we can't throw her into the Mersey for being a witch!"

Shaking himself free of his trance, O'Riley responded: "We can't *do* anything, yet, at least not directly against her. As 'Lillian' she's probably got a legal identity sorted, and through Von-Hesse, a support network, probably even minders."

"But Kevin, she's coming to Eden to see you!"

"Yeah, how ironic… 'Eden' I wonder if that amuses her…" O'Riley smiled unable to help himself: "Adam Mitchell… Adam Teal... Adam… in Eden…could it *really* be him?…"

"And, there's Sean!" gasped Claire, her mother's concerns overlooking O'Riley's crucial insight: "It's a familiar pattern isn't it? Remember with Dominique and Rowena? They get into the families of their victims! Kevin, we *must* do something!"

O'Riley's eyes darted about from side to side as he thought: "Let's chip away at them… work on Adam Mitchell at the Museum."

"How, he's madly in love with her?"

"Oh… get him to do something that draws things out…"

"Such as?"

"Why, a séance… let's see if his ancestors will speak to him!"

Sean was in his usual dream-like state as he wandered about the corridors between classes – the throng of variously motivated, or un-motivated fellow students, passing him like shoals of disturbed fish on a coral reef. Then just as in the waters of the Red Sea the waves parted, and there *she* was: "Lillian! What you doing here?"

"Me? Oh, just going about my business."

"But you're not a student are you?"

"I'm… a researcher"

"*Researcher*… researching what?"

Lilith smiled: "Why *you* of course!"

Flattered beyond his capacity to be rational, Sean grinned like an Alsatian puppy.

"I'm going over to Liverpool, want to come with me?" she asked.

He couldn't refuse: "Definitely: we can get the train, from here, from Conway Park!"

"Hmm… no, I prefer the Ferry…"

"The Ferry! It's November! It'll be bloody freezing!"

"Oh I don't feel the cold… do you?"

"He did, but then he was a 'man' so: "Nah, course not!"

"OK, let's walk to Woodside."

Sean realized that it was nearly a mile walk and thought to complain, but he couldn't: he really did want to impress her.

The journey proceeded at a pace. *Lilith* liked to breeze along quickly: "Do yer always walk so fast Lillian?" Poor Sean was having trouble keeping up.

"I knew someone when I was younger, called Adam, he couldn't keep up with me either. He was in love with me you know."

"In love!" Sean was outraged. How dare anyone else be in love with *his* girl: *his* Botticelli's Venus?

"Yes, we used to walk to and from the Chapel together."

"The Mormon one?"

"No! This was a *very* long time ago… there weren't any Mormon Churches then."

"Eh?" Sean may not have been the best informed youth of his generation, but even he knew they'd been around at least since the early nineteenth century.

Lilith changed the direction of their conversation: "I don't think your mum likes me very much."

"Mum? Oh she's a daft awld girl, always having these 'psychic' experiences an' stuff like that. I don't believe in any of it me-self. Lizzie, my sister, she does: but even she thinks mum's a bit weird."

"She'll try and stop you seeing me you know."

"Mum? Nah… and even if she did, I wouldn't take any notice."

"Do you see much of your granddad O'Riley?"

"Er… not these days, when I was a kid. Me Nan's always been good ter me. She's a 'glamorous granny' yer know, just on sixty years old, but still very nice lookin!"

"So… good looks run in your family?"

"Yeah me sister's pretty… for a sister… she takes after me auntie Mary: *all* the women are attractive in our family."

So the chat went on, as *Lilith*'s flattery gradually got all the information she needed about Sean's extended family…

Claire had taken the séance idea on board: "OK, firstly we need to check our list of effective and reliable mediums, and then we need to persuade Adam."

"That's a job for you Claire" smiled John "you can use your womanly wiles to win him over!"

"At forty-five! I'd risk being like his grandmother!"

"Nonsense… you still look very good… for your age! Anyway, I've gotta get on with tracing your family tree."

"I'll make contact with the mediums" said O'Riley.

Claire looked at them both and smiled: "Yer worked that one out well between you!"

"Bye Claire!" grinned John.

3.30pm and Claire found herself descending the stairs to the basement of Liverpool World Museum. Claudia was out at an appointment and had left Adam to mind the store: "Adam!"

"Oh… hello Claire: what can I do for you? It's only me here I'm afraid; 'her majesty's' out."

"That's OK; it's er… you I want."

Adam thought he'd make a joke of it: "Cool: I like older women!"

"Like 350 years older perhaps?"

"Ah: yer got me there!"

"Seriously Adam, about the past-life regression… have you thought anymore about how you might like to take it further?"

"I've spoken with Dr O'Riley at Eden, we decided to work together with you on it… has he mentioned that to you?"

"Er, not in any depth no… except… we were wondering if you'd like to take the next logical step?"

"Which is what?"

"A séance…"

"A *séance!* What with crystal balls and sitting in a circle holdin' hands with old ladies an' stuff like that?"

"Possibly, it depends who's available, and who'd be willing to do it. You see, it's not something to undertake lightly, it has its risks."

Adam half smiled quizzically: "You're serious aren't you!"

Claire breathed out hard: "I am Adam, I am."

"No… *me* Adam, *you* Professor Lattimer!" he joked in word-play.

"Well at least you're in a jovial mood. Have you seen 'her' again recently?"

Adam's face fell: "No… nothing since Derby Square."

"Then perhaps a séance would help encourage her."

Adam looked closely at Claire's face, trying to read behind her persona: "Does that mean that *you* believe me too, like Dr O'Riley does?"

"I'd be wasting my time here if I didn't."

Reassured on that particular point he asked: "OK, so how will a séance help, ah mean, she ain't dead: unless; yer sayin that she's a ghost!"

Claire smiled her most winsome smile to put him at his ease: "No! She's 'real' enough, it's more the other people, in your regression, if we could get them to come through, that might help us all understand what's going on."

"Cool, it'll be like that TV archaeology Show with Julian Richards: 'Meet The Ancestors' only it'd be 'live' ha ha!"

Claire laughed with him at the thought.

Adam felt a sudden chill: "Suppose it frightens *Lilith* away."

"Adam… do you really think that *anything* could frighten her?"

"Jesus it's frickin freezing!" The wind along the Mersey estuary bit hard and deep into Sean's otherwise genteel body.

"Fresh air will do you good. You want to be a policeman like your dad and granddad don't you?"

"Well… yeah!"

"Then this will toughen you up won't it?" she said in her inimitable coquettish style.

Sean was by now visibly and uncontrollably shaking in the icy estuarine wind: "We shudda got the train!"

"If you had lived, oh say three hundred and fifty years ago, then this would be the only way to cross the Mersey."

"Well I live in the 21st century not the bluddy 17th!"

"Don't knock it till you try it!" smiled the Mona-Lisa smile.

Lilith looked over at the Liver Building's. Water Street, and the site of her former home address, ran up the left hand side of the famous building towards the Town Hall. The old Castle long gone, and the ancient Pool, now filled in and built over.

"Do you still think I look like Botticelli's Venus?" she asked impishly of him.

Sean grinned and then cast his eyes down in embarrassment of revealing the depth of his attraction to her: "Sure… dead beautiful!"

"There is a beauty in death Sean… I said that to Adam once: and I'll show *you* one day."

Sean was perplexed: "Eh, don't get yer?"

Her beautiful eyes scanned his, revealing an almost human compassion: "You know nothing about me, and yet you *trust* me so completely."

Sean's voice quietened: "That's coz, well…" he muttered his words: "I *love* you Lillian…" his eyes pleaded his innocence.

Lilith smiled ever broadly, her dimples making her lovely face even more appealing: "I've saved a lock of my golden hair for you" she said opening her hand to reveal the shimmering strands… platted… like a hangman's rope.

"Wow!"

"You must wear it always, and *tightly*, around your heart…"

Taking the plait from her, he tingled at the touch of her skin, the braided rope lock was heavy, like real gold, but spun into the finest of filaments.

"It'll change colour… with my mood" she said.

For just a moment, Sean's grip relaxed, and the braid nearly fell to the mercy of the wind, and the waters of the Mersey. He saw a flash of alarm on her face, and pulled the plait safely back: "I'll keep it by my heart *Lilith*, forever…I promise!"

The Mona Lisa smile broke out again, washing the shadow of concern from her eyes: "Then, you'll always have me nearby, Sean, won't you… for in my hair, is *all* that is me…"

Wednesday 22ⁿᵈ November 2006: North Road Birkenhead 6.00pm

"Good evening Dr O'Riley; here on ESP business are you?"

O'Riley smiled: "You must be psychic!"

"If the spirits are with me Dr O'Riley… Is it a sitting you require?" Alfred Hulme was a rather short and unkempt man of around fifty years of age, a local healer and medium, he had been on ESP's 'books' as a psychic for nearly twenty years.

"For me individually… no, but you are right, I am here on behalf of ESP, they have an interesting case active, one that involves information obtained under past-life regression hypnosis."

"Ah!" Hulme exclaimed "Are those ESP people *still* using that stuff? They'd get much better results from a sitting!" He shook his head in judgement, but softened it with a smile: "OK, it can get a bit crowded sometimes: if the spirits are willing to show up, but then at least its sociable!"

O'Riley smiled warmly: he liked Alfred's rather charming old-fashioned ways. In return, Alfred had a lot of respect for O'Riley, especially as he had been told by the spirits during a sitting about O'Riley's past mentorship by *Viridios* the 'Green Man' - the nature spirit of life and re-birth who had made the Wirral his home in protection of an ancient and sacred site.

Hulme was one of the very few people outside of Kevin O'Riley's most intimate circle ever to find out about his past. For his part O'Riley was comfortable with Alfred's knowledge of it – he had always been discrete, and reliable with ESP, and, he would never have been informed of the Green Man's mentorship, had the *spirits* thought him unworthy...

"This young man..." O'Riley began.

"No, hush please! I don't want to know *anything* personal about the fellow in advance... let the spirits greet him without any prior knowledge from me interfering!"

O'Riley nodded in assent: "Shall I get Claire Lattimer to call you to arrange a time?

"Ah dear Claire! Such a brave soul isn't she, the spirits have told me all about her, and how you both met!"

Despite his advancing age O'Riley blushed. Twenty five years ago, when Claire was barely out of her teens and a young policewoman under his command, their 'friendship' had been very close...

Alfred put a warming hand on his shoulder: "Don't let me embarrass you Dr O'Riley! Claire would be very welcome to call!"

St Stephens Road Prenton

Sean arrived home cold and wet, but nevertheless elated. He'd been in Lillian's company for several hours, doing a grand tour of Liverpool – precisely why she'd done that he couldn't figure out, but just being with her lifted his heart. She'd even given him that lock of her magically lustrous hair, which true to his promise, he would keep in a locket and chain, close by his heart... forever Now though, he feared he was about to get some ear-ache from his mum: but it was not, this time, for being late home for his tea:

"Sean?"

"Hi Mum!" Sean was still on his high "Sorry 'bout bein' late!"

Claire had been sitting on the 'Lillian' issue for some hours now and she felt it was time to get up and at it. This wasn't just a matter of an 'unsuitable girl' this was a terrifying demonic power that had ingratiated itself into her son's life, no doubt with the intention of killing him: "We have to talk Sean, right now, about Lillian!"

Sean did his 'Harry Enfield' impression of a recalcitrant teenager - he'd just age-regressed five years again - "Aw that's so unfair! I've just come in, an' I'm starvin'!"

Claire, despite herself, was inducted into the act: "I remember your dad at your age being just the same, he was slow on the uptake over danger too!"

"My dad! He's *never* been my age!"

"At eighteen he was more 'you' than you are believe me! And, that's the point: you're under the same kind of threat that he was!"

"Well stop bullyin' me then!"

Claire shut the living room door: "You've *got* to listen Sean, 'Lillian' as you know her to be isn't who, or even what, she seems to be!"

"I like mysteries!" he retorted.

"Really, does that include one's that end yer life?!"

"Don't be daft mum, ah *love* her!"

"Love! You hardly know her... or 'it' as she really is!"

Claire was losing her ground. The emotion of being a frightened loving parent had scuppered all of her plans to be rational with him.

"What would *you* know 'bout it? If you'd *ever* been in love, then yer'd understand!" Sean was almost screaming in anger and frustration - *Lilith's* lock of golden hair was already coiling serpent-like about his very heart...

But the challenge to Claire's emotional capacities for love suddenly sent her mind reeling back across the years. Faces, times, places – conflicts of the heart and even of the soul. Her husband, Kevin O'Riley Junior, was without question, the love of her life, her 'true' love, but he hadn't been her *only* love...

Sean read her dissonance and made his own interpretation of it: "See! I'm right aren't I: ye've got no bloody idea; just leave me alone!" He stormed out.

Blind-sighted by her own psyche's unconscious reaction to the issue of 'love' Claire froze to the spot. To go after Sean might just make it worse; he may even leave the house and be lost to any possibility of help from her.

Ruefully a part of her mind reflected on how impossible it could be to help a member of your own family with 'professional' matters of the heart - especially when unfinished business from your own past had suddenly intruded...

Claire had kept most of the developments away from her husband – 'young' Kevin O'Riley. He'd been through a great deal early on in his life; massive emotional and psychological trauma's – culminating in an intense battle against a malevolent force that he'd shared with Claire, his dad and John Sutton. It was the seminal event and turning point that had led to where each had subsequently gone with their lives.

Young Kevin had settled for a conventional if relatively high-flying career in the police. He'd had enough for one-lifetime of the supernatural and the occult, and anyway he could hardly imagine anything ever coming near to the impact and meaning of those early experiences. He and Claire were bonded for life – no question, but he'd moved away from personal involvement with 'parapsychology' and its related fields.

As usual, he was late in from work, this evening, but now Claire would have some unwelcome news for him. The past had quite literally come knocking on his door...

John Sutton powered up his laptop and logged onto the net as soon as he got in through the door of his home. His old police instincts were guiding him now, and he was determined to make every possible connection and join up every possible dot until the picture became clear. Kevin O'Riley senior had led the way by example and he was determined to be no slouch now in following it.

He managed at last to trace Claire's family back across the generations back through births marriages, deaths, census returns, and parish records until suddenly, right there before him on his computer screen was the missing link: Nathaniel

Lattimer was ten generations back from her, her seventh-times great-grandfather. That confirmation scared him, it must, inevitably mean that 'Lillian' would try to kill her, and... her children.

Back at St Stephens Road, Claire had given her best account of events to her husband: "That's the picture of it Kevin, it's shaping up as something frighteningly evil!"

Kevin junior's eyes shifted about as he stared at the carpet: "Why... why did you wait to tell me?"

"Well love, to be honest, you've not shown any interest in the details of my work for years now..."

"True: but this about our family!" He'd conveniently buried his wife's point beneath his indignation. He was scanning his mind to see what could be done: "But... there's no 'real' evidence, how can I act!"

He was thinking as a policeman still.

Claire understood: "I know love, but it's like last time isn't it? The battle will have to fought outside of common conventions like the law..."

Young Kevin held on to what he was familiar with: "Where do they live do we know?"

"Apparently a big old house of some-kind in Oxton. Claudia at the museum may know."

He braced himself upright in his chair, and took a sharp shallow breath: "I'll call over and see her myself!"

Claire felt a rush of anxiety about too precipitous a reaction: "No, love, we have no idea just how much control Von-Hesse has over her – except that he seems to be able to induce amnesia's in people – Claudia at the museum and Susan at Eden. That suggests a *powerful* skill in hypnosis, and one that's certainly augmented by occultism. He's got to be considered as *very* dangerous, he may even have the capacity to project a bio-PK field"

Kevin was flustered, both by frustration over inaction, and, by his ignorance: "A what?"

"Sorry love, the ability to project energy from his body at a distance and to use it to cause disruption and harm – a kind of psycho-kinesis aimed at changing a person's physical and mental state... I say that, because of what passed from him into me through his handshake and an experience I had out of the blue recently at ESP. Now, if they've given 'Lillian' an identity – created one for her through hacking internet databases, then we may be able to trace her that same way!"

Relaxing, just a bit, he nodded: "I'll get on to it right away. But, there's one other thing... and this should really concern us, what about Lizzie, has anyone made a move on her? Remember what happened once to my sister Mary!"

Outside in St Stephens Road the Black Mercedes Benz Limousine pulled away. Von-Hesse had been watching the house, but not with his outer 'eyes'. His mind had reached out, drawn by the increased emotional energy.

Finding hot and cold psychic spots in the house, he'd singled out the one person untouched thus far – the pretty sixteen year old daughter of Claire and Kevin, who was innocently absorbed in her homework up in her bedroom.

The rest of the house was emotionally hot, but she was cool, and thus marked herself out as a figure-ground distinction. Von-Hesse's darkly handsome face smiled. His mistress would thank him for taking her.

Now, it would be just a matter of time...

John Sutton was pacing up and down in his converted attic – the place he used as a study. Should he ring Claire now and tell her, or wait until the morning? Should he contact O'Riley senior? The implications of the situation now began to filter through from the back of his mind; his 'police' instincts could no longer restrain them. He had his own family, a son and daughter the same age as Claire's kids, and he had his wife; Carla – a very special person in her own right, and someone whom he should be sharing all this information with…

However, as with Claire and young Kevin, the magical moment that had joined them together in their first great battles against evil had long passed – and they'd settled into an 'ordinary' life. Carla was a senior manager in the NHS, a nurse by primary training, who had an almost miraculous 'healing touch' - he'd benefited from it himself. She also had an uncanny background – one that now seemed more like a dream than an everyday reality.

Should he tell her?

Thursday 23rd November 2006: ESP Rodney Street, 9.30am

"Here's the proof Claire, and if *we* know then we can bet our bottom dollar that *they* know!"

Claire's mind was shifted, this name before her on the screen, the details of a life, it was *her* blood ancestor, *her* family: "He's my great-grandfather seven times over… he was real…" she spoke softly in realisation of the truth.

John pursed his lip: "Yeah so freakin real – if yer pardon the expression – that what he got up to 350 years ago is likely being pinned onto you, now, today!"

Claire's head jolted slightly as the mixed channels of thought crossed one-another: "The sins of the great-grandfathers shall be visited upon their great-granddaughters?"

"According to Adam!" John exclaimed "er sorry 'Adam' I meant to say...."

 "Kevin's got the agreement of Alfred Hulme to do a séance" Claire added, quietly.

"Alfie: good, he's one of the better mediums!   When for?"

 "I have to call in at the Museum, and see Adam first, he does know about it, but not that it's definitely on yet. I'll ring Alfie this morning and confirm a time before I go to the Museum.

My Kevin's worried about Lizzie, even more than Sean…"

John's eyes widened, that remark had caught him out on his fears for his own children.

His eyes met hers – and nothing more needed to be said…

Liverpool Museum

10.30 am and Claudia heard the now familiar footfall of Claire in the basement corridor: "Morning Claudia! Adam about?"

 "Hi Claire, he's hiding in the storeroom I think. He's been dreaming out aloud at work again about that girl from his past-life regression hypnosis – You know that I've encouraged him to get his head sorted, don't you?"

"Yeah… he told me." Claire neglected to add that his 'shrink' was her father-in-law.

 "To be direct, I regret ever having agreed to that stunt" said Claudia in a matter-of-fact way

"Stunt?!"

"It could've ruined the reputation of the department!" Of course Claudia meant *her* reputation, but… false modesty made her broaden it out "And, his head's in a right mess now: not that it wasn't before of course…but it's even worse!"

Claire thought it obvious that she'd get no cooperation now with Claudia on a séance for Adam, so she struck back – obliquely: "Has Dr Von Hesse returned the finds yet?"

Claudia' jolted, her eyes immediately glazing-over: "It is necessary for Dr Von-Hesse to have the samples a short while longer…" Claire recovered from her surprise at this strange reaction, and recognized Claudia's robotic monotone response as the result of a post-hypnotically triggered command."

She scanned her for a moment and confirmed that she was indeed still deep in trance. Figuring that it'd be of no advantage to say anything further, she decided to head off and find Adam. Claudia would be amnesiac anyway when she came round – naturally, so it'd be safer to just let her be. Maybe John could speak with her and see if he could use 'covert' hypnotic methods to break Von-Hesse's hold over her…

She found Adam, just as Claudia had said, holed up in the storeroom: "Claire, what a nice surprise! I thought the dominatrix had come for me!"

 "Dominatrix?" Claire shuddered slightly as an old memory took hold of her.

"Yeah, dear old Claudia!"

Claire smiled to release the effect of the unpleasant memory: "No, sorry, only your favourite 'older woman', er sorry *second* favourite – if you count that 350 plus year old 'young' thing you keep bumping into!" Claire smiled again as she spoke.

Adam appreciated her warmth: "Actually, as its 'safe' to say so, you are quite a 'looker' but don't tell Claudia. Yer know I reckon behind that gruff but buxom and marmish exterior, she's gotta secret crush on me, and I'd hate ter make her jealous of you as well as of my *Lilith*!"

Claire's smile broadened and shed the decades from her face: "Thanks, but… I've come here to tell you about the séance."

"Ah… so yer mean that ye've gone ahead and booked me one?"

"You make it sound like a trip to the dentist to have root-canals on yer wisdom teeth!"

"Wisdom teeth… Yer know, I don't think mine are all through yet?" Adam stuck his fingers in his mouth and wiggled about: "No, one's wonky, one hasn't come through at all, one's half way there and one's OK! No doubt on the wisdom scale Claudia would say that makes me a quarter-wit, not even addin' up to a half-wit yet!"

Claire laughed out loud, openly. There was something funny about a Ph.D student hiding in a storeroom from his marmish-dominatrix supervisor who had a secret crush on him, whilst he prepared for a séance by wiggling his wisdom teeth: "Well, I must say you're cheering me up! Anyway… it's… tonight."

"What!?"

"Well we can't do it here, Claudia would lay dinosaur eggs."

"Yeah, *Raptor* eggs!"

Claire laughed again: "It's over in Birkenhead, in North Road, I can pick you up from here if you like?"

"Birkenhead: the 'One-Eyed-City!' Jeesh, couldn't you have picked somewhere *this* side of civilization!"

"See you after work; you can come back to my place for tea."

Adam grinned: "Good job I'm in love with *Lilith*… otherwise an offer like that would make my… let's see… lifetime?"

"Mistress, the daughter is untouched, innocent and emotionally naïve. She would be... perfect."

Lilith hadn't met Lizzie yet, but she was becoming intrigued: "Hmm we could have many uses for her... a hostage, a breeding host: or even... as a stand-by, in case *this* body became damaged... If so, I require her to be *beautiful* Maximilian; this form I inhabit now, is so... agreeable to my taste...

Very well, when I am at full strength, and just before the contagion, you may... take her, if she is of no use, then she will suffice for entertainment.

Her disappearance would cause Claire Lattimer extreme distress, and that, is one of my priority goals.

What else have you found out?"

"Yesterday, Adler followed Dr O'Riley to an address in Birkenhead, a psychic in North Road known as: Alfred Hulme."

"His purpose?"

"Not yet known... but Hulme is a practitioner of spiritual healing, psychometry, channelling and séance."

"Very well, channel into *his* activities, particularly if O'Riley returns there."

"But Mistress... the energy required of me for that, is considerable!"

"Then expend it Maximilian: expend your energy... in my service! That is your *raison d'être* is it not?"

Uncharacteristically, The Bavarian betrayed himself with a pursed lip - but he conceded with slight bow of his head...

Claire's Saab saloon car rode over the cobbled surface of William Brown Street as she looked for a parking place outside Liverpool World Museum. If you timed it right, parking was usually easy, but if not, it meant cat and mouse with the predatory traffic wardens. "How mundane" she mused, there she was trying to save humankind and her most immediate concern was a traffic warden...

At last Adam emerged, still wearing a long white lab coat, walking erratically and deep in animated conversation with... no one.

"There's a nutty professor in the making!" grinned Claire.

She sounded her horn, and Adam walked straight past staring myopically towards St George's Hall: "Here Adam!"

"Ah!" he exclaimed "I thought you'd be in a... well maybe a big Jaguar or somethin', or perhaps a Mercedes!"

"Just shows how we project our fantasies onto people doesn't it Adam? My husband drives the Jag, an S-Type..."

They laughed together as Claire's car left William Brown Street and crossed the roundabout into the 'Queensway' Mersey Tunnel to Birkenhead.

Behind them: on the old Museum steps a man on a Blackberry mobile phone stared intently after them.

Von-Hesse received the call: "Very well, Meier will follow them from the tunnel exit, you can return to Oxton."

The hooded black-brown eyes narrowed. This was no innocent kindness of the part of Professor Lattimer; she wouldn't be wasting her time picking up a young Ph.D student, and especially not *this* particular Ph.D student, unless the ESP team were making their next move – imminently.

Adam made himself at home at St Stephens Road. It was a nice house, with a warm atmosphere. Young Sean was there, and was still in his 'Harry Enfield' teenager mode, which was a relief to Claire, as she'd have had a potentially explosive situation on her hands if the two young men actually spoke to one another in any depth and they were to suddenly realize that they were *both* in love with the same girl.

Wisely, Claire had asked Adam to mention nothing about the purpose for his visit, other than it was on ESP business. Her husband Kevin, of course knew, but he'd been briefed well by Claire, and managed to keep the conversation away from any 'hot' topics. Adam nearly gave the game away when he found himself making lengthy stares at Lizzie. He was just about to say how like '*Lilith*' she looked, when Claire distracted him. It wasn't beyond possibility, that Sean would have heard '*Lilith*' as 'Lillian'.

7.30pm and it was time to set off for North Road. Young Kevin was pensive. He knew that his dad and John Sutton would be there, but deep inside he longed to be there too. Memories of the final showdown with the Harlequin at Woodchurch Parish Church flooded in, as he watched Claire drive away into the night. Someone had to stay with the kids… It wasn't beyond the bounds of probability that an attempt may be made to take either or both of them.

He was of course correct; it would now only be a matter of when…

John Sutton had picked O'Riley up from Prenton Lane in his Lexus GS430h: "Blimey, these 'hybrid' engined cars are quiet John!"

"Makes a change from the old days in the police with Rover SDI's and Vauxhall Cavalier's eh?" he grinned.

O'Riley smiled: "I saw Von-Hesse get into a big Mercedes S-Class Limo – it was black of course…"

"Of course! A step up from The Harlequin's 7-Series BMW though eh?"

"Ha: careful John, you know what they say about Lexus's!"

"That's 'Lexi' in the plural Kevin, and yeah according to 'Alan Partridge' they're the *Japanese Mercedes!*"

The two enjoyed their banter as they made their way to North Road. So much so that they completely failed to see the ostentatious, big black, S-Class Mercedes Benz Limousine three cars behind them…

Alfred Hulme was all smiles as he met them at the door. They'd parked over in Rocky Bank Road, so were within direct sight of the house. Standing behind Alfie was his wizened old-Irish psychic door-keeper: Bridget. Her more obvious duty was to act as receptionist, but she also served to screen visitors, psychically and make sure that the sanctity of the building was maintained.

It was a busy healing-practice and patients would be on site and receiving treatment from Hulme's 'helpers' whilst the séance was being held in another part of the impressive Edwardian building.

Adam found the atmosphere rather strange, but quaint. He certainly didn't expect anything substantial to come from it – a belief betrayed by his perma-grin visage as he entered the hallway. Alfie, of course, not only saw right through him, but was completely at ease with the Ph.D. student's naïve scepticism: "You must be the young man who wishes to communicate with the spirits?"

"Yeah, I'll have a whisky!" he joked.

Alfie smiled beneficently "Old Jock will look after you."

"Old Jock? Woz that, some kinda euphemism fer Scotch?"

"He's Alfred's spirit guide, Adam" Claire was trying to save him from himself.

"Spirit guide!"

Alfie raised an eyebrow: "Is that so strange, here, at a spiritualists? Is it any more strange than re-living a past life under hypnosis?"

Adam's eyes darted about as he tried to formulate a response: "Er…"

Bridget's spinsterish persona took on an indignant air: "Please do not waste Alfred's valuable time! He has set aside healing sessions with sick people, including children to give up his energy to you!"

Adam was used to chastisement from marmish women. So well trained was he that he immediately rounded his shoulders and adopted a 'naughty schoolboy' look on his face.

Alfred was content that appropriate boundaries had been set: "We can go to the séance room soon: I just need to get changed into my mediums clothes… I also have my circle of sitters waiting to help. Claire, I take it that you've told the young fellow what to expect?"

Claire had given him a broad outline but… "No fine details, Alfred, just as you requested, just as I've not given you anything on his background, or even formally introduced you as yet."

Adam shook himself from his torpor: "Yeah, why is that? No one's even introduced me yet!"

Alfie smiled again: "The *less* I know about you before-hand, the better the 'proof' for anything that the spirits reveal!"

"Oh yeah… hadn't thoughta that…"

"The best thing to do is to simply go along with it.
Alfie has agreed to us tape recording the séance – which is a rare privilege Adam!" O'Riley emphasized "Oh, and er… the sitters, and of course Alfie himself, will all have… ahem 'Edwardian' dress… it's part of the protocol demanded by Alfie's spirit guides."

Adam's eyes widened in amused disbelief at the prospect of theatrical Edwardian trappings but with an erratic nod of his head and curled lip, he confirmed his acceptance.

Adam followed the human-train as it snaked its way up the stairs to the top of the house. "Hardly a stairway to heaven" – he mused quietly to himself as he ascended.

The room had a 'period' feel to it: early Edwardian, with thick cloth drapes, heavy wallpaper and old photographs – whose frames hung from black string rather than on modern picture hooks. The large circular table was covered in a plum-red cloth – matching the patterned curtains by shade if not by pattern. On the gnarled dark wood sideboard was a crystal ball and an old 'Parlophone' record player, complete with its antique brass horn style speaker.

If not quite Dickensian: then H.G. Well's would certainly have been at home here….

"I see you've created the right atmosphere!" said Adam with a trace of anxiety in his voice, as Alfred entered the room followed by his all-female, regular circle of séance sitters.

"The spirits prefer it this way… Old Jock likes the photographs of Roxburgh in Scotland – he's from there you know, from Kelso."

"He is?" Adam's mind was dividing between his twenty first century scepticism and the effect of the room's ambiance: "I don't like Dr Who…" he said incongruously.

"Eh?" queried John.

"The new Doctor Who… I liked Tom Baker, or at least what I've seen of him on DVD…"

Alfred understood what was happening, but John's bluntness hadn't caught on: "Dr Who? What are yer goin' on about now Adam?"

He fumbled: "Er…"

Claire offered an explanation: "The new series has had a lot of 'Edwardian/Victorian' stories in it, I know coz Sean's a fan. The stories are a bit 'spooky' in a psychic sense. I think that Adam's psyche has been… 'stimulated' a bit by the room."

Alfred reassured him: "Apart from 'time travel' there's nothing like Dr Who going on in here young fellow!"

"Time travel… oh yeah… I've done that already haven't I, in my past-life regression …"

Claire put her arm round his shoulder: "Remember when you joked with me about it being like that archaeology programme: 'Meet The Ancestors' only it'd be 'live'!"

"Ha! Yeah! Silly me! OK, let's do it!"

Outside, just on the rise of Rocky Bank Road, Von-Hesse had settled in comfort in the back seat of the Mercedes limousine. Meier, the 'hard' man out of his two assistants was his chauffeur. Looking at the façade of the North Road building, Von-Hesse once again reached out with his mind, seeking the location of his prey. At first, activity in the basement healing-sanctuary overwhelmed his extra-sensory perception, but after a short while he was able to mark out who was who, and where they were in the house.

"It's shielded!" he suddenly exclaimed "It's actually shielded!"

"Master?" queried Meier.

"That medium: Hulme, he has attempted to block all psychic intrusions with occult devices… Well, well, he's not so much the labile urban amateur after-all… Nevertheless, I shall *penetrate* his defences!"

Alfred had asked them all to sit at the big, round, table. With the ESP team, plus Adam, Bridget and Hulme himself, the circle numbered nine: "I'd prefer twelve sitters, the combined energy would facilitate things, but, the 'quality' of our circle should more than make up for numbers!

Now… all I know about our… 'enquirer', is that his name is Adam! Let me just explain to you Adam, a little of what will happen… Bridget will start up the old gramophone record player in a moment – the 78 rpm record is 'Absent Friends' by Monte Rey."

"Oh, I thought that was by Genesis… Yeah it is! Me dad's got it on an old vinyl LP by them called *Nursery Cryme*!"

Alfred was still patient with him, putting his intrusion down to anxiety: "It's a little further back than that young fellow… you see 'Old Jock' was an absent friend to his family: he was in the Battle of The Somme in the First World War, but never came home. The song, by the Scottish Tenor Monte Rey, was popular in the Second World War, and Old-Jock's bereaved sweetheart still played it for him then in his memory…"

"Oh… stupid me…"

Alfred nodded to Bridget, who closed the heavy drape curtains: "When Bridget re-joins us, we must join hands, and form an unbroken circle… no matter what happens… keep the circle closed!"

"Adam… you'll be just fine, hold on to my hand" soothed Claire.

He scanned her eyes and in the gloom, he saw her lovely face as it would have been at his age. Without further ado his hand reached out for hers…

Bridget placed the needle arm on the scratchy old record, as the orchestra played, the hollow but strident Scottish voice hailed all to make 'Toast to Absent Friends'!"

Outside, Von-Hesse detected a build-up of psychic energy around the target room: "It begins Meier, let us see who answers the invitation!"

Adam's hands began to sweat especially his right as held by Claire. O'Riley was on his left and the veteran's hand remained cool and steady. Feeling dissociated, almost like an outside observer, Adam watched the medium Alfred Hulme closely as the old record player's tune rang out across the room in some stirring echo of a bygone age. The medium's eyes had suddenly closed as he took a sharp intake of breath; so violently in fact that his nostrils flared visibly, even through the gloom of candlelit shadows.

Adam thought he could hear a faint hum, very deep, almost inaudible, but certainly unsettling. The tone bottomed out into infrasound – just at the frequency that affected the fear-centres in the human brain. The crystal ball on the sideboard jumped as if nudged by an unseen company, the needle on the Parlophone adding one more scratch to the seventy year old record. The vibration now rang into Adam's very bones causing him to tense his muscles – at the same time Hulme started to hyperventilate, not too quickly but deeply as if gasping to draw in the living breath of some ethereal presence. Adam felt his eyes widen as adrenalin surged through his bloodstream. Claire gently squeezed his hand in reassurance, her thumb caressing the back of his – distracted by her tender touch he almost missed the arrival…

"Och tis good ter see ye all here this evenin' mah friends'!"

The Scottish accent boomed through the medium's mouth as through a gaping ventriloquist's dummy.

"Thank you Jock!" said a perfectly calm Bridget.

"Ah feel that Alfie is in good health aye! He has a question fer me?"

It was clear now that Alfred's style of medium-ship was that of a complete possession state – 'Alfie' was now totally subsumed by 'Old Jock'.

"He does Jock… on behalf of a guest, someone you haven't met before."

The mediums eyes suddenly opened and his head traversed slowly round to face Adam. His eyes seemed lifeless, almost jet black in their intensity – Adam felt a surge of fear in the pit of his stomach as the hair on the back of neck stood erect:

"Och so we have! A wee young fellah… Ah, he's nay alone is he!"

"We have John, Kevin and Claire with us, old friends from ESP."

"Ah nay woman, I didna mean them! Och no, standin' behind the wee laddie, we have anudder guest!"

Adam jolted as he looked quickly behind him but all he could see were shadows. Bridget looked too – followed together by the ESP team – all saw nothing: "We… can't see any other visitor, Jock… who is he?"

"Can yer nay? Ah, well he can see ye that's fer sure… a tall man, dark hair an hooded eyes… ay but he's not ye usual visitor, he's half-in-spirit an' half in-flesh!"

Claire looked over at John who leant towards her – silently and almost unbelievingly mouthing a question: "Von-Hesse?"

Bridget continued: "Is this person a friend Jock?"

"Och nay! He has a mission, a mission of many years standin!"

"Who is he Jock?"

"He's a Frenchie, aye, from the south, in the Languedoc, a corrupted soul who lives still in his earthly body… a fallen Cathar *Perfecti* whose family go back to the ancient land of Armenia and the *Paulicians!*"

Bridget was lost… none of this meant anything to her: "What does he want Jock?"

"Och come on fellah, don't be shy! Come in ter tha' circle!"

O'Riley, the better informed of the group at the sitting, had been holding back, but thought that he now had to break with convention: "Bridget, can you ask Jock if I can talk directly with him?"

Bridget bridled, enough for the indignant tension in her hands to waft through the linked sitters: "That's highly irregular Mr O'Riley! You of *all* people should know how dangerous it can be for Alfred!"

"'Tis fine lassie, let tha' man speak, he's welcome… an' is a gud friend ter mah fellow countrymen!"

That reference momentarily stalled O'Riley – it may have been in acknowledgement of his late Mentor, the border Scott, Dr Bruce Irving.

"Thank you… Jock. This fallen-Cathar… can he hear what we say at this sitting?"

"Aye that he can, he's very interested so he is! Come along ye wee Frenchie join us!"

Out in Rocky Bank Road, the Bavarian was struggling to free himself from 'Old Jock's' psychic grip: "Damn! Loosen your hold!" he shouted aloud. Meier turned sharply around at the sudden outburst and saw his Master, with his eyes screwed tight and writhing as if in an invisible straight-jacket.

"He's nay bein very sociable!" came the spirit guides voice through the slack and open mouth of the medium.

"Jock…" continued O'Riley "Can you shut him out?"

Claire interjected: "No Kevin, bring him in, we need him here, exposed!"

"He's' ah diggin' his wee heels in so he is!" came the sniggering response from the spirit guide.

O'Riley nodded… "Jock, can we *compel* him to appear here?"

"Why ah course we can, look ye now afore yer very eyes!"

Everyone stared straight ahead, which of course around a circular table, meant to its central point. An image like a hologram slowly resolved – faintly at first but definitely the form of a male human head, followed by his clothed body, revolving slowly as if on a turntable: "That's him! That's Von-Hesse" exclaimed John "What the hell is he wearing?"

It was indeed The Bavarian's head and face, and immediately recognisable as such, but his 'apparel' was unfamiliar. It was O'Riley who answered: "He's wearing the *Perfecti* black-robes and cord belt – he's dressed as a Cathar who has received the *Consolamentum*!"

"What? Is he dead, or is this some kind of vision from the past?" asked John - suddenly 'concrete' in his thinking and his perceptions.

Old Jock answered through Alfred's mouth: "Och his name in spirit is *Guy de Montpellier*, an before yer is the last moment tha' his soul lived freely and without corruption: that part that *has* died but *not* died, trapped like ah spark ah life inside the husk of ah still livin', but dead body..."

The image shimmered and then... was gone.

"He's got away!" shouted Claire.

Indeed, he had.

"Meier, take the car back to Oxton. The Mistress will know of this – they almost trapped my essence, this 'medium', Alfred Hulme... must die!"

The medium was still breathing in a laboured fashion, mouth gaping, eyes shut tight. Bridget was all for calling it a day: "That's enough, I'll ask Old Jock to pass back into the spirit world!"

Claire squeezed poor Adam's hand again – he was petrified with fear at what he had witnessed so far, and yet the original purpose of the séance hadn't yet been addressed: "Bridget... if we can wait just a little while longer... please; our questions on behalf of this young-man, we haven't been able to ask them yet!"

Bridget dithered, but Old Jock was direct: "Aye, ye can ask, I'll take a look see who wants ter come through fer him!"

Claire looked past Adam to O'Riley: "Kevin... would you do it?" Claire was standing aside in recognition of her father-in-laws experience. O'Riley nodded: "Thank you, Jock... do you know this young man?"

"Ah do... he is nay withoot friends, and nay withoot enemies in spirit!"

Adam's stomach churned: "Enemies!" Claire caressed his hand again – passing some calming energy into his body: then slowly, as an unforeseen consequence, Adam's biochemistry began to attune itself to hers…

O'Riley continued: "We have come to ask about a past-life Adam may have had, in Liverpool, a long-time ago, in the seventeenth century."

There was silence, then Alfred's body convulsed dramatically, causing everyone to tighten their grip. The mediums face changed taking on a mournful light."

"Who's there?" asked O'Riley.

"Who asketh of me?" said the voice of a young man.

"That's Adam Teal!" whispered Claire urgently. Adam Mitchell felt light headed, he'd only heard his voice before on audio tape or on digital video, never from the wide open and gaping-still mouth of a spiritual medium…

"Do you know me?" asked O'Riley.

"I doth not! Wait… I hath a memory, thou camest with others unto mine town: a visitor and thou didst not know even the year!"

"The regression hypnosis!" said Claire.

O'Riley paused a moment to make certain of his next question: "Your name, can you confirm it for us please?"

"Mine name? Why tis Adam Teal of Liverpool Town!"

Adam Mitchell was swaying as if about to fall into a dead-faint. Claire gripped his hand firmly. O'Riley continued: "Adam Teal, we must ask you of someone, of *Lilith*…"

Alfred's body jolted as a moan came from 'Adam': "*Lilith*! Mine love eternal!" Hearing these words, even Claire and John felt a chill. The state that poor Adam was in *now* had been foreshadowed even *then*. Could this truly be 'proof' of Adam Teal reincarnated as Adam Mitchell?

"Kevin!" Claire drew O'Riley's attention with a loud whisper. O'Riley looked as Claire gestured with her head towards Adam, who was almost slumped unconscious in a seated position. Realizing Adam's predicament O'Riley nodded.

"Thank you Adam, you have been a great help… Jock… can we ask if someone specific is able to come through for us?"

The mediums face broke out into a smile: "Och aye ye can, there's a whole bunch ah them here – form an orderly queue now!"

"Thank you Jock…" O'Riley looked over at Claire; concerned he searched for permission from her eyes: "It's OK Kevin…" she said. Nodding in acknowledgement he turned back to face Alfred:

"Jock… is Nathaniel Lattimer – Witchfinder there?"

Alfred's face furrowed into a deep frown: "Who callest now upon me? By what foul devilry is this done?!"

O'Riley checked Claire's reaction before going ahead. She looked intense, perhaps even a little startled, but she nodded in assent for him to proceed.

"We seek… your help Nathaniel, your help over a resident of Liverpool town, called *Lilith*…"

Then as before, an image formed in the centre of the table… an image of a dark, menacing figure set against the background of another place… a room seemingly inside a building… in another time.

Von-Hesse had arrived back at the Lake Hall in Oxton. Agitated he made his way to the attic room, where he expected to find *Lilith*. Sure enough, there she was, reclining on the chaise longue. Her head tilted in trademark style as he burst in: "Such haste Maximilian! This can only mean that you've made some monumental faux-pas."

"Mistress! That medium, they are using him now!"

"And did you do as I instructed?"

"Yes Mistress! But his guide is too strong, they nearly entrapped me in their circle – they have seen me in my original form as the Cathar *Perfecti* Guy de Montpelier!"

Lilith nodded slowly: "Who is present at the circle?"

"The woman Lattimer, her accomplice Sutton and father-in-law O'Riley, also... the youth Adam Mitchell."

Lilith's eyebrow raised at the mention of Adam's name: "Adam..."

"Mistress, the medium Hulme, he is dangerous, he must be eliminated!"

Alfred's body was vibrating violently as Nathaniel Lattimer sought to free himself: "It is by her entrapment and evil power that I am brought here?"

"No, Nathaniel, it is... for a descendent of yours, her name is Claire, she *needs* your help to defeat *Lilith*!"

The mediums' body gave one final jolt: "Descendent, then tis *Lilith*'s curse upon mine issue henceforth and for all time?!"

O'Riley straightened as he answered: "Yes, Nathaniel, we believe that it is. She has returned, and is about to strike down your living family, the people of Liverpool, and perhaps, all of humankind!"

"Then to action! At once I say!"

"How Nathaniel, how may she be defeated?"

There was a lengthy pause – the holographic image froze and flickered: the sitters began to fear that 'Nathaniel' had gone. But then he spoke: "There be one here amongst thee who doth have affection for the witch..."

O'Riley looked at Adam whose eyes were closed and his head slumped forwards as if unconscious: "He is... entranced by her" he said, choosing his words carefully.

"The witch hath weaknesses... she must steal unto herself the vitality of man, or of a woman. If she doest not, then she mayeth be taken."

"Vitality?"

"The very semen of the male and the secret desires of a woman's body!"

"Sex?"

"Art thou then so uneducated?! Demons feedeth upon the base, common and particular in the nature both of man and also of woman! *Lilith* accursed *Lilith*, cast out from Eden, who wouldst also taketh the child from every woman's womb and then impregnate the mothers as *incubus* with accursed and satanically cultivated semen harvested from the base-dreams of wretched men!"

"So... we have to catch her when she is weak? Does that mean when her energy is low?

"Cast her into the waters!"

A sudden chill filled the room, even Adam gasped and came round so sudden was its effect: "Wha... whaz goin' on, wha 'appened? Christ its cold in 'ere!"

The ESP team understood the significance – it could only mean the sudden intrusion of an uninvited guest...

"Adam… Adam…" came the softly feminine whispered voice.

"*Lilith*! *Lilith* it *is* you!" The hapless Adam sat upright; a huge smile broadened his face.

"Who is this?" demanded O'Riley with authority.

Bridget was alarmed: "No! Go back! Old-Jock, close the portal!"

Too late.

"Adam… you have found me again… just as I promised."

Adam Mitchell gasped and wept as he became 'Adam Teal': "Oh *Lilith*, why didst thou leaveth me!"

"Our enemies Adam, those who hated us, hated us for the purity of our love…. our love since we were first together in Eden itself…"

Claire spoke out: "Purity! You want to destroy all of humankind with your evil and yet you speak of purity!"

"Claire!" O'Riley tried to calm her.

Claire's concern for Adam soaked through to him as water through a permeable rock – his hand glowed with it, triggering the already primed reaction to her that had unwittingly passed between them.

"So… Claire Lattimer… descendent of the accursed Nathaniel, you would take Adam from me for yourself?"

Claire wanted to say 'No!' but her energy wouldn't let her: "You won't have him, and you won't have anyone else, we'll stop you!"

"Really? You really think so? My spite is worse even than my vengeance Claire Lattimer, and this you *will* live to understand, I promise you… and… I *always* keep my promises, don't I Adam?"

Claire's maternal fears broke through: "Keep away from my Son!"

Adam responded to *Lilith*'s voice: "*Lilith*… take me, don't go, take me with you!"

"No!" Claire sensed that Adam's soul was in great danger "Bridget! Bring Alfred back, now!"

Bridget tried to call on Old-Jock: "Jock! Close the portal – keep her out!"

"H aha ha, you really think that I can be stopped by such as he?" *Lilith*'s lovely voice had turned into a malevolent laugh.

Claire's sense of urgency overwhelmed her: "Break the circle!"

"No Claire, it's too soon!" yelled O'Riley.

Claire let go, both of Adam to her left and of John to her right.

Alfred gasped as if the air had been sucked right out from his lungs and collapsed face-first on the table-top. Bridget screamed in terror at the sight of her healer and medium, his eyes wide-open and yet unconscious, no breath moving in his chest. The other female sitters screamed to, and in their panic ran in disarray out from the room. John was over in an instant and working hard to resuscitate him.

Adam too slumped as he tried to stand up from the table, slumped and fell in an apparent faint to the floor. Claire caught O'Riley's eye, as pausing for a moment, she took hold of the young man checking for his heart-beat: "There's no pulse!" checking his breathing – "No respiration either!" Opening his mouth with her fingers she cleared his airway:

"You're *not* going to take him *Lilith*!" she started cardiac massage and then mouth-to-mouth resuscitation. Adam's heart was still; his mind, and his soul out of his body, viewing the scene as if from some high vantage point.

To his left, he saw her… "Lillian? *Lilith*?!"

The golden vision stretched out her porcelain perfect hand, her uncanny green-eyes as beautiful as any Botticelli or pre-Raphaelite painting – the Mona-Lisa smile more inviting than at any time before… He stretched out his hand to touch hers and then…

He felt her warm moist lips against his – sealing them with a living breath that filled his lungs. His heart suddenly pounded into life as involuntarily, he opened his mouth wider, and his tongue penetrated her mouth, touching hers and causing his belly to rush with excitement.

She felt him come to life in her mouth, and just for a moment they both paused, holding their contact. Slowly their reluctant lips parted, peeling away softly, even tenderly.

"Wow!" Adam made a whispered gasp. Claire sat back shocked at herself. Looking up, she saw O'Riley staring deeply into her eyes.

A quick glance over to John confirmed that he'd brought Alfred back. He was now having to deal with an over-excited Bridget who had suddenly found her County Sligo accent and was babbling incomprehensively at him "Bridget! Bridget Calm down; Alfie's fine now…just fine!" he urged.

But Alfred was far from fine. Drained: the effort prior to his collapse had been bad enough, but his cardiac arrest had terrified him: "We must keep the circle closed, keep her out, she's too strong: she just brushed Old Jock aside like he was nothing!"

He looked over at O'Riley: "You must make contact again!"

"Contact?"

"Yes! Contact with your mentors… It may be that no one else and no other power can stop her…"

"There you are Maximilian, their little get-together has been disrupted: you might even say that I'm the 'party-pooper' ha ha ha!"

"Mistress, we need to finish them: *all* of them; but especially that medium!"

Lilith smiled at him: "He bothered you didn't he?"

Von-Hesse was indignant: "He nearly trapped me. And, he revealed my original name and status to those ESP bumpkins!"

"Perhaps, but he is not the real threat. If one exists, it is the older man, Kevin O'Riley senior."

Von-Hesse's eyes narrowed: "Why, because of the blacksmith?"

"Why? You mean that you've not studied this place Maximilian?"

"This place? You mean The Wirral? It's…just a peninsula: over the Mersey from Liverpool, a nowhere place: a backwater, stuck between an English city and the Welsh coast."

Lilith smiled: "A 'little corner of English-nowhere'? Oh no… it's much *more* than *just* that. You see, others have been here in the years since my last animation, others… of my *family*… skilled in the supernatural and the occult. They had… uncovered its *special* significance, and this man O'Riley has been intimately involved in defeating them. There is no question Maximilian, he is the *one* great threat to us."

"Then… he must be killed. I will not tolerate such an individual to live!"

Lilith tossed her hair and smiled at him again:

"Not so easy… Maximilian, you see he is 'protected', we would have to entice him, to come to his doom: by his *own* hand…"

"We can't let Adam go home alone in this state; he lives in a flat near the city centre. He needs to be watched, for his safety. I can take him in to work in the morning." Claire was making her argument to O'Riley and John.

"We do have a duty of care" said John "Especially as we now know for certain just what we're up against. *Lilith* could make a move on him at any moment."

O'Riley was watching Claire closely: "He can stay at Prenton Lane" he said, still scrutinizing Claire, for her reaction.

"I can put him up!" she protested.

"Yes... you could... but then you have a full house, whereas at Prenton Lane, there's only Maggie and me – and there's no chance of him getting embroiled in a dispute with an eighteen year old lad who's in love with the same girl as he is, is there?"

Claire scanned O'Riley's eyes and knew that he had seen deeply enough into what had happened between her and Adam. Her positive reaction to him was still scaring her: "You don't have to worry... I know the boundaries."

"Yes... but does *he*? He's just been in an intensely charged environment – he'll be *very* vulnerable and open to the slightest *hint* of suggestion."

John who'd missed what had happened during Adam's 'resuscitation' sought clarification – in his usual blunt way: "Yer wha?"

Claire decided to get her side of things across – just to avoid any misunderstanding: "I think that young Adam's forming a bit of an attachment onto me... I know, I know I'm old enough to be his mum, but he has no other 'real' woman to anchor himself to... to resist 'Lillian'."

John bought it: "Oh… well it's understandable: you are a nice looking woman Claire, and, powerful – in his life. He's young, and as Kevin says, he's *very* vulnerable.

O'Riley replied: "There is another advantage in Prenton Lane of course – the protection it offers, by grace of our 'mutual friend' against the supernatural and the occult…"

That night a dazed Adam was made welcome at the O'Riley home in Prenton Lane…

Friday 24th November 2006: ESP Rodney Street, 9.00am

The team assembled early for their post-séance de-brief. O'Riley had taken the still stunned Adam into work at the Museum and then drove to the Eden Institute to ask Susan to cancel all of his appointments for the day: "Adam got in OK, I am a bit worried about him, after-all he's vulnerable almost wherever he is at the moment."

"Yeah… and like how do you explain that to Claudia?" spluttered John.

O'Riley looked over at Claire: "How are you today, OK?"

She wondered how widely O'Riley was casting the net of his question to her. She certainly wanted to avoid any further discussion about her and Adam: "I'm OK, it was a bit shocking… hearing my ancestor speak out like that., and then actually *seeing* him… like, like he was hologram or something… But, I can't get my Kevin and the police involved, it's not like we've even got any evidence yet: that the everyday world would sit up and take notice of!"

John sighed: "It's always been the way Claire, with what we do: and it's particularly hard for us, we've all come into this from law-enforcement – and yet we've had to leave behind the one way of making sense of the world that we'd all previously shared and understood."

O'Riley's brow was furrowed with reflection: "And yet… we *have* to act. Let's go over what we've learned from last night."

"I feel a flip chart coming on!" grinned John.

"Cheek! My flip-charts have stood me in great stead for two whole careers!" O'Riley stared at the centre of the A2 sized chart and put a big question mark bang in the centre: "That… for me is Von-Hesse!"

John nodded: "A Cathar *Perfecti* it was said… called *Guy de Montpelier*. Doesn't sound very 'Bavarian' does he?"

"No John, he doesn't. But then, it seems he's been around for a *very* long time… here's what I think from what was revealed at the séance: We know from the past-life regression that 'Von-Hesse' was an 'alchemist'…"

Claire interjected: "And we know from the sarcophagus that *Lilith* was apparently buried in it after her execution, and that it contains alchemical spells and inscriptions in ancient Aramaic and Latin concerning 're-animation'…"

"Right, so, 'Von-Hesse' – I'll keep calling him that for the moment, was an alchemist in service to *Lilith* for occult purposes, but, it seems that he was already very old, in everyday terms by the time he arrived in Liverpool in 1665, perhaps as much as three or four *hundred* years old."

"Why that old?" queried John.

"Because of his 'French' name and dress as a Cathar *Perfecti*. They flourished in the Languedoc area of southern France between the eleventh and fourteenth centuries…"

"So that could take him up to the Black Death period?"

"Middle fourteenth century – yes, possibly, but he could have been 'old' even then…so the range estimate for his origin must be from the eleventh to fourteenth centuries, but certainly no later than that."

"And then he turns up in Liverpool bang in the middle of the Great-Plague!"

"Yes! And of course we know that *'Lilith'* is linked to contagion and pestilence…"

John stroked his chin: "Don't bode well do it!" he said with deliberate understatement.

Claire had been listening closely and was scared: "It fits, I don't want to believe it, but it fits!"

"So what's with the Cathars then? Just *why* was he involved with such a group in the first place?" asked John.

O'Riley sighed: "Well, 'Old-Jock' said that this *Guy de Montpelier* was a 'corrupted' Cathar *Perfecti*, so, that means that he must've in the religious vernacular of the time: 'sold his soul.' The Cathars were a heretical Christian movement – heretical in the eyes of the Roman Catholic Church that is – but they regarded themselves as simply *Bons Hommes et Bonnes Femmes* the 'Good Men and Good Women'.

Their beliefs are rooted in Gnosticism, particularly the *Paulicians*, of, of all places; Armenia."

"Armenia! That's where the soil samples were supposed to be from" said Claire.

"And, given that *Lilith* is supposed to have been Adam's first wife before Eve, some sources believe that Eden itself was in Armenia!" added John.

"Yes, that's right; in fact it's now the favoured location according to Biblical scholars. So… we have *Lilith* 'created' from the soil of The Garden of Eden in Armenia, we have ancient Aramaic inscriptions; and we have a 'Cathar' apparently called *Guy de Montpelier*, who follows a religion with its roots in Armenia."

"So, what about his *Perfecti* status, Kevin, what's that all about?" queried John.

The Cathars had a ceremony called the *Consolamentum*. The Consolamentum was the baptism of the Holy Spirit, baptismal regeneration, absolution and ordination all in one – so the *Perfecti* were the Cathar moral exemplars and teachers – the equivalent of ordained priests, even though they rejected the idea of a 'clergy' as such. Most Cathars though weren't *Perfecti* but rather *Credentes* which means believers."

"You said it was a branch of Gnosticism Kevin… that's a kind of heretical Christianity that's based not on *faith* but on *knowledge*, a knowledge derived from a direct experience" said Claire -so how do you square the idea of 'faith' as in being one of those *Credentes* with the 'certainty' of *Gnosis* or 'knowing' - as the word means?"

"Well, they - the Cathars didn't actually regard themselves as Gnostics, it's a kind of retrospective label put on to them by our modern times. Of course in all usual respects they *were* Gnostic - but with this singular exception - that the majority of them were believers rather than knowers. But yep…to answer your point about it being held at the time to be a heresy think how 'occult' their beliefs would seem to the orthodox Christians of those more superstitious times…

You see, the Cathars, in common with other kinds of Gnosticism –considered the Lord Creator of the physical world not to be the true or highest God: but was called 'The Demiurge' by the Gnostics, and the *Rex Mundi* that is: 'King of the World' or even Satan by The Cathars: indeed both Gnostics and Cathars thought of the world as a *prison* for the soul. They believed that their essential and pure spark of spirit was trapped in the material world and they had to seek their ultimate redemption through liberation of that spark: back into the highest realm of pure spirit – called The *Pleroma* by the Gnostics, where it would be reunited with the true godhead. The Cathars also believed in reincarnation – with spirit forced to return and live in the material world until it reaches the 'perfected' state – that of being a *Perfecti* which, given Adam's apparent previous life as 'Adam Teal' is interesting. It also gives us a different angle on the 're-animation' of *Lilith*."

"Catharism sounds like a form of Western Buddhism!" responded Claire.

"It does, yes, in fact like Buddhists, the Cathars were vegetarian too, in-fact many were what we would today call vegan."

"But they *were* Christian?" asked John.

"They certainly considered themselves as such. However, they were very different from the Roman Catholics or the later Protestants or Puritan 'Reformed Christians'. For them, Jesus wasn't a 'real' human being, more a kind of 'phantom' or projection of spirit into the physical world where he operated to liberate souls from their entrapment in matter, just like a Buddhist *Bodhisattva*.

Naturally, these beliefs brought them into direct conflict with the Roman Catholic Church and Inquisition. There were even military expeditions against them which the Cathars sometimes violently resisted. Many Cathars were excellent professional soldiers – at least when pushed into fighting – otherwise they were essentially pacifist."

"OK…" said John "So we have our Von-Hesse who's really not 'Bavarian', but a Frenchman from Languedoc: called *Guy de Montpelier* – a *Perfecti* who somehow is corrupted, presumably by contact with *Lilith*?"

"That's what we have John. A complication is that Catharism spread into Germany and into Lombardy in Italy. It depends whether 'Von-Hesse's' original identity was as a French Cathar, who later took the identity of a German, or was it the other way around? He may even be older still of course, if we consider the Armenian link. The séance simply identified his identity as *Guy de Montpelier* at the last moment before the final corruption of his soul. The question is how was he corrupted? Was there a flaw in his basic character? Or maybe there was something of a 'revelation' from *Lilith*?

Lilith stands for everything that Catharism rejects. She is of this world, made from the very earth that the Cathars despise as a prison and the entrapment of spirit. She is highly sexual and wants to repopulate the world. The Cathars would be horrified by that – and see it as an extreme form of evil to take spirit and force it to live a material existence."

"OK… so where does his alchemy come into all of this?"

"Remember that Alchemy is closely allied to Hermetic Philosophy, and *Hermeticism* is itself very closely affiliated to the Gnostic traditions – hence the Cathars. It's what you'd expect of someone who'd had a very long life… He's seen a great deal, been 'transformed' through his contact with Alchemy, and… corrupted… as you say by his contact with *Lilith*.

The Cathars are also amongst the supposed guardians of the *Christian* version of the Holy Grail, so you have another link with Alchemy there."

Claire had been pondering the bigger picture: "So, what it boils down to is that we don't know who 'Von-Hesse' really is, or was – just that he's somehow mastered the arcane wisdom of alchemy enough to halt the ageing process and to sustain his life over centuries?"

"Imagine how much knowledge you could gain over such a huge amount of time!" said John.

"And how dangerous you would be!" added Claire "He's possibly the most 'experienced' individual alive today – a continuity of life that bridges ancient *and* modern wisdom."

John asked the obvious question: "If that's so then what does he need *Lilith* for? What's his cut on the deal?"

"That, I think" said O'Riley "is the question that we must answer."

Claire… joined the dots: "*Lilith* wants to repopulate the world with her off-spring and descendants. She was Adam's first wife but was cast out from Eden and as a result curses all of Eve's kind… so now… she needs a new Adam!"

"Von-Hesse!" exclaimed John.

"That's obviously what *he* wants…" replied O'Riley.

"Who else then?" asked Claire.

"Of course, it's 'Adam Teal' now as Adam Mitchell: and she said about their love going all the way back to the Garden of Eden!" interrupted John.

Claire shuddered involuntarily: "She actually said, that they'd first been *together* in Eden… What did she mean by that: that somehow Adam Mitchell is not only Adam Teal, but really also *him* the first Adam… the *first* created man?"

"I think that's stretching things a bit too far" said O'Riley "I can accept that he's Adam Teal… but for him to have been Adam in Eden himself! It'd be like saying that some woman, somewhere alive today, is the reincarnation of Eve!"

He didn't notice that Claire had shuddered again.

O'Riley paused: he'd gained some insight from his brief personal-development encounters with 'Lillian': "Perhaps, *Lilith* has chosen Adam Mitchell, or… maybe…

it could even be Sean…"

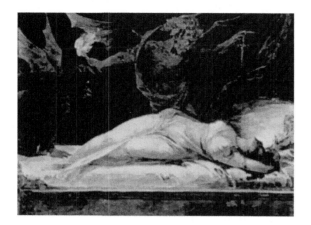

10

Incubus

laire had been stunned by O'Riley's reference to her son Sean as a possible candidate for being *Lilith*'s new Adam. It had hit her blind spot dead-centre. She had believed *Lilith*'s interest in him to be mere occult sexual predation – that, or a simple malevolent strike against her loved ones. She had not expected this, and even less had she anticipated her internal response. Her eyes cast downwards as an instinct more basic than any consciously contrived morality made itself known. O'Riley sensed it, and perhaps indiscreetly, gave voice to it: "It shows how human we are doesn't it Claire?"

"I'm sorry?"

"Human in that fundamental sense that seems so in-human to our sensitivities…"

"Sorry Kevin, I'm not with you?" She was, and she knew it, but instinct and outer morality are never comfortable bedfellows.

"To be the mother of Adam?"

"What!"

"All very Darwinian really, a kind of genetic opportunism…"

"That's a disgusting suggestion!"

"Didn't you feel it: just for a moment?"

She had, of course, but her attempts to suppress it from her consciousness required that she deny it totally: "No!"

O'Riley felt for her all-to-human reaction: "Sean, is your son, but he's also my *grand*-son."

"Then speak for yourself and yer own 'genetic opportunism'!" she exclaimed.

"It's an opportunity for another kind Claire, for insight…because it gives us a perspective on other parts of the mystery."

John thought that he'd better get involved and try to avoid an emotional spiral between Claire and O'Riley: "Oh, you mean the mystery about Von-Hesse and his relationship to *Lilith*?"

"No John, not exactly: I meant the mystery of existence, our *personal* mystery – and just what it means to be human, especially when faced with the *in*-human."

"Kevin, I didn't ask for gratuitous psychotherapy thank you!" Claire was getting well annoyed now. Only part of her anger was directed towards O'Riley, but as he was within 'reach' psychologically – he was getting all of it.

O'Riley was feeling a certain pressure within himself, and as he had always been taught – he decided to trust it, and let it roll: "It's a complex situation this, for everyone involved. Only *Lilith* really knows what's going on, and she'll rely on human psychology to be her unwitting ally – that's why we *must* analyse ourselves and how we may be being affected by her."

"Meaning?"

"Meaning that there are at least three males that we know of, who are perhaps being groomed by her as a potential new-Adam. If she were just an ordinary girl, getting involved in ordinary relationships with three male partners – then that'd be complicated enough, but here, the stakes are incalculably higher.

We are a team, and to defeat her we have to work together, that means there can't be the slightest micron of space between us. Yet, because she operates through human psychology and relationships, it's easily within her reach to drive us apart, and what better way than by exploiting close family and personal relationships… through the unconscious desires of biology, and… of sexual attraction…"

Claire scanned his face: "You're skirting around the edges again Kevin!"

O'Riley knew that he was. He'd hoped to make this a gentle and progressive discussion: "You're at the centre of this Claire – for a number of reasons. You're descended from Nathaniel Lattimer, so *Lilith* has an unbounded hatred of you – and yet, Sean may be her 'genetic' choice as father of her off-spring.

Then… of course, there's Adam."

Claire visibly blushed at this, which was of course noted by the two men.

O'Riley continued: "Adam is… if he's a 'candidate' a genetic rival to Sean. I know, that's got nothing obvious to do with how we as professionals work with him…"

"You're patronizing me Kevin; I know full well what you're implying!"

O'Riley's neck straightened: "It *has* to be said Claire!"

Claire looked over at John – who simply looked puzzled.

O'Riley continued: "*Both* Sean and Adam, in their different ways, have an emotional bond to you… You've said so yourself that Adam only has you to anchor himself to, in order to make any possible stand against *Lilith*. With Sean… it goes without saying, you're his mother…"

"And?" Claire asked, almost defiantly.

"And… *Lilith* will play you off against both of them, in order to destroy you and whichever one, or both of them, she eventually discards."

"And there's still Von-Hesse in the equation" said John.

"Indeed… and he'd happily kill all of us."

O'Riley had decided to spare the final humiliation against Claire – but John, not being privy to all that had happened outside of his view at the séance unwittingly put his foot in it: "So how would *Lilith* play Claire off against Sean and Adam?"

O'Riley coughed to clear his throat, and then paused.

John looked puzzled again: "Was that such a hard question?"

"Because Claire… has an emotional bond to both of them."

"Well of course she does, she's Sean's mum, and… er… professionally related to Adam."

Silence followed. John scanned his friend's faces: "Wha yer mean what Claire said about Adam forming a bit of an attachment to her?"

"That's enough!" shouted Claire "We should be getting on with the job in hand, not this pseudo-Freudian crap! You've been a therapist too-long Kevin, it's about time you remembered what the real world's like!

Claire wasn't just embarrassed, she felt betrayed.

She stormed out.

O'Riley looked over to John: "I'm sorry."

"What's gotten into her Kevin? The talk about genetic opportunism seemed to piss her off quite a bit, but, there's something else isn't there?"

O'Riley breathed out hard. He knew that there was, and he knew that it was more complicated even that that…

Having stormed out of ESP, Claire was at something of a loss. She could go into the university and distract herself with the mundane tasks of lecturing and paperwork, or… she could follow the energy of her argument with O'Riley, and come here to William Brown Street, and Liverpool Museum.

She knew what O'Riley had been up to, and, she knew that he was right – it did have to be confronted, if only because of her shock at her own reaction to what in effect was a shared kiss with Adam. Not an ordinary kiss either, she had brought him back from the dead – not for nothing is it called 'The Kiss of Life' and the deep symbolism of that life giving exchange in such a highly charged and dramatic atmosphere as a séance – all added up to something that couldn't be ignored.

Feeling like a schoolgirl fighting a forbidden crush, she walked in through the automatic doors of the Museum entrance. Looking around she decided to turn left and sit down in the ground-floor café – it would give her time to think… and to be rational.

She was lost in her cappuccino and scones when she heard a voice call her name.

Upstairs, Adam was mulling quietly to himself over the previous night's traumatic events. It had been a great shock to him. He had literally been scared to 'death' and then brought back to life by the most arousing sensation he'd ever physically experienced.

His young mind was flooded and confused. His emotional, even spiritual love for *Lilith* had, it had been revealed to him, spanned the centuries. Everyone around him then and now, had called her evil and wanted her destruction. He'd seen the evidence for himself – in his past-life regression and then at the séance – but he could not free himself of his love for her: could not, and would not. Yet, he was also aware of his attraction to Claire Lattimer, a woman old enough to be his mother, yet still stunning in appearance. More than that, she'd been kind and gentle with him, passing an unmistakable energy into his being through her hand just as he was at his most terrified during the séance, and then with her lips – passing life-giving breath – *her* breath into his lungs – as if she had breathed his very soul out from her body and back into his.

Thinking back, he'd remembered how they'd shared jokes… flirted even, in the days leading up to the séance. He'd resisted her attractiveness, thinking only of his love for *Lilith*, but, in that crises he had been unable to resist being aroused, *very* deeply by her, and… he sensed, she had been aroused by him too.

Digging his pencil into the desk it eventually snapped, snapping him too out from his reverie.

Claire was caught by surprise by the sound of her name. It was an unwelcome voice that called, especially now that she'd just walked away from ESP and was alone…

"Lillian!"

"I'll sit down… you don't mind do you?"

Claire's spine chilled: "I do actually!"

"Then what a shame that it's a public place, I can sit anywhere I want to!" *Lilith* smiled with an expansive wave of her arms."

Claire wanted to stand up and walk to another table – but she realized that would be a too ordinary and everyday thing to do. Lillian was not after-all either of those things: "What do you want?" she asked aggressively.

"Oh Claire… isn't it more a matter of what *you* want… and why you're here at the Museum this morning?"

Claire felt herself blush again.

"That's so becoming in an older woman, blushing over her crush on a younger man!" smirked *Lilith*.

"There's no crush; only a deep concern for your corruption of his soul!"

Lilith shook her head: "Oh dear, poor Claire… you don't do jealousy very well do you: did his lips taste sweet?"

Claire's anger nearly burst beyond her control: at the last moment she was able to divert it back into her body so that she shook with a jolt: "Keep away from my son!"

"Sean? Oh he's in love with me, didn't you notice?"

"Love!? You've bewitched him!"

"Yes… love does that to people doesn't it? Just like between you and Kevin…"

Claire glared into *Lilith*'s limpid green-eyes. Despite herself, she couldn't help but notice their beauty: "My husband knows about you, and in time he'll bring the full force of the law against you and that 'Bavarian' accomplice of yours!"

"Your husband? Oh him! I think you'll find that he has absolutely no capacity to act in any way against me. In fact, dutiful fellow that he is, he's busy checking the internet right now… He'll find… he'll find… that I really *do* exist. Records of my identity are everywhere, all 'genuine' and validated. I am a citizen by birth of this country of yours, and *protected* by its laws. He has no evidence against me: I have committed no crime that can be proven against me. What are you going to allege Claire; that I'm an evil supernatural entity who wants to wipe out the human species? That'd be the quickest route I can think of for you to be sectioned under the mental health act!" Lillian smiled and continued "But anyway…no, I didn't mean him, I meant the other Kevin, his father… and… your former lover…"

Claire blushed again.

"My you're making quite a habit of that aren't you.
Does 'young' Kevin know about your affair with his dad?"

"That was before he and I were together, years before!"

"Yes… you were so young weren't you, but, you haven't answered my question: *does* he know?"

Claire didn't reply.

"Wondering how I know are you Claire? Well, I know *all* about you. You see, I read hearts, not minds… I know exactly what you hide in there…"

"Then you know the answer to your question don't you!"

Lilith sat back in her chair: "Yes Claire I do. He'll be upset to find out won't he; especially after all you went through together at the beginning of your relationship."

Claire scowled at Lillian: "He won't believe you!"

"Really: you really think so? Doubt is enough to poison a relationship, even a marriage that's lasted over twenty years."

Claire tried to turn the conversation away from her painful memories: "What is it you want Lillian, or *Lilith*, or whatever you're called?"

"Want? Whatever, and *whoever* the fancy takes me to have – whilst it amuses me, and then…" her voice trailed off as her face showed a cold dismissal. The fate of her playthings was not only predetermined, it was inconsequential to her.

"You really think that you could possibly succeed with this campaign of yours of hatred and destruction against the whole human race?!"

"Really Claire, you should know better than to ask that. Haven't you been checking up on me: on the collective human memory of their encounters with me? Of course you have! It's just a matter of time – when I'm ready, it *will* happen. Along the way, I will… strengthen and amuse myself."

It was Claire's turn to sit back: "Oh yes, on the subject of the collective human memory – you're remembered as a *succubus* aren't you – taking men's sexual energy and vitality like some kind of vampire!"

"Vampire? Oh Claire how crass, 'vampires' are just figments of you humans imagination – the projections of your sexual desires perverted into the biting and sucking of life-giving blood… I'm *real* Claire… I *really* do feed off sexual energies, and *not* just men's either, for I am also the *incubus*… I can have women too, I can even fertilize them…" Lillian smiled her most 'Mona-Lisa' smile.

Claire felt a nausea in her stomach.

"That's right Claire; I could even have you… oh daughter of Eve…"

"No!"

"No? Are you so sure? You've been vulnerable before, haven't you?"

Claire's body twitched as Lillian's words found another weakness in her defences: "I was seduced, bewitched… it wasn't what 'I' wanted."

"You don't have to want it Claire, I can just… *take* it."

"No, never!"

"I don't even have to force you… just wait until you become very *tired*, and start to yearn for *sleep*…"

Claire's eyes blinked, but she fought back: "No, it won't work, I know what you're trying to do!"

"Think that you can stay awake forever Claire? All you have to do is to fall asleep once, just once, and I can come to you. Don't you think I'm attractive Claire… aren't I the most beautiful girl you've ever seen? I asked Kevin – Kevin senior, that is, if I was as beautiful as Rowena was. I found her in his heart – right there with you – all cuddled up… you looked so sweet.

Look at me Claire… *look* into my eyes… wouldn't you love to taste my mouth…"

Claire closed her eyes and turned her head away. She felt trapped: if she walked away Lillian would have won, if she looked at her, then Lillian would win. In her mind she sought out another image – an image of a protector…

Claire's concentration was broken by Lillian's mocking laugh: "Well, well, well… and you thought *that* could protect you? Ha ha! Oh poor Claire! Green Claire, green is what grows, grows in the *earth* the very soil itself – But I am that *soil* Claire, without me, the land itself wastes away and dies, oh yes, *all* of it, all of its 'greenery' – why do you think that in the ancient texts; I bring the desert and the wasteland to humankind?"

Claire chilled at Lillian's words. *If* true, then not even Kevin O'Riley's ancient protecting spirit and mentor could help them, not this time.

The porcelain hand stretched out and touched her. Caught unable to move or open her eyes Claire's hand felt Lillian's energy penetrate her body seeking out her glands, her hormones – her energy: "You're still fertile Claire… I sense it, in your ovaries, still… very viable!"

Light headed Claire's eyes were beginning to sink into sleep; Her body glowed with an arousing warmth, her labia swollen and engorged with blood, her vulva moistened, her nipples and clitoris tingled and firmed: she was being seduced…

Then:

"Lillian? Claire! What you two doin' 'ere"

Over at ESP John had played back the audio tape from the séance the night before: "There! The spirit guide 'Old-Jock' he quite clearly says that Von-Hesse's family are from Armenia, they were Paulicians!"

"That answers the question of his family's origin John. Maybe they had something to do with *Lilith*'s transportation to Europe in the first place?" replied O'Riley.

"Cosmopolitan fellow isn't he!"

They carried on listening.

"Crikey! Listen how Old-Jock just gets shoved aside like he didn't matter – this *Lilith* is one 'mother' – if yer pardon the pun, of a spirit!"

"Mother…" O'Riley mused "Oh no! I've just remembered something!"

Claire stood up, finally able to move after Lillian withdrew her energy: "Adam, you must get away from her now!"

"Wha?" Adam looked around the very large and open café. Some of the sparse spread of customers had turned to look: "Oh… er, best go upstairs Claire, if you wanna see Claudia." He mumbled.

Claire took hold of his hand, her warmth passed into him, her bright blue eyes pleaded: "Come away with me now!"

"Come away with you?" His heart skipped a beat as their eyes scanned one-another's.

From the corner of his eye he saw the glowing russet-blond wavy hair, the heart shaped face, the dimpled Mona-Lisa smile.

His hand loosened… and fell away.

"What?" asked John looking over at O'Riley's ghastly expression.

"*Lilith*, she *can't* under all usual conditions mother children herself, at least not *human* children. If she's going to 'breed' with a human male, then there's only one way that she could do it"

"What?" asked John again– being characteristically blunt.

"By impregnating human women with her harvested sperm – the sperm she takes from men as a *succubus* and puts into women as an *incubus*!"

"But… but that'd mean 'farming' people like battery hens!"

"Yes…" said O'Riley grimly "it would."

"So, even if she chooses one male as her new 'Adam', she'd need to incubate the semen in… well… thousands, or hundreds of thousands, even millions of women!"

"And there I was lecturing Claire about genetic opportunism!"

Claire's heart sank. One look into Lillian's eyes and Adam was lost.

"You see Claire; you can't compete for Adam with me… No woman can. I may let you live, *if* you please me… that would be your only chance of survival."

Adam shook himself: "Lillian my love, no, please… don't hurt her!"

Lillian tilted her head into her trademark coquettish pose: "You have affection for her Adam?"

Adam looked back at Claire – her eyes now moist with emotion: "I… don't, I don't know…" his head spun as memories from the past flooded in, memories of being Adam Teal. He turned back to the pre-Raphaelite vision: "*Lilith*, you are my eternal love, there can be *no* other!"

There was nothing more Claire could do without help. She backed-out through the café doors, not daring to take her eyes off Lillian. Once in the museum foyer, she turned and ran for her car, and for ESP...

Claudia was in her office and as usual she was picking over Adam's paperwork with a fine-toothed comb. Her attention was taken by the footsteps in the corridor. One was a soft, slow regular pattern – the other erratic heavy and bungling.

"Adam!" she yelled, ignoring whoever he may be with "Come into my office please!"

His right eye peered round her door: "Yes Claudia?"

"Is the rest of you attached to that beady eye? If so allow it to follow you in!"

"Oh!" a foot appeared and then the right half of his body.

"Are you stuck or something? I said come-in!"

Reluctantly he slid completely through the door which he kept as nearly closed as he could. Claudia tutted in exasperation, but her irritation was forestalled by the sudden appearance of a shock of russet-blond, wavy hair...

John and O'Riley were still on the flip-charts: "So... we should expect an outbreak of bubonic plague then are you saying Kevin?"

O'Riley nodded slowly, his eyes staring into space.

"Surely it can be easily treated these days, with anti-biotics?"

Once again, O'Riley nodded.

"Well then, if that's the worst that she can do..."

O'Riley's reverie was broken by the sound of running feet through reception: his eyes cast a glance over to the door, which immediately burst open: "Claire?!"

Claudia was taken aback by Lillian's sudden appearance. Her porcelain white complexion set off perfectly by her lustrous hair and uncanny limpid deep-green eyes: "Who's this?" she muttered.

Adam's eyes betrayed a fear as he looked away from Claudia and then at Lillian.

The pre-Raphaelite vision spoke: "My name... is Lillian, I'm Adam's friend..."

"You're the girl he's been telling everyone about!" exclaimed Claudia as she at last recognized her description. She struggled to shake off her surprise: "Be that as it may, these are private offices and without permission... Lillian... you shouldn't really be here!"

Lillian smiled her Mona-Lisa smile: "But *you* brought me here Dr Moore..."

Claudia's brow furrowed: "I'm sorry?"

"Oh yes..." continued the demon Goddess "You raised my sarcophagus, and my bones, from the hard packed clay on the old Liverpool shore-line..."

"What?!"

Claudia's incredulity was the window to bypass her defences. The limpid green-eyes fixed hers: "I really should thank you, intimately..."

Claudia's head started to feel light as the room appeared to spin before her. She struggled to keep conscious as the darkening tunnel of her vision caught a final sight of Adam's horrified face.

"Claire!" O'Riley's exclamation came as a second attempt to get her to respond had failed. She had collapsed into a chair; her breath was shallow and laboured. Slowly she looked up from the floor: "I'm sorry… sorry for storming out."

O'Riley smiled softly. He was glad that she'd returned. It must have upset her, to have heard what he'd said:

"I'm sorry too…"

Claire stopped him with an exhausted wave of her hand: "Listen, please, both of you… *She*'s at the Museum, right now, she's with Adam!"

"You've just been there: after you left us?"

"Look, no questions now, please… Just let me tell you, I spoke with her myself, the two of us alone…" Claire paused as tears filled her eyes: "She can read into people Kevin, she says she reads their hearts, not their minds. She read right into my past… *our* past…" The urgency in her eyes caught O'Riley as she continued: "She says that she'll tell my Kevin, about us…"

"What!" mouthed O'Riley: "She knows about that? How?"

Tears streamed down her face: "I told you, she reads people's hearts, you don't have to even be thinking of something, if its 'there' she finds it… she told me she'd read yours!"

A sharp sense of alarm gnawed at O'Riley's stomach as he recalled Lillian's 'seeing-through' him.

"Remember? You even told us about it yourself?"

O'Riley nodded in acknowledgement.

"She knows about Rowena too. She was trying to seduce me Kevin! If Adam hadn't come in, she would have!"

John, who knew about Claire and O'Riley's past joined in the conversation: "You mean, like an *incubus*?"

Claire nodded as her face contorted in distress: "There's more. Kevin… she knows about the Green-Man. I was thinking of him, trying to get an image in my mind to protect me, to resist her with: but she just laughed. She said that 'Green is what grows' – grows in *soil* and that she *is* the soil, she can destroy anything that grows even turn the land into a barren wasteland or a desert!"

John nodded: "It does say that about her in ancient middle-eastern texts, Kevin."

"And we were thinking that bubonic plague was the worst she could do…"

Claudia sank deeply into a dream-like state; her body paralysed her breathing seemingly disconnected from her conscious will. Struggling to move she at last half opened her eyes. She seemed still to be in her office – which was bathed in an eerie grey-white light. She tried to speak – she could feel her larynx move but her mouth only fell open and became still. Desperately her mind tried to make sense of what was happening. Her body registered fear as a shimmering shape moved into view – at first without definite form, but then slowly resolving into focus: a womanly shape with billowing long hair that seemed to hiss and rush with a deafening roar that filled her ears. The shape closed ever nearer, a naked woman with a classic hour-glass figure seemingly emitting the bathing grey-white light.

Claudia strained to look, fascinated, like an animal frozen by car headlights. The limpid green-eyes were now a silvered hue, unblinking and inhuman but transfixing: the Mona-Lisa smile overlain onto her face like a mask. Claudia felt the unmistakable sensations of sexual arousal in her body, her breasts firming, her nipples and clitoris becoming erect and tingling – her labia swelling and opening... her vulva moistening…

Her one last attempt to resist was in vain, overwhelmed by the spectral presence whose ghost like form began to merge with hers. Her paralysed muscles could feel but not move as the demons labia opened to reveal her own enlarged clitoris – so enlarged that it unfurled as a scorpions tail its sting bent and hooked sought Claudia's vulva.

Unable to gasp, she nevertheless felt its penetration – deeply and with fullness as it curled back against her G-Spot, the sting stimulating her so completely that she orgasmed immediately. Her lubricating juices gushed as the Scorpion Tail ejaculated harvested semen into her fallopian tubes…

O'Riley held his head in his hands. Shutting out the world may help him focus his mind.

John as ever the action-man, spoke first: "Let's get over there and sort her out!"

O'Riley's head emerged: "How?" he asked flatly.

John shrugged: "I don't know… just sort her. If we go over now, we'll think of somethin' before we get there!"

O'Riley shook his head. Claire responded for him: "She knows the score John, she even said to me that her identity is now so well recorded that she's a full UK citizen by *birth* and protected by its laws! If we go and 'harass' her or otherwise try to harm her, then *we* end up on the wrong side of the law!"

John grimaced in frustration: "I wanna see this… girl… thing… or whatever 'it' is!"

"She'd eat you alive" said Claire bluntly

"OK… so what the hell do we do?"

O'Riley at last sat upright: "We plan; we carry on exactly with what we've been doing already this morning, use the flip-charts, plan, and especially, anticipate her next moves. We also do everything we can to protect our families…"

Adam had watched as Claudia slipped into apparent unconsciousness. Looking at Lillian he saw only her intent and unblinking gaze. Claudia's astral-impregnation was outside of the capacity of his physical senses to detect: "Lillian… what's happening?"

"Happening? Oh… dear Dr Moore is receiving her reward for helping me… I feel tired Adam, I must restore my energies. She won't remember anything when she awakens: best that you carry on with your work."

Adam felt a sudden panic: "You're going!"

Lillian smiled: "I'll come back for you: don't worry.

Of all the people of this city, I *will* come back… for you…"

7.00pm and Von-Hesse was watching *Lilith* as she rested on the chaise Longue: "Mistress how went your… outing, today?"

"Well Maximilian, very well. I have sown my first seed."

The Bavarian narrowed his eyes: "Did you have enough already stored?"

"I shall need… replenishment. But it was good after such a long time."

"Mistress, if the contagion is to be refined sufficiently to defeat their medicine, then we must store more transformative energies!"

Lilith shook her head: "Always so anxious Maximilian. I've a mind to play a while before we move to the next stage. I'm curious as to how humans enjoy their sexuality."

Von-Hesse had feared this would happen: "But Mistress, you *must* preserve your bodily purity!"

"Must did you say? Must! Maximilian, you know better than to say that."

"But you promised… that it would be me!"

"It will be Maximilian" she soothed "*If* you do my bidding."

Von-Hesse's alarm sought an urgent clarification: "But I was to be the first, the *only* one!"

"Worry not, I'm still a 'Virgin' in *that* way – only in Astral form have I yet taken human sex…"

"Mum it's Friday night!" Sean was battling with his mother over his regular Friday night jaunts on the town.

"Sean, you've not been well, you've been looking pale and exhausted!"

"What? I'm fine… just fine, let me get past will yer!"

Claire was in mortal fear over her son's likely predation by Lillian, but she knew that in his 'possessed' state, she'd never have the physical strength to stop him: "Keep your iPhone on, if anything happens, anything at all, ring me, or your granddad!"

"Granddad!" Sean couldn't believe his ears. His mother fussing was one thing but being asked to ring his sixty-eight year old grandfather if he got into trouble was too much: "Bloody hell mum!" He paused in his retaliatory tirade then looked puzzled: "What about me dad? Shouldn't I ring him if I get me bollocks kicked?"

Claire sighed: "No, not this time, leave your dad out of this."

"Not *this* time? Yer sound like yer expectin' me to get done-over or somethin'?"

She knew that without further and as yet impossible explanation, she couldn't even *psychologically* stop him now. Nodding she moved out of his way.

Sean saw her nod as her affirmative response to his question: "Oh thanks! Have a nice 'safe' night-out Sean!"

"Where are you going?" she asked, hardly expecting an honest answer.

He read her face and decided to be truthful: "The Krazy House, in Wood Street."

"Wood Street, you mean Liverpool city centre?"

"Yeah! It's a hard-rock and heavy metal club!" Sean's reply was voiced as an assertion.

"OK…" Claire was now resigned "Just be careful eh?" She hugged him like she may never see him again…

Adam's flat off Smithdown Lane in Liverpool

The black Mini-Cooper S pulled up in the darkened street below. It's occupant scanning the windows for signs of movement. Sure enough, from behind the back-lit curtains a lonely round shouldered figure stooped. The Mona-Lisa smile widened as Lillian opened the car door.

Adam was lonely. Not an unusual condition for him, but one increasingly less bearable. His long hair was at last free of the pony-tail he was forced to wear for work at the Museum. Like thousands of others he'd been very much taken as a schoolboy with the TV archaeology show 'Time Team' as presented by the eccentric Tony Robinson and his team. They were 'real' archaeologists, he thought, plenty of hair, dirty digs in mucky

British fields, loads of beer and… on the periphery of filming, ample glimpses of attractive women. In contrast, his career was stuck doing his Ph.D. through Liverpool University and his academic supervisor at Liverpool World Museum: Dr Claudia Moore.

Claudia must have been young once, he mused. She was even attractive when she let her own hair down: indeed underneath her austere suit she had a very decent figure. But… despite his suspicion that she held out some kind of forbidden flame for him, she was still the main complication in his life – or at least she *had* been until recent events had blown some closed and locked doorways in his mind clear off of their hinges.

His apparently chance meeting with the beautiful and spectral Lillian, his past-life regression as 'Adam Teal' where he again met Lillian, this time as '*Lilith*', the séance where yet more details of his apparent past-life emerged, and, where he had shared a most intimate moment with the lovely Professor Claire Lattimer, as he'd collapsed and received the 'Kiss-of-Life' from her…

He almost laughed to himself at how he'd felt such strong attraction to those two very different but stunning women, and yet how here he was now, all alone in his run-down first floor flat on a Friday night. His private musings resolved down to an assessment of the relative merits between *Lilith* and Claire.

Claire was the kind of woman who if she had but been younger – around his age – and single, he would have fallen for in a big way. He could even see himself as married to her – one of those 'just-so' facts that are simply there and that seem to need neither reflection nor explanation. He simply 'knew.' However, she wasn't close in age to him, far from it indeed; she was in fact old enough to be his mother – and, she was also married… *very* married.

Lilith, however, was different. Despite how ESP had revealed her dark side to him, he was as captivated in this life as he had been in the last: *Lilith* or Lillian; Adam Teal or Adam Mitchell – underneath the same souls (he felt) were there; there and bonded together for all future lifetimes – just as she had promised to him.

His meandering mind reached its conclusion: even age-adjusted, there would be no contest between them, it could only ever have been *Lilith* first: and Claire second.

Little did he know…

He was startled by the knock on his front door: "Hold-on, I'm comin'!" Wondering if it was one his university mates he rushed to the multi-lock and chained door. He didn't own much in a worldly sense, but he didn't like the idea that he could lose it either. The area where he lived was notorious for burglaries. He paused momentarily: "I should get one of them spy-hole thingies" he said to himself. Then with a firm grip he opened the door: "Lillian!"

Her deep-green eyes shone their radiance, drawing her smile out broadly into attractive dimples: "Good evening… Adam Teal…"

"*Lilith*!" he breathed.

Sean was out on the pop with some of his heavy-metal friends. Bemoaning the fact that he'd soon have to cut his hair, maybe even down to a fashionable 'slap-head' length in order to join the police – he'd drowned his sorrows with booze and raised his spirits with music. He'd intended to go straight to the Krazy House, but found himself in nearby Seel Street first. By now quite drunk and separated from his mates he thought to at least attempt to be honest to his word to his mum. Reaching the door he paused as if to throw up – not wanting the bouncers to see he turned away and took a few steps to get out of sight. Purging himself of his Chinese takeaway, he returned feigning the capacity to walk upright and unaided. The front of the night club seemed blurred now – the lights bright, almost searing to his heavy eyes. So searing; that they formed a halo around the girl's lustrous russet-blond hair as she emerged in company with a tall long haired male companion: "Lillian!"

Adam was high as a kite. Here he was out on the town with Lillian. She'd called in out of the blue and whisked him away in her stylish Mini Cooper S. She'd insisted on seeing the town's night-life. She'd even dressed in tight-black biker leathers for him – so well cut that she looked like she wore a cat-suit. The cry of her name from the wobbling drunk caused him to glare: Get lost!" Adam preferred not to be too antagonistic with drunks – so long as they got the message.

The drunk didn't get the message: "Lillian! Wha yer doin' with tha' Muppet?"

"Muppet?"

"Yeah, Muppet!"

Adam's back bridled. Pausing to look over his shoulder towards the bouncers he saw them busy with some other drunks. Satisfied he put on his 'brave act': "Piss-off home yer tosser!"

The 'tosser' wasn't listening: "Lillian, don't yer recognize me? Itz me! Sean!"

It irritated Adam that Sean looked very like a certain good looking film and TV star much admired by women.

Lillian forestalled him: "Hi Sean, this is my friend Adam."

"Friend? Ya downt mean *boy-friend* do yer?"

That was red-rag to a bull to Adam. Of course she meant that: didn't she? "Yeah, she is, so fuck-off!"

The two young men squared off as if to fight it out over her. Lillian intervened: "Sean, I'm out with Adam tonight, we're old friends, he's been showing me around Liverpool."

Adam was becoming annoyed with the placation: "Lillian, we don't need to justify anything to the likes of him, come on, let's go!"

Lillian turned with him but looked back at the barely perpendicular Sean: "Be seeing you!" she smiled.

"Shit!" Sean was not impressed. He watched them go in the direction of Bold Street, and then followed gravity's least line of resistance and wobbled on down Wood Street. Wrapped up in self-pity and disappointment, he didn't see the gang on the next corner...

Lillian was scanning the young people as they passed by. Her smile seemed to take-in every exotic sight as a breath of inspiration: "I didn't know that Liverpool girls were so open about their bi-sexuality."

Adam frowned: "Oh... that's just the norm these days; girls go out with their mates, have a few drinks, and then have a bit of fun."

"With each other?"

"Well, yeah... it's like... fashionable I suppose."

Lillian smiled: "Good, it'll make things easier..."

Adam let out a gasp of disbelief, but as he watched her watching teenage girls kissing and fondling each other openly in the street, then he remembered: he remembered that as well as being 'Lillian' she was also '*Lilith*' that enchantress from another lifetime.

"You didn't see this kind of thing then..." he heard himself say."

She turned to him: "No, but it's really quite tame compared to the Greeks and Romans."

"Who?" Adam's trance had already evaporated.

"Why, Adam Teal have you forgotten? I used to tell you of long-ago times, of the beauty of the Queen of Sheba and of Salome, step-daughter of Herod and descendent of Hellenistic Greek Kings."

Lillian's words bathed him. A memory, a distant memory of lanes and green fields, of a sunlit summer's sky – of a walk home with her from the Chapel: "Toxteth Chapel…" he said, "I can see it… I remember!"

Lillian turned to look at him: "Your memories live in *both* times Adam Teal. You wanted me then… and I kept you waiting… Do you still want me now?"

"Want you?" he whispered "Of course I want you!"

Her eyes widened as she read both his face and his heart: "Even though you know me for who and what I really am?"

"Yes… I loved you then, and I love you now."

Lillian's porcelain white hand stretched out and caressed his face: "I nearly killed you Adam Teal… with the contagion…"

"But you lifted it from me…" said Adam, with Adam Teal's voice.

Then as *Lilith*, she smiled again: "Very well Adam Teal, you may take me: be the first, and the last… take me… tonight!"

Sean saw two of the gang walk towards him – the two he was supposed to see. His attention thus taken away, the other three moved to blind-side him. Angry at his earlier encounter with Adam and disappointed in Lillian, it was all more than his overloaded and drunken brain could deal with. He fell for the bait as the first two shouted something incomprehensible at him: "Yer wha?" he said stopping and glaring into the gloom.

The impact shocked his consciousness out from his body. Now just a spectator he watched as the rag-bag of a human form was cruelly kicked and stomped on the floor...

As Adam Mitchell, he would have been embarrassed at bringing Lillian home to his modest and rather unkempt flat, but as 'Adam Teal' anywhere he could be with *Lilith* would have been as the Garden of Eden itself: "Your flat... it's on our old route back from the Chapel. The fields we used to walk together, their soil is still here, just below our feet..." Her voice was softer than the finest silk. "I'm still a Virgin Adam Teal, no man has ever taken me... now *you* are my choice."

All he knew was that an indescribable bliss awaited him...

In the early hours of that now Saturday morning, Claire Lattimer was in a state of fitful sleep. Intense dreams wrapped her in their entanglements; false awakenings imprisoned her as her psyche fought within itself – pregnant memories reaching their term: She was aware of his warmth, his hard lean form, even his scent – the scent of a body washed in toil and sweat. The room was dark – the night silent – heavy bedclothes gave her comfort from the cold-air. She felt her body welcome him: gasping as his fullness entered her. Her whole world seemed contained in that moment. At last he climaxed – she could feel his member twitching as he ejaculated – grasping his body to hers she kissed him and saw his face, Adam's face..."

Sean didn't so much as come round, as half-come round. In that betwixt state, he passed through the hands of the ambulance and the casualty department at the Royal Liverpool

Hospital. His leather jacket cruelly sliced by gratuitous blade slashes, his face beaten and swollen, his hair matted his blooded scalp patchy from where hair had been torn.

He'd been lucky, he hadn't been stabbed. His leather jacket deflected the knife sufficiently for his body to survive without penetration. His attackers had run-off as two police-officers happened across the attack. He had been perhaps only seconds away from a lethal knife wound.

He'd been identified from personal papers found in his wallet, now it just remained for his family to be informed. Stable in his hospital bed, his half-closed eyes saw the ward's night-light suddenly dim almost to complete blackness before taking on an eerie grey-white hue…

Adam was deep in dreamless sleep. Wrapped in Lillian's perfect body he had literally entered paradise. So ecstatic was he that he would gladly have died there and then. He could imagine no greater purpose, not truer fulfilment to his life than this. *Lilith* had given of herself to him as to no one ever before. He couldn't possibly know that this supreme moment of his life had put him in mortal danger from the power of another, a rival he didn't even know that he had – a 'man' transformed by centuries of ardent alchemical labour who's own existence had been directed towards that which *Lilith* had given without restraint unto him.

The hooded black-brown eyes sought her out. *Lilith* was easy to find – her energy signature was so intense that it shone like the sun amongst mere candles. Von-Hesse did not know about what had happened between her and Adam, yet, but his darkened heart was suspicious. After so much time and so much effort, he would tolerate the life of no rival.

He and no other would be *Lilith*'s Adam Kadmon!

At last the hold of Claire's fitful dreams was broken. Her husband 'young' Kevin had got up from their bed, his movement shaking her into wakefulness. Kevin was not best pleased: "That's the front door: who in hell can that be at three in the morning!" He looked out the bedroom window: "It's a Bobby: couldn't they have just rung me up if it's a problem at work!" Still muttering as he went downstairs: "I'm not on-call; so this had better be important!" Claire's intuition told her: Sean hadn't come home, it must be him...

She was of course irresistible, but in his very weakened state even more so. Feebly he tried to cry-out before the rapture overwhelmed him. Behind her shimmering form he could see his nurse – oblivious to the predator on her ward. At last he resigned himself – the inhuman beauty of those Botticelli Venus eyes mesmerized him as the hissing rush of astral-energy enveloped his whole body. His mouth tried to gasp as the intense pleasure first convulsed him and then evacuated his testes, draining him of libido and his last vestiges of life. His mind swam as he heard the cardiac alarm sound and the shout of his nurse for the crash-team.

Lillian stirred. Adam was soundly asleep. His energy had come to her – naturally, but her needs were greater than that. Only in astral form could she be replenished. In mock pity for the rejected Sean, she had sought him out – battered and bruised, the stability of his life would be compromised by her *succubus* desires. Nevertheless, she had callously emptied him. Now energized, she would leave her sleeping 'Adam' and return to The Wirral. She had developed a taste for human sex – it had its diversions: and through it she had even uncovered a new and intriguing source of pleasure in herself. She would play a while longer before dealing in pandemic death...

Claire and Kevin didn't know that Sean had cardiac arrested. That had happened after the police were asked to contact them. Concerned parents they left straight away leaving sixteen year old Lizzie alone and asleep, with just a brief written note of explanation by her mobile phone at her bedside.

Kevin's Jaguar purred along at high speed down Borough Road Birkenhead going towards the Queensway Mersey Tunnel. The couple were silent and lost in their concerns. Kevin, as a father, Claire as a mother. But other thoughts too, insisted themselves upon Claire's consciousness – thoughts of Adam and the incredibly 'real' dream she had just had of him. So real that her own arousal was as full and enduring as any outer sexual and emotional experience could ever have been.

She squared her thoughts by telling herself that she just wanted to avoid the pain of thinking about what had happened to Sean – she even believed herself as she thought it. In truth however, something more real than she could ever have guessed had returned into her life.

The Jag descended down the tunnels winding turns into the long steep straight that bottomed out at the half-way point between Birkenhead and Liverpool. In the distance a lone car approached. As she watched it draw near, Claire casually noted the wish to be making the return journey with their ordeal safely over and done with – and with Sean coming home with them… home, and safe.

The dark car loomed ever closer – a black coloured Mini Cooper S Claire's eyes momentarily passed over to the Cooper's driver – a long haired young woman.

Failing to recognise her consciously, Claire's heart nevertheless missed a few beats in alarm.

Out of the tunnel, Lillian's Cooper slowed for the automatic toll booths and then smoothly accelerated away, heading for St Stephens Road in Prenton…

Claire and Kevin parked their car in the Royal Liverpool's car park and made their lonely way into the casualty department. Each step wearied them emotionally as they prepared themselves as best they could for what they were about to see. The hospital was busy, the process of getting help and directions laboured. At last, they found their way to Sean's ward. Casualty had telephoned ahead, and a junior doctor was there to meet them, directing them into a small side room. Claire's maternal instincts were fully aroused: "What's happened! Has he got worse?" Her face was furrowed with concern, her eyes fearful.

"Mrs O'Riley… Mr O'Riley, he's 'safe', but… as well as his injuries – which I'm told you know about, he had a complication after he arrived on the ward…"

"Complication?!"

"Yes… as I say, he's stable now…"

Claire wasn't getting her answers: "What happened!" She was normally patient with medics – appreciating the difficulties they faced, but this particular doctor simply wasn't getting to the point.

The medic sighed and twiddled with his stethoscope: "He… arrested."

"Arrested! Cardiac arrest you mean?"

"Yes, but he's OK, we're just doing some tests now, as far as we can tell he'll recover fully. We had a crash team there very quickly."

Kevin asked for background clarification: "This *was* as a result of his injury wasn't it?"

The medic stalled – again: "Er…"

"That's not good enough doctor!" Claire was awash with conflicting emotions: fear for her son, rage at his attackers and frustration with this uninformative doctor.

"There was a further issue…"

"Go on!"

"Something else seems to have happened, around the time of his cardiac arrest, or immediately before, something that had also happened to one other admission some days ago…"

Claire's frustration was boiling over: "Where is he? I've had enough of this stalling! I want to see my son!"

The medic dithered. He'd drawn the short straw and had been bundled off to intercept the parents whilst his more senior colleagues tried to figure out what had happened. The junior doctor's inexperience had reached its own limits: "He's had some kind of reaction… in his groin area…"

"Groin area?!" Claire hadn't caught on yet. Kevin though had guessed; he'd heard about the 'other' incident from Claire in conversation with her at home:

"You mean like Dr Teal from the School of Tropical Medicine?"

Looking downwards the young medic nodded: "Yes…" he said quietly.

Claire was aghast: "How in hell did that happen in a hospital!"

"We don't know Mrs O'Riley; all we can say for sure is that there was a voluminous discharge, including some blood. There doesn't seem to be any crush or other external trauma injury, just… as I say, an excessive bloody discharge. We're doing tests to make sure that he's OK, internally."

Claire exchanged a deeply concerned look with her husband: "It *must* have been her!"

"Her?" queried the medic.

Claire just shook her head: how could she explain? "Never mind; please just take us to him."

Lillian's black Mini Cooper S pulled up directly outside the O'Riley house in St Stephens Road. Proximity was no barrier either way to her original purpose; she could just as easily have returned to Oxton and 'projected' her astral form from there. Another urge however was rising up from within her, one more visceral, than astral.

Her limpid green-eyes scanned the external façade of the house, and sensed Lizzie's presence – her sleeping body's energy as easily detectable as with an infra-red remote sensing device. These eyes however saw more than the infra-red, they sought out the vital essence of a human soul and read its character, its nature and… its vulnerability.

Lizzie was very vulnerable.

Lillian opened her car door and walked through the gates of the house. No protective spirit barred her way; no occult talisman's raised the alarm. Just one lonely human soul lay oblivious in its innocent sleep.

Lillian's Botticelli-Venus eyes radiated an angelic, but inhuman beauty as her form dissolved, shimmering as particles of fairy-light and passed wisp-like through the permeable walls of the house.

Sean was unconscious as his body closed down in a primal effort of recovery. Trauma had followed insult leaving his psyche no option but to follow into unknowing sleep. Claire stared at the pitiful sight – the memory of her last hug with him as he left the house, irritated at his mother's fussing, was replayed to her as if she could somehow change the outcome.

Kevin's eyes saw the wounded surface, her heart the wounded interior: "Have the police been called yet?" Kevin's police superintendent's persona was rallying to his aid.

"They have, but they've been advised that Sean's in no fit state for any interviews.

"Right! Then there's not much more I can do here. Claire, I'm calling in at Copperas Hill police station and see what in hell, if in anything... anyone's doing about this!"

Claire let him go without a word. The police was his world... a place where he could operate with authority. Kevin could do the 'man' thing; she'd have to stay by her son's side. So attuned was her being to her son's ordeal that her psyche's whispering warning of her daughters imminent peril passed unheeded.

Lizzie murmured as she lay dreaming. The source of her alarm was outside of her dream-world experience. Her instincts tried to rouse her but her brain was locked in to its wave-like dream rhythms. Only her quiet cry betrayed a subliminal awareness of what approached her: her call out to her mother as instinctive as that from any isolated prey animal.

The fabric of her dream began to break-down, like the frame-rate of an old cine-film, until at last one final frozen image dissolved away, leaving Lizzie in a half-awake state – aware now that she had been dreaming, but unable to fully wake herself up. The rushing sound in her ears was uncomfortable, the grey-white light eerily unfamiliar. Trying to move she felt herself make the effort, but an odd sensation of involuntary relaxation seemed to make it impossibly difficult. Her eyelids could open – just half way. Her breath became dissociated from her conscious control as her muscles finally relaxed into a profound paralysis.

Lizzie's heavy eyes stared into the now shimmering light. Gradually a naked woman's shape resolved itself into view; her long locks of flowing hair waving like a nest of silver serpents – no human-soul stared from behind the visions mesmerizing and uncannily beautiful eyes. Lizzie felt the grip of terror surge through her body – as spectral-like the woman floated through the solid foot of her bed.

The figure approached ever closer: Lizzie's fear and her remaining willpower escaped like evaporating mist – replaced by an erotic stirring in her belly and vulva.

The astral apparition's smile broadened as it sensed its prey's submission, yet a curiosity linked the malevolent form to its physical counterpart of Lillian, – a curiosity about the young girls behaviour outside the night-clubs on the Liverpool city streets: a curiosity too about how easily she had teased Claire at the museum… a curiosity about the rapture of physical sex with a virgin girl…

"Mum?"

Claire heard the faint echo of her son's voice as it struggled to speak her name; his dry lips chaffed and congealed as he gasped out his words: "Mum… Lillian… in my sleep… she… comes to me, in my sleep!"

Claire's worried face flattened and became smooth as she heard her son's confirmation of her suspicions: Lillian, or *Lilith* as she was also known, was a *succubus* and *incubus* demon – who *must* feed on the libido of humans for the maintenance of her physical form. What had happened to Dr Teal had also happened to Sean – it was all becoming clear to Claire – Lillian was targeting specific people – people related to, or descended from her enemies in seventeenth century Liverpool: "Hush Sean… relax love… she can't get to you now, I'm here… you're completely safe…"

He was of course, but only because his demon lover was occupied elsewhere, with yet another member of the family: an innocent young girl with no sexual experience at all, and now completely in the enthralment of a merciless *incubus*…

The astral forms spectral beauty enveloped Lizzie – who now surrendered utterly to her paralysis and her mounting state of arousal. The Scorpion Tail had unfurled – its stinging clitoris poised for penetration... and insemination.

And yet... something had changed. Lizzie now felt the increasing pressure of a real physical weight on her bed, the serpent hair glowed in hues more golden than silver, the yellow-grey Botticelli eyes turned at first pale and then to the deepest of limpid green opalescence.

The rushing sound in Lizzie's ears dimmed and she began to feel the warmth of a physical body, a naked girl, seemingly only a little older than her, but with porcelain-perfect skin and alabaster turned curves.

The girl's body had permeated her bedclothes as easily as mist, gradually becoming warm and alive as soft flesh gently laid itself upon hers – still aroused: the girls lovely face and mouth teased her ever more with her scented breath.

Used only to the ungainly and forceful kisses of adolescent boys – the moist, full softness of this girl's mouth was electrifying – so enrapturing that her paralysis melted away as her excitement pulsed through her veins and washed – tingling over her skin. Lizzie's on-going experience was now a seamless continuum, she could no longer discriminate where dream had left off, and outer reality had begun – her receptive physiological state led her mind into willing participation.

For now, Lillian withheld her serpent-tongue from Lizzie's mouth; instead she softly licked at her firm breasts slowly circling her areole then drawing back along the length of her erect nipples – finally enveloping them with her lips in a gentle teasing suck. Lizzie's legs instinctively parted as her labia swelled and opened – allowing Lillian to gently press and then rub her vulva against her. Even for Lillian, this was a new experience – it took an effort of will for her not to unfurl her

Scorpion Tailed clitoris – instead she wanted to enjoy this young virgin as a purely physical, and all too-human erotic encounter. Lizzie's own arousal was such now that instinct guided her; taking the lead in stimulating and enjoying *Lilith*'s unbelievably lovely body.

Timing her own arousal with perfection, Lillian chose the precise moment to penetrate Lizzie's receptive mouth with her serpent tongue – both girls felt the surge of imminent climax and rubbed their clitorises together passionately – Lillian's tongue causing Lizzie's vulva to ripple in pulsed contractions – her orgasm lengthened almost indefinitely by the serpents power.

Then as mist, Lillian's physical form faded, leaving the faint sensation of its warmth and physical presence impressing on Lizzie's hot and sweating body. Lizzie's paralysis returned: her mind swirled as dream images paraded before her inner eyes in a slide show of still's before blending into one continuous stream. In moments she was in normal rapid-eye movement sleep, her psyche processing through dream symbols the most intimate emotional and physical experience of her young life.

Outside – in physical form, Lillian's Mona-Lisa smile broadened in appreciation of this novel sexual experience. Her Scorpion Tailed clitoris tingling in anticipation of her next bi-sexual encounter – which Lillian resolved would be fully in the flesh – and involve the all powerful vigour of her impregnating…sting.

Over in Liverpool, Adam's body shook involuntarily, rousing him from a deep and dreamless sleep. The bed next to him was cold: his mind dissonant between the earlier emotional and physical fulfilment of his life, and now, the emptiness of being alone. Lillian had gone…

Throughout the long night Claire kept vigil at her son's bedside. The passage of the hours, combined with her exhaustion allowed her mind a degree of focused concentration. Going over every single fact she had about Lillian, she tried to form a mental map of her relationships and likely plans. Oh how she wished she had one of Kevin O'Riley seniors' flip charts and red pens now!

Suddenly, the hair stood on the back of her neck: "Lizzie! Lizzie's all alone!"

Saturday 25th November 2006: Oxton Wirral 8.00am

Lillian was in near exhaustion after the adventures of the past 24 hours. She had seduced Claudia, Sean and Lizzie, lost her physical virginity to Adam, nearly seduced Claire – enjoyed a night on the town – but most importantly, she had squandered some of the precious libido she had taken from her male victim Sean, libido she would need to transform any harvested sperm, incubate her contagion and maintain her physical shape. Her fatigued state did not go unnoticed by her would-be New Adam; Maximilian Von Hesse: "Mistress? You've been away all night... you look as if you've been overdoing things..."

Lilith as Von-Hesse knew her to be, was too tired for his fussing: "I just need rest Maximilian, give me the space to achieve it."

Curious, the hooded black-brown eyes narrowed as he sought to penetrate her mind. This impertinence roused *Lilith* to anger: How dare you! Did you think that I wouldn't know!"

Von-Hesse attempted to placate her; he knew that despite her weakened state she could easily find enough energy to end his existence: "Mistress... forgive me... it was out of concern!"

He did manage to see into her most recent 'charged' memory however, and saw the face of Lizzie. His curiosity took the further risk of asking for clarification: "You have penetrated the Virgin mistress?"

Lilith's green-eyes narrowed in mocking parody of Von-Hesse's stern inquisition: "And is that *any* of your particular concern Maximilian?"

"Only that she's the daughter of the woman Lattimer, and blood descendent through her of Nathaniel Lattimer... the Witchfinder..."

Lilith managed a Mona Lisa smile: "Not yet... I have merely toyed with her. As for her relationship to that accursed man I know of it, and it amuses me that his descendants are my playthings. I'll have her mother too before I kill her, just to see how grateful her face is for the orgasm I'll give her before she dies!"

Von-Hesse appreciated the sadism in giving death as the price of indescribable bliss. He smiled: a rare experience for his face... "That would be most... appropriate Mistress..."

Lilith was too tired to continue: "I'll sleep now Maximilian... but tonight, I will go again to Liverpool's club-land. You... can follow me there, openly this time, but at a discrete distance..."

Sean's condition had remained stable over-night so by 11.00am Claire decided that she should return home and get some much needed rest. In the night she'd called Kevin on his mobile and begged him to go back to Prenton Lane and check on Lizzie's safety. Reluctantly, he'd agreed, he'd been busy interviewing the police constables who'd found his son and was arranging for CCTV recordings to be checked for any sightings and possible identification of the offenders. He'd found his daughter sound asleep, but on Claire's insistence, he'd stayed with her. Now he was being asked to call over at the Royal Liverpool Hospital and collect his wife. He wondered if Claire had given any thought that he too needed some sleep…

Claire and her husband arrived home by 11.00am: "Kevin, we're both tired…"

"Oh… you've noticed?"

"Please love, that's not helpful… let's take it in turns to sleep, whilst the other waits up for news on Sean, and… keeps an eye on Lizzie. I have this awful feeling that Lillian will move on her next!"

Kevin had been too long a policeman. His heart had forgotten the special value of relating during times of crisis – he was a more 'practical' man. But, he did find it in him to hear the logic in Claire's argument: "OK… You sleep first; I'll doss-down in the early evening."

Claire crashed out in bed and no sooner had she blinked twice than her inner cinema ran the trailer for the coming dream – a period drama about seventeenth century Liverpool…

5.00pm and Lillian stirred un-replenished from her sleep. She knew that if her plans to exploit the Liverpool club scene were to come to fruition – then, she'd need to harvest another victim. Adam, of course, was available, but… she had chosen him as her future consort. No, she would have to find someone else, someone who was asleep or at the very least too tired to put up any kind of resistance – someone with a good quality of semen for use in the effortless impregnation of licentious Liverpool girls, unwarily open about bi-sexual experimentation.

Over at St. Stephens Road, Kevin exchanged places with Claire and fell into a deep, and available, sleep...

Claire heard nothing. Wide-awake the astral sounds were outside of her ken. Even as she softly crept into the bedroom to get some clothes she was completely unaware. No warning chill, no erect hair at the base of her neck. A quick glance at her sleeping husband lying on his back – his breathing the shallow and rapid cycle of a man within a dream.

She passed right through Lillian as the spectral demon leaked through the curtained window – only *he* saw her, constrained by his paralysis, unable to call out to Claire for help, unable to raise a desperate hand. The bedroom door closed – and the beautiful Botticelli Venus face filled his eyes – just as he had warned his son about the famous painting: an inhuman light shone from the yellow-grey eyes...

"I'll be in Wood Street and the surrounding area... hmm about... midnight onwards. You *may* follow on if you wish Maximilian, it is my intention to spread seed in unwitting soil ha ha!"

"You have harvested again today Mistress?"

"I have... not fully to his detriment: he'll be sore, but *not* fatally harmed, as yet... I'll probably take some more of him; the quality of his semen is unusually high, better than his son's. In fact... I think it would be as well to make alchemical analysis of a sample from him... something 'other' than *just* human has passed through his birth-line..."

"This is Kevin O'Riley Junior?"

"It is."

Maximilian was still in calculating mood: "So… the man who threatens you, must be his father! It cannot be O'Riley junior, otherwise you would not have harvested him. So, O'Riley senior has some special occult or supernatural quality passed down *differentially* through his bloodline, perhaps some of his offspring are carriers, but do not express the quality individually, and in full!"

Lillian smiled her trademark smile: "You are far *too* clever for your further guaranteed longevity Maximilian: curiosity doesn't just kill cats – it takes fallen Cathar *Perfecti* too!

Von-Hesse wasn't listening – the alchemist in him was intrigued: "Maybe… it passes through the female line – or at least is capable of doing so… That could mean that the girl Lizzie…"

"That would mean" interrupted Lillian "that at some near future time – Lizzie will have to be taken, from her family, for my… personal investigation… as a potential higher-incubation host. Meanwhile, we will test a sample from her Father. Other, more 'normal' female humans will suffice for basic incubation hosts – we will need shall we say 'basic' hybrid demon-offspring for menial tasks…"

Von-Hesse scanned Lillian's face trying to detect any sign of a plan he was unaware of: "The contagion… the impregnated hosts, will they be vulnerable?"

"Of course not! Just as before, in past times, those who host will be immune – for the duration of their usefulness…

Now, I am going out – and I do *not* wish to be followed Maximilian, so inform Adler and Meier. You may meet up with me later, in case… in case I have need of your *baser* skills…"

Claire thought to check on Kevin. She'd spent the last hour on the phone to her father-in-law and to John, telling them in detail about what had happened to Sean. Of course she knew nothing of Lillian's nocturnal seduction of Lizzie – for even Lizzie herself remembered it only dimly as a dream. Still less had she known of the demons predation of her husband, until now that is... as she tried to rouse him from his sleep.

Adam had spent the day dissociated – even for him; he was in an unusually fractured state. Lillian had given him her virginity, and her love – or at least as much as '*Lilith*' was apparently capable of in that regard. His memories of her: memories stretching back from before his birth; were of his own fawning love and in return, her sometimes cruel teasing.

Sitting watching his little portable TV he stared in impassive reverie through the passing images as if he were looking at raindrops as they wended their way down a winter's window pane. His thoughts drifted and he found himself wondering if he really did exist, or was Adam Mitchell just some awful nightmare that Adam Teal was dreaming sometime back in the seventeenth century. His stomach twinged with adrenalin as he heard the knock at his door. Could it be... could it be her?

His answer came through her lips. Gasping his legs went weak and folded at the knees. Her smile broad and dimpled. She had never looked so human, so ordinarily beautiful: "Lillian!"

"Adam!" she replied.

"*Lilith*..."

As 'Adam Teal' Adam Mitchell embraced her – and a warmth of love passed between them: "*Lilith*... you've come back, I was *so* afraid that you'd gone from me!"

Lilith's heart had opened. Her decision, her choice, had been made. Von-Hesse had followed her for centuries, but 'Adam' had loved her for lifetimes.

"I'll never leave you now Adam Teal... your fate and mine are entwined, as entwined as if my golden hair were wrapped tightly around your heart..."

Tenderly she caressed him and led him back through his shabby flat's bedroom door...

Claire quickly ascertained that Kevin was still breathing and had a heart-beat. Terrified, she managed at last to rouse him. the blooded semen discharge had soaked the bedclothes. Shocked, he hung on to Claire as he had not done so since they had first struggled together to defend their love against evil: many, many years ago.

The experience had indeed shocked Kevin, shocked him out of his remoteness and his identification with his police persona. He needed Claire's love now, and he understood finally just what peril his children were in.

But something had changed in Claire too. Her love for him hadn't abated in the years he'd been distant – no it wasn't that. It was more what had made itself known in her heart in recent days and weeks: something unbidden, that had stepped in through that unwitting gap in their intimacy: something that seemed to rival, rather than as yet, replace: her love for her husband…

For even this very day, with her son Sean recovering from a near fatal cardiac arrest, physical assault and predation by a malevolent *succubus* – her *own* dreams had betrayed her, she had dreamt, emotionally and sexually, about Adam…

Later that evening at St Stephens Road

John looked over at O'Riley; concern was written across his older colleague's brow like hieroglyphs on an Egyptian tomb: "This is a *real* attack now Kevin, we've *got* to take it seriously!" said John.

O'Riley nodded but still stared blankly ahead. His inner-vision sought a complete picture of the threat: "Green is what grows in soil… That's what Lillian said to Claire…"

Claire was shaking. Her son was still in hospital, her husband laid out and recovering upstairs. Her daughter Lizzie grounded in her room for her own safety: "She's telling us that we can't win this time!" said Claire in obvious distress.

O'Riley turned around: "Years ago, my mentor, and briefly John's too – the late Dr Bruce Irving – he told me that evil always gives itself away – true evil, destroys everything, even itself in the end – he said – so, we should always expect that it will tell us, as if it couldn't help itself, just how we can defeat it."

Claire's fear filtered out the meaning in his words: "She'll never do that! She's dangerous Kevin, she's nearly killed your son and grandson – and just for sport too!"

O'Riley's age and experience – his own narrowing life-span had given him a strongly defined reflective edge: "I would think that Bruce would have said that she's probably already told us, it's just that we didn't listen properly."

"What? Oh not now, leave the philosophy for yer patients!"

O'Riley continued: "Why hasn't she played the *succubus* card with me?"

John couldn't resist a half smirk: "Well… no offence, but perhaps 'younger' stock is… yer know… kinda… better?"

"Ah! The 'genetic quality' argument… But then that presupposes that her *succubus* activity is *solely* for some kind of reproductive purposes."

"Well, what else?" asked John bluntly.

"Think about it… it's pretty pointless prematurely killing your 'farm animals' – for that is what the genetic argument presupposes that her victims are. Remember the fairy tale of the goose who laid the golden egg?"

"I think you're wandering off-track a bit there Kevin" said John "She could take *any* male she chose – there must be a surplus of good genetic stock out there – so she can afford to milk a man once and then dispose of him."

"John please!" Claire was uncomfortable with the milking analogy "My son and husband have been 'milked' as you put it!"

"Oops, sorry Claire, that was insensitive of me."

"But young-Kevin wasn't killed was he, and neither was Dr Teal. Yes, he *nearly* died, and so did Sean, but they *didn't* die.

You see, we're making a number of assumptions: reasonable ones given the fear involved, but assumptions nevertheless.

I agree, John, she could have any man she wanted, it seems they only need to be in a state of sleep, or perhaps traumatized in some way, into unconsciousness.

However, she's met me… she 'read my heart' she knows about my past, she recognized my talisman but she *hasn't* directly attacked me – indirectly through my family – yes, but directly, no."

Claire responded: "So you're saying that there's something about you that she's recognised as a threat?"

"Yes, it's the logical conclusion – and – we have the comment at the séance from the medium Alfred Hume – the comment that I should consult with my 'mentors' as only they would be powerful enough to stop *Lilith*."

"But… none of us have had any contact with 'them' in years – Bruce is dead, and only you have ever had any communication with him since– and that was more than twenty years ago… and as for the Green Man, and his Avatar 'Crazy Horse' as he was nick-named – likewise, he vanished in the 1980's and hasn't been seen or heard of since!"

O'Riley became quiet again, sighing he sat down into Claire's deep leather high-back armchair: "Then… it might be up to me to seek them out again…"

"Will they come back?" asked Claire.

"Who knows? I'm reminded of that quote from Shakespeare; it's that delightful scene in Henry IV, Part I. Owain Glendower, trying to impress the Prince, says, 'I can call spirits from the vasty deep.' And Henry Hotspur replies, 'Why, so can I, or so can any man; but will they come when you do call for them?'

That's our problem isn't it…"

Adam's love for *Lilith* had worn him out into a state of blissful natural sleep. Fondly she stroked his face. Despite her words to him, she would indeed leave him again – this very evening. Adam both as himself and as Adam Teal surely knew now of her true nature, and what she must do. She would rise up from their bed and make her way by car to the city's club-land and there smile her Mona-Lisa smile as she 'farmed' the naïve young girls of Liverpool…

Von-Hesse was dropped off by Meier in the Audi R8 Supercar at Duke Street: near to the junction with Colquitt Street. He'd make his way from here on foot – skirting the chosen area as if a patrolling shark. His military mind and it's literally centuries of experience made him methodical in his approach to human problems. The hooded black-brown eyes sought his Mistress's energy – and sure enough her intense signature revealed itself as if a beacon-light from a misty shore.

He allowed himself a smirk of self-satisfaction and then drew up the collar on his black Abercrombie overcoat. His tall angular but muscled figure was an impressive sight as it moved in and out of the shadows – impressive and also of interest to those who thought he might be carrying something of value for them …

Lillian had dressed for the occasion in her black biker leathers. Their darkness contrasted perfectly with her porcelain white skin and russet-golden locks.

Groups of 'Emo' girls passed her by, doing the 'buddy-gay' thing with one-another. Lillian was obviously not an Emo, but then what Lillian *really* was, wasn't obvious to anyone. 'Goth's' too, some of them openly relating bisexually – but Lillian was looking for victims less likely to be bizarre – more likely to be ordinary college girls, vulnerable but open to experimentation

– it wasn't long before Lillian's stunning looks and obvious 'by herself' status attracted some interest…

Von-Hesse too had attracted attention. The five youths on the street corner made sure that they were out of shot from CCTV as they watched for the approach of a potential victim. Their habit needed funding, and Saturday was always a good night for a quick mugging before they ran off and assembled at their favourite club for doing drugs. It was the same five who had attacked Sean O'Riley the night before and it was their tried and trusted tactic of distraction and blindsiding that they were to employ now. It was just that unbeknown to them, this particular *victim* had fought on the streets of Liverpool before, fought… and killed…

Von-Hesse's attention was taken with tracking his Mistresses energy signature – detected at a distance and through solid walls, he could 'see' through his unearthly black-brown eyes that she was now in company with a group of others, and by their mass and general shape – they were female.

His peripheral vision caught a sudden movement from his left. The mercenary soldiers instincts operated immediately as he quickly scanned the threat: "Gotta ciggie mate?" asked the voice. Von-Hesse ignored it – he knew the tactic. Quickly he looked to his rear 'blind-side' and there saw three shadowy figures closing on him. Realizing he'd rumbled them they rushed – the first two drawing lock-back box-cutter style knives. Dispassionately, the Bavarian relaxed his right arm allowing a concealed combat knife to descend from his sleeve and into his open grip. The first youth swung his knife wildly at Von-Hesse's face. Leaning back slightly he allowed it to pass him and then quickly stepped in so that his body blocked the yobs arm above the elbow. Gripping the attacking arm with his left hand he punctured the youth's throat with his concealed blade. Not even bothering to check the outcome, he spun the collapsing body into the path of the first two yobs as he angled himself to counter the threat from the remaining 'blind-siders'. The second knife wielding yob jabbed desperately at Von-Hesse – who's response was a swift slash across his opponents grip with his razor-sharp blade – the youth screamed and dropped this knife – but was too late to escape as Von-Hesse continued his counter-strike dropping the knife point-first behind his enemies collar-bone and severing the base of the carotid artery. Expertly, he removed the blade in one continuous motion and closed against the remaining yobs who'd now had enough and ran for their lives.

The Bavarian hadn't even broken into a sweat: "Had this been

last time, I'd have chased and cut you *all* down!" he shouted after them.

He'd always preferred cold steel at close quarters. He hadn't even been inconvenienced enough to draw his silenced semi-automatic Glock 18, 9mm pistol...

Satisfied, he emerged from the gloom and resumed his cyborg-like protective scan on behalf of his Mistress.

Over in Prenton, the St Stephens Road cadre were still deep in discussion. Claire had checked on Sean's condition by phone, and having ascertained that he was stable and resting – she made the reluctant decision not to travel to Liverpool and leave her vulnerable daughter and husband alone at home. O'Riley and John had volunteered to cover for her, but she wouldn't go, she had a 'confession' to make, and now was going to be as good a time as any. Indeed, at the rate things were developing, she may not get another chance for some time – perhaps not even ever…

"Look, Kevin, John… this may not seem the best time to raise this… but, I've been having strange dreams."

John, not always the most thoughtfully tactful of individuals spluttered a guffaw: "Well of course you have Claire! Yer a parapsychologist, be odd if yer didn't!"

Claire's face told O'Riley that she was serious, and was asking for help: "I'd be interested to hear about them Claire" he said.

John apologized: "Sorry, it just seemed surreal in the middle of all that's going on… yer know, you sayin' that…"

Claire nodded slightly and stared at the carpet: "They're about Adam…"

"Adam? Young Adam Mitchell?"

"Yeah… you see, you were right, there *is* an issue between us, I wasn't sure… but my dreams are telling me that there is.
I have felt an attraction to him… I'm ashamed really to admit it, it's not something I wanted, it just happened… Obviously this is especially difficult for me, as you're my father-in-law…

The dreams seem to be in the seventeenth century, about the time of Adam's past-life regression."

"Go on…"

She sighed again: "They're sexual… really sexual, yet so 'ordinary' and everyday, almost well… repressed and *Puritan*."

O'Riley's long experience told him that when someone made a 'confession' that they were becoming perhaps infatuated with another person outside of their marriage or relationship – then it was either in an effort to genuinely sort it out: or, to indulge it by getting other people to talk with them about it. With Claire, now, it could be either of those, or perhaps even something else… "Claire, it's a feature of infatuations that we like to place the 'beloved' in our *personal* context: weave them into the fabric of our lives, as if we've somehow *always* known them."

Claire looked at him, reading his face for signs that he could be trusted with where she was going with this… He was after-all her father-in-law, and, long-ago, unknown to her husband, her one time passionate lover… "I know that Kevin, but go on…"

"You've now met Adam…"

Claire's body jolted involuntarily at these words, which of course O'Riley noted: "You've met Adam… in a highly charged atmosphere, highly charged and highly *suggestible*. We both know how the psyche can react to that kind of energy-field – deep unconscious fantasies get projected out onto the people we meet, and, they can trigger a reciprocal projection back, onto us. That, can create an illusion: the illusion of true relatedness – whereas it's just a kind of 'product' of the mix – the emotional and psychological mix that we find ourselves in. We're particularly vulnerable if our own relationship has been treading water for some time. It's as if we need a life-giving spark back in our lives…"

Again Claire's body jolted at his last words.

"And that did pass between you didn't it? A life-giving spark – at the séance, in a *very* highly charged emotional and psychological atmosphere – quite beyond those that occur in normal everyday life…"

Claire replied: "But I don't have an *ordinary* or everyday life! The stuff I get involved in is by definition *extra-ordinary* and... this... whatever it is with Adam... hasn't happened to me before, not in over twenty years of marriage!"

"Only you can answer this Claire, but you have at least to look inside your marriage and ask yourself what's been happening between you both... not on the surface... that's too easy to distract yourselves with – the everyday stuff of raising a family and getting on with your careers – no, I mean deeper than that: down where whatever it was that brought you both together in the first place still resides. If you've drifted apart at that level..."

Claire's unconscious mind seized the chance and caused her body to twitch in reply. She had to smile: "Looks like a part of me is agreeing with you!"

O'Riley smiled in acknowledgement: "Or... your dreams are *not* fantasies."

Claire looked puzzled – but her belly churned with expectancy: "I'm sorry?"

"Or, they're telling... or perhaps *reminding* you... of something that really happened."

Claire's face contorted as she replied: "I've not been 'unfaithful' to my Kevin, it's just an emotional thing; I've *never* physically betrayed him!"

John had been listening closely: "He didn't mean that Claire love... he meant that maybe, like Adam Mitchell as 'Adam Teal', *you* had some kind of past life yourself...a past life *with* Adam Teal."

Claire's eyes widened as she took on board the implications: "But... that would mean, you know... in the dreams... that before I knew my husband, in 'this' life, I'd known Adam and..." She couldn't bear to say the words, her eyes filled up with tears. Then at last composing herself she said: "I've got to know the truth – I *have* to do a past-life regression!"

Liverpool Clubland

Lillian had ingratiated herself with a trio of drunken girls – attractive and in their late teens, they were students at Liverpool John-Moores University. Living in student accommodation: they'd be ideal victims – once back at their flat she'd begin their Lesbian seduction and impregnation. The sperm harvested from Kevin O'Riley junior had been alchemically transformed within her body: and now her clitoral, scorpion sting, tingled with anticipation:.

She'd enjoy delivering this particular act of insemination in the 'flesh' rather than in her astral form…

Von-Hesse understood his Mistresses needs. He would recover her car and leave it near the students flat for Lillian's return to the Wirral. Meier could take the Audi Supercar back over to Oxton with him from there.

On his way back to Duke Street he walked past the gloomy alleyway where the two dead bodies still lay undiscovered and gave them not a single glance…

11

Death
Hath not
Parted us

Sunday 26th November 2006: Prenton Lane Wirral 11.00am

 ohn had stayed at Claire's overnight – to act in support should she need it, with protecting Kevin junior and Lizzie. The remainder of the night however passed uneventfully, and by 8.00am he was able to rouse himself from the sofa and make his way home to get cleaned up before he had a private meeting with O'Riley in Prenton Lane

Like O'Riley, John too had a protective talisman – given at the same time to them both by the late Dr Bruce Irving – way back in 1984. A simple red coloured knight's-shield necklace charm with a gold pentacle design and some Celtic 'Ogham' script symbols writ in gold at the five pentacle points. Originally they'd had a third, but that had been lost during an intense showdown with a malevolent psychic force at a local church – a battle the like of which that none of those involved hoped that they'd ever have to endure again.

Caressing the tiny shield with the pad of his right thumb he wondered whether it would be strong enough to protect him this time. It would only work if he wore it around his neck continuously, and its power could be circumvented if he allowed himself to be tricked into harming himself – either through an accident or otherwise 'by his own hand'.

Memories flooded back as he passed the chain over his neck and secured the little shield over his heart.

"John! Welcome! O'Riley was all smiles as he opened the door to his old friend and colleague. They'd come a long way together and although John had developed and matured over the years the changes in O'Riley had been immense. He'd moved on from being a young, deeply insecure and neurotic police-superintendent – a very ego-centric individual, utterly given over to ambition and yet with a personality cracked like an old dinner plate from the rim to the very centre – to being an elderly and highly respected psychotherapist with a great gift of insight and wisdom. His journey had been an odyssey of self-discovery as the very land itself had reached out to him revealing its most intimate occult and supernatural secrets.

His development had attracted attention from sinister forces that sought to exploit the self-same mysteries of the land for themselves. In the battles that followed O'Riley at last came to an understanding of himself and like a developing photograph, his true self finally emerged – only it was not the picture of a senior police officer that finally resolved. His re-birth was made complete when he resigned from the police in 1985, just as he was about to achieve his life-time ambition of becoming a Chief Constable.

His 'after-life' involved taking up training as a Jungian psychotherapist at the Eden Institute in Rodney Street – inspired by his late mentor Dr Bruce Irving – and by a bizarrely surreal but 'humble' police-constable nick-named 'Crazy Horse' who it turned out was really a mysterious avatar of The Green Man – the nature spirit of rebirth, whose 'Green-Chapel' was revealed as being an ancient grove of trees in the dale of a local beauty spot.

In the twenty one years since, O'Riley had worked as a depth psychologist and psychotherapist, dedicating his life to helping ordinary everyday folk find their true path in life: and discovering their potential for realizing their own inner 'holy-grail' of becoming who they really were.

O'Riley had watched as Claire and John had gone on to work in parapsychology at Liverpool University, and especially at ESP. Occasionally their professional work overlapped with his; as parapsychological phenomenon are a natural by-product of examining the depths of the human soul. Any inner voyage of self-discovery that penetrates deeper than the surface of the mind inevitably uncovers these archetypal powers and processes – and O'Riley's great experience had always been on hand to assist the researchers at ESP.

Recent events however, had a different 'feeling' to them, more as they had been years before, back at the beginning, when truly evil and destructive forces had contrived to bring about the utter destruction of humankind...

John always felt at home in Prenton Lane. Maggie, O'Riley's wife was at just fifty-nine years of age still a very attractive woman. She wore her hair long: as she had all of her life – and still had her slender hour-glass figure. An original 'Hippy' in the 1960's, she'd shared her husbands' journey and through her own many trials and tribulations had matured into a very fine woman.

She greeted John with a hug: "Lovely to see you John!"

O'Riley sat down with him in the front room: their eye contact prepared them for what was to come: "Is this wise Kevin?" he asked.

"Probably not…" O'Riley replied "but, she's in a state anyway: if we don't at least try then it will simply intrude as 'unfinished business' into everything we try to do subsequently to defeat this *succubus* demon!"

John looked thoughtful: "What about going straight into a séance?"

"It'd have to be with Alfred Hulme – at least for continuity, and there's no guarantee that he'd agree. He was traumatized after last time – he nearly died remember!"

"As did Adam… hence Claire 'sparking' with him: of course, there's young-Kevin too, and his feelings about all of this."

O'Riley rubbed his chin: "About Adam? Well… as far as I know, Claire hasn't told him, and in my opinion, she shouldn't tell him, yet. If she did, it'd only add another layer of complication and stress. It'd be far better to get this sorted first, and then if she wants to tell him later she can: It'd be a difficult enough thing to deal with on its own…"

"Then it's looking like it'll be me who does the past-life regression hypnosis?"

"Yes, and I don't envy you on that. The friendship between you both may subconsciously intrude. Claire will know that: she'll also know that her own psyche may simply 'perform' and act-up to subliminal expectations. The only way we could be sure that we had a 'result' would be if something new and valuable came from it that could be verified later."

"Yeah… bog-standard post-termination follow-up research."

"Bog-standard? Hardly John, the stakes here are very high."

John accepted the point, but he still had reservations about *only* using hypnosis: "Kevin, I think we should do a double-header on this – OK firstly we attempt a past-life regression, but then, we do a séance – preferably with Alfie. It's the same protocol we followed with Adam."

O'Riley nodded: "I agree, but it'll be subject to Alfred agreeing: there are risks – obviously the same ones as last time which are more than bad enough on their own of course; but there are others…"

"And they are?"

"The effect on Claire and her marriage. Hypnosis is a powerful experience: any emotions or attachments she may trawl up for Adam as 'Adam Teal' are likely to persist after she comes back out from trance. Then, there's the effect on Adam himself. Do we even involve him? My own answer to that is definitely not – at least not yet, but what if Claire *tells* him – precisely because she can't help herself? And then there's the final question – that of Lillian… does *she* know of the emotional bond between Adam and Claire?"

Neither man could answer that…

"How do we beat her Kevin? We can't use the law, at least not yet; we have no kind of evidence that would be taken seriously."

O'Riley pondered the question: "Well, like I said last night, I may have to make contact with 'him' again…"

"The Green Man?"

"Yes, or his avatar. Trouble is I have no idea where to start. Every time he's helped us in the past, he was always there already: in the background true, but still 'there.' However, as you said yourself, he vanished years ago…"

"You could go back to the dale…" said John, referring to the mysterious Barnston Dale, site of the Green Man's Chapel from the fourteenth century poem *Sir Gawain and The Green Knight*.

"Yes I could… but something in me is holding back. I've not visited it for years. It's as if… as if…I've moved on somehow, and lost my connection to the land: almost as if the portal that had opened for me all those years ago, has closed again, and my time to benefit from that special place has passed…"

Lillian was sleeping-in to recover her physical energy from the effects of her over-night exertions. Von-Hesse didn't approve of her latest escapades – physical sex with human females was only a short step away from losing her bodily virginity to a human male – and that he could not tolerate. The prize of *Lilith*'s virginity had been promised of old to him, and to him alone – for by taking her side 'against Adam and his choice of cursed Eve' he would be given the reward of being the 'second' Adam – *Adam Kadmon* the 'father' through *Lilith* of the new human race.

He'd also been troubled by the existence of an apparently mortal threat to *Lilith* – and therefore to himself, in the shape of the elderly human male Kevin O'Riley senior. *Lilith* would not disclose the details, but gradually he was piecing things together from the few scraps of clues that she had left for him.

Accordingly, today he would take Adler and Meier out with him in the Mercedes and reconnoitre the Wirral – seeking out these 'special' places that this peculiar peninsula was said to contain – places so ancient and so deeply connected to the mysteries of the land and of the human soul, that their guardian spirits still resided there and watched closely over their chosen people.

If *Lilith* would not help him to destroy O'Riley, then he would surely take it upon his own initiative to bring about this recalcitrant psychoanalyst's death…

O'Riley and John were still working on the details of the past-life regression: "OK, we're agreed on it then Kevin, it's just a question of when, now."

"Yes, It'll depend on Claire's resources of course, but I'd say the sooner the better, and before Monday."

"Monday? You mean before tomorrow? That means today!"

O'Riley smiled: "Yes, I mean today, before we have to worry about Adam again. Now he's back at work at the Museum, Claire may just find herself going over there to see him. We should really get this out of the way – analyse the results and then move on – take the initiative… before our enemies do."

Midday and the latest news from the hospital was that Sean was doing fine with test results showing no evidence of myocardial infarction. His heart was stable and he was ready for discharge. The police had made a preliminary visit and taken a statement – sadly however Sean's drunken state, the night-time shadows and his subsequent trauma in hospital had meant that he had little memory of the attack.

There was other disturbing news on Liverpool's Radio-City however, two men in their early twenties had been found dead from knife wounds in the Wood Street area of the city. Only one victim had been identified so far – Ryan Edge of Wavertree Road. Claire listened with distress to the news bulletin thinking that the two young men must have been victims of the same gang who had brutally attacked Sean.

She could not know that Ryan Edge; leader of the gang of drug-addicted muggers who'd attacked her son – was the direct-line male descendent of one Abraham Edge – ironically also killed by Von-Hesse, some three hundred and forty-one years earlier, on that exact shore-line spot, of the old town's ancient pool...

The black Mercedes wafted along Arrowe Park Road from the direction of Upton Village. Meier was driving with Adler in the front passenger seat next to him. Seated alone in the back was Von-Hesse. Using a paranormal sensing technique derived from dowsing he passed his hand over a map of the Wirral waiting for a tell-tale 'magnetic pull' which would indicate a psychic 'hot-spot' in the landscape. He'd followed a response all the way from Oxton, which was becoming stronger by the moment: "We must be near, take the next turn left!"

The Mercedes purred into Pool Lane on the Arrowe Park estate: "Straight ahead Meier..." The road turned down suddenly to the right as a medieval church tower came into view, the church itself on a raised circular walled outcrop overlooking a large housing estate. Von-Hesse knew at once that this must be the place – the magnetic pull from his dowsing hand was at its fullest intensity: Meier, take the car to the lych gate and then stop."

The Mercedes silently rolled to a graceful halt as Von-Hesse's experienced eye scanned the church: "It says... Woodchurch Parish Church... Meier, you are the best archaeological expert amongst us... what do *you* make of this?"

Meier's eyes narrowed: "I'll take a closer look Master." Getting out he noted the circular wall – a sure sign of an ancient foundation. A brief avenue of yew tree's led from the lych-gate to a solid medieval door.

"Well?" snapped Von-Hesse from behind him.

 "Most of the building you see before us is medieval, but... the site is of great antiquity... yes *very* great antiquity."

Von-Hesse nodded: "Indeed, the energetic concentration here is *extremely* high… My clairvoyant senses… my *retro*-cognition can see…" his voice trailed off *"Mein Gott!"* The sudden outburst in German startled Meier; his master was not one temperamentally disposed to call out to 'God' in exclamation in *any* language.

"Master?" he queried.

"Never, have I seen so much in one place before, n*ever!"*

Meier watched as Von-Hesse's clairvoyant vision responded to a sight unseen by his own merely 'human' eyes.

"He has been here Meier… this O'Riley… he *and* his blood-line. But there is more, so *much* more!" Von-Hesse's breathing had become shallow as his face contorted, almost aghast at what his inner eye had revealed to him. At last turning away – "We are… fortunate… this place has been 'inactive' for some years. It is as a Cauldron of psychic and spiritual energy that periodically erupts – and then may be tapped into by those gifted enough to understand its power.

Hans Meier

We are fortunate indeed... that it is for now, beyond our enemies use..."

Meier looked again, and saw only the surface features of a medieval church on a raised mound of earth surrounded by a circular sandstone wall: "This place is *that* special?"

Von-Hesse nodded: "It is... and we must away from it! I would rather *not* disturb its sleeping spirits... See, the road names 'Pool Lane' and 'Druids Way' – they are a memory of

what was here before even this... ancient... Christian church!"

Back in the Mercedes and the Bavarian closed his eyes passing his hand again over the map. His sensitive palm picked up lesser impressions, some so faint as to hardly register, others

Gustav Adler

merely 'background level' – to the extent expected of an ancient landscape. A few registered higher, but then suddenly, just as before an intense magnetic pull drew his hand like a dowsing rod to the south west of the map: "Meier! Go back to Arrowe Park Road, and head for Barnston!"

"Today? You mean we should do it today?" Claire was taken a little aback – she'd have no time to prepare herself – but then was that a deliberate ploy on O'Riley's part? "Don't want me to get my story straight eh Kevin?" she half-joked.

O'Riley coughed: "Ahem… Maggie can watch Lizzie over at Prenton Lane: I'd recommend that young-Kevin go and pick Sean up from the hospital."

"I see… you really want to cover all the bases don't you."

"It's best Claire if you do this whilst young-Kevin is otherwise engaged. I'm sure you wouldn't want him to hear some of the things you might say?"

Claire saw the logic in that: "Yes, you're right. How about you John, are you OK with doing this?"

John nodded: "Sure love, no problem, in who else's hands would you be as safe… as in mine… eh?" he smiled.

She smiled in return: "OK, I'll get Kevin to go pick Sean up. Maggie's OK with this is she? I mean, us doing the regression hypnosis in her home whilst she entertains Lizzie?"

O'Riley laughed: "Maggie is the consummate hostess, and she's always got plenty of time to give for her granddaughter!"

"Right then… let's do it!"

The Mercedes perfectly tuned suspension allowed a most comfortable ride as Von-Hesse concentrated his mind on following the psychic reading from the map. As the journey proceeded along Barnston Road the energy field increased in amplitude until at last as the limousine descended the brief winding curves of the road passing through Barnston Dale, Von-Hesse's hand almost burned with its intensity: "Here! It's here! Meier, find a place to stop!"

Meier squirmed uncomfortably at the harsh command but as the road suddenly climbed the Fox and Hounds pub came into view on the right: "Perfect!" pronounced Von-Hesse "quickly, into the car park!"

Meier pulled the Limo across oncoming traffic and took the sudden inclined right turn. The car park was bordered by large trees and was positioned conveniently close-by the area of the Dale – from where the energy had spiked so powerfully. Von-Hesse breathed out hard as he stared out from the Mercedes double-glazed window. The hooded black-brown eyes took in every visible feature of the landscape: "It's over there – beyond the wall... I detect... a stream and a grove of tree's..."

The Bavarians got out of the car – a strange sense of foreboding gripped them as they gathered together: "Master" said Meier "I have a feeling of unease: almost anxiety about this place!"

"Me too!" said Adler.

Von-Hesse ignored them – his eyes strained to penetrate the surface features within his view: "It is the land… it reaches out to us…" he murmured. Walking towards the tree-line he suddenly stopped – the spectral outline of a large dog - a 'Harlequin' Great Dane, shimmered into clarity, its dead-looking eyes frozen like a still photograph. Von-Hesse stared quizzically at it.

Meier was puzzled: "Master? Are you alright?"

Von-Hesse realized that Meier couldn't see the spectral animal: "Yes… a predecessor of ours has left an impression of his *familiar spirit*. The creature could go no further than this. The land prevented it… How very interesting, it seems this place is shielded from certain psychic energies…"

Von-Hesse chuckled quietly to himself: "Come, we must cross the road and then over the wall and into the Dale!"

Adler and Meier exchanged unsure glances.

Von-Hesse would have none of it, snapping his fingers in the old-fashioned continental-German fashion he strode purposefully onwards.

The approaching figure puffed away on his large black pipe. A tall athletic looking man of about fifty with a mat of tight black bushy curly hair and beard: "Och gud mornin' ter ye!" he said in a border-Scot accent. Von-Hesse responded with a curt-Germanic nod.

"Is it ter the wee dale ye ah thinkin' of goin'?" asked the Scotsman through a cloud of pipe smoke. The Bavarians halted as Von-Hesse took a second look at the stranger. His mouth widened slightly into a half-smile as he saw deeply into the Scotsman's eyes: "That… is my purpose" he said quietly.

"Och tis a bonny place fer sure… even in winter-time, it's still *green*."

Von-Hesse picked up the emphasis in the Scotsman's voice: "That must make it very *magical*" he emphasised in reply.

"Aye, that it is… but it's easy fer a man ter get himself inter difficulties there… ye see… the dale… it takes ter sum folks, an' not ter others."

"That, is what I intend to find out for myself!" replied Von-Hesse curtly.

The Scot chuckled: "Och gud day ter ye then!" Giving a slight bow Von-Hesse walked on. Meier and Adler followed, with Adler having a last look over his shoulder at the stranger:

"Eh!?"

Adler's outcry drew Von-Hesse's irritated attention: "What is it now?"

"That man, he's vanished! Vanished from the middle of an open car park!"

Von-Hesse shook his head: "That 'man' was *never* there Adler… have you learned nothing in your years following me?"

"A ghost?" Adler's face betrayed his fears.

"In his case… yes. I recognised his 'form' immediately. It has been perhaps twenty or so years since he passed-over into spirit."

"But Master… he warned us about the dale!"

Von-Hesse looked at Adler like he was an uncomprehending child: "In life, he was known to the man O'Riley senior, as one of his earthy mentors… Of course he tried to prevent us from approaching the dale… there is *something* quite extraordinary there, and I want to find out just what it is!"

Claire arrived at the O'Riley household in Prenton Lane in trepidation, but feeling about as ready as ever she would for the coming attempt at past-life regression hypnosis. Maggie had prepared in advance to keep Lizzie company. Despite her years she related naturally and well with young-people and could draw easily on her own youthful experiences. John however was more anxious even that Claire. He was a very competent hypnotist, but Claire was no naive subject. His approach would have to take that into account, and be novel and unpredictable.

O'Riley had provided dual tape-recording facilities and a high definition digital video-camera: it would be important to have an accurate record of events: "All's ready John" he announced.

The room was darkened with Claire seated comfortably in a reclining leather armchair. Giving John an acknowledging nod of assent – she closed her eyes and waited passively to hear the sound of his voice…

Von-Hesse had reached the old sandstone wall that bordered the dale from Barnston Road. Sensitive, he'd already picked up invisible tendrils of psychic energy probing his mind, and now even his body. His two companions were reacting to the same intruding force but they didn't have Von-Hesse's iron mental constitution: "Master!" Adler was feeling dizzy "My mind, it is spinning!"

"Nonsense, resist it! It seeks to undermine you through fear!"

"I can't…" Adler had now broken out into a trembling cold sweat

Meier was hyperventilating – his chest tightening with each step. Von-Hesse was implacable: "Over the wall: both of you!"

They made a cursory attempt at responding but at last he could see that his order was impossible for them to obey. A minute more and they'd be reduced to gibbering idiots: "Damn! Back to the car then, both of you!" Cussing, the iron-willed Bavarian climbed over the wall and brushed aside the winter bushes. Having disappeared from their view, his two companions gratefully obeyed their last order and retreated back to the Mercedes.

Von-Hesse continued on and noted how the sparse winter bushes at the periphery of the dale gradually transformed into greenery as he probed deeper and deeper. Despite himself, the hair on the back of his neck raised and tingled as he saw trees in what appeared to be their full summers spread of green leaves. His feet became entangled as he tried to push through the thickening greenery – ahead he could hear a babbling brook: "Not far now!" he exclaimed

John knew that Claire's psyche would try to second-guess his induction technique. She was experienced enough to be able to do that – even though it could defeat her own purpose. Such 'involuntary resistance' was common in people familiar with hypnosis. John had the added disadvantage of being her long-time friend and colleague. It was always easier to be hypnotized by someone you didn't know – someone you couldn't put up any 'personal' barriers to.

"When you're ready, just allow yourself to *go inside*" John's instruction put the ball in Claire's court. So long as he was patient, she'd dictate the pace – that way whatever resistance came up would at least be minimal.

O'Riley kept in the shadows and out of Claire's line of sight, but nevertheless giving the process his whole attention.

Claire's eyes blinked. She knew that this was a signal from within, that her unconscious mind was ready. For a moment she wondered if she should test its resolve by resisting, but no sooner had the thought crossed her mind than her eyelids felt heavy and tired. Going with it, she closed her eyes but strained to keep her eyes staring as if straight ahead from behind her lids. John saw the motion of her eyes and noted its significance as a degree of subliminal resistance. Nevertheless, it gave him something to work with.

"Now... Claire, one of your eye-balls will start to feel *heavier* than the other, so heavy that it will want to drift down and to one side behind your eyelids."

He was giving her an apparent choice – she could notice and then allow 'one' of her eyes to sink down behind her eyelids... But of course, if one goes, then both will go... In a moment of preoccupation Claire's mind tried to make the choice and then experienced the impossibility of it: her left eye started to move as she 'let-go' of the desire to keep it staring straight ahead – and almost immediately her right eye followed.

"I'm *not* speaking to Claire... Claire needn't listen to my voice, rather... I'm speaking to another part of the deep unconscious mind... a part that lives in memory... memory of a time that is... that *was*... past..."

This was a far more rapid attempt at accessing the part of Claire's mind that 'remembered' a possible past-life than she had anticipated. John, she thought, was always slower and more paced than that. This was just a sufficient amount of the unexpected to open the door to her soul.

Her body suddenly convulsed in a groan as she let go of being 'Claire'

Von-Hesse found his way far more difficult with each attempt he made to penetrate the living greenery. Imperceptibly at first the branches began to lengthen and entwine his feet and legs. A sense of alarm gripped The Bavarian as suddenly his arms were wrapped tightly to his body, His feet left the ground as he was spun like a cotton reel – passed from branch to branch and bush to bush –so rapidly did he twist and turn that he was compelled to slump limply into unconsciousness…

His first sensation was of a damp, wet and rough surface chaffing through the thickness of his black Abercrombie overcoat. Through his tightly closed eyelids a slow methodically blinking light shone – orange-yellow in colour it drew his attention until curiosity at last opened his eyes.

With some surprise he found himself staring up and behind him at a car hazard warning light. Looking back to his left he saw the other, together making a flashing pair, His hands stretched out and felt the rough road surface – confirming the sensation he'd felt through his back. Moving to sit up and turn around the deep rumble of a car's engine filled his ears as the first of a short line of vehicles passed to the offside of the car parked besides him.

"You alright mate?"

Von-Hesse looked to see the concerned face of a man in his thirties. The Bavarian quickly scanned his visage and read him as no threat.

"Thought yer'd been knocked down! I've called up for an ambulance on me iPhone!"

Von-Hesse ignored him. Hauling himself to his feet he found that he was in Barnston Road as it crossed the bottom of the dale. Nodding to himself in understanding he re-orientated himself to the task of returning to the Mercedes.

"Oi wha about the ambulance?!" said the Good Samaritan.

Von-Hesse looked around and having ascertained that no one was about – he cruelly discharged his frustration by striking the man with a 'Karate' style chop to the throat: "Indeed, it would be a shame to waste an ambulance call… so have this one on me!"

The irritated Bavarian strode purposefully back to the pub car park leaving the Good Samaritan lying stone dead the bonnet of his own car.

Claire's face showed the birth pains of her 'other' self as she drifted in to awareness from the far recesses of her psyche. John knew that proper timing was all important now. If he questioned her too soon, then the past-life personality may become lost in confusion – too late and the moment may likewise be missed.

At last, although not exactly gone, the convulsions settled – and John seized the moment with a question bland enough to direct the attention of the emerging personality: "What can you see?"

"See: see sayeth thee?"

Both John and O'Riley felt their bodies tingle at the sound of her words. John always likened past-life regression voices to receiving a message from an alien civilization: "Yes… before your eyes now…" By *not* asking the voice if it recognised him, John was keeping the process focused on Claire's on-going and immediate *internal* experience – keeping her concentrated on whatever it was she could see at that moment – rather than to test Claire's reaction to him as a hypnotist.

"I see mine home, tis in… Liverpool Town…"

"And your name is?"

"Sarah… Sarah Teal, wife of …" Claire's voice trailed away into muttering.

Rather than pursue the obvious, John asked a clarifying background question: "What was your maiden name Sarah, your family name before you were married?"

"Mine family name? twas Tennyson… Tennyson of Birkdale."

"Sarah Tennyson, from Birkdale in Lancashire?"

Claire nodded.

"What year were you married Sarah?"

"1670" came the clear as day reply.

O'Riley was making handwritten notes as she spoke – 'Five years after the plague…' he mused silently to himself.

"Tell me about your husband…"

Claire's face lit up: "Oh he be a fine young reformed Christian man! Good in business – he hath taken over from the family of Matthew Hopgood – after they didst die from the Great Plague. Now, he doth make import and export of goods with the colonies."

"The colonies?"

"Aye, New England!"

John looked over to O'Riley. He hadn't yet asked the obvious question. O'Riley saw the purpose in John's eyes and nodded in agreement.

"Sarah, can you tell me your husband's name?"

"Adam! Adam the love of mine life!"

Claire's face was radiant as if she had shed the years back from middle-age to glowing youth.

"Adam Teal?"

"Yes!"

"Thank you Sarah… now I want you to move forward in time… to a time and place where you are comfortable and safe… comfortable… and safe… still as Sarah Teal. When you are ready, you can tell me what you can see."

Claire smiled: "Children… young Jonathan and Benjamin!"

"You have two sons?"

"I do… they are as Adam is: tall and strong and godly in their reformed Christian faith!"

John decided to risk a deeper line of questioning about her relationship with her husband: "You and Adam… you are very much in love?"

Claire's body jolted again – this time her head moved sharply from side to side – but there was no verbal answer from her. John recognised its significance and probed further: "Sarah, you can *allow* yourself to tell me…"

"Adam… hath loved another afore me… not with his body, but he didst within his heart…"

"Who was this Sarah?"

"I curseth her vile name!" Claire spat her words venomously "She was called *Lilith*… *Lilith* Hopgood… she bewitched mine poor Adam with enchantments!"

"But he loves you now doesn't he?"

She nodded slowly "Yet shalt I always be as second in his heart? I fear very much that he hath kept her memory fondly unto himself… I saw her once… when I was in Liverpool afore I knew my Adam… She was so young, and *so* very beautiful… Her hair was endless, her face as perfect as porcelain…" All the men-folk wanted her, for they were beguiled!

John stopped himself from being gratuitous over 'Sarah's' feelings for Adam. She'd made that obvious by saying that he was the love of her life. He also wanted to avoid amplifying any post-hypnotic attachment 'Claire' may feel for 'Adam'.

"Thank you Sarah… can you move forward in time, once again… to a time when you are comfortable and safe… comfortable… and… safe…"

John inserted the suggestions about being 'comfortable & safe' in order to try and avoid 'Sarah' from reliving any trauma in her life through Claire's mind and body. Hypnotists are often piously simple in their beliefs about the safeguards they attempt to build in – today, John, despite his concerns that Claire could violently abreact was no different.

'Sarah' however – had intentions of her own…

Von-Hesse reached the car park at the Fox and Hounds pub and found his two Bavarian compatriots waiting anxiously for him: "Master?" Adler looked disbelievingly at his uncharacteristically soiled overcoat and generally dishevelled appearance. Von-Hesse was not amused. Despite years of military service in all manner of climates and conditions, he was proud of his 'everyday' persona and liked not a single hair out of its immaculately groomed place: "Silence! Silence… and listen… I have… confirmation of the secret of that place. It is *very* interesting. I did not know that *he* was the guardian spirit of this land."

"He, Master?" Meier queried for clarification.

"Yes, Meier… you will know him from your archaeological studies and from the history of the Romans – that dale is in Latin appropriately called: *DEO VRIDI SANCTO* 'To the Holy God *Viridios*' the Chapel of the *Green-Man!*"

"*Viridios?* Ah! The masculine deity of 'verdure' of vigorous lush greenness and vegetation: that the Romans discovered in ancient Celtic Britain!" Meier's education hadn't been wasted.

"The same, but he has many other names… now commonly called… 'The Green Man'. Understand this… *both* of you: he is the enemy of our Mistress – *Lilith* – *Lilith* who's elemental spirit is the very earth and its soil. What grows within soil may thus be destroyed *by* soil… Only one of them can survive the coming contest, so mote it be!"

John waited as patiently as was required as Sarah fast-forwarded through the events of her life. Internally Claire watched the flickering images like the frames of a speeded-up silent movie. At last 'Sarah' gave out a mournful cry as Claire's back arched up from the recliner.

"Sarah? Sarah… tell me what's happening!" John was concerned now that his safeguard had failed, or had even been intentionally by-passed.

"I am… I am…" The words faltered from Claire's gasping mouth.

"Yes Sarah?"

"I am… abed. I am abed… I am dying…"

"John! Bring her back!" O'Riley dramatically interrupted."

A twinge of fear struck at John's belly as he composed himself: Sarah, you are going back *from* that time, back to a happier time, a happier place…"

Claire's head shook as her face betrayed a cold sweat: "No! I *am* happy! I am to be with my beloved, with Adam!"

"Adam has already…?" John couldn't find a suitable word for 'died'… he was very concerned now that his question may reinforce 'Sarah' into re-enacting her death agony through Claire's living body.

"I wouldst join him! He hath told me that his death *hath not* parted us! In mine dreams, he comes unto me: death hath not parted us… I shalt join him, be again with my beloved Adam, be with him *forever*!"

O'Riley was leaning forward urgently in his seat: "John disassociate her from Sarah *now*, bring Claire back!"

"Claire… listen to my voice… only my voice…"

But Claire wasn't listening, Claire had *become* Sarah…

John desperately tried all that he knew to anchor Claire back to his guiding voice: but Sarah was now too strongly associated: and in effect now *possessed* Claire's body:

"I *must* be with Adam!"

"Claire… you *will* listen to my voice… separate yourself from the memories Claire… you are married to *Kevin,* you live in 2006, you have two children; Sean and Lizzie…"

"No! I'm Sarah, Sarah Teal, I must *die* and be with Adam!"

Claire's breathing became laboured. John looked to O'Riley in desperation.

"Sarah! If you truly love Adam, go back to him 'in life' now, and free Claire!" O'Riley commanded.

John looked askance at O'Riley.

"No!"

"Sarah! Adam would not want you to hurt Claire… let her go… go back in your memory to the happy beginning of your romance together – relive the memory, *allow* yourself to remain there in peace, and *allow* Claire to come back to *her* body… for Adam, Sarah… do it for your love of Adam…"

John watched in amazement as O'Riley's commands led to a calming of Claire's breath, and a relaxation of her body, until with a slump, she entered a clam and peaceful hypnotic sleep:

"Ahem, back to you John…" said O'Riley apologetically.

John gave him a grateful smile of acknowledgement: "Now Claire... rest contented and happy; allow yourself all the time you need to return back to your normal consciousness – being completely safe... safe and well..."

She slept for twenty minutes whilst her body recovered its composure; and her mind its stability...

Von-Hesse arrived back at Lake Hall in Oxton looking not only the worse for wear, but increasingly care-worn as he pondered his discoveries. Last time he had been in Liverpool, he had known nothing of those ancient, sacred places. *Lilith* had mocked him for his ignorance of the localities *special* features and that had spurned him to reconnoitre the area, but what he found was utterly beyond his expectation. Meier asked the obvious question: "Master... does The Mistress know of those supernatural sites?"

The Bavarian nodded grimly: "She must do, Meier... her sentience is without bounds in such things."

Meier was troubled: "Then, she knew what danger we were in, simply by approaching them?"

"Of course" came the curt Germanic reply.

"Doesn't that make you feel... well... a little angry?"

Von-Hesse glanced at his student. He was never a *little* angry – it was all or nothing: "Not angry Meier, but *concerned*. You see, the Mistress likes to amuse herself, sometimes at our expense; sometimes at the expense of others. To my taste such diversions are trivial in their motivation... *I*... am serious minded, and work tirelessly to achieve my goals. That is why I have survived for as long as I have."

Curiosity moved Adler's lips: "How long is that precisely Master? You've never actually told us."

A knowing smile smoothed The Bavarian's handsome features: How long? How long...." His voice trailed as his mind recalled the passing centuries with their processions of events, personae, strife, achievements... and... frustrations; "I have seen many things, too many to tell off. Suffice to say I first knew this land, this England... before their precious Great-Charter was delivered to their King..."

"Great Charter? You mean The *Magna Carta* – of 1215!?" asked Meier, in surprise.

"Yes... I mean precisely that, but... that was in my 'middle years.' Now enough of this, we must speak with the Mistress, I would compose a plan for dealing with our enemies!"

Claire's eyes had opened but she felt no great desire to move.

No one spoke.

As well as giving her the necessary time to come back to normal consciousness – the two men had taken time to analyse their own reactions to what had happened. Everyone was shaken...

Claire spoke first: "I need... I need to know more John."

John shifted in his chair: "Not another regression hypnosis Claire, this one was a little too close for comfort!"

"You're telling me!" she exclaimed "No, not another hypnotic regression, but maybe a séance, like we did for Adam?"

O'Riley interjected: "I doubt that Alfred would agree Claire, and it would really *have* to be him if anyone – just for continuity's sake. We need to remember that two people suffered cardiac arrest last time! Not something to be taken lightly."

Claire nodded: "I understand Kevin, but I have to do this, even if I have to find another medium."

"Alfie's the best there is, he's well known to us and has always proven reliable. It'd take months or even years to check-out and accredit another medium up to his standards" said John.

"You feel that strongly Claire?" asked O'Riley.

"I do… yes" she sighed… OK then, I'll have to ask him myself…"

O'Riley nodded in acceptance. "Claire should at least have the opportunity to ask; if Alfie agrees, then he accepts the risks: anyway… we need to meet up tomorrow morning to de-brief. Meanwhile – Sean's probably home by now!" he smiled.

Lillian was waiting patiently for the Bavarian trio. As Von-Hesse had said, she liked to amuse herself by watching people struggle to discover the truth – even if those people were her very own supporters and their enforced curiosity had put them into danger: "Ah Maximilian: my you are resourceful aren't you? How well you used your occult skills! You actually managed to find the two most significant of Wirral's *five* 'special' locations!" She was smiling broadly.

Adler and Meier exchanged a nervous glance – it was as if she had been watching them all along…

"Mistress… I thank you for your… compliment, but… what I have found out requires our utmost and most urgent attention!"

"Dear Maximilian…" she smiled "always so impatient to kill and destroy aren't you?"

The frustration level was in danger of exceeding The Bavarian's tolerances: "Mistress! We have O'Riley, the medium Alfred Hulme, and now I discover that the *two* most powerful occult and supernatural places in this damnable country are here on our very doorstep – *and* they are hostile to our purpose!"

"The church, Maximilian, is indeed as Meier deduced, and you 'sensed' of great antiquity... it is built upon a natural sandstone outcrop that once contained a deep, black watered pool, and a grove of sacred Druid's oaks. The church was built over the site when the Christians, in their fear, attempted to suppress the 'old faith' of these islands. The pool, and outcrop were a cauldron, Maximilian – known to the ancients as The Cauldron of Britain, and... The Cauldron of Rebirth."

"That which became the Christian's Holy Grail?!"

"Yes, and not a common cup or chalice, but set within the very land itself. You should have studied the local myths – all you'd have needed to know is writ there for anyone to find, if they would only but look and see..ha ha ha!"

"Then it *is* connected to O'Riley senior?" queried Von Hesse.

"Indeed it is: you see, he is the hereditary 'Keeper' of The Cauldron – and its secrets, hence his mentor is that cursed 'Leaf Head' – *Viridios* whose 'Green Chapel' you entered both uninvited and unwisely. But O'Riley has lost his connection to the land, and *Viridios* dares not to stand openly against me. As O'Riley loses his will to fight, he will sicken and die, the only way he can – by his own hand, or more precisely, by his own loss of heart...

When our victory here is complete, I will turn this Wirral peninsula – once the sacred enclosed retreat of a Celtic heroes into the *New* Garden of Eden... then..."

"Then I will stand with you against *him* in the final battle?"

"Him? Yes... against him... the self-styled *Rex Mundi* of this physical world...and perhaps too, even against my brother..."

Von Hesse straightened: "*Lucien*... will he return?" but then refocusing on more pressing matters "However unless we act, against the medium, Hulme: and against O'Riley and his clan, directly – then we may not prevail long enough for the final battle!"

Lillian tilted her head in her inimitable coquettish style: "For a soldier of great experience you are both a poor strategist and negligent tactician Maximilian."

"Mistress?"

"Our enemies are divided, disconnected and so unable to rally their collective strength against us. When *we* move fully against them, it shall be in such force that they cannot resist us! Not for us to be trifling about with irrelevant distractions. My strength grows daily, and before their mid-winter Christmas festival I shall release my contagion – and that, Maximilian, will be their doom…"

Von-Hesse didn't reply. He'd heard his mistress, and he'd understood her reasoning: but he was now resolved to act quite independently.

Target practice would help his meditations…

Adam managed to drag himself into work on time despite his now constant preoccupation with *Lilith*. He found a sullen-in-mood Dr Claudia Moore, head in hands at her desk: "Hi Claudia, you look cheerful... er not..."

Claudia slowly raised her eyes to meet his and sighed.

Then Adam put both feet so deeply into it that they emerged in Sydney Opera House: "Cheer up Claudia: anyone would think you'd gone an' got yerself pregnant and didn't know how it'd all happened, or... even who the father was!" he enthused.

"*How* did you know!?" came her both irritated and astonished reply.

"Eh? Wha? I wuz just jokin' that's all! Tryin ter cheer yer up!" he said waving his arms about theatrically.

Her face showed more than a lack of engagement with his breezy sense of humour.

"Crikey: yer serious aren't yer!" he gawped.

Claudia slumped back in her chair: "It doesn't make sense! I have *no* idea how it could have happened, it's all out of phase with my cycle – I've just had my period and now... I'm putting on weight, and I've got all those... symptoms!"

"Oh don't worry: yer always like that! Moody... yer know... that kinda stuff..." he smiled pathetically.

"When you grow up Adam you'll make a very good 'man'!"

"Really? I will? Wow thanks!"

"Get out Adam."

"Eh?"

"Go take the morning off!"

"Oh… OK… by the way, is it a girl or a boy? Adam's a good name fer a baby boy – the 'first man' an all that!"

Despite her familiarity with Adam's idiosyncrasies and harmless intent, Claudia was incredulous: "What! It's early days Adam, how on *earth* would I know what sex it is?"

 "Can I be the God Father?"

Little of course did either know, but the pregnancy wasn't even human…

 "Out!"

Receiving no further reply, Adam did as his supervisor had told him; he put his stuff away and headed for the main entrance.

Claire had taken the day off work. She needed to recover from her traumatic past-life regression hypnosis – and, she had to be there at home for her son Sean. Maggie had kindly helped by driving Lizzie to school at Wirral Grammar. Young Kevin had gone into work to follow up any further news on the investigation into the assault on Sean, only to find that the double knife-murder in Liverpool's club-land had taken up all available resources. Believing that the two incidents were probably related, but as yet having no idea in just what way, he'd accepted the facts as they stood and stoically got on with his day-to-day police responsibilities. For Claire this was to be a day of reflection. Sean, despite his ordeal, was still fixed in that altered state of consciousness he'd been in since first captivated by the ethereal Lillian. Claire had a fight on her hands to reach him *and* to face up to the after-effects of discovering her apparently former-life as the seventeenth century wife of one Adam Teal… aka Adam Mitchell…

O'Riley made a mid-morning visit to the home of Alfred Hulme in North Road. Reasoning that time was of the essence he knew that although Claire was exhausted after her recent ordeal, that they must maintain the initiative. If they faltered now, then their enemies would certainly gain the advantage. Walking up the path to the impressive Edwardian house, he wondered how his request for a second séance would be received.

His answer came in the form of wizened old psychic door-keeper: Bridget; native of County Sligo in Ireland and near impermeable barrier to accessing the great mediums presence: "You'll need to make an appointment Mr O'Riley!" came the opening salvo.

O'Riley smiled; Bridget was Alfred's equivalent of his very own Susan, the doorkeeper to the psychoanalytic mysteries in Rodney Street: "Thanks Bridget, but this is an emergency."

The wizened face cracked into lines forged by decades of sentry duty: "It's *always* an emergency Mr O'Riley; no one ever comes here for any other reason! I'll tell Alfred that you called, he'll ring you when he's free."

"It's life or death Bridget!" O'Riley emphasized.

The wizened eyes narrowed as if in synchrony with her narrowing patience: "As you well know Mr O'Riley, Alfred is a spiritual healer and not just a psychic medium – *all* of his work is a matter of life or death!"

Chewing on his lip O'Riley was about to give up. Short of making a forced entry he wasn't going to get past the formidable Bridget: "It's OK Bridget, I've been expecting Kevin." O'Riley looked with relief past the doorkeeper as the familiar smiling visage of Alfred Hulme popped around the door: "Old Jock told me what you lot had been up to!" he said: "I did warn you not to mess about with all that hypnosis nonsense!"

O'Riley broke into a huge grin – this was going to be Alfie at his best…

Over at ESP John was busy following the now well-trodden research lines on the internet genealogy websites: ancestry.com and familysearch.org. Sure enough, by re-tracing the already established path back to Adam Teal, he was quickly able to find some brief records concerning his wife Sarah Tennyson: "So… she *did* exist!" With the evidence finally before him, John's reserved nature now allowed him to contemplate the implications: "Bloody hell… we've got ourselves a three hundred and forty year old love-triangle!"

That morning, Lillian had left Lake Hall as early as 7.00am. Normally Von-Hesse would have been nervous at his Mistress going out so early without telling him what she was up to – not that Lillian ever felt obliged to justify her movements to anyone – but today he was grateful for her being otherwise engaged as he wanted some time alone and undisturbed with his alchemical equipment. Adler was curious about his mentor's activity: "Master, you are preparing something?"

Von-Hesse was irritated by the question but this soon passed as he explained his purpose: "Indeed… I am preparing a chemical toxin for use against an enemy."

"A poison?"

"Yes… a poison against a psychic opponent who would otherwise be protected against occult procedures. Its effects will of course be fatal."

"Won't that arouse suspicion?"

"The death will appear natural – the toxin will break down almost immediately."

"Does the Mistress know?"

"She does not, but of course she will eventually as nothing ultimately is beyond her omniscience."

Lillian had been paying discrete visits to her farmed victims – ensuring that their 'pregnancies' were developing without hindrance. The girls would proceed to term rapidly – within a few weeks – giving every appearance of theirs being a previously undetected or even a concealed pregnancy. None of her victims – apart from Claudia were already mothers, making this far easier to suggest to families or boyfriends. As the pregnancy progressed the 'host' mothers psyche would become attuned to the demands of their demon foetus, forcing them to defend the growing beast and to care for it until shortly after the birth.

The demonic children would have the appearance of being human, but would rapidly grow into *Lilith*'s monstrous functionaries. These chimeras would not be the 'new human race' of *Lilith*'s ambition but an elemental sub-species; familiar to times and cultures past as demons, witches *incubi* and *succubae*: the hand maidens and servants of their mistress.

This 'first wave' of chimera births would be timed with the spread of the pandemic contagion, at which point the 'New Adam' would be impregnating *Lilith* with his seed so that she may incubate it, and then pass it on to other especially selected host mothers. *Lilith*'s insemination by her New Adam' would be 'natural' not astral, and he who was chosen would thus become the father of the new race of humans.

Von-Hesse had worked for centuries for this privilege, but The Bavarian had reckoned without the power of an emotion hitherto absent from his Mistress – love.

Leaving the museum, Adam had crossed from William Brown Street and into Dale Street; unconsciously directed to tread the modern road surface of old-Liverpool town. He was glad to be out in the fresh air – even if it was late November. In a dream – as usual - as Dale Street reached the junction of Castle Street and Water Street – his mind felt the pull of far memory, and gradually his ruminations on Lillian became 'recent' memories of *Lilith*… as Adam… once again, became 'Adam Teal'…

"Good mornin' Adam Teal!"

He stumbled and tripped as he heard the soft, feminine voice. In a heap at her feet he looked up at her lovely pre-Raphaelite face: "*Lilith*!"

She held out her warm porcelain perfect hand and hauled him to his feet. Their eyes met, and they embraced. He gasped as his whole body tingled with love for her. *Lilith*'s caressing hands took his shape into her mind, cherishing her most human moment of affection.

In her unguarded and all too human state, *Lilith*'s supernatural eyes failed to penetrate Adam's heart. If she had done so, then in a corner reserved especially for her, she would have found Sarah… Sarah, as Claire…

"A séance Kevin? There are alternatives you know."

"There are?" O'Riley had been allowed to cross the portal and into Alfred's private living quarters above his healing sanctuary – and was enjoying a morning cuppa courtesy of the irritated and chastised Bridget.

"Yes, a simple 'reading' for example. There would be less chance of an upset like last time…"

"Would it be as accurate, or, productive?"

"Yes, it could be."

"Could be?" O'Riley didn't favour a 'could-be' what was required now was a guaranteed certainty. Alfred sensed his disappointment and turned the proverbial tables: "I had hoped that you'd have fallen back on your own resources Kevin."

O'Riley knew immediately what he had meant; then sighing he said: "I haven't been there in some years; I don't even know now, how, if at all, that I'd be received."

Alfred smiled: "Your covenant will last longer than life Kevin."

O'Riley smiled ironically in return: "I'm afraid I've got 'form' for breaking my covenant Alfie. In the past, I got myself into very hot water for it. I'm not a little troubled by the possibility that my subsequent neglect of it has brought about its end."

Alfred's sixth sense formed an impression: "Shakespeare… Henry IV…" he murmured.

"Ha: you really are a mind reader Alfred! Yes, that's been in my thoughts: that quote from Henry IV, Part I Act-3;

Glendower: I can call spirits from the vasty deep.

Hotspur: Why, so can I, or so can any man;
But will they come when you do call for them?"

Alfred chuckled: "That's the well-known bit, but it continues;

Glendower: Why, I can teach you, cousin, to command
The devil.

Hotspur: And I can teach thee, coz, to shame the devil—
By telling the truth. Tell truth and shame the devil…"

"Tell the truth?" quizzed O'Riley.

"Yes, it's the one thing you can't expect from that demon. She will have a golden tongue fer sure, but don't hold out for any open truth from it."

"How will 'shaming' her with the truth help?"

"How? Oh that's easy! She'll rely on her allies whilst she's building up her strength. The truth of course is that she'll deceive and use all of them, casting them aside when they're no longer needed. Strike now, work on them with the 'truth' and if possible turn them against her!"

"Her allies? Do I even know who they all are? There's The Bavarian – that Von-Hesse fellow… and, I suppose even Adam Mitchell now, as he's so obviously in love with her."

"They'll be the main one's Kevin: both men who are potential consorts for her. But they're natural rivals too. Play them off, if you can. Von-Hesse is *very* dangerous, but that could be to your advantage. If he can be turned against his mistress…"

O'Riley smiled: "Alfie I never took you for such a schemer!"

"Ha! Well you see Kevin that's my point about the last quotes from Shakespeare. You asked for a séance – perhaps to 'command' the Devil – so to speak. But the second part of the quote suggests another way…

O'Riley drifted off into trance staring at the pattern in Alfred's living room carpet: "She said that we *can't* beat her Alfie… and that she can devastate and destroy even my old mentors…"

"And you believe her?"

"I really don't know this time. She's an unknown quantity, virtually a stranger to me. Every time I've had to battle against evil on a grand scale before – I've always *known* who and what I was up against. This time… it's somehow different."

Alfred looked closely at O'Riley as he processed his deepest thoughts. Then, on an intuition he said: "Very well Kevin, you can tell Claire that she can have her séance."

"Alfred!" exclaimed Bridget in protest.

Alfie took Bridget's hand and soothed her: "Shush now Bridget. It'll be alright, we'll more than have the measure of our 'friends' this time. So… then, what could possibly go wrong eh?"

That evening Claire was preparing herself for a séance centred not on Adam, but on *her*. O'Riley had telephoned from Liverpool and told her that Alfred was willing to help – that very evening – O'Riley had suggested strongly to Claire that it should be sooner rather than later. His reasoning had considered both Claire's fatigued state, which could be an advantage in that she'd have an already lowered threshold of consciousness: and the fact that they simply couldn't afford to wait any longer before Lillian gained her full strength.

After the meeting with Alfred, O'Riley had headed to ESP and brought John up to date. They knew the risks; whatever came up could be so strongly identified with by Claire, that her marriage may even fall apart – never mind the more obvious dangers of triggering an occult reaction from their opponents.

Lizzie and Sean went with Young Kevin to be with Maggie at Prenton Lane, where the house itself – being 'protected' offered a degree of safety for them. This occult protection had been conferred many years previously and had never been breached. Satisfied that as much had been done as could have been done, Claire waited for John to pick her up and take her to North Road. Her mind was racing; confused between her professionalism and love for her family and her 'other' love, one that was now reaching across the centuries to claim her.

This time, Adam was *not* to be involved in the séance; he wasn't even to be informed about it. Lillian's reach was far too deep for him to be entrusted with the information. Officially, the purpose of the séance was to uncover and identify the complex web of interrelationships between Claire, Adam and Lillian, and to gain whatever intelligence they could to help them defeat her. Unofficially of course, it was an indulgence for Claire's highly charged emotions of attachment to Adam: and of course, young-Kevin was not told about his wife's new found romantic and sexual affection for him…

John and O'Riley could only hope that they'd be skilful enough: and lucky enough; to manage the process…

Lillian had spent the day and now the evening with Adam. Quite distracted from her other tasks, she'd allowed herself to enjoy being a normal human girl. She'd shopped for food and was now cooking some exotic French cuisine for him. Adam was elated. He'd been given the day off work, spent it with the love of his life and now here she was back at his humble flat cooking up a special evening meal. Life he thought just didn't get better than this: "Where did you learn to cook French food Lillian?"

Lillian's Mona-Lisa smile was at its most appealing: "Oh… I've travelled a lot and learned things here and there. My friend Maximilian likes French cuisine – especially from the Languedoc in the south-west. This is a Languedoc recipe."

The mention of Von-Hesse's name chilled Adam out from his elation: "Maximilian? You mean The Bavarian, Von-Hesse?"

Lillian's coquettish pose betrayed some slight irritation with her lover: "Oh Adam you know Maximilian isn't really Bavarian: he just likes to use that crafted Germanic persona to intimidate people; and now he's become so fond of it that he's long forgotten who he really was!"

The chill spread through his body as he recalled his séance: "Lillian… all of this scares me; I don't understand what's going on. People tell me that you're some kind of evil force and that you want ter repopulate the world or somethin' I don't get it… me heads done-in with it all…"

Lillian wrapped her arms around him and held him close so that her firm pert breasts pressed against his chest. His fear started to melt immediately: "Adam… you *know* the truth about me… you always did. You've remembered our past life together – when you were Adam and I was *Lilith*… you've remembered your love for me then and how I made my promise to you that we'd be together in future life-times…"

Her voice was so soft, so seductive, so full of love. He turned his head from resting on her shoulder and caught the full beauty of her almond shaped opalescent green eyes. At that moment, his heart opened fully, not just as Adam Mitchell, but also as Adam Teal. Lillian saw the enduring love he had for her – the love that had returned his forlorn soul to this earthly plane after more than three centuries. She saw that he was indeed her 'New Adam' her true choice – but then, in a quiet corner of his heart, outside even of his own awareness, she saw Sarah…

Claire's mouth was dry as she walked up the path to Alfred's house in North Road. Physically and emotionally drained by the scale and pace of recent events, this was to be yet one more great demand on her resources. John put his arm reassuringly around her shoulder: "We're all with you on this Claire."

"Thanks…" she smiled faintly "I don't know how I'll handle what may come up – I just know that whatever it is, I *have* to know."

Bridget, ever the guardian of the portal was tight lipped. Resigned but unwelcoming she moved to one side as John and

Claire passed into the hallway. O'Riley called from the third floor landing: "Come up folks!" John led the way, drawing Claire away from Bridget's unhelpfully draining energy.

Alfred joined O'Riley on the landing to greet them: "Don't worry, Bridget is just over-protective of me… she'll join us in due course. When she sees that Old-Jock is happy with things then she'll come round."

Claire smiled as best she could: "Thanks Alfie, I realize how much of your energy this'll take."

Alfred smiled in return: "It's OK love, I've known you these many years; you've a good heart… the spirits will help you I'm sure!"

As reassured as she could be, Claire went in to the séance room.

Lillian's penetrating vision had now read deeply into his heart. She settled back and slightly away from his arms, their embrace fading: "So… you got married after I'd gone… I never knew…"

 "Wha?" Adam was still in his present day mode; he hadn't a clue what she meant.

Lillian looked deeper still: "Her name… yes, I can see it… Sarah… Sarah Tennyson."

Adam suddenly went weak at the knees as 'Adam Teal' remembered within him: "Sarah, yes… I can see her too, I *remember* her!"

The reluctant if not quite recalcitrant Bridget had joined the little circle round the old Edwardian table. The heavy folded curtains blocked out the streetlights below and helped muffle the sound of passing traffic. The sitters joined hands as the now familiar voice of Monte Rey singing 'Absent Friends' wafted out from the brass horned Parlophone record player. The almost inaudible hum of an infra-sound vibration struck deeply at Claire's already worn nerves – her adrenal-glands dumped their hormones into her bloodstream as a feeling of terror gripped her. John was seated to her left and O'Riley to her right. Both felt her hands break out into a cold sweat. O'Riley's steady hand held hers firmly, but John's subconscious fears that Claire may not be strong enough to endure the ordeal made his own hand weaken.

Alfred's eyes suddenly closed as he took his customary sharp intake of breath – his nostrils flaring widely giving his features a grotesque form, as cast in the flickering candlelight. Suddenly the Scottish accented voice of 'Old-Jock' – Alfred's spirit-guide boomed through the mediums gaping, motionless mouth: "Och tis good ter see ye again this evenin mah friends'!"

"Thank you Jock!" replied Bridget.

"Ah feel that Alfie is not in such good heath tonight, he's a wee bit drained so he is aye! But… he has a question fer me?"

Bridget shook and swept an indignant glance around the visiting sitters at Old-Jock's comment about Alfred's health: "He's not recovered from last time Jock… I advised against another sitting for these people, but he insisted!"

"Och, if Alfie's happy then ye shud be too Bridget! I see tha' someone *important* is missin' since last time… one who has affection fer the demon…"

O'Riley decided to speak out – irregular as it was to do so: "Jock, Adam Mitchell has fallen under the spell of Lillian, but what we've come to ask tonight does concern him."

"Kevin ma old friend, the wee lady, Claire, it's she that has the question is it not?"

"It is."

Claire was shaking almost uncontrollably now.

"But… she's very upset, and exhausted with things: if I can ask her questions of her behalf?"

"Och aye of course ye can…"

"Thank you Jock, It concerns the spirit of someone who passed-over some long time ago, someone who was married to Adam Teal, who lived in old Liverpool town: Adam Teal who's spirit came forth at our last sitting."

"Hold on keep an orderly queue!" came Old Jock's voice "Och there's a great rush ah spirits here tonight Kevin, an ah good many ah here fer the wee Lassie! Come forth Adam Teal!"

Adam's mind flooded with 'new' memories and impressions. He saw Adam's wife Sarah – her natural blond hair and fresh complexion – light blue eyes and fine bone structure – her pretty features: "Shit" he gasped in recognition its Claire Lattimer!"

Lillian stepped back from him, her green-eyes darkening – 'Lilith' would suffer no rival for her chosen man's affections.

His lips silently muttered as Adam Teal's memories suddenly evaporated as if vanishing into a vacuum…

"Who hath called me?" came Adam's voice through the gapping mediums mouth.

"Adam Teal?" asked O'Riley

"Tis me, ye hath disturbed upon mine rest once again!"

"Yes, Adam, I apologize for that… but it is a matter of great import and concerns Sarah…"

"Sarah? Thou meanest mine wife?"

"Yes… Sarah Tennyson."

"Oh sweet Sarah, such a fine, fair an' lovely lady, never was a woman kinder or such a homely mother or comely wife! What asketh you of me about her?"

"She has passed into spirit, yes?"

"Yes… after my death, she didst follow, and didst suffereth greatly, afflicted with a broken heart. I didst say unto her, in mine lifetime… I didst say that death wouldst *not* part us."

O'Riley braced himself for his next questions. He felt Claire's cold shaking hand in his, growing increasingly limp. A quick glance at John passed the message for him to be ready to catch hold of her should she pass-out: "And *after* you lifetime Adam?"

"After? After… I didst visit upon her in her dreams, and through my love for her I comforted her thus: 'Death hath *not* parted us… sweet Sarah…' These words didst I speak as mine promise unto her."

Claire moaned and then fell into a faint.

"John keep hold of her hands – we must maintain the circle!" O'Riley exclaimed. The two men held her firm and managed to support her bodyweight in the chair without letting go: "Adam, I must ask you this… I must ask you about *Lilith*."

"Oh *Lilith*, my love eternal!"

"Yet… you loved Sarah too?"

There was an extended, pregnant pause. O'Riley exchanged yet another look with John. It seemed that Adam was working on his answer – which could only mean that the emotions involved were far from being clearly resolved for him.

At last the answer came: "I hath love for both, differently, but yea, for both. *Lilith* was mine first, truest and most natural love – yet she was taken from me, and with her went the paradise of my youth! Then, heartbroken and bereft, I didst plead unto God's good grace, and he sent me Sarah unto me, who became mine loyal and loving wife."

"Sarah knew of your love for *Lilith*?"

"Aye, that she did: twas never kept from her, and yet even so, it didst not affect her love for me. Greatly hath God blessed upon my soul!"

"Adam… do you *still* visit Sarah?"

"Still sayeth thee?"

"Yes… do you visit Sarah, now, in her dreams?"

Alfie's body jolted and then appeared to go into a spasm. Relaxing itself, Adam's voice continued: "How canst I, for she hath already passed hence into spirit!?"

O'Riley's breath shallowed as his questioning reached its climax: "Has she Adam? Has she really? Or is she *still* on this earthly plane?"

Alfie's face contorted as his mouth silently murmured Adam's reply: "Can you repeat your words Adam, I couldn't hear you…" said O'Riley.

"I… I canst see her! She is here with thee, here now! Sweet Sarah!"

Claire moaned again as she came round to Adam's voice.

"Adam, do you visit her still?!" insisted O'Riley.

"I… I do!" came the reply "I do… I… I must warn her… must protect her…"

"Protect her? Protect her from *who* Adam?!"

"No! It canst not be so!"

"Adam you *must* answer me – for *Sarah's* sake: protect her against *who?!*"

"Oh *Lilith* my Love! I will come back for thee, when thy time is nigh, I shalt be upon the earth again… *Lilith!*"

Alfie's body gave one final convulsion and then Adam Teal was gone…

12

Angel of Death

he séance had ended. Claire was visibly shocked as well as drained, but O'Riley thought that at least they now had an answer: "Claire was right… Adam *has* been visiting her in her dreams."

John nodded: "Yeah… and we know why now too!"

Alfie was also recovering from his ordeal. He was a 'physical' medium – one whose body, whose very physiology was taken over as a host by the spirits. Nevertheless, exhausted as he was he found the effort to give warning: "Kevin…John… this is *very* serious. Claire is in mortal danger. The demon will know now, even if she didn't before. In fact we're *all* in great danger, she's the Angel of Death!"

O'Riley read the concern engraved across Alfie's face: "You'll be OK won't you?" he queried.

Alfred sighed: "I will, if I'm careful. Obviously, I've drawn attention to myself now. I hope Old-Jock can protect me… after all, that Demon just brushed him aside like paper!"

O'Riley tried to reassure him: "You're no threat to her Alfie; it's us she wants – in particular Claire… and me."

Lillian was troubled – not a state of mind she was accustomed to. She'd made her choice for her consort – Adam, over Von-Hesse, and yet now she'd discovered a corner of Adam's heart as 'Adam Teal' that concealed a memory of another woman – Sarah – Adam's 17th century wife, who it seemed had been reincarnated as Claire Lattimer – the biological descendent of the Witchfinder Nathaniel Lattimer.

It was clear that Adam and Claire had affection between them: so Lillian's usually dismissive air towards her enemies would no longer be appropriate. This Claire Lattimer was a threat – in a way that Lillian had never encountered before, she was an *emotional* threat, a rival for Adam's affection, and yet protected from Lillian by *his* reciprocal feelings for her. If Lillian was too quick to kill her rival – then she ran the risk of emotional rejection by her chosen 'New Adam.' Not something that would have bothered her once, but then, for the first time in her long material existence, *Lilith* as 'Lillian', was in love…

All of this, and she had to ensure that her still 'useful' servant Maximilian Von-Hesse, didn't suspect that she'd made her choice. The insult would certainly spur him into killing Adam, even if that meant his own immediate destruction and damnation by *Lilith* herself.

Lilith's one true weakness then, was her all too human, but long repressed capacity, for love. Pondering the consequences she decided to secure her relationship to Adam: she'd test him and see if he would set aside 'Sarah' as Claire. "Adam, you must be careful of Maximilian. He doesn't yet suspect that you're his rival for my… affections."

Adam was still wrapped in his newly associated 'memories' of Sarah and how alike Claire Lattimer she was. Being 'Adam' it still hadn't fully dawned on him – the dots weren't joined: "Eh, Max? Yer mean Von-Hesse? He's gotta thing for yer himself?"

Lillian took all three questions as one: "Yes. He's *very* jealous, and is quite capable of killing you."

"What!"

"You have to make your choice Adam Teal, if you want me, then that means that not only must you conceal my love for you from Maximilian – it also means that you must set aside *any* feelings you have now, or have ever had in the past, for *any* other woman."

One look at her angelic pre-Raphaelite face and then into her, almond-shaped, limpid, opalescent green-eyes and it was as if no other woman had ever existed…

North Road Birkenhead

From the shadows over in Rocky Bank Road a tall dark figure watched as O'Riley, John and Claire left Alfred Hulme's North Road healing practice. Claire with John in his Lexus, and O'Riley in his Honda Legend. A single lone vehicle remained parked out on the road: Alfie's blue Volkswagen Passat. Waiting a few minutes until the coast was clear – the tall angular figure emerged from the cover of the overgrown bushes that billowed out across the pavement. Von-Hesse had many skills; by-passing vehicle security was one that he'd acquired recently, but nevertheless expertly. In just a few seconds he'd opened the driver's door…

Tuesday 28th November 2006: Eden Institute Rodney Street 9.30am

"You've been neglecting you patients Dr O'Riley!" scolded Susan.

"I have?" O'Riley actually sounded surprised. He knew he had of course but rather like a late-payment bill, he'd hoped no one had noticed.

"The whole day's appointments are clear – everyone's fed up of being cancelled at short, or even at zero-notice!"

"Oh…" Despite his apparent gloom, O'Riley was actually relieved. His work load with the ESP team had grown to the extent that it now governed his life completely. Susan's chastisement was just the excuse he needed: "Right… OK, well, I'd give you the day off Susan…"

"But there are nine other therapists working here who need their reliable receptionist in place" she continued for him.

"Er… yes… Right, I'll be off then, have a nice-day Susan!" O'Riley exited the building post-haste. Susan smiled as she watched him go. Dr O'Riley was her favourite analyst at Eden, a kindly gentleman with many long years of experience behind him. He'd even helped her when she'd been bereaved with the death of her husband.

Little did she know that she would never see the good Doctor again…

Outside, O'Riley went immediately next-door but one to ESP He didn't see the black BMW Mini Cooper S pull in to the parking space opposite – nor the lustrously long haired pre-Raphaelite vision of a girl driver who's Mona-Lisa smile settled upon him as if a laser gun-sight, as he walked along.

Inside ESP: "John! Claire! Great to see you both, especially you Claire – no offence John" he smiled "How are you today?" he asked of Claire.

Claire's face was her only reply; looking drawn with black rings under her eyes – her usually full mouth thin and turned down.

O'Riley sat opposite them on a low back red leather settee: "It must have been an ordeal for you last night Claire."

She nodded.

"But we *did* get an answer" added John.

At last Claire responded verbally: "Did we? I'm just left with this state of dissociation… *Am* I Claire Lattimer… or am I really Sarah Tennyson? All my life before, I've never doubted my identity… never, not once in all that I've been through… but now…"

O'Riley pursed his lips: "Whatever doubt you're in, it'll be fuelled by the emotions you've been feeling."

"Psychoanalysis 101 is that Kevin?" she replied less than graciously.

"Not exactly Claire… more pre-term Jungian depth psychology. We all know how hypnotically inductive emotions can be."

"This is *real* Kevin, not some trance-state fantasy or cryptomnesia… its real!"

"Yes… 'it' is… whatever that 'it' is precisely, and that's what we should be looking to discover."

"Claire's had a double whammy on this Kevin" said John "first, she finds out that she's descended from a seventeenth century Witchfinder who'd apparently drowned *Lilith* – who then turns up as Lillian wanting revenge – and then, she finds that she's a reincarnation of this Sarah Tennyson – who was married to Adam Mitchell in his previous life as Adam Teal!

It'd be comedy if it weren't tragedy…"

"More like pathos and irony I'd say, John" replied O'Riley. "Pathos as notwithstanding the occult and supernatural overlay – this is a very *human* story. Irony, as there's an element of being mocked by fate…"

Claire stared in disbelief at him: "That's your take on this? Like yer some kind of theatre critic?!"

O'Riley smiled: "It's a *psychodrama* Claire – and that's the key to how you work your way through this."

"What?" Despite her challenge, a twinge of hope stirred in her heart – O'Riley had skilfully teased her emotions – raising their temperature so that she would become receptive to stepping just a little outside of feeling sorry for herself, and seeing the bigger picture.

"This whole 'human-triangle' thing that's emerging between you, Adam and Lillian – it'd be so easy to get swallowed up by its emotional drama. But that would be the quickest way to literally 'lose the plot.' Lillian, or *Lilith* as she's more properly known, may be just as involved in the drama as you are – emotionally, and *that* is our surest way to defeat her."

"By making it a 'psycho'-drama?"

"Yes… Her vulnerability needs to be exploited."

"Vulnerability? Does she have any vulnerabilities?" asked John.

O'Riley nodded thoughtfully. "You know, I really think she does… *Lilith* needs a 'New-Adam' a male *consort*. It seems that our Bavarian friend coverts this role for himself… and yet… Lillian – looks to have chosen Adam Mitchell…" Claire's heart skipped a beat at the idea of Adam being *her* chosen man "And…" he continued, "if you don't mind me saying so Claire, your reaction just then probably reveals not just *your* attachment to Adam, but very likely mirrors that of Lillian herself…"

"So, you're saying that we can get to *Lilith* through Adam?"

"Yes, John, I'm saying precisely that – and that's where Claire can use what she's going through emotionally, both to model Lillian's or *Lilith's* feelings for Adam *and* to exploit them to bring about her downfall. If Adam has *just* the right amount of reciprocal affection and attachment to Claire then it'll work…"

"Cool… But, what about The Bavarian?"

"Von-Hesse? Well, it was Alfie's idea to play him off against Adam."

"No!" Claire interjected "Von-Hesse would kill him!"

"Exactly! And that's a fear that *Lilith* must feel too. So – she could be manipulated into taking care of Von-Hesse for us, which is one dangerous enemy out of the way. You see, by testing Claire's feelings we also get an angle on how *Lilith* is feeling – with respect to their joint object of affection – young Adam!"

"Very clever Kevin, but… it's not the *whole* picture. Others are involved too: Young-Kevin, and Sean, maybe even Lizzie. And then there's *Lilith's* broader plan for the destruction of humankind!"

"One step at a time John. We can't lose sight of the larger-scale of things but, we have to have a place to make a start. I'd suggest that as Claire is a focal point – then we start with her. If we don't utilize what she's going through, then the energy tied up within her will drag her down deeper and deeper into withdrawal and depression. That would affect all of us, you, me, and Claire's family – we'd all lose our energy and capacity to react. That's why I said we should make this a psychodrama – we have to be fully conscious psychologically of what's happening. So, be a part of it, yes, but not be contained by it."

"OK, but what about Lillian, won't she see Claire as a threat to her over Adam: especially if she already knows about her apparently being the re-incarnation of this Sarah Tennyson – wife of Adam Teal?"

"Yes, she will, but there's a double whammy for her too: if she harms Claire – at least prematurely, then she risks rejection by Adam. She'll have to avoid that… no I think that it's much more likely that she'll move on to the next stage of her plan without directly harming Claire or her family."

"And that is?"

"If I'm right… she'll start the serious work of pandemic contagion… and *that* is something we'll all have to worry about!"

Over in North Road Birkenhead, Alfie was getting ready for a visit to The Pyramids shopping mall. Grabbing his car keys he made his usual cursory check of the outside of the car – leaving it on the road always mean that it was vulnerable to damage overnight – especially as it was parked directly opposite a junction – that with Rocky Bank Road - and because of the risk of vandalism or theft. Everything seemed fine until he used his remote sensor to unlock the car and switch off the alarm: "Funny… I mustn't have set the alarm last night…" a quick look inside and all seemed fine. His stereo and CD player were still there and nothing looked disturbed. It was chilly this morning so he switched on the air-conditioning. He didn't notice the minute particle-fine mist that instantly filled the cabin, and then his lungs…

Lillian's Mona-Lisa smile had watched O'Riley disappear into the ESP Institute. Satisfied that he'd be gone for some time, she paid for her parking ticket at the nearby machine and nonchalantly strolled over the road towards Eden. In reception Susan saw her approach and recognised her immediately as that strange ethereal girl who'd tried to enchant her favourite staff-member: Dr O'Riley. With a look of grim determination, Susan prepared to confront the young girl – she wouldn't get past her this time…

Lillian's coquettish tilt and dimpled smile floated into view around the door.

"Miss Hopgood isn't it?" came the deeply registered voice from Susan.

"Of course!" she replied breezily "who else!"

"Dr O'Riley is otherwise engaged and he has no free appointments for the rest of the week."

Lillian's smile broadened at Susan's obviously defensive reaction to her: "Oh… that's just as well then isn't it."

"I'm sorry?"

"Just as well that he won't be needing you anymore."

"What?"

"Did you get that flu jab Susan? You mentioned it last time we met. Remember, when I said how *ill* you looked?"

Susan was off-balanced by Lillian's strange line of questions: "Er… I did actually… if that's any business of yours!"

"Oh shame… you needn't have bothered: it won't help you now, you know." With her smile broader than ever, Lillian passed her porcelain-perfect hand across Susan's eyes…

Midday: Paradise Street; at the building site where the sarcophagus had been discovered.

Dermot O'Brien and Callum McHugh had made much of their 5 minutes of fame. Many pints of Guinness had been downed on the strength of their story about how they'd discovered the mysterious stone sarcophagus – subsequently whisked away by the buxom and marmishly glamorous Dr Claudia Moore of Liverpool Museum: "I quite fancied her so I did!" declared Dermot.

Callum shook his head: "Yer'd have yerself more chance wid dat supermodel Kate Moss so yer would!"

"Nah… I likes me women ter be curvy… Now, that Dr Moore *she* was curvy! Anyway, time fer a bevy, you comin or wha?"

McHugh spat into the wet concrete filled foundation trench before him and nodded: "Yeah, come 'ead then!"

Smiling, the two friends turned around, and then, abruptly stopped: "Who are yous!" exclaimed O'Brien.

The massive frame of Hans Meier stepped closer: "Your names!" he demanded.

"Yer wha?!"

The ice blue Germanic eyes glinted in the low winter's midday sun: "You are the workmen O'Brien and McHugh?"

"Yeah, so wha's it ter yous like?"

"*You* discovered the sarcophagus!"

O'Brien puffed himself up: "Yeah, we did: wanna buy us a pint?"

As last words go, they were in keeping with how he'd lived his life. The silenced Glock 9mm pistol clicked in two short bursts. One bullet each to the head and to the body – a classic double-tap: "Gustav, help me by pouring more cement into the trench..."

Smiling, psychopathically, Adler operated the machine to release the entombing concrete.

1.00pm and O'Riley was still at ESP. He'd managed to talk further with Claire and gradually she was re-orienting herself back to the task in hand: "So, I have to play up to Adam you're saying?"

"A little, and that's where you have to be strong. Whatever you feel for him, or believe that you feel for him – those emotions belong in the past – in another time, and in another life. Simply falling for him all over again as 'Sarah' did back then, will just make you a victim: you, your husband, your children... and possibly, the whole human race!"

Claire's eyes darted from side to side as she struggled to stay focused: "You *are* right, Kevin... my husband... he's the true love of my life... of *this* life... but... I still have these other feelings..."

O'Riley continued – he wasn't going to be distracted by Claire's appeal to her infatuation with Adam: "Then there's Sean... we must keep him away from Lillian. For a start, she's not interested in him, no matter what he may feel for her – she's made her choice and that choice is for Adam. Then, Lillian could still use him to get at you, or even to entrap Lizzie. That's not beyond the bounds of possibility... and neither is her seduction of young Kevin...your husband!"

Claire's body jolted as an unconscious blind-spot was hit by O'Riley's words: "I hadn't thought of that! Stupid me! Of course, he was attacked by her in his dreams!"

"Yes... as a *succubus*: and this is why I've been earnestly trying to get us all orientated towards just how complicated the permutations of this are!"

Claire put her face in her hands: "Oh god it's too much, I can't follow it... I only get one part of the picture at a time!"

"That's a feature of your emotional involvement Claire, and that's why we must as far as possible set that aside, *except* where for the sake of the end result... you *must* indulge it... "

John had been thoughtfully rubbing his chin: "And that too is why we have to seize the initiative Claire. Kevin's right: if you can keep Adam just a little interested in you, then that would be enough to 'rain of her parade' – she couldn't risk his rejection by harming you – and – you'd get a kind of 'proxy' protection for your family too. Meanwhile, we get on with the task of exploiting her weaknesses and hopefully... stopping her!"

John was looking pleased with himself.

Just then O'Riley's mobile phone buzzed announcing that he'd received some text messages: "Oh damn, thought I'd switched it off... sorry, er excuse me..."

O'Riley had two new texts, one from Maggie and one from Eden. Opening Maggie's his eyes rapidly scanned the content: "Maggie wants me to ring her urgently, something about Alfie..." Then the second: "This one's from Eden... Christ! Susan's collapsed at work and been sent to the Royal Liverpool Hospital! I'll have to go back and see what's happened – I'll ring Maggie and let you know what the other problem is..." So saying, O'Riley leapt up with a vigour that denied his advancing years, and ran a quick pace back to Eden.

Lake Hall Oxton

"You're looking pleased with yourself Maximilian" said Lillian with a raised eyebrow and half-smile.

The hooded eyes narrowed and looked down the Bavarian's noble, aquiline nose: "I have... attended... to the problem of that medium Alfred Hulme."

"Attended?"

"Yes mistress an aerosol administered through the air-conditioning system of his car – it has a very short half-life,

460

both in and out of the human body. It will break-down rapidly and become utterly undetectable – the effect will appear natural."

Lillian smiled: "Putting your alchemical skills to good use I see."

"Indeed Mistress, I am particularly pleased with this er… preparation. Also, Meier and Adler, have consigned those Irish workmen to the foundation trench of the new building in Paradise Street... A simple old-time sentiment: to make a human sacrifice towards the future good fortune of the building. My medieval ancestors would have understood..."

"How *apropos* Maximilian, the symbolism amuses me. As I was buried there – then so shall they replace me!" Lillian swathed herself over the Chaise-Lounge: "I too have been active in 'administration' as you call it."

The Bavarian's eyebrows rose: "The contagion? Was it ready so soon?"

"A trial run: it *was* effective. Now I just need to maximize my energy reserves – which of course means more harvested semen, not to mention… impregnations of this cities naïve and licentious young girls."

"I see. And where was this trial run Mistress?"

"Oh in Liverpool, at a certain address in Rodney Street…"

O'Riley was as pale as a ghost. Arriving back at Eden he'd been met by Dr Mike Bradley a fellow analyst, who gave him the staggering news: "I found her collapsed behind the reception desk with large black swellings on her neck. Her breath was rattling – she looked in a gawd-awful state! I've no idea what was wrong with her, and neither did the ambulance or paramedics."

O'Riley had an idea, but it was too terrifying to mention… "So, we don't have a diagnosis yet?" He knew they hadn't. If they had then all hell would have broken loose…

"No nothing, nothing at all."

"If there's any news will you let me know?"

"Sure Kevin, don't worry…"

"I'll be next-door-but-one with my daughter in-law; otherwise you can reach me on the phone…" O'Riley's return journey to ESP was virtually in slow motion.

"Get on to the School of Tropical Medicine and tell them to send Dr Jonathan Teal over." The junior hospital consultant wasn't sure, but his unconscious patients' presentation strongly suggested what he feared her condition to be.

"Dr Teal: he's a plague specialist isn't he?" replied the senior registrar.

The consultant nodded grimly: "Yes, he is… and I'm afraid that could be precisely what this poor lady is suffering from…"

"Kevin, you OK?" John hadn't seen his old friend in such a visibly shaken state in decades.

"It's Susan John, she collapsed at work, although its' not been confirmed the description of her body – large black swellings on her neck…"

"Buboes!" exclaimed Claire

O'Riley nodded: "What else... this can only mean that it's started, *Lilith*'s contagion has started, started right here bang in the middle of our territory. It's her calling card: she's telling us that she's approaching the height of her power, she's telling us that she can reach out to any one of us, anytime, anywhere! Alfie was right... she *is* the Angel of Death..."

Maggie hadn't had a reply from O'Riley yet after she'd sent her urgent text message, so she rang him on his mobile.

"Oh that's my damn phone again. I'll just see who it is... It's Maggie... Hello Love..." his voice trailed as her urgent words broke into the polite niceties of conversation.

"What! Oh no!"

John and Claire exchanged worried glances.

"Where? At the Pyramids multi-story car park?"

"That's in Birkenhead" remarked Claire in response to overhearing O'Riley's question.

"Oh shit... OK love, look, something's happened here too, I'm OK, so are Claire and John, I'll get back on to you as soon as I can... OK... bye... love-you... bye..."

O'Riley pressed 'end-call' on his mobile and looked round at his companions' expectant faces: "That was Maggie... Alfie Hulme, he's had what appears to have been a heart attack whilst out shopping in Birkenhead... he's dead..."

By the time Dr Teal arrived at The Royal Liverpool Hospital, Susan had already died. Tissue and fluid samples had been taken and had confirmed the presence of the *Yersinia pestis* bacteria: "The clinical presentation and the confirmation of *Yersinia pestis* completes the diagnosis… it *is* bubonic plague."

Dr Paul Chambers felt his blood chill at Dr Teal's words.

"The question is: how did she pick up the infection? Also, what do we know about her contacts within the last five to seven days? The DoH must be notified immediately, and the World Health Organisation! We must execute our emergency procedures – all family members and anyone else she has been in contact with must be given antibiotics immediately including medical and ambulance staff. Contact the pathologists: we require an autopsy straight away – and carry out tests to check that this is bubonic, rather than pneumonic plague. If it's the latter, then we may already be too-late to stop it spreading…"

"Which antibiotic?" asked Chambers.

"As a prophylactic we can start with Streptomycin 30 mg/kg by intra-muscular injection, twice daily for 7 days. If we have any established cases presenting then either Gentamicin given as intra-venous or intra-muscular, or, Doxycycline, orally – which is suitable for both adults and children: we can use the oral antibiotic prophylactically too." Dr Teal looked around the circle of deathly faced junior doctors and registrars: "Well! Don't look so despondent! This isn't Liverpool in 1665 yer know, we have 21st century medicine and antibiotics at our disposal. So long as we act promptly and efficiently we can stop this in its tracks!"

At Lake Hall in Oxton, Von-Hesse was staring out of the loft-space window across the Fender Valley: "They will bring their medicine to bear upon the contagion Mistress."

Lillian was breezily cheerful: "Oh let them. They'll find the bacterium and then believe that their antibiotics can stop it. But we know differently don't we… we know that *our* pestilence evolves and changes – the more they try to fight it – the more intelligent it becomes…

Now… the list Maximilian, I must have the completed list. They will be the first to die! The stupid medical authorities will see familial patterns emerging and mistake the epidemiology as being due to social contact between family groups – instead of the truth – which is that the victims have been *chosen* to die as descendants of my past enemies!"

Von-Hesse nodded: "Adler has completed the list; it is ready for your use. May I ask, about the children? Will you strike them down as of old?"

"The children Maximilian? Why, of course. I shall visit the Royal Liverpool Women's Hospital and pass my hand over the pregnant mothers bellies!

Those whose foetuses I choose *not* to replace with my demon seed will die as stillbirths or spontaneous miscarriages. So, soon Maximilian, soon, and my vengeance against cursed Eve and all of her kind will be complete. First that pitiful city of Liverpool, and then…"

With a Mona-Lisa smile she turned to leave: "Anyway, I'm off to have fun in the night-clubs now Maximilian, I think I'll harvest a few more men this evening: ha ha!
Be a good-boy while I'm away won't you?"

"It must have been her!"

O'Riley shrugged: "Let's wait Claire until we have the results from an official post-mortem. As far as I know, Alfie was in good health – with no history of a heart condition."

"Come on Kevin!" said John, "it's got to be 'reasonable suspicion' as we would have said back-in-the-day!"

"Maybe… but then why not use this plague of hers?" replied O'Riley.

"Perhaps it wasn't her… perhaps it was Von-Hesse. We know he has *bio-PK* ability. It'd be within his reach to cause a fatal cardiac arrhythmia" offered Claire.

O'Riley nodded in acceptance: "Yeah… he could. He's also an accomplished alchemist, so he could have administered some kind of poison. Whichever it was, being connected to us probably sealed poor Alfie's fate. He knew it too: he was genuinely in fear."

Claire sighed: "The place we should all be right now is with our families." She'd spoken for the whole team. The notion of *Lilith*'s plague on the loose: and perhaps 'assassinations' via *bio-PK* or poison by Von-Hesse was terrifying.

"Let's adjourn then… but, let's not separate from one another – that'd just play into their hands" said John.

"Agreed: we should meet up here again tomorrow morning and plan our next move. Lillian has the initiative again, we must take it back!"

Any plans the team may have had for the previous evening had to be forestalled. The local health authority had kick-started their emergency procedures and it wasn't long before O'Riley was contacted to be given prophylactic anti-biotic treatment. Although they hadn't been near Susan in the relevant period, O'Riley had managed to persuade the heath authority officials that the ESP team *had* been in contact. Accordingly, they and their immediate families were given their preferred 'oral' rather than intra-muscular injection, course of antibiotics.

The test results from Susan's autopsy which thankfully confirmed bubonic rather than pneumonic plague –the latter spreads through coughs or just simple person-to-person airborne transmission. No other cases came to light overnight and the authorities decided to suppress news of the incident, to avoid alarming the populace.

Despite their antibiotics though, the ESP team knew something that the health-authorities did not. This particular contagion was supernatural in origin, and tragic though Susan's death was, it was only just the beginning of a terrible plague that no antibiotic could ever hope to stop.

"Given what we know, was there really any point in undertaking all that antibiotic stuff?" asked John.

"There was. Firstly, the authorities would insist – at least in my case as I work at Eden and had regular contact with poor Susan. Secondly, it sends the right kind of signal to our opponents. They'll think we're scared."

"We *are* scared!"

"Well of course, but there's an element of poker in all of this,"

"As in they'll think we're ignorant – and don't realize that antibiotics are useless, or we haven't even figured out that Lillian is behind it all" offered Claire.

"Right!"

The phone rang and intruded into their contemplation: O'Riley picked it up: "Hello? Oh, hi Mike.. What?! OK, Cheers, bye... That was Mike Bradley over at Eden, he obviously doesn't know what's going on, but on a hunch he said he thought I should know... Remember those two Irish navvies who'd become minor local celebrities?"

"The two who found the sarcophagus?" asked John.

"Yeah... them... they've gone missing off site, just vanished from the face of the Earth, like Dr Flynn did from his home..."

"It's *Lilith* it must be, Kevin: this means that *anyone* associated with the sarcophagus find is in immediate danger... like Claudia... and... and *Adam!*" gasped Claire.

"Yes, it's her or our Bavarian friend: or maybe either of those two henchmen of his, that Adam told us about. She's playing with us, trying to get our attention divided: we must stay focused and remember it's the contagion that's the *real* threat."

"What's the next move then? We did agree that Claire should try to win Adam over" asked John.

"Yeah... but to pull that off safely, we're going to have to fall back onto some of our old skills" said O'Riley.

"Old skills... you mean like police-style surveillance?" queried John.

"Yes; as in locating Lillian and Von-Hesse and making sure they're out of the way whilst Claire does whatever she has to do."

Claire had been mulling over the general line of O'Riley's argument: "No..."

"Sorry Claire?"

"No, it's too *conventional*, she'd know what we were up to and simply play games with us. It'd also take up too much time and resources and we're short on both."

O'Riley raised his eyebrows and pursed his lips: "OK, do you have a better idea?"

"Don't know if it's better... but if I'm to see Adam, and try to get him to move away from Lillian; then it can only be at one or both of the two places where he spends most of his time: the Museum or his flat... I'll just have to be spontaneous and turn up - unannounced."

Lillian was sleeping in after her exertions. Physically exhausted, she was re-charging her 'astral' body – the energetic supernatural form of existence through which she operated when acting as either a spectral *succubus* or *incubus*. Recently, she'd taken to physical sex with human girls – seducing and then impregnating them through her scorpion-tailed clitoral sting; delivering alchemically altered semen harvested from her male victims – a feared attribute of hers long ago recorded in the collective human memory of ancient near-Eastern religious texts. Her growing powers were such now that she could incubate large volumes of semen: carrying out alchemical transformations of them within her astral body. Still not at the height of her powers, the effort exhausted her physically – as did her own lust and desire for physical sex with her 'chosen man' Adam Mitchell aka Adam-Teal: the man to whom she'd readily given up her bodily virginity – the man whom she truly loved... It was at Adam's flat that she'd slept-in this Wednesday morning. Her energetic lust had near burned poor love-sick Adam to a frazzle. He'd managed to crawl out of his

bed, his fatigue being merely human rather than astral – and had gone into work at the Museum.

Claudia was off sick – apparently through her pregnancy, so Adam was effectively unsupervised. By 11.00am he'd found his way down to the Museum's ground-floor café. His large mug of black-coffee steamed like the vapours within a mediums crystal ball – his eyes seeing faces, patterns and possible futures:

"Argh! Claire! Where'd you come from?" He'd been so engrossed he'd not seen her come in and sit down at his little table.

"On your own today Adam?" she asked.

"Uh… yeah… Claudia's threw a sickie… well, not literally. Or maybe she has? That's what happens isn't it when yer pregnant… yer throw-up a sickie?"

"Pregnant! "How'd that happen?"

"That's what she said! She's in a relationship…but it ain't 'his'…" Adam looked up at Claire: "No! It ain't mine!"

Claire laughed: "Not been sowing your wild oats then Adam?"

Adam's back straightened: "Well actually, I have!" he declared proudly. But he caught the faint trace of a reaction in Claire's eyes: "Er… it's Lillian… or *Lilith*… I get mixed up… all these different names yer know…"

Claire's heart sank, but she struggled not to show it – failing utterly in the process: "That's nice…" she managed to lie.

Adam's emotions side-tracked him as his heart read hers: "I do love you, you know?" he heard himself say as his hand reached out for hers: "Bloody hell did I just say that!"

Claire gave him a dimpled smile: "You did…"

Their hands touched, fingers tenderly entwining. Courage from another lifetime welled up in him: "Look, Claire, this is gonna sound well weird, but, I've seen you, seen us… together… in a past life…."

"I know" she said "I've seen it too".

"You have!"

"Yes. It started in dreams, and then I did a past-life regression, and a séance with Alfie."

"So it *was* real!"

"Real, but I always came second didn't I…"

"Second…"

"Second to *her*, second to *Lilith!*"

"Sarah…" His mind flooded with Adam Teal's memories.

"Yes?" she said…

Lillian had got up and got ready. She did eat, but more for conventions sake than for nutrition. Her preferred nourishment was human libido – the life-force itself as expressed through sexual energy. Effortlessly beautiful she was completely ready in just moments. Pausing to look at her reflection she noted with a Mona-Lisa smile how her hair colour was changing – the russet tones now almost auburn-chestnut as her natural angelic-blond highlights blended and faded: a sure sign of her growing power. A quick look out of Adam's flat window to check her car, it was still there. She was just about to turn away when her eye caught sight of another vehicle, not one she'd seen around that street before, but one she recognized immediately – a light sky-blue metallic Lexus: distinctive with its new-model enlarged grill badge…

Adam was struggling with his emotions: holding Claire's hand and feeling her fingers caress his; he felt again that energy that had passed between them at the séance: "Oh this is too weird, it can't be true… I can't be in-love with two women at the same time!"

Behind Claire's smile – she wondered too, how could *she* be in love with Adam when she was still so in-love with her husband? "Do you remember what you said to me... back then, when I was Sarah?"

Adam's memories resolved and focused: "Yes, I said that we'd never be parted, even after death" he murmured. Then continuing he said: "Is that it? Is that why we've met up again, and felt this amazingly powerful attraction, one that neither of us in this life knew that we had for one another?"

"Maybe, you've come back as 'Adam' so that this time 'Adam' can see through *Lilith*; see who and what she really is."

Adam shook his head: "No... *he*, Adam, he knew what she was, but it didn't stop his love for her, not even his death could stop it – and *Lilith* promised him, promised him that they'd be together again in future lifetimes."

"But Adam promised Sarah too, didn't he... didn't *you*. You said that death wouldn't part *us*... and it didn't... did it?"

Claire's words were taking her further than she'd planned. She'd hoped to sail close to the wind, but keep herself on course, and not lose herself... to herself.

Adam shuddered as his hand tightened around Claire's: "Make love with me" he said, pleading with his eyes and he looked into hers.

"Oh Adam... I would... but..."

"But what?" he begged.

"I'm married... I'm married to Kevin, and I love him, he's the love of my life!"

"Of *this* life Claire, he's your husband in *this* life, but we were together *before* that, we were together *first!* And we made a promise: from me to you, and you've been waiting for me, haven't you, all this time! In your heart, you know you have!"

Claire's eyes filled up as 'Sarah' came closer to the surface: "And yet, its *Lilith* that you love the most isn't it? You'd be asking me to throw away everything in this life that means something to me, just so you could still pine for her – just like last time!"

Adam sat back and sighed. What could he do? He *did* love both, but both differently. Was it just his ego that wanted to take Claire to bed? Or was it his soul trying to save him from the fate that awaited with the ethereally beautiful, but demonic Goddess *Lilith*?

John saw the girl emerge from the flat. He'd never actually set eyes on her before but he knew her immediately. The hair colour wasn't what he'd expected, but there could be no question about this girl's identity. Quite apart from her stunning beauty, her ambiance was unearthly. The Mona Lisa smile and coquettish tilt of her head – the perfectly formed hour-glass figure – the heart-shaped face, the porcelain perfect skin, and opalescent-green almond shaped eyes – all combined with an intense femininity that only great master painters could ever have hoped to catch.

He shook his head as his psyche recalled the last such woman he had met – the memory was itself hypnotic and dangerous – particularly as Lillian had sensed it immediately – as she closed with her prey.

John pretended not to notice her – a give-away in itself. Lillian was *always* noticed. Walking along the pavement her dimpled smile broadened as she opened his car's front passenger door, climbed in and sat down. John was stunned into a frozen regard. She spoke for him: "Well, you must be Dr John Sutton. I wondered when we'd meet. Of course I knew that we would, I know simply everything!"

John managed a question: "Lillian?"

"Oh come now John Sutton, you know my *real* name. But you can call me Lillian if you like."

John felt his head becoming light as he stared into her fascinating eyes.

"That's right; if they were brown they'd be like hers wouldn't they John?" Lillian teased him, reading both his mind, and his heart.

"Rowena…" He couldn't help but say the name. Lillian's power had fully penetrated into him.

"I asked Kevin O'Riley about her… she's engraved on his heart too, and on dear Claire's. Now I find her inside you. Was she as pretty as me John?" Lillian's lips parted emphasising their fullness – her sensuality now radiated, its energy bathing John like a summers-day sun. Lillian's smile opened broader than ever as she sensed his body giving in to her.

Then… "You're wearing one of those charms!"

John gasped, and then reflexively clutched at the little red shield suspended on a fine gold chain around his neck: "Back-off *Lilith*… I know what you are!"

Lillian laughed: "Oh what a big strong macho ex-policeman you are, needing that little necklace to protect you from a mere girl like me; ha ha!"

"You're no mere girl *Lilith*!" said John, his voice raised in fear and relief "I know you killed Alfie Hulme, and Susan!"

Lillian pouted: "Oh John! How could you say such things? Maximilian killed that interfering busybody of a psychic medium – not me. As for Dr O'Riley's receptionist… well, she was my business card – you might say."

"We'll stop you *Lilith*, just like we've stopped all the others before you!"

"Stop me? How? I haven't even started yet. You'll find me far more dangerous than Rowena was, or that Harlequin – You see, unlike them no part of me has *ever* been human: ha ha! Careful Dr John Sutton, you have a family don't you, and my reach is unbounded – even to that 'unusual' wife of yours…"

"Get out!"

"Why of course. Now, don't forget to call Claire on your mobile after I leave, it'll give her time to get away from Adam before I arrive. You see… you're like an open book, you can hide *nothing* from me John Sutton!"

Laughing, Lillian left and made her svelte-like way over to her BMW Mini-Cooper S.

John reached inside his pocket and turned off his radio-mike.

"Claire… Sarah, all I can say is that as Adam Teal, I genuinely loved you. Loved you as my wife; the mother of my children, and, my best and truest friend. I had *none* of those things with *Lilith* – barely a few summers of youthful and unrequited enthralment – until, at the very end, when the Witchfinder cast her into the pool – she gave me acknowledgement of my feelings for her – and her promise that one-day we would be together. She's kept that promise, Claire… she was my first love, I can't change that, it's just been my fate… She was my first… but not my *only* love…"

Claire felt her mobile vibrating inside her suit jacket. Reluctantly withdrawing her hand from his, she nevertheless kept eye contact with him as she answered: "Hi… John? How long ago? Are you OK? Sure? Right… catch you later."

Claire looked worried as she pressed the 'end-call' button.

"Problems?" asked Adam.

She nodded briefly: "I have to go; your girlfriend is on her way over."

"She'll be jealous…" he murmured.

"She'll happily kill me, Adam: and then she'll destroy you!"

"No! No, she wouldn't do that… she loves me… And that means she *couldn't* ever hurt you!"

Claire realised that it was now or never, but she knew too that she wasn't in control of her own heart: taking his hand and looking him deeply in the eyes she said: "Come to me…and I won't turn away…"

Adam became Adam Teal again: "Oh Sarah… what do I do?!"

"See her for what she is, and what she's going to do!"

He withdrew his hand: "I can't… I won't! How can I? I really *do* love her!"

Claire gasped as she felt her heart sink.

Adam reached out and took her hand again: "I still want you Claire… even if… even if only the once… just for the past and how we were…"

She scanned his face, her mouth fell open. Part of her wanted to say yes, as she silently, and unconsciously mouthed the word. Then speaking out aloud: "I have to go… *Remember me… Adam…*"

Then with moist eyes she left.

Adam watched her leave. Gradually, the Adam who had known and loved Sarah faded back once more into his subconscious – with it went the elder Adam's maturity, and back to the fore came the bungling young Ph.D student. Mixed emotions resolved into a single tear as his heart gradually quickened in anticipation of *Lilith*.

A quarter of a mile away from Adam's flat, O'Riley turned over the engine on his dark blue Honda Legend car. His receiver had picked up the dialogue in the Lexus – and he was now playing its recording back through the Honda's top-of-range sound system. The old ways had worked after-all he thought… He and John had eventually persuaded Claire that to simply turn up at Adam's flat would have been dangerous – just in case Lillian was there. A part of Claire seemed to relish the encounter – almost like a spurned wife. O'Riley had persuaded her to see how that feeling was an echo from a former life-time, and that they should – for now at least – work rationally. There would be plenty of time for the irrational – later….

Feeling that the job had been well done O'Riley's Honda purred back onto Smithdown Road and turned towards the city centre for his rendezvous with Claire and John.

What he didn't see were Adler and Meier following on after him in their grey Range Rover SUV.

Adam was still in the café when Lillian arrived. Vision-like she floated in through the glass doors – her lovely smile gladdening his heart: "Hello my love: *nearly* caught you out with another woman didn't I?" teased Lillian.

Adam's eyes soaked up her beauty. How could such a sweet face be the angel of death?

"There's no one else for me *Lilith*... so long as you're here how could there ever be?"

"Then Adam Teal, there *never* will be anyone else for you: because now that I'm returned, I'm here *forever!*"

"Ok... but it'd never stand-up in court – it'd just sound bizarre!" Claire had been listening to the tape-recorded conversation between John and Lillian in the Lexus.

"True..." said John "But it tells us that Von-Hesse killed Alfie, which confirms beyond any shadow of a doubt that he's dangerous".

"And" said O'Riley "It confirms that *Lilith* or 'Lillian' killed Susan with the plague." O'Riley sighed before he continued:

"The starting gun has fired – and the race for the continued survival of the whole of humankind is on..."

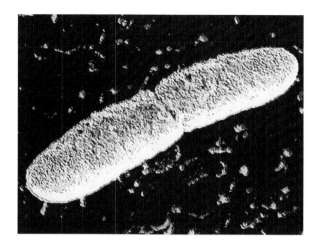

13

Animus Pestis

Thursday 30ʰ November 2006: School of Tropical Medicine, Pembroke Place, Liverpool 10.30am

r Jonathan Teal was feeling much better. His concerns about the mysterious case of bubonic plague had abated enough for him to feel that the authorities were in control: "No further reported outbreaks, and, the cultured *Yersinia pestis* bacteria have responded to simple first-line antibiotics. Good... early days but we should be able to get on top of any further outbreaks. The main thing will be swift diagnosis of any new cases."

His senior assistant Dr Michelle Wilson nodded: "But we still need to know where on earth the victim contracted the infection."

"Oh it will likely be the traditional way – an infected animal flea: with a bit of luck the original host animal is already dead, and any fleas have themselves perished. Anyway, it's been a long night... I need to get to sleep."

Michelle was worried for her boss. He'd recently had a mysterious illness himself: an unexplained cardiac arrest following some kind of seizure at home, and, it was rumoured around the university-hospital – a strange bloody evacuation of his testes.

Since the plague casualty had been admitted to hospital he'd barely been away from work. It was his specialist field, and he felt the need to prove to his colleagues that despite his unexplained illness, he was more than up to the demands of his job. Now at last, he felt he could go home.

Michelle smiled: "Get some good rest and sleep you deserve it!"

Teal smiled in return: "Thanks Michelle, I couldn't have kept going without you: unless there are any further developments, I'll see you on Monday!"

Blearily, he made his way out from his office and into Pembroke Court: finding himself unable to recall where he'd parked his car – the effort and fatigue of days and nights of concentration had all but overwritten his memory. He'd just realized where it was when his attention was taken by the approaching figure of a girl. Squinting as his heavy eyelids strained to stay open he could see her almost endless auburn chestnut hair, streaked with natural blond highlights – framing a heart shaped face. His belly churned out a warning as his subconscious mind recognised the pre-Raphaelite symmetry of her features: "I… know you…" he muttered

Lillian's smile was perfect: "Hello again Dr Teal" said her silky feminine voice.

Her opalescent green eyes were mesmerising: "I… know you… from somewhere…" he faltered.

Her dimpled smile seduced the last of his defences as she passed her warm hand across his eyes.

"Well?" came the curt Germanic demand from Von-Hesse.

"We were able to follow him undetected Master" replied Meier.

"And the electronic scanning: Adler?"

"It was successful Master. He used a radio microphone receiver to pick up a message from the target Sutton in his Lexus. We also recorded his mobile-phone conversations."

"You have made a transcription?"

"Of course Master, it's here in writing and on audio CD."

Von-Hesse took the written report from Adler, his computer and electronics expert. The hooded black-brown eyes narrowed as he read the words: "The fool!" he exclaimed suddenly.

Adler was concerned – did he mean him? "Master?" he queried.

Von-Hesse glared at him as would a public schoolmaster at a dunce: "Not you, the Mistress! She's told Sutton that I killed the medium Hulme!"

Adler couldn't help himself: "Master, be careful! We shouldn't say such things about the Mistress!"

Von-Hesse trembled with suppressed rage at this hint of insubordination: "Shouldn't! Shouldn't did you say? A *fool* is a *fool* Adler, howsoever elevated that fool may be!" But there was more than Lillian's breezy disclosure behind his concern:

"She is getting *too* close to Adam Mitchell!" Visibly shaking he simply had to vent himself further: "If I get the slightest further suspicion concerning her affection for him, then I will kill him, immediately! Go, both of you, watch him closely and report back any contact they may have. I will *not* accept this!"

Young Sean had recovered enough to feel the need to get away from his mother's 'protective custody.' As his body started to regain its strength, his mind paradoxically became weaker, it's will-power to resist the memory of Lillian's beauty evaporating like autumn mist. His dad was at work, his mum over at ESP, and Lizzie safely at school. Trusted to make his way to his grandmother's at Prenton Lane, he instead found himself catching a bus to Hamilton Square in Birkenhead and the underground tube-train to Liverpool…

"There you go Superintendent, there's the same man again walking up as if to go past the alley this time." The civilian employee of the police was showing Young Kevin O'Riley CCTV recording's from the Wood Street area in Liverpool taken on the night of the double knife murder: "Can we enhance the image?" asked Kevin.

"Yeah, we've got someone working on that now. What we can say is that he's male – obviously – height about 6ft 3" in old money – he's wearing a long dark overcoat – he has swept back collar or maybe even shoulder length hair – looks well-built, but slim, probably athletic. He has a distinctive gait, strident or 'ramrod' like he's had military training."

Young Kevin shook his head: "My son Sean was attacked by a gang of youths, so it can't be this fellow. We don't have anything else to place him with the two victims?"

"No… but he's the only clear image we have from during the material times. There've been no new eyewitnesses either, except other sightings of our tall angular friend – from bouncers. We're getting night-club CCTV checked out to see if we can trace his movements. I wonder who he is...?"

Young Kevin wondered too.

Sean emerged from Lime Street tube-station just following his intuition. He had no idea where Lillian would be, he just 'felt' that it would be somewhere near here, in the heart of the city. He'd heard his mum and grandfather talking about her as if she was some kind of evil creature, intent of destroying him. Whilst he'd been very ill, he'd even believed it, but now that had begun to pass, and the bruising from his attack had begun the slow process of recovery – he felt differently again.

Despite the cold damp weather, he wandered into St John's Gardens – the little patch of greenery behind St Georges Hall that occupied a commanding position overlooking the city centre. Down to his left, beneath the Old Hay Market and on into Whitechapel – lay the bed of the ancient Pool of Liverpool – now dry and built over it was as far from his conscious awareness as the embodied spirit that now approached him from the multi-storey car park built on the head of the old Pool.

"Hello again!"

Sean jumped as he sat round-shouldered on the park bench: "Lillian! God, I was looking for you, and then suddenly here you are!" He was embarrassed by his still badly bruised face.

"You must be psychic" she smiled.

"Nah… don't believe in all that crap. Me M'am does, but not me."

"Then how do you explain meeting me here?"

Sean was stumped: "Er…"

"I'm going to the Museum for a coffee, want to come along?"

"Wow, you bet!" he said. Lillian smirked her coquettish grin. She knew who was watching them from the bushes…

"Oh and by the way… do you still have that lock of my hair?"

"Alfred's funeral is next Wednesday, at Landican cemetery. Susan's is the same day, and at the same time but in Allerton. I can't be at both. Susan had very few family left to speak of, so I'd better go to hers" said O'Riley.

Claire felt compassion for her: "Such a shame, and such a nice lady. Look, I'll go with John and represent us at Alfie's."

"Will you be OK? Fairly or otherwise, Bridget's blaming us for what happened you know."

"I know" she said. "It's understandable, Alfie was her whole life – being a spinster and having no kids…"

They fell into silence as their thoughts reached out to her. Claire was next to speak: "I'm worried about my Kevin" she said flatly.

O'Riley had been expecting this: "Does he know about your feelings for Adam?"

She nodded: "Yes… he does now, I couldn't live a lie with him. He knows that it's not 'real' in the sense that our love was, and is – of course… but he's not reacting like I thought he would. He's going deeply into himself, and last night he went out somewhere on his own – gone for hours, wouldn't tell me where. It wasn't a pub, he doesn't drink. I'm worried that whatever happens now with Lillian, things will have changed between us… maybe forever."

John could of course always be relied upon to bring things down to earth, with a bump: "Whatever happens with Lillian will change *everyone* Claire – with respect, your marriage can't be top of the agenda right now, because if she wins, then none of us will be left around to worry about *anything*!"

Claire looked at him astonished.

O'Riley came to his aid: "He is right Claire, hard though that is for me to say – especially as Kevin is my only son and you are my daughter-in-law. We haven't included him enough as things have gone along – so he's bound to feel rejected, *very* rejected – but we have to go on as we are and worry about putting the pieces back together later – *if* there is a later..."

John kept the focus on practicalities: "So, what do we do now? We can't afford to let our own concentration and effort slip for a second."

O'Riley sat back in the red-leather settee: "Haven't got a clue... but that's never a bad thing... it lets inspiration fill the void, and that's what we could do with now, some inspiration..."

Sean was chatting animatedly to Lillian as they walked in through the entrance to the Museum: "Wow! Haven't been in 'ere since they did the place up, it's brill!"

"Isn't it" she smiled "Going to buy me a coffee Sean?"

"Absolutely!" he enthused - then he remembered Adam: "Look, what happened to that 'friend' of yours – yer know... the one I saw you with when you wuz out clubbin' it?"

"Don't you think it's rude to ask a young lady about her male friends?"

"Er... I'll get the coffee..."

Lillian was enjoying teasing Sean; she also enjoyed Adler's attempts to take secretive digital photographs of her companion from the Museum foyer.

Sean brought over a tray with two huge mugs of black coffee, a jug of milk and some brown sugar: "Don't know if you have it black or white, I should've asked!"

"Black: don't you think that people who dither between opposites are so boring?"

"Eh?" she'd lost him completely.

"Your Mum would know what I meant – she had a problem once with someone who tried to master the eternal opposites within nature – good idea, if it'd worked. Trouble is, it can backfire and all that energy just blows you away… Pity, I'd have liked to have met him… again. Your Mum's memories of him suggest that he d become *very* powerful…"

"Again?" Sean was confused, did she mean The Harlequin?

She smiled her dimpled smile: "Oh yes… I *do* know him… in fact… he's my favourite 'son'."

Sean gaped in astonishment, but Lillian merely pouted and blew her sweet smelling scented breath across his face: his body responded immediately, which of course Lillian knew that it would: "You're becoming aroused Sean…"

Sean blushed: "I…"

"It's alright… men are always like that around me… women too, if I want them to be."

"Crikey! Yer mean that yer do that… yer know, with other girls and stuff?"

"Why not?" she breezed "You've been around the clubs here, its normal these days for girls to experiment and enjoy one another… Why do you ask, don't you approve?"

Sean did approve, he just didn't approve of Lillian with any other man: "Wha, er well, do yer have any sorta… yer know with other men?"

"Do I have a boyfriend do you mean?"

"Well… yeah… like."

"Would you be jealous?" she teased.

Sean squirmed but at last coughed up the obvious: "Of course!"

"He works here actually."

This wasn't the reply he'd hoped for: "Here! *He* – whoever he is works here?"

"Yes, you met him with me that night around the Clubs in Wood Street."

Sean's face fell flatter than a pancake that had just dropped from very high on the ceiling to very low on the floor. Looking around, Lillian had noticed Adler leave with his digital photographs: "Don't worry, I still like you" she soothed.

"*Like* me?"

"Yes, isn't that enough? You might live a little longer that way."

Sean was confused: "Wha, sorry I don't get yer meanin'."

Lillian just carried on: "How's Lizzie?"

"Lizzie? Oh she's in school." His hair stood on the back of his neck "Yer don't fancy *her* do yer!"

"Have I ever even met her?" came Lillian's evasive reply.

Briefly, his mind toyed with the idea that if Lillian fancied Lizzie, then maybe that'd be a way in for him.

"Hmm nice idea…"

"Wha?"

"What you were thinking. I've never done a threesome: or at least… not a brother-sister one…."

"*Shit!* You knew what I was thinkin'?"

"Of course, I read people's hearts – what's hidden in the very core of their being."

"Bloody hell!"

"So… to answer your question, yes, I might: if it amuses me, and before I finally settle down. After-all I'm so inexperienced, I've only just lost my virginity."

This was worse still: "Only just? You mean it could've been me!"

"I did consider you yes: you and the other two. Don't you remember, I told you about the man where I'm living in Oxton? Well, he was one I'd had short-listed for simply centuries. He's very jealous though, you know. He'd have killed you if I'd have chosen you. The other one: Adam, works here. Your Mum fancies him too; in fact, she's in *love* with him."

"Me *Mum!*"   This was all becoming to much…

"Yes, she's the jealous type as well, in her own way – and now the poor-thing, she wants to destroy me."

Sean's head swam: "Oh yes… I've heard her say that to my Granddad O'Riley…" he murmured.

"Ah… dear Dr O'Riley. He's very handsome for his age – in fact he wears his experience well – makes him *very* sexy. It must be him that you get your good looks from."

"Me Mum's nice lookin' too: especially as age-adjusted" Sean protested as only adolescents can.

"Yes… she is, and she's had quite a life your Mum, in fact your Granddad could even have been your Dad."

"Wha?"

"Oh silly me!" mocked Lillian "You didn't know that they'd been lovers before your Mum married your Dad, did you?"

Sean couldn't… didn't… want to believe her: "No! That's crap: why are you sayin' that to me?!"

"You should ask your Mum about bisexuality too, she's had quite a bit of experience there. Still, she had good taste, they were both very beautiful. I'll have to ask her if they were as beautiful as me… I've asked your Granddad, and your Mum's friend: John Sutton, but they wouldn't say. They both knew them, and they knew about your Mum's Sapphic dalliances."

"Sapphic?"

"Yes Sean, from Sappho: poet of Lesbos, don't you young people of today have any education?"

Overwhelmed, Sean tried to back away and stand up – but Lillian's beauty paralyzed him: "Poor Sean… never mind, I'll let you go now. Maybe, we can meet again soon… in your dreams?"

His eyes bulged: "Then it *was* you! My Mum *said* it was!"

"Of course… and I've had your Dad that way too. And as for your Sister Lizzie: oh she's so sweet – so… virginal. You see, I was a virgin myself, in the body Sean: but *not* in astral-spirit… It was so nice to enjoy her. Poor girl thinks it was *just* a dream… Maybe I'll have you both physically before I'm through with the final destruction of your human-kind…"

Sean's fear found the energy to stand him up. Terrified he ran crashing through the glass doors.

Lillian's Mona-Lisa smile bathed him as he left: "Thanks for the coffee Sean… don't forget to look after that lock of my hair…. I'll be seeing you…*very* soon!"

Dr Jonathan Teal had had a lapse of memory. Putting it down to his fatigue he'd eventually found his way to his car and drove home to Childwall. It'd only been a few days after his mysterious seizure that the plague scare had broken out. His testes were still sore – but the damage had not been as bad as first feared. He felt that he'd proved a point by answering the call from the Royal Liverpool Hospital – he was still 'the man' when it came to matters of plague – and he was still healthy and strong – despite the gossip. It was just that he'd had a strange and disquieting lapse of memory since he left the School of Tropical Medicine that morning – he remembered a girl walking towards him and then all went hazy… a girl yes… a familiar girl, like someone he'd seen in his nightmares…

By the time he arrived at his well-appointed detached house – he'd noticed that he felt ill. Perhaps it was seasonal flu? There was a lot of fuss going on at the Tropical Medicine School about a possible avian influenza pandemic – H5N1 or 'Bird Flu' as it was known in the press – but hey, Liverpool had just had its first outbreak of bubonic plague in years – the last being amongst some quarantined merchant seamen in the 1950's: and he, Dr Jonathan Teal, had successfully treated the cultured bacterium with common front-line antibiotics. OK… the patient sadly died, but then clearly she was at the end of the disease's progression. He at least deserved credit for identifying the pathogen quickly and avoiding mass panic amongst the city's populace didn't he?

As he walked up the path to his front door, his final thoughts were of recent work by two colleagues from Liverpool University: Professor Chris Duncan and Dr Susan Scott – whose research had suggested to some scientists that the fourteenth century *Black Death* pandemic either wasn't bubonic plague – or bubonic plague was in fact caused not by the *Yersinia pestis* bacteria, but by an emergent viral pathogen, which had somehow simply become dormant – and was ready to strike again; "Rubbish!" he muttered as his temperature climbed rapidly "I've demonstrated that bubonic plague *is* caused by *Yersinia pestis* and so have countless other clinical and epidemiological studies… and of course The Black Death *was* bubonic plague… what else… could…" his ramblings faltered as his aching body suddenly became limp: "it be…"

Collapsing in the hallway – his anxious wife saw the already erupting black bubo swellings on his neck.

Over at ESP John took a call from their Liverpool university colleagues: "Yer what! Oh shit… OK fucking hell! Thanks for telling me, yeah Chas, will do… OK, I'll tell her, and Kevin too, OK, bye… bye…"

Claire looked at John expectantly. It would take quite a bit for him to 'revert-to-type' on the telephone in the style of his former career: "What is it John?"

"That was Chas at the university!"

"Yeah I gathered that much, what is it?"

"It's Dr Teal... he's dead!"

"Dead?!" Claire instantly suspected Von-Hesse "It's that Bavarian killer again!"

"It was plague Claire."

"What!"

"Yeah... and he'd had all the prophylactic treatments too. They're doing tissue tests on the bubo's right now. It's weird, all the infectious disease specialists say that it takes four to seven days to kill an untreated case – but his signs and symptoms were virtually instantaneous!"

"It's Lillian..." said O'Riley quietly "It must be, and more than just that, she's been able to control how the disease progresses – its speed of onset... The folks at the university don't know that... how *could* they know that!"

"Rather you tell 'em than me Kevin" said John "They ain't exactly gonna take any notice of us are they – I mean medics aren't the most approachable people when it comes to their own area of expertise, never mind some parapsychologists coming along and saying 'Oh by the way, this plague outbreak is caused by a demon witch who was last seen in Liverpool in 1665 – before some Liverpool Museum archaeologists dug her skeleton up on the built-over dry bank of the old city Pool!"

"How we going to stop her Kevin?" asked Claire urgently.

O'Riley was silent. Staring into space he knew that he simply had no idea…

Dr Michelle Wilson was as stunned as the rest of the staff at the School of Tropical Medicine: "His last words were what?"

"He was delirious, and kept rambling, but he said something in Latin just before he stopped breathing: *Animus pestis*."

"*Animus pestis*! I don't know of any pathogen by that name… literally it translates from Latin as, well… as 'Pestilential Spirit'…some kind of spirit that brings a contagion…"

"Maybe, but that's what he said" replied the young male registrar "He was delirious after-all. Main problem now is finding out how in hell he caught it, and how his signs and symptoms didn't show until virtually the very last hours of his life? It's certainly not the way bubonic plague classically presents!"

Michelle's knew that only too well, but deep down below the level of her conscious mind, her psyche *really* knew… Her spine tingled as she repeated Dr Teal's final words: "*Animus pestis…*"

Claire was feeling ill herself – her exhaustion was beginning to tell: "I don't know if I've got the resources for this Kevin" she said to O'Riley "It's got to have been the most intense fortnight of my life since – since… The Harlequin and his sister…"

No one needed to reply – O'Riley and John remembered that all too clearly.

"Just one more straw on my back and I think it'll break" she added - her voice flat with certainty and resignation.

O'Riley took a sharp intake of breath: "Which is why we can't give up! Remember how you rallied for me Claire: and you too John: twice in the past we've had to face evil on a huge scale and both times we won through in the end."

"Don't wanna be the party-pooper here Kevin" said John "but we were a hell of a lot younger then *and* we had help – from our 'friends'. We don't have that now…"

"He hasn't asked!" exclaimed Claire "For whatever reason… he hasn't asked them!"

O'Riley bridled, despite his usually cool persona: "We've had this out just the other day Claire; I said then that I've not been near the Dale in years, and I haven't so much as seen a glimpse of *him* in maybe twenty years. I don't even know if the place would receive me again – never mind… The Green Man himself. You see, it's like I've done it again, you know, like what happened last time and the time before that… I've forgotten my *covenant* with him. What if I get rejected? What if it's already too late?

"*If* it's too late Kevin, then trying isn't going to make any difference, but if it *isn't* too late then it'll make every difference in the world!" Claire was straining to emphasize her point "we can't do this alone Kevin!"

"Can't! What do you mean can't? Wasn't that what *he* taught us, that when faced with the greatest evil, we *can*?"

"If I were you, I'd go, I'd go cap in hand… not for me, not for my *ego* but for everyone… for everyone out there who'll be her next victims – for the old, the sick, the children Kevin… think of the *children*!"

The phone went again breaking into their charged atmosphere. As before John took it: "Hello Dr John Sutton at ESP? Oh, hello again Chas... his last words? You got this from the registrar... *Animus pestis*... OK, thanks... any more cases? No, OK, how about his family? I see... OK, thanks again, keep us updated please... cheers, bye."

John looked at his two emotionally drained colleagues: "You probably got that – the registrar's reported his last delirious words as: *Animus pestis*"

"The Pestilential Spirit... That's what it says about her doesn't it... in the old Middle-Eastern texts – about *Lilith*... This contagion is psychic... supernatural... a pestilential spirit..." O'Riley spoke quietly "She's claimed to be stronger than *anything* we could muster against her, stronger than anything that could grow in *her* soil, *her* very earth – made as she is from the soil of Eden itself..."

"Kevin come on! Now who's 'delirious'? She's spooked you; we've got to get going on this. I'm nearly finished, I've almost nothing left – my family are under attack – my husband, my son, probably even my daughter – I've got this 'thing' with Adam... I'm drained... You've *got* to make the effort!"

"So... he is the O'Riley boy, Sean?"

"Yes Master" Adler was at The Bavarian's dockside warehouse hideaway: reporting back to Von-Hesse on Lillian's movements and contacts "The digital images confirm it. They were at the Museum together, perhaps her other contacts with Adam Mitchell are no more significant than that?"

Adler's attempt to put his master at ease was not only unappreciated, it was totally ineffective: "Fool! She plays with the O'Riley boy, *and* with us! Do you forget how long I have known her? Every time, she is the same… she toys with people and then *destroys* them!"

"Forgive me Master; there was no offence intended, merely an attempt to put your mind at rest."

"At rest? At rest! I have *never* known rest Adler – these many, many years beyond your simpleton's comprehension! She has released the contagion again – a concentrated attack against a *single* individual… when she does this the onset is very quick – hours, perhaps even minutes. But it is wasteful. We need a blanket contagion – which will have an orthodox incubation period, but will strike down many more victims. So you see, she *is* 'playful' and that, equates with 'wasteful.' Bah! I am tired of her games…"

"But surely, when it comes it will be unstoppable Master?"

"It will… The science of this century is advanced, but, misinformed. What they call bubonic plague is not a single disease – as many of them believe, but a spectrum of pestilences of which the *Yersinia pestis* bacterium is but one single pathogenic element.

Her contagion is far deadlier as it utilizes *all* pathogenic agents, including bacteria, viruses and even prion proteins - and causes them to mutate under conditions of any medical resistance. If their scientists and doctors try to defeat it – they will simply strengthen it. The only way for it to be overcome is by the will of *Lilith* herself – or – through her destruction… But… she makes mistakes Adler, already twice before in my company she has forestalled herself and on both occasions this was due to her infernal delight in playing with people and their emotions!"

"Twice Master? I knew about the Great Plague of 1665, here in Liverpool but…"

"The other? That Adler was the *Black Death* of 1347. We had travelled to Genoa in Italy, after initiating the contagion in Asia. She became embroiled in Genoese and Florentine politics and was discovered and cursed for witchcraft.

I barely escaped with my life. I then had to make the perilous journey back to Armenia, to a location now known only to me, but revealed previously to me by *Lilith* herself as the source of her blood-soil, and therefore her great-powers. Then after many difficult labours was I able to make the necessary refinements, until the time and place I judged were right for her return. But I tell you Adler, this is the third and *final* time that I will assist her against the force of her wilful nature. Her rewards… they are of course incalculable, but the long centuries in between weary what is left of my soul!"
Then Von Hesse's eyes suddenly softened as in an unguarded moment of memory he made disclosure of the distant past: "You have both asked how 'old' I am… well… know now this… truly, by my 'birth' I am not Maximilian Von Hesse, but *Guy de Montpellier* a Frenchman of the Languedoc, in the south of France - I was a Cathar, a *Perfecti*, a 'priest' of the Cathars… and their master of the secret Hermetic arts of Alchemy… I made a discovery… a great book… hidden at the castle of *Montsegùr*… this book, was a so-called Satanic heresy to the Roman Church."

Adler shifted on his feet: "But Catharism was itself a heresy, Master… what could be so special about a book?"

An ironic smile broke out across Von Hesse's handsome features: "It was 'the' Book, Adler… The Bible."

Adler thought he understood: "Ah… and The Cathars believed that unlike in the Roman Church; that the Bible must be writ in the language of the ordinary people… not Latin!"
he smiled feeling pleased with himself.

Von Hesse's hooded eyes darkened, chilling Adler: "Fool! This was not the Bible as accepted by either Rome or the Cathars! It was… the *Codex Lucifer:* The Devil's Bible…"

Adler's eyes bulged. His mouth had opened but no words came out. Von Hesse shook his head in near contempt and continued: "*Lucifer* - the bringer of light - the Fallen Angel… the book was his secret transmission - with an alternative Genesis, an alternative account of Christ… and an alternative Revelation of this world's end… and… also other, most secret knowledge, concerning the mother of all Demons herself… the immortal and uncreated Goddess… *Lilith!*"

At last Adler understood: "Then that is how you first made contact with her!"

Von Hesse nodded - this time approvingly: "Yes… through a most careful study, I deciphered the meaning of the ancient texts… and so… brought her back into the world of flesh. But… the timing was shall we say unfortunate. The Roman Pope had launched a Crusade against the Cathars: and the fortress of *Montsegùr* was stormed. In the battle, the book was lost … I had to flee: but at least I knew now, *how* to summon forth Great *Lilith*… Already, my studies in Alchemy had artificially extended my life, but from her, I had the promise of *eternal* life as her *Adam Kadmon* - her New Adam – and through that union, to be the new father of the world!"

Adler was now so inducted by his curiosity that he just had to ask more…

"But The Devil… *Lucifer*… he is not just the Fallen Angel is he, Master? We, who follow you, and the Mistress, we know his *true* identity… He is The Demiurge – 'The Lord Creator' of this physical world who first entrapped the divine spark of spirit into matter – the divine sparks of individual human souls!"

Now Von Hesse smiled: "Adler, *still* you mistake the one for the other..." he said softly.

"But The Demiurge, he is *Lucifer!*" exclaimed Adler – "This, you have taught us!"

Von Hesse shook his head: "He is as *if* Satan... to The Cathars, for as they believed, and as some believe still: that the *Rex Mundi* or otherwise the 'Lord Creator' is merely a lower God: someone who through either accident, or more likely evil design, created the world; to as you say, entrap, sparks of the divine Godhead... The Gnostics; would agree with this, but they do not mix up either The Demiurge with Satan, or... indeed *Lucifer* with Satan. The latter conflation is the mistake of many orthodox Christians, although their mystics down the ages have periodically discovered something of the truth for themselves."

"Then who authored that book: the *Codex Lucifer* Was it the Fallen Angel, or Satan, or.... 'him' The Demiurge?"

Von Hesse smiled again, his preoccupations now thoroughly distracted: "There is much that you still do not understand: following The Demiurge's creation of the world, something happened... something unintended... As the Gnostic Gospels have their Christ saying: 'If flesh comes into being because of spirit, then that is a great wonder... but... if spirit comes into being because of flesh, then that is the wonder of wonders!'

You see, once formed, this world fashioned a soul of its own..."

"What?!"

"Oh yes Adler: where else then did you think that that cursed 'Leaf Head' *Viridios* came from? Him, and all the other 'nature' deities?'"

"Ah... er...."

"From the Earth itself!" exclaimed a suddenly irritated Von Hesse "from its soil, from its waters!   You see, those 'New Ager's are actually right about something: they call 'her' *Gaia* – the Goddess of the Earth, but 'she' has many names and many faces, just as does *Viridios*.   But our Mistress, *Lilith* was the *first* Goddess to enter creation – she is the primordial feminine principle, and she should have triumphed – right back at the beginning of time: but her recalcitrant nature forestalled her, her damnable wilfulness, that which *always* gets her in trouble!"

Adler was lost: "You mean, that *she* wrote the book?"

"No! Attend carefully now as I explain, and think yourself fortunate that I make this most *secret* revelation unto you!

Early that evening Claire arrived home far more exhausted than when she had left. The frustrations in the team had finally broken through to the surface – including an extraordinary reluctance in O'Riley to call upon the one source of help that had always proven reliable.

Coming home to the 'normal' demands of family life, Claire felt that she was on the edge of mental collapse. She really didn't need what was about to happen…

"Sean? You OK?"

Clearly he wasn't: "I need ter talk Mum."

Claire could see from his face that something was seriously troubling him. Drawing as deeply as she could on the dregs of her energy she nodded: "OK, come in the front room."

"What's happened Sean?" Claire correctly guessed that this wasn't something that had arisen spontaneously in her son, but rather was as a result of something that had happened from the outside. Sean sighed, as tears filled his still bruised eyes: "Mum... just tell me the truth..."

"The truth? I always tell you the truth Sean; I've *never* lied to you about anything. What is it, what's troubling you?"

He shuffled his feet – preferring not to sit down. Claire though had little energy left so she slumped onto the settee: "Well? It's OK son you can say whatever it is that's bothering you!"

Staring at the carpet Sean muttered: "I saw Lillian again today."

"What! Sean! You were trusted to go straight to Prenton Lane!" Claire's voice was raised so loudly that it drew the attention of young Kevin who paused by the living room door.

"Just tell me the truth Mum!" tears were flowing freely now.

Claire rallied her compassion: "Then just *ask* me Sean, I don't know *what* it is that's troubling you?!"

"It's about you... you and granddad..."

Claire felt her heart pound and miss a beat – she really didn't have the strength for this: "Go on..." she said faintly.

"Lillian said that before you knew dad, that you and granddad... that you and him had a relationship, a *sexual* relationship, and that Dad doesn't know, but John Sutton does."

Claire let out a moan, a moan of existential angst – this was the one secret that she hoped would *never* come out. Her voice trembling she said: "That's what that evil cow told you?"

"She did Mum, an' she said that you'd had Lesbian love affairs and that granddad and John knew all about them. She's sayin that now yer in love with her boyfriend from the Museum!"

Pale and drawn, her voice breaking she asked: "Is that what you want to believe, from *her* after all the harm she's done to our family, and very soon now to the whole world?"

I just want the *truth* Mum! I'd have ter live with it, she mocked me an' said that granddad could've been me Dad!"

Claire tried, she desperately tried to gather enough up from within herself to deny it, but she couldn't. She'd never lied to him, never in his whole life, instead she said nothing, and cast her eyes down to the floor.

"Mum, yer not answerin' me, if it's not true just say so!"

Out in the hallway, young Kevin, propped himself up on the wall – his whole world teetering on the brink…

Von Hesse's warehouse hideaway at Birkenhead docks

Von Hesse was concluding his 'revelation' to Adler, who'd now been joined by an astonished Meier:

"Yet… her nature is… as mercury itself… and she toyed with me Adler… toyed with me and led me through great dangers all over the world, from these Britannic isles to far Cathay itself and beyond - until… she made her mistakes and was once more 'forestalled'. But now, my patience with her is near all done through… After the passing centuries, my own powers have grown greatly: which is how you Adler, and you Meier have come to be 'changed' by my knowledge of Hermetic Alchemy.. so that now, your own lives are, to some

extent, increased, even unto your – 'reanimation': should that become necessary. My power is such that soon I shall have neither need nor desire of her patronage: nor indeed even of her love… .

 Yet…know this: I will *not* stand for any man to be consort to her other than myself, even if that means destroying her, as well as him!"

Over in Liverpool, the Mona-Lisa smile, smiled…

Later...

Lillian breezed back to Lake Hall in Oxton, giving nothing away at how she had 'overheard' her servants little tirade against her, and his unauthorised revelation to them about her origins and destiny. Von-Hesse had worked himself up after his talk with Adler and Meier, but by now he'd calmed down again. Nevertheless he sought to probe his mistress's activities: "Been busy Mistress?"

Lillian tilted her head and smiled her Mona-Lisa smile: "Why of course Maximilian, I'm *always* busy. I had a lovely coffee at the museum. It was nearly spoilt by a strange shaven headed man taking digital photographs of me – but then I am so irresistibly attractive aren't I? Still... next time he does that, I'll just smite him down instantly with plague."

"Argh!" came the terrified cry from Adler.

"Then... I ticked-off some people on the list... the Teal family, some Lattimers', some Pennys', Longfields', Tarletons' and a few others who are related but with different family names." The incubation will be about 24 hours then they'll show up all at once! That'll be nice... it'll distract the authorities just as I spread the contagion widely at the weekend!"

"Then it *is* to be this weekend Mistress?" asked Von-Hesse.

"Yes, Maximilian, it is – and then early next week, I will begin to exact my most *personal* revenge. Dear Professor Claire Lattimer is to be sacrificed... as I was by her great-grandfather of seven times: sacrificed to the murky waters... Draw up an appropriate plan Maximilian, I want it to be *special!*"

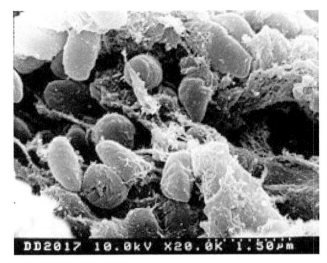

Working late at the School of Tropical medicine Dr Michelle Wilson was looking at the test results from poor Dr Teal's tissue samples: "The cultured *Yersinia pestis* bacteria are not responding to the front-line antibiotics – they're immune!"

"But they weren't before!" replied her assistant.

"Quickly, let's try Doxycycline and Gentamicin!"

Perversely, Lillian had ensured that Streptomycin and Tetracycline – which she had 'allowed' to be effective in culture after poor Susan's death, would now no longer be effective after Dr Teal's demise. This time, Dr Wilson would find Doxycycline and Gentamicin to be effective, but by the height of her contagion no antibiotic would be effective and the disease pathogens would not only mutate but broaden to include not just the by-then pneumonic bacteria, but also viruses and fast-acting prion proteins... There could be no successful human response to *Lilith*'s plague.

Over in Prenton Lane, Claire heard a gasp from the hallway. Fearing the worst – that she and Sean had been overheard - she left the front room to find her ashen faced husband putting on his overcoat and her daughter Lizzie looking on scared as her Dad went to leave.

"Kevin Love! Wait! Let me explain!"

But Kevin didn't wait. Silently, and slowly he walked out. Paralyzed by guilt she had no energy to follow him, but enough to turn on Sean: "See! See what you've done!"

Sean shouted back: "Me?! It's not what *I've* done, Mum, it's you!"

Lizzie burst into tears. Sensitive and introverted – the complete opposite in personality of her brother – the impact of the whole situation had struck deeply into her.

"Right! You've asked for it – you asked what happened, well, I'm going to tell you kids – *both* of you!"

Claire sat them both down in the living room, their mugs of tea unattended and steaming symbolically into the atmosphere.

"I was your age Sean… eighteen going on nineteen. A young probationary policewoman: that was just over twenty-five years ago… The police were different in those days, misogynistic, male-dominated, hard – even brutal. Policewomen were sometimes used and abused sexually and hounded out of the job if they didn't 'deliver'. To many Bobbies back then you were either a 'bike' or a 'dyke'.

Bikes were there to be 'ridden' whilst the dykes rode each other - there was no middle ground!

I was being bullied by a certain Sergeant – Frank Carver – who had a reputation for forcing young police-girls to sleep with him or get sacked. I'd started a relationship with a Bobby, Steve Lewis – who was a few years older than me, and much more experienced. Carver just about tolerated that, but when he found that I wouldn't do as he wanted – he tried everything he knew to intimidate me and to get me to resign.

Our Chief Superintendent – who was later to become your granddad, was an eccentric character, even for the police. I didn't know just how eccentric though – and especially, I had no idea about what had been going on in his own life – the occult and supernatural events that had turned his world upside down. That had all started about four or five years before I'd joined the job. Another Bobby – John Sutton – yeah *that* John! He was working with me at Birkenhead and he had worked with your granddad when it had all started over at Upton five years earlier.

They had an issue between them in those days – a policewoman called Petra George. I never met her, but John was in love with her, and, she had a certain 'affect' on your granddad. Anyway, it turned out that she was connected to the odd things going on at Upton – her and a male Bobby nick-named 'Crazy-Horse' who had odd coloured eyes: one blue and one-green. It all came to a head at a siege when Petra was shot and killed – your granddad was shot too, through the heart and should have died, but he didn't – instead he had a 'Near Death Experience' within which all the strange things that had happened were explained to him.

It's hard to put in ordinary words; we've kept this stuff away from you – not for any reason other than it'd be so hard to explain. Anyway – it turned out that your granddad's family on his grandmother's father's side – if that's as clear as mud? Were called Strongbow, and they were a local family who had been involved in some of the strange secrets of the landscape – connected to the 'Green Man' the nature spirit of rebirth.

Your granddad although he didn't know it had been 'chosen' to carry on the tradition of his ancestors – but – he was a career mad and ambitious man in those days, and he resisted any understanding of what was going on – so… as you do… he started going insane, and having all kinds of paranoid delusions, hallucinations, seeing ghosts – that kind of thing. He was having all kinds of therapy and getting involved in weird Tantric Buddhist stuff through your grandmother Maggie – who was a very attractive ex-hippy in those days…

Anyway after his Near Death Experience, he seemed to understand what was going on – he made a *covenant* a sacred agreement with The Green Man – he'd carry his 'unhealed' wound and as a 'wounded healer, would himself become a healer of peoples souls, but, as time went by and his career took off, he forgot, and as he forgot, things started to happen – this time much worse things as evil occult and supernatural forces focused on him drawing on events happening outside of his life – feeding on their negative and destructive energy – your granddad learned that it was 'Manichean' – these dark forces were attracted to him – to the light within him – compelled to destroy it and him. They were led by a mysterious woman, someone called 'Rowena', who was a lot like Lillian, everyman she met saw a different woman – she was a chameleon-like demon: very powerful and dangerous, and it was just as she started to work on your granddad that I came along.

He was very low: his marriage was sadly in a mess, Rowena had even penetrated that —and she'd even allowed John to believe that she was Petra come back for him!

Anyway, I saw her for what she was: I tried to warn your granddad, but at first he didn't believe me. I watched as he crashed, so vulnerable and afraid. Maggie – your grandmother left him – yes she did! Hard to believe now I know – but it happened.

He was a handsome man, I'd just been dumped by Steve Lewis – after Rowena put him up to it – so… there we were both vulnerable, and I fell in love with him – simple as that. I didn't plan to, you never plan these things they just happen, its… chemistry… 'alchemy' as your granddad would say.

Well… I fell for him, and… he did for me, but… not as much. You see, he still wanted Maggie back. But you know what… she was with Rowena! Oh yes, she hadn't left him for another man, but for her. Rowena was a sexual predator, a bisexual predator, who like Lillian fed off people's libido. She was more too; she had a mission, a goal to exploit what was happening in the country at that time – the social unrest of the early 'Thatcher years' the mass unemployment, and the terrible riots. She even murdered a man with spontaneous human combustion."

 "What?" Sean had been listening intently but this sounded well weird.

"Yes, it's also called human auto-oxidation – he caught fire – burnt to charcoal leaving the chair he was sitting in untouched.

She liked fire; she used it during cover of the Toxteth Riots over in the city. Anyway… like I say, she was a sexual predator, and had seduced both your granddad and your grandmother – but to hurt him she took her away from him –

all caused by a powerful mesmerizing hypnosis – she even tried it with me. I didn't want it, but she was too powerful – I was so young remember. Her effect on Maggie was even stronger.

Kevin – your granddad, eventually turned for help to The Green Man – but he'd come back to him by a roundabout route – through someone who knew all about him himself, independently – this was Dr Bruce Irving. Bruce was a Jungian analyst – yeah just like your granddad is now! But he'd been drawn to the Wirral through a dream – he was a Border-Scot from Annan, in Dumfries.

He'd worked out just where the Green Man's sacred grove was: – it's at Barnston Dale – he got the information from clues in a fourteenth century poem *Sir Gawain and The Green Knight* which is set on the Wirral but even more so from much older Celtic and Irish folklore.

Anyway – he and the Green Man's spirit helped Kevin fight against Rowena and the even darker forces that gathered behind her… I helped too; even though I knew that if we won, then I'd lose him… lose the man I loved. I knew that really, he wanted Maggie back, and because I loved him, I helped him.

The fight was hard, and the battle was fought in many places but in the end we did win, Rowena, apparently was destroyed in a fire, and I helped Kevin save Maggie by dragging her out of the burning building.

John, who was with us through all of this, met a nurse called Carla, who it turned out really was Petra… a kind of reincarnation."

"Kind of?" asked Lizzie

"Yes love, you see, she too was part of the mysterious powers of the land that had gathered round to fight against the evil forces that stood arrayed against Kevin. He hadn't any idea what was happening at first… John's love for Petra, was so strong, so pure – that in the end she did come back, as a nurse, when he was injured by a blow to the head in the riots.

"This Carla, that's not the Carla who John is married to is it?" asked Lizzie.

"It is… she's an NHS executive now on the Wirral."

"Well can't she help against *Lilith* now?" replied Lizzie

"It seems not… you see, her 'powers' are specific, or were specific, to something that happened in a special way and at a special place: that time is past, and what she did can't be called upon again until the time is right."

"So that's why 'Lillian' can say what she says about my affair with your granddad, and about my so-called Lesbian affair with Rowena, it wasn't an affair – it was a supernatural seduction."

"Lillian said 'affairs' in the plural, Mum."

"Well, that came later – around the time I met your Dad. I'd left the police and gone to university to do psychology. What happened then surprised the life out of me, I'd got my degree and was reading for my Ph.D. in parapsychology. After all I'd been through up until then it was the logical thing to do, the police couldn't offer me anything more – but I'd seen another world – through knowing your granddad.

Anyway, by then, your Dad, who I'd not met before, was a Police Cadet – nearly five years younger than me. I was lecturing at the police college at Mather Avenue on the psychology of interview techniques, and there he was… it was love at first sight for both of us. And my god what a ride we had then! Little did I know it but an even worse evil than Rowena was on the scene, a Harlequin character of quite extraordinary power: calling himself Dominic Magister. It stretched all of us, even The Green Man himself... the whole thing was a nightmare. His 'sister' Dominique, who was really an avatar of him – a projection of his mind in female form, drugged me and then used me sexually – hence – yep, the second of Lillian's allegations about me being bi-sexual.

The story – I'll tell you it one day was amazing – the battle against that Harlequin and his entourage. As I say, it was far worse than Rowena – who it turns out, had been his occult consort. In fact, he'd been in the background all the time we'd been busy fighting her!"

We did win... John then left the police and followed me into academic psychology – your granddad resigned just as he was promoted to Assistant Chief Constable – and went to the Eden Institute to train as a Jungian analyst – inspired by his mentor the Border-Scot Dr Bruce Irving – who the Harlequin had murdered by his three thugs: men carved out of living stone.

Your Dad became a fully-fledged constable in Merseyside police and has ended up a superintendent. But me... I went on to join ESP and John followed me there a few years later, and we've worked together ever since."

"What about this Adam character from the museum Mum, Lillian's boyfriend?" asked Sean – now feeling that he understood things a little better.

"Adam... well, you see, we have biological ancestors, and we have 'spiritual' ancestors. So, you have a family tree – that's your parents and grandparents and so on... all the way back that's your genetic inheritance. Then, you may, also have a past life or lives – a kind of spiritual family tree if you like. Now, during all this recent stuff, I'd been having strange dreams. I followed them up with a past-life hypnosis and a séance and discovered that inside me is a 'memory' of a past life, of being someone who was married, married it seems to someone called Adam Teal, who, it just happens has turned up in Adam Mitchell's life as either a reincarnation, or a 'spiritual memory' it's hard to really know which it is – for either of us. But, the point is, when you find this stuff inside of you, you find *all* the memories and emotions that person had – so there's a risk that they become more real for you than the life you have now."

"Don't you believe that you actually were this woman in the past then Mum?" asked Lizzie

Claire sighed: "That's the problem love, you can't *know* that you are, or were, *but* it still 'feels' that way… and that's where Lillian gets that from."

"So you're not in love with him then?"

"Not in love? I can't explain it any better, you feel that you are, and just like with your Dad and your granddad, it's not something you can help. I've never fallen out of love with your Dad… never, and I've never been physically unfaithful; but, no one, no one in the world, can help the power of how they feel when those emotions just overwhelm them!

There's one big complication in all of this – and that's Lillian. You see *she* really is an evil demonic entity, and, she really did know Adam Teal – who it seems became Adam Mitchell, and I'm a biological descendent of someone called Nathaniel Lattimer, someone who had Lillian drowned as a witch in 1665!

That's why she wants to destroy me – she hates all descendants of her tormentors from the past – and – she sees me now as a threat to her and Adam – because she's *chosen* him, chosen him to be the father of her demon-human hybrid offspring and the new human race that will come after the great extinction!"

"Didn't Dad know about this... I mean in detail?"

"No Sean, he didn't. You see, over the years, your Dad and I drifted a little apart over psychic things. He's become very much the kind of policeman his father wanted to be, but never quite succeeded. What I do, is a reminder of the past and all the pain we went through together. Make no mistake, he is the true and absolute love of my life... but, he didn't keep up with the rest of us in the field of parapsychology.

What's happened tonight is that he overheard something that wasn't fully said, or not said in its proper context. Now, he's walked out... gone... and I've no idea where to!"

Sean felt sick: "I'm sorry Mum, I had no idea: I was stupid!"

Claire hugged him in forgiveness: "It's OK love, you only said and did what you thought you had to, given what you thought you knew. Your Dad didn't know about my relationship with his Dad – that must have cut him up inside very deeply – how could I explain... what do you say to someone about that? It'll be like he's been betrayed by me *and* his own Dad. Of course he wasn't, because all of that happened before we even knew each other. I don't know what he'll do now... if he confronts your granddad then Maggie too will get to know about his affair with me.

We decided between us that for your Dad to know and for Maggie to know would hurt them too much, it would've just been gratuitous. We didn't want to deceive them about things, just not to hurt them; but now... I have no idea what your Dad will do. The main thing now is that we draw back together and beat Lillian, before she destroys all of us...

Friday 1st December 2006: ESP Rodney Street Liverpool 9.15am

Young Kevin hadn't come back home the previous night. Not wishing to add yet more stress to her extended family, Claire hadn't rung round to see if he'd turned up anywhere, especially not at Prenton Lane. If he had, it would certainly have meant a showdown with his father and acute embarrassment for his mother. Instead, Claire had opted for a 'conservation withdrawal' putting herself into a state of protective rest. One thing was certain; her enemies wouldn't rest, if anything they'd be gaining in vigour and determination. Young Kevin would have to be allowed his feelings – and be trusted not to do anything to hurt either himself or others. If he didn't turn up for work this morning then she'd certainly hear about it. If he did, then he'd have to be considered as 'OK' at least for now.

However, now that she was face to face with O'Riley himself, she did think that he should be told.

"Sean said that to him?!"

"I'm afraid so yes. Young Kevin walked out leaving me to explain to the kids – which just about took all the reserves that I had left. Sean's gone to Maggie – I made sure this time, and I dropped Lizzie off at school – Maggie will pick her up on the school run."

O'Riley slumped: "Great, bloody great!"

"Talk about karma catching up with yer!" offered John bluntly.

"That... ain't helpful."

"Oh I don't know Kevin, depends on how you look at it. It's an example of the past still meaning something today"

"Meaning?"

"Meaning that perhaps you really *should* go to the Dale."

O'Riley turned his head away as he rested it on the back of the leather settee: "If he was going to help, then he'd have shown himself by now, that's how it's always worked before. He hasn't shown himself: ergo he isn't going to help, QED!"

"Then... what next?"

"What next? That's up to our opponents, they have the initiative... It's like this in any war; the waiting is always the worst part..."

Lillian had been busy overnight. She'd spent time with Adam, until he fell asleep exhausted from their love-making, then in astral form she'd re-charged her energies draining the testes of sleeping men and inseminating the wombs of sleeping women.

By midday she'd arrived back at Oxton refreshed and ready for what was about to come: "Ah Maximilian! The first of our new wave of plague victims should appear late this evening..."

"Excellent Mistress..."

"Isn't it!" she breezed. "Now, here's what I require you and your associates to do... The girl Lizzie O'Riley must be taken – we can hold her hostage to ensure that Claire Lattimer later surrenders herself to us for sacrifice. The girl's a very suitable 'reserve host' should I need another body, so she must not be 'damaged' in the abduction".

Von-Hesse nodded: "A simple enough task – we can take her as she's en-route home from her school."

"Good… You may use whatever violence is necessary to secure her from any 'protection' that she may have.

For myself… I'll be visiting a hospital… the Liverpool Women's Hospital NHS Foundation Trust to be precise…Such a self-important title don't you think?
You see Maximilian; human women are deeply instinctive creatures. Beneath the façade of their sister-hood – the 'collective mothers' hide a competitiveness and jealousy about one-another – especially over childbirth. Well… I'll simply be assisting them… those unborn children my psyche deems suitable – I will 'enhance' with my spirit, so they are born as my demonic-servants: those whom I deem unsuitable, will be spontaneously terminated. What a stir that will cause!

So…The Liverpool authorities will be hit with a triple-whammy: an outbreak of plague, a disaster at the children's hospital and an abducted sixteen year old girl!"

Von-Hesse smiled – this was the "*Lilith*" he loved, cruel, efficient and ruthless: "It will be my pleasure Mistress – to act decisively at last!"

"Good Maximilian – then this evening, I'll strike at the night-clubs in Liverpool. After that we can rest a while and watch our enemies struggle to cope – before the contagion goes beyond mere epidemic – to global pandemic!"

"And Claire Lattimer?"

"Ah yes… *you* may deliver the message to her about her daughter – let her and her stupid-policeman husband be in no doubt that any attempt to rescue her will lead to her death – instantly, by plague. They will be contacted in due course with our further instructions."

Von-Hesse straightened his back as he prepared his 'big question': "Then Mistress… for me and my promised reward?"

"Oh fear not Maximilian, your reward is guaranteed, you will receive all that your loyalty to me deserves!"

"How unusual…" Dr Michelle Wilson mused out aloud to her research assistant Laura Cunningham.

"What's that?" Laura queried.

"Here… the DNA test results from Dr Teal – he carried two copies of the Delta 32 gene… that's hypothesized to give protection against bubonic plague, just as it does against West Nile virus, and HIV."

"Oh yes… a study found that a higher-than-average number of the descendants of the Eyam 'Plague Village' survivors in Derbyshire – from the 1665 Great Plague, carried two copies of that mutation… obviously it didn't help him…"

"Obviously not. I wonder if he was a descendent of anyone who survived the 1665 outbreak here in Liverpool? Ah well, guess we'll never know."

Michelle was deep in rumination when the phone went: "Hello? Oh, already? He's early… OK, send him up, OK, bye."

"Is that the reporter?" asked Laura.

"Yeah, Donald Lithgow from the Daily Post & Echo – they've got wind of the Plague story and want an interview.

Don Lithgow was an 'old hack' used to sniffing out the truth behind the flannel you so often get from people in authority. He'd known Dr Teal, but had yet to meet Michelle: "Dr Wilson?"

"Yes! Come in and take a seat."

"Thanks, call me Don… Donald makes me feel like a duck!"

They shook hands.

"Should I wash my hands afterwards?" he asked semi-seriously "After all, you guys are handling bubonic plague aren't you?"

Michelle smiled dismissively: "Don't worry Don, we don't handle it directly – and anyway the infective agent is just a simple bacteria – we have it safely in culture."

The hack grinned: "Is it Dr Wilson? I've heard that quite a number of scientists don't accept the bacteria model for bubonic plague, they think it's a virus." Lithgow was pleased with himself at showing his pre-interview research.

Michelle grinned back: "Don't get confused Don: *some* scientists in this very specialized field, don't believe that the 'Black Death' of 1347 and 'The Great Plague' of 1665 were Bubonic Plague – they think that it was an Ebola like virus that caused a haemorrhagic fever. The bacteria *Yersinia pestis* was positively identified with bubonic plague as far back as 1894. It also causes pneumonic plague and septicaemiac plague."

"So I can't write a story saying that there's a 'Black Death' outbreak in Liverpool?"

"If you do, then don't quote me! There have been two cases, both sadly fatal... We're looking into any possible infective contact between the people involved, although it must be said that the classic 'reservoir' of bubonic infection is from rat-fleas and *not* from human-to-human contact. Just to be safe, we've administered antibiotics to family members of the two victims, but no further cases have emerged, and we have no reason to expect that any will."

Don sat back and narrowed his eyes as he smiled his journalists crocodile smile: "Suppose... just suppose that this bubonic plague mutates – that's what you medical guys call it don't you? Yeah... you do... suppose, it becomes 'pneumonic' and gets spread by people coughin' an' sneezin' over one-another?"

Michelle paused before answering. She'd expected awkward questions and had hoped this wouldn't be one of them: "We've no evidence that will happen" she compromised.

"Hmmm... but... if it does? And... you mentioned it yerself, that septicaemia form of the disease... isn't that where people bleed to death, on the inside, yer know internally-like?"

Michelle pursed her lips: "But that's *not* what's happened Don. We've had two cases – tragic, but not what would count as anything like an epidemic."

"And yer not expectin' any more?"

"That's right."

"OK... But *if* there are any more, can the authorities cope?"

"Well sure. We have stocks of antibiotics available. You see, in the twenty-first century Mr Lithgow, not the seventeenth – we have the benefit of effective antibiotic medical treatments. Promptly diagnosed, very few people should die of bubonic plague; perhaps as few as between 1-15% of treated cases, with the likelihood being in the lowest end of the range."

"That's what you tried with Dr Teal and Mrs Susan Patterson is it?"

Michelle blushed: "They didn't present for medical treatment until they were in the terminal stage of the disease. Normally, you have a period of anywhere between four to eight days of signs and symptoms before an untreated case could be expected to die – and then, in simple uncomplicated bubonic plague, the mortality rate is around 40 -60%.

"And in pneumonic plague?"

"We aren't talking about pneumonic plague Don, but it's significantly higher.

"Septicaemiac plague?"

"Again it's higher than bubonic plague – perhaps between 60 and 90% depending on the pre-morbid conditions in the patient and if the septicaemia is primary or secondary."

"So I can put the Daily Post and Echo's readers at their ease can I?"

"Well, certainly. We've had two cases of uncomplicated bubonic plague, no other outbreaks; and we have sufficient antibiotics to meet *any* contingencies."

"Good! OK, I'll write my article up… be seeing you Dr Wilson… I hope!" Grinning, the journalist left; leaving a worried and embarrassed Dr Wilson. Laura spoke for her: "We didn't tell him that the antibiotics failed did we…"

"No" murmured Michelle "Let's just hope that there aren't any further cases…" Sighing she returned to mulling over her paperwork. Lost for a few seconds in matters scientific she at first barely noticed the telephone ringing: "Get that for me will you Laura!" she said. Seconds later, Laura had the news: "Michelle: *twenty five* new cases have just been admitted to the Royal Liverpool Hospital! We've got an epidemic!"

Lillian retired to the Chaise Lounge. It was her favourite place to step 'out-of-body' from. Closing her eyes she started the *seperatio* process – the de-coupling of her astral form from her physical body – the reconstituted physical body created from the skull of *Lilith* Hopgood and the distilled essence of her blood soil – taken from the Garden of Eden in Armenia.

Becoming as still as a statue – her body appeared lifeless – her psyche, reaching out in its elemental shape. In an instant she had arrived passing silently and invisibly through the main Crown Street entrance to the Women's hospital. The hustle and bustle of the corridors noticed her not – the hurried march of a physiotherapist passing through her spectral form as through air itself.

Only a small child saw her – her innocent eyes catching a Mona Lisa smile as *Lilith*'s hand passed over her mother's belly: "Mummy who's that nice lady?"

"What lady, little love?"

"That lady... she looks like a fairy princess."

The mother smiled: "It must be the good-fairy bringing your new baby sister!"

"She smiled at me mummy – then she went through that wall over there."

"That's nice love... maybe she's bringing all the mothers their new babies! Isn't that lovely of her!"

At the Liverpool Health Authority a state of near panic had set in. Some manager's reactions to the now obviously serious outbreak settled on their own personal complexes about responsibility – would they be blamed, or sacked even? The Department of Health, The Health Protection Agency, even the World Health Organisation were immediately notified. At the School of Tropical Medicine, Michelle Wilson was stunned. Within minutes though she'd rallied herself to the task and had headed over to the Royal Liverpool Hospital to offer her help.

Over at The Liverpool Daily Post & Echo offices, Donald Lithgow smiled an ironic smile as he updated his story on his laptop…

Maggie had heard the news on the local BBC Radio Merseyside. The details were sketchy but what had been released was notification that a number of Liverpool residents had been admitted to hospital with what was described as a 'mystery' infection. Perhaps naturally enough, most callers to the radio station thought that it was Bird Flu, the Norovirus vomiting disease or perhaps SARS – it was winter after all.

A few suspected the truth – rumours of two plague deaths had been circulating publicly for a few days now, but the health authority had effectively blacked-out the initial reports – and Don Lithgow, the authorities favoured local newspaper 'hack' for releasing difficult stories to, hadn't got his report out yet, so most local people were still oblivious.

Maggie guessed that it was plague; she knew what had been going on with the ESP team. Deeply concerned she could barely concentrate on her journey to pick Lizzie up at Wirral Grammar School. The return trip was one of broken concentration too as she tried to make light chat with her granddaughter whilst the stress of the school run traffic overloaded her already frayed nerves.

By the time she reached Mount Road for the final half-mile home she'd had enough and completely failed to see how the Black supercharged Range Rover in front was positioning itself to force her to turn left into the sheltered and tree-lined avenue of Burrell Road.

The Range Rover braked suddenly – inexplicably blocking her way. She tried to drive past on the inside but the Range Rover turned slightly making the manoeuvre impossible. The open turn into the secluded Burrell Road beckoned – as Maggie could reach Prenton Lane through this 'back' route. Sounding her horn at the blacked-out windowed Range Rover as she made the turn, she didn't see the Mercedes limousine turn directly behind her.

Her little Honda shook suddenly as the Mercedes wafted past and pulled across the road forcing her to stop. Now seriously alarmed she reached for her mobile phone – as the Range Rover roared to a halt behind her, both cars now completely blocking her in.

In an instant and well before she could scroll down her mobile phone 'names' to O'Riley's number, the driver's door was pulled open. A sickening smell of chloroform was her only sensation as her mind swirled into blackness.

Meanwhile, at the Liverpool Women's Hospital a sudden rush of complications with natural deliveries and elective caesareans had resulted in a wave of stillbirths…

14

The Fisher King

ater that afternoon the waiting for the ESP team was over. John's contacts at the university rang him with the news that around thirty new admissions with advanced plague symptoms had come in overnight and through the course of the day. They also told him about the Women's hospital... Grimly he passed the information on to his colleagues:

"It's started... almost thirty new cases since last night. They're trying to keep it quiet to avoid panic – they'd given an interview to a selected Daily Post and Echo journalist, just before this spike of cases – and then just to add to it; as if by cruel coincidence, there's been a suspicious cluster of spontaneous terminations and still-births over at the Women's Hospital in Crown Street!"

"Well Kevin?" asked Claire "There you go – just what you wanted: they've taken the initiative!"

O'Riley seemed to dither. Drumming his fingers and lost in indecision he at last brought himself to reply: "The authorities would never believe us... What would we tell them? We'll just have to find some other way of fighting *Lilith* ourselves..."

John, usually impetuous and the older archetypal 'action-man' introduced some reality into the equation: "With respect, Kevin, precisely *how* do you intend that we fight them? Every caveat we identified before is still in place. We have no *evidence* and we have no *authority*. In short, we've got no 'orthodox' weapon at our disposal. The only possible way to go would be through the help of those you've been keen to avoid contacting…"

John's words pushed O'Riley into the gap in his mind between the realization of the truth, and, his fear that the help wouldn't be there… "And if they don't help? If the Dale is empty… and dead? What then John? It's like it's all resting on that, what if there *is* no help to be had!"

Claire felt a sudden twinge in her stomach as her psyche sensed some terrible alarm. By the time it reached consciousness her instincts were urging her to go to her family: "Look… I've just had an awful sense of foreboding… I know it's irrational but my intuition's telling me to get home to my kids!"

"It's not irrational Claire – it's natural that you want to be with your family when something like this is happening" said O'Riley.

The intensity of her feelings now drove her to lash out: "Oh don't be so *wet* Kevin! Yer just speaking a load ah patronizing crap! My husband – *your* son, has walked out on me and the kids, right when we need him the most; of course I want to be with my family: it's *your* family too!

You know what? You won't do what's right because you're scared; scared that we'll have to make this stand alone – and yet that's exactly *why* we are alone, because you won't move yer butt – you're like that '*sick Fisher King*' in the Arthurian myths who doesn't realize that the land sickens and dies with *his* apathy!

He's the wise-old-man – the Grail-Keeper, yet he's lost his way and sits with his old 'unhealed wound' unable to move!"

Stunned by Claire's outburst O'Riley shuddered as his body jolted at her words. Head in hands he struggled to release himself from the turmoil of opposites tearing away at his soul. In truth *Lilith* had 'spooked' him. Her suggestion that she *was* the soil, that she could destroy anything that grew within it – anything... had cut away at his unconscious reliance on his old mentor. More than that, he'd become settled in his ways, relaxing into his later years he'd gradually forgotten the purpose of the covenant he'd made at the Green-Chapel – the ancient and sacred Dale. He'd forgotten 'him'... had *Viridios* too forgotten him? If so, he feared, then all he had left to fight with was himself; an old man, tired and careworn without the energy and stamina of his youth and middle years.

Once again the immortal bard's words repeated themselves to him:

Glendower: I can call spirits from the vasty deep.

Hotspur: Why, so can I, or so can any man;
But will they come when you do call for them?"

Getting no reply from O'Riley, Claire followed her instincts and left ESP. Running to her Saab parked in Knight Street, her sense of urgency tunnelled her vision. So much so that the peripheral shadows perfectly concealed the tall, dark angular figure who now stepped out across her path.

Claire screamed in shock as the hooded black-brown eyes literally arrested her: "You! Keep away from me you killer!"

Von-Hesse's head tilted back slightly – allowing him to regard Claire with obvious contempt: "My Mistress commands me to pass a message to you!"

Claire clutched at her chest her heart racing with fear: "Message? What message!"

A smile now broke out across the Bavarian's handsome face: "Woman…listen carefully… your daughter Elizabeth is enjoying my Mistresses hospitality…"

Claire gasped as maternal rage overcame her fear – she lashed out at the tall powerfully athletic figure – who simply caught her hand in a near wrist breaking grip: "It would be my pleasure to end your life Lattimer! However, my instructions… for now… are simply to pass this message; Elizabeth is *safe* upon the contingent requirement that you and your… relatives and associates… comply in full with our conditions. If not, she will suffer unimaginable pain and death from the pestilence!"

Claire's horrified face was taken as her understanding.

"So… you will make no attempt to recover her, you will take no action to resist our further purposes, and… when my Mistress decides the moment has come, then *you* will surrender yourself as replacement for her!

Understand, woman?"

The grip on Claire's wrist was sickeningly painful. Crying in desperation she nodded. Von Hesse let go, causing her to gasp with relief. "So… to reiterate, you will not inform the authorities *and* you will not interfere in any way with our… progress… Then, we will exchange the girl, for *you*. And, just so you don't unduly worry, you may tell Dr O'Riley that Elizabeth is accompanied by his wife… likewise to be exchanged at the appropriate place and time – of which… you will be informed in advance!"

O'Riley was still in a state of stunned torpor. John had left him to it, figuring that he'd learn more about what was going on inside himself if he was left alone to experience it. Meanwhile he'd rung his contacts back and got some more information: "Well, that *is* interesting…" he mused.

"What is?" came the murmured question from within O'Riley's reverie.

"Oh the er… names of the latest plague victims… they're clustered into five family groups. Dave at the university reckons that's to be expected as it's an infectious disease… but… the names are: Teal, Lattimer, Tarleton, Penny and Longfield."

O'Riley stirred like a sloth: "Teal and Lattimer! Obvious why it's them… don't know about Tarleton, Penny or Longfield though."

"Yer need to sharpen yer wits Kevin. What's obvious, as you seemed to hint, is that the Teals' and Lattimers' have been *selected* by *Lilith*, or Lillian as she's known; and that suggests that the Penny's and Longfields' must be connected by descent to people in seventeenth century Liverpool too. We'd better ring Claire… just in case any of the Lattimers' are close relatives of hers."

Before O'Riley could answer the sound of Claire's running feet could be heard in the corridor. The door burst open and her terrified face came into view: "Kevin, John… they've taken them! Lizzie and Maggie!"

Meier couldn't resist the temptation. The chloroform had been effective in seconds and they now had two unconscious women at their mercy. Maggie in truth to her 'glamorous granny' status was still a stunningly beautiful woman – and Lizzie had inherited a mix of her mother's and grandmother's looks and figure. As Adler watched, Meier groped at their breasts and passed his hands up Lizzie's skirt.

"Careful! The Mistress said that the girl in particular was to be unharmed!" Adler was in terror of *Lilith*'s displeasure.

By now very aroused, Meier was almost past restraint: "Ah she won't know… and these two won't be complaining – why not… the mother is still attractive… maybe I can…"

"Meier!"

The *Furor Teutonicus* in Von-Hesse's voice electrified Meier causing him to cry out in startled fear.

"You fool! Have you learned nothing from your time with me? There is no surer way to spoil your occult progress than to indulge in lustful passions… All I have achieved with you would be undone – and then there would *no* possibility of your re-animation! Remember that your value to me, is in my prior investment in time, and effort. If things go wrong… then I will consider 'reconstituting' both you and Adler. But, if you insist on throwing my 'investment' in you away… then I will simply dispense with you myself!" Mark me: only the Mistress may exploit libido… but we… we must… divert its energy into our transformation – *that* is the true Alchemy! I myself have no such passion. Sexual lust is simply beneath me. Only with the Mistress…. And then only for the supreme privilege of being her consort… But base desires Meier! Besides… the Mistress would destroy you instantly if you despoiled the girl. She is to be retained as a potential host – should any 'misfortune' overcome the Mistress's present form."

Meier felt embarrassed but not shamed: "I was thinking of the older woman… such a temptation – she'll be wasted after-all… the Mistress will kill every woman she does not use!"

"Indeed, but it is not your place to submit to carnal lust. If you still desire it then you have not made sufficient progress. Beware… the Mistress is particular about her servants. She may allow you to kill the woman later, let that be enough!

Now… Adler, you will maintain their unconscious state – administer drugs as required until the Mistress returns."

"Yes Master… when will that be?"

Von-Hesse breathed hard: "I don't know. She's in the city readying to strike down the young and licentious in the night-clubs. Soon, the authorities will realize how great the contagion is. When they do that, the city will likely be quarantined. This may be the last best opportunity she has to spread the pestilence en-mass to the city's youth…"

Lillian was indeed in Liverpool – she was with Adam at his flat off Smithdown Road. The news about Claudia's illness was that it was pregnancy related – *late* pregnancy, and despite her protestations – no doctor would believe her when she said she'd gone from just having her period to near full term in a matter of days. This was despite a glut of similar reports from local girl students – all in the eighteen to twenty one age range – who although behind Claudia in term, were likewise apparently pregnant as if out of nowhere.

Being unsupervised – Adam was a virtually free agent, and he readily responded to Lillian's mobile phone call to meet her back at his flat. Her psychic energy was low… she'd expended a great deal of it in her astral interdiction at the Women's hospital – but her physical energy was high – her libidinous physical energy… Soon, she would be ready to conceive herself – although she was holding back until the contagion was fully released. Meanwhile… she'd enjoy herself with her one and only human love – Adam Mitchell the reincarnated soul of Adam Teal and her chosen New Adam…

Adam's mind swam as it drank her beauty. Responding as two people – Adam Teal and Adam Mitchell – conjoined within a single soul – he marvelled at his great good-fortune: "How did I *ever* come to deserve you *Lilith*? You're absolutely perfect… the most beautiful, most radiant, most feminine girl I could ever imagine!"

Lilith gently caressed his face. Snuggled together beneath his fraying bed-sheets – even the grubby walls and rotten window frames seemed to her to be as rich and opulent as the Ptolemaic palace of Cleopatra, in ancient Alexandria. Only with him had she ever found the peace and love that was – she believed – rightfully hers. Rightfully hers from Eden, and yet denied to her by that first Adam who forsook her because of her essential, wilful and independent nature –for that *other* second woman…

From Adam's rib was Eve forged and from their union the cursed 'human' race. But *Lilith*, out of the Earth itself was fashioned and none of true humankind had thus far issued from her – only demi-gods, demons, witches and shades. Now – this would change; this one, innocent, bungling, but lovely young man: this 'New Adam' had reached her heart through the enduring purity of his unconditional love.

The ESP team were at St. Stephens Road – with them were Sean and… Young Kevin. Responding to a desperate plea from Claire, the Police Superintendent had arrived to find his wife in a state of almost inconsolable distress. Misreading the situation at first as being as a result of his walking out on her – he prepared himself for a confrontation with his father about Claire's revelation about their relationship. It took John to take him aside and break the news about Lizzie and Maggie's abduction.

Just on the cusp of middle-age, 'Young' Kevin still had the vigour of his youth – and it took a Herculean effort on John's part to physically restrain him from leaving right there and then in an effort to rescue his daughter: "Kevin! Think! Just for a moment think! They'll kill her, and Maggie too, if we so much as breathe within a mile of her!" John's impassioned and pleading eyes, plus his physical strength – caused Young Kevin to resign himself. John continued: "We don't even know where they're holding them… it's unlikely to be at Lake Hall They could be anywhere, this side of the Mersey, over in Liverpool, or somewhere else altogether.

Now… whatever it is that's been eating away at you – then fer Christ's sake let's put it to one side until all of this is over! We can't win if we don't fight together as one… yeah? United we stand, divided we fall!"

Young Kevin nodded "OK… alright…" then with a last outburst of frustration: "Shit! I'm a senior police-officer! I've got all their resources at my disposal… and I *can't* use them!"

"Things are gonna go pear-shaped on a huge scale Kevin. Within another twenty four to forty eight hours, the police will be so overwhelmed with this outbreak of plague that they simply won't have the resources to go look for Lizzie and Maggie… we'll *have* to do this ourselves…"

Young Kevin shook his head as the enormity of the task sank in: "Where, where do we start?!"

John sighed and looked over his shoulder at Kevin senior: "For my money… it's down to yer dad."

O'Riley had heard it all. He knew now that he had to go to the Dale. Just as John and Claire had said… and just as they'd said too, he was afraid, afraid that this time, they'd have to stand alone.

"OK… in the morning then, I'll return... to the Green Chapel…"

Late that evening and Dr Michelle Wilson was so exhausted and stressed-out that she was making basic mistakes: "Laura! Help me out here please, I can't remember… I can't remember what this culture is!"

Laura was tired too, tired and scared. She'd been buffered somewhat by Michelle's seniority – for with seniority came responsibility – at least in circumstances like these. In 'ordinary' crises so called responsibility often meant a cover-up or at least 'spin' – but there could be no such devices now – those responsible for protecting the public's health really would be held to account – if… they survived.

"Its *Yersinia pestis* Dr Wilson… simple *Yersinia pestis* found in soil."

"Soil? Oh yes… soil is a natural reservoir for it…" In her fatigued state, Michelle's psyche picked up on the symbolism rather than the science of it all: "Soil… the very earth itself, it's as if even that has turned against us…"

Laura sighed: "The other teams have identified a spread of different strains – it's not one form of *Yersinia*, but several… and, there are as yet unidentified viral pathogens that seem to be working synergistically with them."

Michelle jolted as her psyche again read the deeper meaning: "It's like they're intelligent... or being directed intelligently... some kind of 'mind' is behind this..."

Laura sensed that her boss was losing it: "You need some rest Dr Wilson, go take a break; I can carry on from here."

"Rest! I can't do that, where would I go? No where's safe! Don't you see! This isn't an *ordinary* disease; it's something... supernatural..."

Laura didn't see: all she saw was that her boss had lost it...

By midnight, the authorities still hadn't gathered enough to realize the full scale of the threat. The article from the Liverpool Daily Post newspaper would go out on tomorrow mornings front page, but the reflex reaction from the health establishment had been to scale things down whilst they made their tests. Michelle, in her fatigue driven altered state of consciousness, had been the only one amongst them to intuit the truth.

Meanwhile, the youth of Merseyside made their regular Friday night pilgrimage to worship their Dionysian gods in the night-clubs of Liverpool – unaware that their fatal nemesis was already amongst them.

Lilith worked her way into the heaving morass of young people. Ecstasy alcohol and other drugs fuelling their dance, deafening rhythms played through the sound-system – laser lights and strobes flashing – Dante would have found his inferno in this place, instead the youth of Liverpool found their smiling death.

Adam had accompanied her, unknowing of her intention; he'd drunk enough to require a visit to the toilet and it wasn't long before *Lilith*'s stunning beauty attracted male attention:

"Whaz yer name-like girl?" The 'slap-headed' youth was beguiled – his attraction to *Lilith* heightened by his drugs.

"I'm *Lilith*... and my name is retribution" she smiled.

"Yer wha?!"

Lilith's Mona-Lisa smile broadened to show her lovely dimples as she passed her hand across his eyes.

Puzzled the youth bobbed his head to the music and was carried away by the crowd's human tide.

Adam found her again: "Alright love?" he asked – his eyes showing his devotion to her.

Lilith felt the warm glow of love in her belly. She would protect Adam, he would not succumb to the pestilence – he was more safe in her company than with anyone in the whole world: "Let's try some more clubs… I'm bored with this one: it'll be dead soon."

Adam didn't want his love to be bored: "Bored?! OK, let's go!"

Lilith paused at the door. As if shielding her eyes from the strobes, she passed her left hand over the dying crowd.

15

Lilith

The Redeemer

Liverpool at dawn

dam was deep in the oblivion of sleep – his last recollection was of *Lilith's* soft curvaceous form wrapped about him – but on this early December's dawn it was only her body that he held – her spirit in its primordial *astral* form had left it's bodily host – and as the sun's Easterly rays showered the city with hopeful light – there she stood in mocking parody of Rio de Janeiro's 'Christ The Redeemer' – her arms outstretched atop the 40 storey St John's Tower. Her face turned to the west – was a picture of natural beauty, and: of the coming death....

"Behold... for I am *Lilith* and my name is retribution! Now is the time of mine vengeance come... Arise oh blood-red curtain of death... out of the very Earth itself!"

Then did the western sky obey her command... an eerie coat of
misty cloud – as red as death, drew out from the land –
stretching as grasping fingers – pointing, seeking, touching... it
descended from on high as a veil: down over the river Mersey;
penetrating into and between, the buildings of the world
famous waterfront.

Down onto the Liver Building – and on up James Street, towards Castle Square... Enveloped too was old St Nicholas's Church and Dale Street: even Water Street – the site of *Lilith* Hopgood's home, more than three hundred and fifty years previously.

Old Hall Street and then Paradise Street – her place of entombment – invested by the red vapoured *miasma* until at last, all of the *old* Liverpool Town was shrouded in the killing cloud.

Then the two cathedrals: the Anglican and the Catholic: – the
last possible refuges of hope for the city

The Empire theatre, St George's Hall...

Then the museum itself...

Lime Street railway station, and the city centre...

Even 'Hope' Street

For a while, the Sun itself, was covered with Lilith's blanket of red death

Then as a beacon: she shone from atop of what was now, her tower: *Lilith's* Tower...

"From the very stone of these buildings shall it issue forth – the dusty pores shall bleed with my unseen contagion: out hence from this city until *all* of humankind is consumed! Oh Adam in Eden, how your descendants will wail in their misfortune and curse the usurper Eve's hated name!"

The red mist had settled, and then sank into the very stone of the city – the sky left an eerie hue with blood read streamers, trailing like fingers from horizon to horizon.

The stunned people of the city could not know that *Lilith's* plague would leech out from every pore in every building, even from the tarmac pavements and road surfaces.

Death had already struck at the nightclubs and the maternity hospital, but over the next 24 hours, first their home town, and then, the rest of the world, would succumb to *Lilith's* vengeance...

16

The Green Chapel

Saturday 2nd December 2006

'Riley had risen early. Last night had been a terrible and emotional ordeal for him. Suffering the pain of his wife and granddaughter's abduction he'd also been caught-out on an old psychological complex. He'd lost sight of himself in his maturity as an elder psychotherapist – becoming the rock for others, nurturing them to accept their weaknesses and flaws. Thus had he gradually distilled-out his own capacity for self-acceptance; as if his outer-persona as the all-too-perfect and 'wise' old-man meant that no room was left within for natural and all-too-human failings.

Now that the great emergency of his later life was upon him: could this too-perfect man, come once again to accept his own liberating imperfection? In the still dark morning he drove his car along Barnston Road towards the eternal Dale. The dawn was fast approaching and he hurried to be there as the first-light yawned across the fields. Preoccupied, he failed to notice the strangely dark and reddening sky, that stretched tendril-like over from the West and then sank down fatally into the city. His mind raced with rhetorical questions: "Have you betrayed the covenant? Are you still, in your older years, a flawed and un-integrated personality? Have you left it too late to return to the Dale?"

The road dipped through its winding path bottoming out into the Dale and then rising until the familiar old sight of the Fox and Hounds pub with its tree lined car park emerged from the fading gloom. Turning right – his car ascended the brief rise and drove over to the little corner of the car park that he'd always taken… more than twenty years earlier.

Memories now flooded his mind – fresh and alive, almost vivid 'green' in their lushness.

A final look round the car park – almost aching to see some sign of a friendly presence – he got out and walked his weary way over to the old sandstone wall. At sixty eight years of age, it was a harder task than before – worn joints and wasted muscles no longer bore the exertion so readily. The bare twigs of the broken bushes scratched at his face as he pushed through a silvered frost, covered all: "It's still winter!" he exclaimed "These bushes... should be green!"

Had the Dale's magic died? This special place had a magic... a magic known only to a few, but recorded long ago in the medieval Wirral poem *Sir Gawain and The Green Knight*. As the home of the 'Green Man' the nature spirit of rebirth, and of the living greenery itself – its heart was blessed with evergreen lushness, even in the depths of the coldest and most inclement of winters. Here was that Spirit's 'Green Chapel' and here it was in his middle years, that O'Riley had met his Master: 'The Green Man' - *Viridios* and been inducted by him into the 'Order of Imperfect Man' – a gift that had opened his heart and soul to his true purpose in life, making sense of all that had gone before, and giving him the strength to fight against a wave of evil that had threatened the very land itself.

But... that was then.

Desperately he found his way to the heart.

The great oaks were bare and frost covered: the stream shallow; fast food packaging littered the gentle slopes. No dawn chorus of summer bird song greeted his winter ears. A sad, desolate Wasteland met his tired eyes.

"I'm too late... it's died... the Green-Chapel has died!"

Unbeknown to O'Riley, death had struck elsewhere too. The regions hospitals were filling up as terrified youths in the agony of bubonic plague were clogging the casualty departments. Caught so suddenly and at such intensity – what little preparations the authorities had made were simply overwhelmed. The Saturday morning edition of the Liverpool Daily Post carried Don Lithgow's article on the earlier plague cases – but was now hopelessly overtaken by the speed of events.

Worse still – this fresh surge of cases had all the characteristics of *pneumonic* plague – spread from human to human by aerosol particles sprayed from congested lungs. The infections progress was rapid, unprecedentedly rapid and no available ant-biotic seemed to be effective.

The awful truth had at last emerged – there was a rapid onset, untreatable - 100% fatal and highly contagious epidemic at large with nothing to stop it becoming a global pandemic. Billy Butler the iconic BBC Radio Merseyside presenter delivered the increasingly bad news:

"The authorities have confirmed that they outbreak is a new kind of pneumonic plague – its already spread out from the city and is striking people down in their thousands!

The hospitals and emergency services are at breaking point!"

Lilith had returned from the invocation of her *miasma* and now slept a peaceful sleep in the arms of her lover. Later that day, before the city became quarantined, she would take him to safety at the Birkenhead warehouse. Then, if necessary, she would deal with the recalcitrant Von-Hesse – who must accept Adam's status... or die...

O'Riley felt his stomach heave. Too dignified to give in to it, he turned and made his forlorn way back through the trees and bushes. His last hope had gone. He saw his wife's face etched into the bare trees, her fear and agony gnawing at his soul. His footfall echoed with the hallucinated cries of his granddaughter – abducted and the prisoner of an unbeatable and unbearable evil.

By the time he reached the road his breath was shallow, his heart feeling the emotional as well as the physical exertion. What use was life now? He thought. "I've lost!" he screamed "I've lost through my damned arrogance, and betrayed *everyone* that I've ever loved!"

The little rise to the car park seemed steeper than before, his leaden feet turning into a pain in his left arm and a vice-like constriction around his chest: "Take me now! Let me die I don't want to live!"

He didn't see the car turn into the car park behind him – still less did he hear it. Hyperventilating he lay across the bonnet of his Honda Legend urging his heart to beat its last.

Young Kevin had received an early morning call himself. Sleeping on the sofa he was stiff and sore as his mobile summonsed him to meet the emergency. All police rest-days and annual leave were cancelled as officers were called in to their respective parade stations.

Soon the Mersey tunnels, the tube and even the eternal Mersey Ferries would be closed down. The motorways out from the region would be blocked and all flights in and out of Liverpool John Lennon Airport would be suspended. The port of Liverpool would be closed with crews ordered to remain on their ships. But of course it was already too late…

O'Riley was moaning – his face buried into the bonnet of his car. His heart had refused to obey him and stubbornly beat on. The crack of small pebbles under the tyres of the approaching car drew his brief attention, but he couldn't bring himself to look.

The gentle hum of the car's engine and the faint smell of exhaust fumes in the cold – damp morning air gradually irritated him enough to look up from his car bonnet.

The visiting car was actually a small van. O'Riley read the words printed on the side: "Wirral Ranger Service…" Suddenly he found himself laughing: "Ha! Countryside Rangers! If *only* they knew!" The effort of laughing tightened his chest and he slumped forwards again across the bonnet.

After a moment the window of the van wound down: "That's right sir… Countryside-Rangers. They don't mean much… to people who think they're important… but really… they're nothing…"

O'Riley's spine tingled and shuddered like it hadn't done in twenty years. The voice, and in particular the form of its' words were well known to him: "You! *It's* you!"

The passenger door to the Ranger van opened, the welcoming sound of a heater beckoned: "Climb in!" said the voice. O'Riley hauled himself off the bonnet – his grateful smile just winning against his withered features.

Climbing in to the warmth he turned to look at this Countryside Ranger. Sure enough – there was the shock of red curly hair and beard – and most defining of all – the odd coloured blue and green eyes – the green one seemingly turreted like a Chameleon's and able to swivel about independently of the other.

"You're back!" O'Riley managed to exclaim.

"I ain't never been gone sir… you just didn't look…"

"You were in the police…"

"I left in '86, just as soon as I was happy that your son was settled and on his way. I've been a Wirral Country Ranger ever since."

"You haven't aged… but then you never did, did you." O'Riley murmured.

"Well, that's a bit of a misunderstanding actually sir, I age a little with the year, and then… in the spring, I become young again… I enjoy my work; someone has to look after the countryside, the wildlife and the fields… I'm the Ranger for the Heswall Dales – but, I take in Barnston too."

O'Riley shook himself: "But it's dead, Barnston Dale is dead, I've just been there, it's all frosted in winter's coat, the leaves are fallen away, the stream is shallow and lifeless!"

"Really? Sounds like a wasteland…"

O'Riley sighed: "That's what she brings – The Wasteland!"

The Odd-Eyed one swivelled his green-eye to regard him: "She's certainly brought it to you…"

"To me? To the whole world! She's …a nemesis, the death of all humankind. She even said that she could stop…you: The Green Man – the spirit of life… whatever grows in soil she says she can destroy… because she *is* the soil, the very stuff of the Earth itself…"

The Ranger engaged the gears and drove away towards the car-park exit: "Come for a little drive whilst we talk… Here have some of this" he said handing him a gilded hip flask.

"What's this?"

"Whiskey, it'll warm yer heart and thin yer blood. Good on a cold winter's morn."

O'Riley gulped it back – the burning in his throat soon translating into a whole body glow: "Oh that's good!"

"Best Scotch malt whisky!"

"Scotch… oh yes… like dear old Bruce Irving was."

"He's doin' fine."

"Fine? He's been dead these twenty two years and more!"

"Dead you say? Yes… you did say that… You said that about the Dale too."

"It *is* dead! I've just come back from there… the life in it has gone!"

"You can still say that, and with you being one ah them Jungian psychoanalysts?"

O'Riley's spine tingled again: "You mean it isn't?…"

The Ranger paused as he changed gear and then made a slow right turn: "You psychologist types, you talk a lot about what you call 'projection' don't you?"

"Projection? Yes… that's where someone projects what's really inside their own head onto outside people or places, so that he doesn't see them…." he faltered "as they really are…" Another tingle rippled up and down his spine: "You mean that I *saw* what was in my own head? What I *expected* to see, and not what was really there?"

"You saw… your own desolation mirrored back to you. It was lifeless, just as you *nearly* were back in the car-park.

You see… Claire was right."

"What?"

"Claire: Claire Lattimer – when she said that you'd become the Fisher-King."

"You knew she'd said that?!"

The green-eye rotated and fixed him – answering with its unblinking gaze: "The land sickens with you… or appears to, to your own self-reflection. Those around you who love you, despite their own pain and distress – they sense it, they sense it in you, and see it come out from you – you see you forgot the message of the old myths – the King and the land are one…"

O'Riley felt a surge of energy return to his body: "How do I defeat her? She's so universally powerful!"

"There are two ways: both are necessary – but only one is in your gift."

"Go on!"

"Go back, back to the Dale – see it at it *really* is, as only those who have known its secrets can see it. Gather from the stream bank some of the good earth. Take too some water from the stream – you will need these to mix with *her* soil – without that, she cannot be sustained, or, even reconstituted. Someone must find where her soil is kept and lace it with that of the Dale. Sprinkle the water on it too – that will undo all the alchemical work of that corrupted Cathar."

"And the other way?"

"That, sir, is not yours to use. Only by one to whom she surrenders to, both in body… *and* in heart…"

Claire had received yet more bad news. Watching Sky News and then –BBC News 24, she'd heard about the increasing outbreak of Pneumonic Plague in Liverpool – the number of known victims in the region had now reached over ten thousand – mostly young people in their late teens to mid-twenties, people who only twenty four hours earlier had been perfectly fit and well. That; and her mobile phone had rung with the news that the Lattimers' who had contracted plague in the earlier batch of cases were indeed relatives of hers: uncles, aunts, cousins… Her parents were safe and well in North Wales, having moved to Colwyn Bay when they retired, but surely it was only a matter of time before *Lilith*'s evil found them. The people of the city were ringing in to the local radio stations, speaking of a strange red mist that had fallen onto the city at dawn before melting-in to the fabric of the buildings – dismissed by the authorities as hysteria and superstition – Claire chillingly realised what it must mean...

Worried sick about her daughter – John had arrived early to keep Claire company: "The tunnels will be closing anytime now. Already the trains and ferries have stopped." He told her.

"I don't know what's happened to Kevin – the police will be on the front line as usual… what happens' when the food and essential services stop?"

John shook his head: "I don't know Claire; I don't think anyone can know, nothing like this has ever happened before. Let's just hope that Kevin senior comes back from The Dale with some good news!" John hoped… he piously hoped, but his more rational thinking side held out no such hope at all.

Lilith got through the Mersey tunnel just as the police were closing it. By chance – Superintendent O'Riley - Kevin Junior was there to see the last cars through, and in the midst of his own anxieties, completely missed seeing her. Adam was in the front passenger seat – now in a trance state – inducted by the sheer shock of the situation – and – by his fathomless love for *Lilith*. His head shook in disbelief as he dared at last to ask: "*Lilith is* this really all your doing?"

She smiled her Mona Lisa smile: "A long time ago, Adam Teal, you watched me stand on the shore of the old Liverpool Pool – both cursed and condemned as a witch. You knew then who, and what I was, but I saw in your eyes, heard in your words, and felt in your heart, your *genuine* love for me. Not a love for my beauty, not a love for my power, but a genuine, *true*-love. In that moment, I knew, with all my heart can hold, that we should, that we *would*, one-day be reunited together… in love.

Now… I'm back, and I've chosen you to be my consort – it's a great gift Adam… you will never age, never die, be mine forever – and *our* children will inherit the Earth!"

Adam Mitchell – and within him Adam Teal, felt his objections numb, softly, into acceptance. How could he argue against fate, against such a wonderful love-story, for that is what this was – something more romantic and yet more real than anything he'd ever known of. As the car gently accelerated away from the exit – he felt his concerns slip, as if sucked back into the closing, dark road tunnel.

Adler had been 'maintaining' Maggie and Lizzie under the direct supervision of Von-Hesse. Both were on drip feeds for hydration and for the administration of sedating drugs. The warehouse on the Birkenhead side of Duke Street Bridge had been acquired in advance for this purpose – and also hid Maggie's Honda car – which had been seized with the women at the time of their abduction. Von-Hesse was impatient,

Lilith should have arrived by now – if she delayed much longer then the developing catastrophe would leave her stranded in Liverpool. At last he heard the sound of her horn signalling her arrival: "Meier! Open the gates, quickly!"

Meier, still smarting from his humiliating put-down by Von-Hesse jumped to-it: stepping aside as *Lilith* drove swiftly in through the opened sliding wooden gates. Von-Hesse's Germanic perma-frown expanded into astonishment as he saw Adam sitting in the front passenger seat. *Lilith* was amused by The craggy-one's visage: "Why, Maximilian, you look like you've had a dose of salts!"

"Mistress… you've brought *him* here?!"

She breezed out of the car parting her now hair to reveal her perfect heart-shaped face: "Yes!" she replied in a hissing whisper "And *you* Maximilian will afford him every grace and favour just as you would me!" Her eyes had darkened from green to black, chilling The Bavarian with their clear and present warning.

"Of course Mistress…" he replied soothingly.

Lilith smiled her Mona-Lisa smile and tilted her head in trademark coquet pose – her eyes lighting back into opalescent autumnal green hues: "Good!" she chirped, then added "I'm near the very height of my powers Maximilian… just remember this; I have marked you… and with just a blink of my eyes the wretched remains of your soul will be torn out from the living tissue of your body and stretched into eternal damnation!"

Von-Hesse felt his legs buckle with uncharacteristic weakness: "Marked me mistress? Why!?"

You always underestimated my reach Maximilian. I overheard your displeasure about me in conversation with your acolytes: so now... your continued survival is conditional upon your complete, and unfailing, loyal obedience."

"But... I'm to be rewarded... for my *centuries* of service to you! You promised!"

"Oh yes... so I did... and, so I shall... Place but one wrong thought in your mind and I shall find it... find it and deliver to you the most exquisite torture of living death!
There you are... promise kept!"

Meier and Adler had closed, having hearing every word that had passed between them. They could be could be trusted, but only so long as their Master's power held true. Simple survival would demand that they obey *Lilith* even before him... The Bavarian may have the ability to 'reconstitute' them should they suffer some misfortune and die in his service, but *Lilith's* supreme power of life and death would easily overrule the fallen Cathar's Hermetic Alchemy.

Von-Hesse realized that not only had his coveted status as *Lilith's* consort been lost, but so too had much of his authority over his inferiors: "Mistress! I do not deserve such punishment. I am a man of honour!"

"Honour? Your honour as a human male was left back in the eleventh century – Maximilian Von Hesse... or *Guy de Montpelier* as you were then known! Enough now: your complete obedience or your immediate death – it's *your* choice!"

Lilith turned next to Meier: "Now, Meier, show me the two human females... unharmed and inviolate are they?"

O'Riley was back in the car park at the Fox & Hounds pub. The Odd-Eyed one had dropped him off, and then drove sedately off on his business: as if all-hell hadn't in-fact, quite literally, broken out all around them.

Retracing his steps: fortified now by whiskey and by contact with the *avatar* of the Green Man – he climbed again over the old sandstone wall. The closest bushes were bare – as before, but gradually a most verdant lusciousness revealed itself – at first in little islands of greenery and then at last opening out

into a riot of jade and emerald hues. The old oaks stood
sentinel and proud: leaves firm; and yet in this, the depths of
winter, still full in their summer's health. Out from the foliage
a human face formed: The *Avatar* emerged now fully as The
Green Man; his head, face and body, sprouting luscious vines
and leaves.

As surely as had been his ancestor: young Connor O'Riley, in
old Liverpool Town; Dr Kevin O'Riley, was re-united with his
mentor and master.

The little stream babbled its life giving tune and a great weight
lifted from an old man's shoulders…

17

The Last Temptation of Adam

Sunday 3ʳᵈ December 2006: Chester Street Police Station Birkenhead, 10.25am

uperintendent O'Riley had his work cut out. Not only were large numbers of people on the streets – clamouring for information – but the hospital and ambulance services were strained beyond breaking point with exponentially increasing cases of virulent pneumonic plague. Even the discipline and dedication of the police was beginning to show strain as officers openly talked of walking off duty and returning home to protect their families – not only from the unseen enemy of pestilence, but also from their fellow citizens.

In Liverpool itself, gangs of looters had already started to raid supermarkets as the police's authority finally broke down. The government had created a cordon sanitaire around Merseyside – held firm by out-of-area police officers and backed-up by what little military forces remained in the UK due to overstretched, overseas commitments in Iraq and Afghanistan. Nothing it seemed could stop the rapid progress of the contagion.

The University and School of Tropical Medicine were effectively under siege as armed police-officers protected their scientists from desperate and fearful people clamouring for the now impossible safety of a sure and certain cure.

Out in the Wirral suburbs, the streets were mostly quiet. But soon the few active groups of prowling looters would force others to do likewise in a spiral of runaway competitive panic.

The 'hysteria' the authorities had tried to suppress over the reports of a red-veiled mist that had descended onto the area of the old Liverpool town, was by now unstoppable: for not only had a miasmic contagion broken out in the city, but the 24 hr international television news channels reported a strange phenomenon now affecting the dawn skies of the whole world...

Like some great blood-red, volcanic ash cloud, a rolling blanket of visible, and yet somehow intangible vapour, had encircled the globe – moving from West to East, it settled at dawn, in fingering tendrils, onto the world's great cities and population centres.

But there were no active volcanoes that could explain away this blood-red portent and all attempts at taking samples either in the air or at ground-zero failed... it as was if the cloud were of the ether itself - as it sank into the pores of buildings and the very tarmac of the cities roads. Meteorologists pronounced it as inexplicable, and not a product of any known weather phenomena.

Within 24 hours it had already reached the West coast of the USA striking into: California, Oregon and Washington states.

But one thing was uncomfortably certain, and thus fed into what was rapidly becoming a worldwide, mass-hysteria: the point of origination – the font and fountain head of the cloud was the sky above the 'plague city' of Liverpool in the UK.

All too soon – the dusty pores of the hosting stones breathed out their invisible death, as one by one, the great cities of the world fell to *Lilith's* plague...

O'Riley was at St. Stephens Road with Claire, John and Sean: "So that's it... that's what we have to do, but it's only half of the equation."

John was rubbing his chin, like he always did when he was frustrated: "I've asked Carla to help, but she's torn between our kids and the poor folks pouring into Arrowe Park hospital with this contagion... She's having some effect it seems, at least in holding its progress back – she's a natural 'healer' with great-gifts, as you all know...

But back to the problem: what we do know is that at least *some* of the soil is still at the Museum – which means we'll have to cross over to Liverpool somehow. The rest... I'd guess it's at Lake Hall?"

"Agreed" said O'Riley. "That's the logical place for it to be - which leaves the 'other' part of the problem – how can we use someone to whom *Lilith* has given her body and heart to – to destroy her?"

Claire sighed: "Obviously, that can only be one person – Adam!"

The two men looked at her.

"What?" she said looking from one to the other...

Lilith had been satisfied that the women – in particular Lizzie – hadn't been violated. This was fortunate for Meier as she'd easily read his heart and found therein his hidden lustful desires.

Von-Hesse's efficiency had meant that the warehouse complex had been fitted-out with every necessary convenience – there was sleeping accommodation, plenty of food and water – even its own power supply.

"Everything you need is here Mistress – including the soil and the Skull from Lake Hall." Von-Hesse was keen to demonstrate his usefulness.

Lilith's Mona-Lisa smile bathed him: "And the computers?"

"Yes, everything!"

"Good! Now, I want you to carry out the alchemical analysis on that semen sample – the one from the younger Kevin O'Riley – the police superintendent: it was of a *very* high quality, and I sensed something unusual, something 'additional' within it."

Von-Hesse's scientific curiosity was aroused: "You think that he could have inherited something from his father – something to do with that damnable green Dale?"

"Possibly Maximilian, possibly. Just make sure that you remain useful and I *might* find it within me to... *almost* forgive you. If there is something... in that semen sample, then we should harvest some eggs from his daughter Lizzie."

Von-Hesse's eyes narrowed with ever focused curiosity: "You believe that it could pass through the female line?"

"Well of course!" the coquettish tilt, tilted even more: "Anyway, what I suspect *may* be carried by both the policeman and his daughter does not originate with the O'Riley family... oh no... it came into that line from another – so yes, the female line *is* important.... So, off you go Maximilian!" She dismissed him with a wave of her right hand.

Next she addressed Adler: "I'm to show Adam the two women, in private. There are things he doesn't yet understand. Prepare them, ensure that they are clean nourished and hydrated, but still heavily sedated."

"Mistress!" Adler knew better than to display anything other than efficient Germanic obedience.

Lilith's smile opened out her lovely dimples as she thought of the mayhem and death at that very moment sweeping through the city...

Superintendent O'Riley was down at the Ferry Terminal at Woodside. It'd changed a great deal in the more than twenty years he'd been a police-officer. Gone now were much of the original wood and iron-work – replaced with a pastiche of the pseudo-retro and modern: a recreation of things that were never actually there. With this 'leisure refurbishment' - the soul of the place had almost completely passed away. The ferry boats themselves had changed – extensively refurbished and modernised, even re-named. The 'Woodchurch' – the boat his father had taken in 1985 over to police headquarters to resign as an Assistant Chief Constable, and the ferry where that odd-eyed avatar of The Green Man had opened his father's heart to the future – was now called 'Snowdrop.' The terminal was eerily quiet. The ferries tied up, their crews sent home. The swell of the Mersey tidal estuary rose and fell, transferring a gentle rock to the landing stage. Young Kevin was transported back in memory to his childhood – to happy times with his Mum and sister Mary – the wonder in a child's eyes seeing the Liverpool waterfront from the prow of a ferryboat – the iconic Liver-buildings with its two great 'Liver-Birds' symbols of the cities endurance and permanence.

The tingle in his spine spread to the hairs on the back of his neck – electrified by the voice from nowhere: "Hello young man."

Young Kevin's eyes bulged as he turned around: "You! What are you doin' here?"

"As Spike Milligan used to say – 'Everybody's gotta be somewhere!'" came the reply.

The policeman's face was wide with incredulity: "You… you've *not* changed… you look younger than me!"

The green eye scanned his visage: "And you… 'young-man' are looking far too careworn fer yer age – a lot like yer Dad used ter look these many years passed."

"My Dad… I was just thinking of him…" Kevin Junior's face slumped as his thoughts settled on the betrayal he felt from his father and his wife.

"It must hurt" said the Odd-Eyed one.

Emotions welled up and spilled over into tears: "Years ago, back when I first met Claire… that Harlequin… Dominic Magister… he used to say… he used to say that they'd been lovers – my Dad and Claire. I didn't believe him…"

The Green Man stepped closer – and stood by the policeman's heavy shoulders: "And now… there's someone else from the past isn't there: so long ago that it stretches back into another lifetime."

"That's what she says…" he wiped a tear from his nose "How do yer fight that? How can I get her back? You see… she was my first, my last and the *only* one in-between – there's never been anyone else… OK I knew she was a few years older than me, and 'experienced' before I met her – but I had *no* idea that included my own father: and now, a 'love' for someone from a past-life!"

"You ever watched a tree grow?"

"What?!"

"It takes a long time – the watching – sometimes longer than a single human lifetime. I watch them… I watch them all…
I see the seasons come and go, the leaves flower, fade and fall: how the trees bend before the autumn wind: how they rest in winter and then stretch themselves in the spring. It takes years to watch a tree grow; sometimes *hundreds* of years – but is the tree we see now the same as before? It's everything it was: but now, it's so much more – all its 'memories' are stored there in its rings, but still, it grows on growing. People are like that… we should enjoy them as we find them… for that brief moment in time we are privileged to know them…"

"Oh Claire!"

Gathering himself, young Kevin turned to find he was alone…

Lilith's arms were draped around Adam's neck: "You must know *everything* about me my love: everything, that I am…"

"Whatever it is, I'll still love you" he said "It's my fate, my karma if you like – I loved you as Adam Teal and I love you still now as Adam Mitchell. Nothing can *ever* change that…"
He meant it, his love for *Lilith* was the heart-song of his soul, and he knew it.

Slowly, *Lilith* drew her arms back. Pointing to the door behind her she said: "In there, Adam… are two women… taken by Maximilian – on *my* orders."

Adam's eyes narrowed as he scanned hers: "OK, go on…" he replied.

"One of them you know… Lizzie, Dr Lattimer's daughter… the other is Lizzie's grandmother – on her father's side.

Adam's breath shallowed. He'd had to get used to *Lilith*'s ways: pandemic genocide was all well and good – when he didn't have to watch it happening: hermetically sealed in the warehouse he was too remote from it; it was too impersonal … but this? "Why?!" was all that he could say.

It was *Lilith*'s turn to shorten her breath. Her all-to-human love for Adam was her only source of anxiety, or, of conscience: "Oh a number of reasons… you see Claire Lattimer… whom you have felt some affection for… is the biological descendent of that cursed Witchfinder Nathaniel Lattimer – as indeed is Lizzie. Claire… *must* die in retribution!" *Lilith* looked deeply into Adam for his inner reaction – but an unfamiliar confusion came into her mind – her love for him had paradoxically clouded her sixth sense.

Adam's face gave nothing away.

"Lizzie… on the other hand, is quite perfect… as a potential host… for me…"

That definitely got a reaction: "What?!"

"If, any harm should come to this body – then I can be hosted inside hers – *metempsychosis* a trans-migration of the soul."

Adam's face contorted as he struggled to understand: "But… that wouldn't be you… the *you* I've always known…"

"Oh she is *very* pretty, and it'd still be 'me' inside. She's a virgin too, so you could have me for the first-time all over again! But don't worry; I don't plan on having need of her. You see… *this* form, this shape, that you see now – is not my original, my *archetypal* form… only that which I inhabited when this body was born – back in seventeenth century Liverpool.

I have had others... I can of course 'shape-shift' taking on the *imago* of my victims most secret desires - yet *this* image and its physical body are particularly pleasing – Maximilian chose the parents well – they had good genes – like Lizzie does – from her mother: and in particular, from her father's parents.

You can see for yourself just how attractive Maggie is – despite being... oh fifty nine years old... she looks almost twenty years younger – and yet... there may be something *more* in Lizzie, something that her father and paternal grandfather also carry – something that even her brother Sean does not... Maximilian is looking into that right now. If so... then, we can re-think things.

But, back to Claire and her destruction... it must be a sacrifice – not the plague – that is too common a death since the release of my contagion. Maximilian has come up with a most appropriate plan: Claire will be lured here to be exchanged for Lizzie: except of course that she won't be – instead; she will be seized and bound in chains. Then, Maximilian, Adler and Meier will commander a Ferry Boat and take us to the now built-over mouth of the Old Pool – just opposite The Albert Dock. And there... as I was cast into the Pool by her blood-ancestor, so shall *she* be thrown into the merciless waters of the Mersey – weighed down by chains. It's so *apropos* and symbolic, don't you think?"

Adam moistened his dry mouth: "And what about the grandmother Maggie: why is she here?"

"Well, at first she was just in the way when Maximilian seized Lizzie – but then it became obvious that as Kevin O'Riley senior's wife – she was a useful hostage. You see, although poor Maximilian was late in grasping it, O'Riley was the only man alive with the potential to stop me. Having his wife as hostage as well as his granddaughter, gives me leverage over him."

"He could have *stopped* you?!" Adam's brow furrowed "I've met him... he did some 'personal development' therapy with me... at that Eden Institute in Rodney Street: he's an old man; he must be... what... in his late sixties?"

"Yes, he is... and yes he *had* the potential to 'forestall' me, but the silly fellow had lost the connection to his mentor" *Lilith* smiled again her Mona Lisa smile – "A pity that he didn't try... it would have saved me the trouble of hunting *Viridios* down afterwards... when the human race... is all but extinct...

Still, it'll be amusing to see O'Riley's face as I kill his family..." then *Lilith* suddenly chilled: "But, you must understand my love – *they* would destroy me if they could... and end our love forever!" her eyes shone with an all too human love as she beheld him.

"There's one final thing, and you must know this... I can't kill *all* the human race with my contagion... some, I have to allow to live. I have certain needs... needs that I must fulfil, if I'm to maintain my substance in physical form – in this body that you love and desire so much..."

Adam's mouth was dry again: "What needs *Lilith*?"

She turned slightly away – try not to be shocked, try to understand..."

He shrugged: "Just... tell me..."

"You know the stories about vampires?"

"Vampires! You suck blood?!"

"*No...* vampires are just symbolic projections of humans' erotic lust for one another – that's why they're always depicted as being so... sexual. With me... its sexuality itself that is my nourishment... *libido* is my blood lust. I feed on human sex!"

"Oh my God!" Adam's head swam "I knew, I knew that you *enchanted* people... you always have – even before, in Old Liverpool – people were drawn to you – your incredible intensity..."

"What they were drawn to was my intrinsic energy Adam... but that energy must be harvested from *living* people – male or female: their orgasms are my life-blood – for I am known in human mythology as many things – one is the *incubus* or *succubus*, the sex demon..."

"But you said... you said... you said that I was your *first* lover, that before me, you were a virgin!"

"I was, in my body – my physical body. But I have an astral form – in that shape I have harvested men over the centuries... in their *millions!*"

Adam could only joke: "Well, if yer must be promiscuous..."

Lilith continued: "Since you... since realizing that I *love* you, as equally and truly as you love me... I will have no other human male – you were my first, and you will be my last." Then a further confession: "But... I must have nourishment: I never used you that way – and I never will. Recently, I developed a taste... for human sex in physical form. Not with men, I reserved that for you – but with women... so that I could combine my astral and physical pleasures.

You see – if you are to be my consort – and father of my children – you must finally realize how that can *only* be achieved. You must fertilize me – but my womb can bear no children to term: I must host them in the physical bodies of other women – inseminate them with our conjoined sperm and egg; Your blood in my soil. That way, we can soon repopulate the world: truly you will be the *new* Adam!"

This wasn't what Adam had expected: he hadn't known what to expect – but it wasn't this.

"So... you can't bear my children? I'd always hoped to have kids..."

"Through me Adam... you *can* father the whole world!"

Adam's dissociated state – the progressive shocks of love, of trance, of séance, of realized reincarnation, and the dream-like new-world of *Lilith*'s contagion: had shifted him – but this final temptation – the *last* temptation of the New Adam, took him over the edge: "To father the whole world..." he mused.

"Yes my love... to be the *New* Adam."

She had no apple to give – instead she had a practical example: "See now I'm hungry, so, I'll give you a demonstration. We made love last night Adam... I still hold your semen in my body – watch... see how I satisfy my hunger – and how I inseminate..."

She led him through the doors to the holding room: Adler had indeed prepared the women as instructed.

"Leave us Adler!" she commanded. Swiftly, he obeyed. Adam leant to look past *Lilith*. There were two beds side by side, on each was the naked and unconscious form of a woman – both attached to a computer controlled drip mechanism – supplying hydration, nutrition and... sedation.

Lilith turned towards Adam and smiled, stepping back to one-side to afford him a full view. She watched his face betray a spectrum of emotions: at first disbelief, then as his pupils of the beauty of the female form.

"You know Lizzie" said *Lilith*, stroking her face – "She is attractive isn't she. No man has ever penetrated her – her womb is young and receptive…"

Then, with her trademark coquettish tilt, *Lilith* sat down on Maggie's bed: "You can see just how lovely this one was in her youth – her body is still slender, her breasts full and firm – quite exquisite bone structure. Such a pity she's post-menopausal – hers was a body created for childbearing and for men's lust…"

Adam's body swayed as his subconscious mind fought against itself – the opposite poles of guilt and an expectant voyeurism, clashing hard within him.

Lilith stood up and parted her lustrous long hair. She'd learned many things in her past incarnations – from Salome at the court of King Herod she'd learned how to move… She teased Adam with the most exquisite strip he had ever seen – her body seemed to glow with a golden halo that shone through her corn-yellow hair – her skin as perfect as porcelain – her eyes more opalescent than a pacific coral reef. At last she draped her lustrous hair over Maggie's sleeping face – drawing it back slowly so that its soft-fullness teased her nipples – very slowly – very softly so that when at last the cotton-soft tide had passed – Maggie's breasts were engorged, swollen and aroused. *Lilith* smiled at Adam: "See… only a woman can truly know how to arouse another woman… her orgasm will nourish me."

So saying, she blew gently on Maggie's eyelids – and then pressed gently on the line of her eyebrows – following their arcing length – drawing the energy from between her eyes – outwards across her face. Gently caressing – she expertly massaged Maggie's shoulders – following pathways known for centuries to masseurs, healers and Tantric guru's she energised

Maggie's limp and sedated body – faint moans from beneath the chemical coat of sedation signalling her inner arousal.

At last so greatly was she aroused that she half stirred – her eyes faintly opening and the drip shunted into her left hand jerking with her body's motions: "Oh look Adam... her eye colour is similar to mine... how lovely."

Now enjoying herself fully, and sensing Adam's own arousal, she decided to play no more. Parting Maggie's well-turned thigh's she slipped between her hips –allowing her hair to fall across her face once again. This time though it concealed her passionate lips as they sought out Maggie's nipples. Adam could hear the sound of suckling and the now clear moans of pleasure from Maggie. *Lilith* tilted her own pelvis downwards – so that her buttocks rose into the air – displaying her labia – perineum and anus. Adam's member – aroused fit to burst at the sight of such feminine beauty, throbbed urgently.

Slowly, *Lilith* clenched her buttocks and tilted her pelvis first one way and then another – repeating the process so that Adam saw the motion in her perfectly formed cheeks. Giddy with arousal he didn't see what had 'unfurled' from *Lilith*'s clitoral hood.

Maggie's body, was open and for the taking – and taken she was. The enlarged Scorpion tail parted her labia – its sting just firm enough to seek out and open her vagina – before hardening widening and entering. Maggie's back arched and her full mouth fell open with a gasp as *Lilith*'s Scorpion tail filled her – wider than anything ever had before.

Slowly, *Lilith* lowered herself, until her pubis rested on Maggie's – Maggie's clitoris responding to the delicate but firm pressure. *Lilith* rubbed and swirled through her pubis – as the scorpion tail moved backwards and forwards – faster and independently of the lateral motion through *Lilith*'s hips.

Lilith sensed Maggie was ready – at last reaching for her mouth she sealed it with her own – first licking around the rim of her lips and then – extending her forked serpent tongue so that it wrapped around Maggie's, gently stimulating the most sensitive areas.

Simultaneously – the scorpion tail extended its sting – hooking back against Maggie's G-Spot, it injected its stimulating venom electrifying Maggie's nervous system – causing her to gush and ejaculate – her vulva pulsing as her body went first rigid and then utterly limp. Maggie's eyes rolled back in her head with the incredible intensity – unable even to gasp.

Lilith herself now climaxed rubbing vigorously through her pubis – Adam, recognising his lovers moans of pleasure climaxed himself – conditioned as he was by sight of her lovely body and the sweet sound of her own petal-soft moans.

Maggie's face was red and flushed – her heart-rate dangerously high. Inside her vagina, the scorpion tail phallus unfurled its sting, but not before one final injection of stimulant venom – Maggie's body responding with an epileptic jolt.

Lilith's own breathing was hard – her body moist with exertion. She gave one last serpent tongued lick across Maggie's still erect nipples and then out of Adam's sight, slowly withdrew the Scorpion tail – which rapidly became flaccid and curled up under *Lilith*'s clitoral hood.

Lilith smiled as she stood up: "That's how to fuck a woman my love… I do love kissing them as they come… all that energy… I've taken almost all of it from her body. She nearly died poor thing. She'd need a lot more practice to satisfy my hunger…"

Adam was embarrassed – he'd soaked his boxer shorts. Looking over to Lizzie – *Lilith* followed his gaze. "Oh I won't have her… at least not yet. Just in case I have need of her body… Perhaps as a replacement… or… as a host mother to incubate our children… Poor Maggie, I actually passed my fertilized eggs into her womb – your semen, my 'soil', if only she was still fertile – she'd have the honour of bearing our children…"

Tuesday 5ᵗʰ December 2006: Von-Hesse's Warehouse West Float Dock, Birkenhead 10.00am

Pointlessly, Merseyside was in 'lock-down' as police and military helicopters patrolled the skies and more police reinforcements were called in to secure road blocks. Effectively, the government had made the entire metropolitan county a no-go area for anyone outside of its perimeters at the time the area was closed. Even the coast was sealed by the Royal Navy – with assistance from the Republic of Ireland - so depleted and stretched overseas were British maritime forces. Within those borders – the plague was running riot. But it was of course much too late. The numbers of deaths had now climbed to the several tens of thousands with complete break-down of the emergency health-care system. Looting for food and stocks of bottled water broke out on a huge scale as at last even police officers left their posts to return to their families.

Gradually the gas and then the electricity supplies became intermittent and deaths from non-plague infections increased as seasonal influenza struck at the elderly and isolated. It would now be only a matter of time before the last of the hospitals ceased to function. The population were in terror as the deadly unseen disease seeped like the feared miasma of the Black Death into the very air itself. Disposal of the dead was now a serious problem as mobile freezers and makeshift warehouse mortuaries failed to meet demand. The spectre of mass medieval plague pits was looming...

Von-Hesse was smirking in satisfaction. *Lilith* scolded him in jest: "Take that schoolboy look off your face Maximilian – it always means that you've been up to something!"

"Mistress – we have the results from the semen and from the eggs taken from the girl Elizabeth – they *both* contain the identical non-DNA or RNA genetic element!"

"Good – is its nature as we suspected?"

"It is Mistress – it is a modification – rather than a natural mutation – something introduced many hundreds of generations back – by tracking associated genetic markers, I have estimated that it originates around nine thousand years before the Common Era."

"That long!" *Lilith* was genuinely surprised "That must mean that their blood line has been associated with this backwater of a peninsula since shortly after the re-colonization."

Adam had been listening-in and drew on his archaeological background: "You mean... just after the last ice-age – the late Mesolithic period when modern humans returned to this land as hunter-gatherers!"

Von-Hesse looked down his nose at his rival: "Indeed... this 'modification' has been present ever since. The Mistress detected it in harvested semen..."

Adam blushed – despite his apparent acceptance of *Lilith*'s 'activities' he preferred not to think of her doing such things with other men: "Well... what kind of modification do you mean?"

The Bavarian smiled: "Not something your twenty first century science could readily comprehend – more the province of the supernatural and the occult – in other words of the 'old' sciences."

"Maybe… but that's not a proper answer" Adam had been emboldened by *Lilith*'s favour. Without that he would never have dared risk crossing this war-hardened veteran occultist.

"Spiritual powers of the highest level can easily alter an individual's genotype. At some point, near to the time that I have indicated – an ancestor of the O'Riley's – through the female line, was exposed to the spiritual powers of the land – chosen by it and altered irrevocably by it at a molecular level – leaving its trace as a non-sex linked, non-DNA marker.

If the Mistress endows you as her consort – you too will be so changed." Adam took this last remark as Von-Hesse still holding out in hope that *Lilith* would in the end choose him, rather than Adam. That meant that he was still un-reconciled to her choice – and that… meant that he was dangerous.

Lilith had been pondering: "This means that we *must* keep Lizzie alive, and available for both harvesting of eggs and hosting as a mother. If we can combine her non-DNA genetic marker – with what I already have – then… much will change…" *Lilith* took a few steps as she pondered further.

"Very well… let's not waste any more time! Soon Maximilian, the contagion will be at its maximum, and then, like dominoes every city in this country will fall empty and dead: thence across into continental Europe and beyond from West to East as my red shroud breathes out its miasmic death: finally becoming true global human extinction!"

"Indeed Mistress, your powers are great and your reach unlimited!"

Lilith smiled at Von-Hesse's sycophancy: "Yes… quite. Pass the message to Claire Lattimer – she's to bring Kevin O'Riley senior with her – you may try her mobile – if it's still working – Adler will scramble the message electronically so that the authorities can't listen in."

Von-Hesse was perturbed: "You want *both* of the O'Riley's' Mistress? Surely we only need the young one – now that we've identified what it is that she carries."

Lilith smiled her Mona Lisa smile: "We only *need* Lizzie Maximilian – but I want her grandfather present so I can be certain of killing him. The independence of that ancient blood-line stops now! As for Claire… I am to be her Nemesis, and with her: also that of cursed *Eve* herself…"

St Stephens Road

O'Riley, Claire, John: Kevin Junior and Sean were in a council of war. Everyone was talking at once: and out loud, about their fear; and increasing terror… "We *have* to stay focused! *Lilith's* plague's already spread out from the city. Another 48 hours and it'll envelop the *whole* world!" declared O'Riley.

Suddenly, Claire's mobile phone rang: it was vibrating so hard that it shook itself near clean off the coffee table: "Best answer it love…" said John slowly, and quietly.

Claire licked her lips swallowed hard, and answered: "Hello?! Tonight? OK? I'll ask them… I can't guarantee it… But what if they won't… Hello? Hello!? Damn he's rung-off!"

With wide and staring eyes she looked at her husband: "They want: *just* me…" then looking at O'Riley "And you… He said we're to be unarmed!"

"It's a trap!" snarled John.

"Of course it's a trap!" retorted O'Riley: "Sorry John, I didn't mean to snap at you… oh you *know* what I meant!" Then fully recovering his composure: "When and where?" asked O'Riley coldly.

"Now! Down at the West Float dock: we'll be met there" replied Claire.

"Kevin, son… *you'll* have to deal with her blood-soil!"

"It's *my* wife and daughter dad!" protested Kevin Junior.

"*And* your mother too! *My* wife! Von Hesse will kill them *all* if we don't agree to his terms!" asserted O'Riley paternally.

Kevin junior nodded silently in resignation and defeat.

"Take young Sean with you: go to Lake Hall. Use the mixture from the Dale: do *anything* you have to, to survive! Whatever else may happen: you *and* Sean must carry on with the family's ancient and sacred heritage. If not: then *everything* our ancestors struggled for will be lost!

Sutton raised a questioning eyebrow to O'Riley, challenging him to do the right thing by him.

O'Riley sighed as he responded: "We need a mobile reserve John: some muscle to back us up!"

John grinned and set his face determinedly:

Pulling out an automatic pistol; he cocked it, dramatically.

Ever reliable, John was *ready*.

O'Riley give a tight lipped nod and smile in recognition:

Then taking out his pentacle charm from behind his collar he mused: "Stay with me old friend..."

Von Hesse was well concealed. With him Meier – the indisputable 'heavy' of his two understudies. The pilot boat chugged in: its two-man crew had been stalwarts in the crisis – keeping to their duty – recently extended to include recovery of plague victims from the Mersey. Callously, The Bavarian waited until they'd tied their boat up – and then cold bloodedly drew his silenced pistol. One 'double-tap' each, delivering a single bullet to both the head and body, and two more corpses floated in the Birkenhead docks. His Mistress needed the pilot boat…

8.30pm and The Team gathered for a final time at St Stephens Road. Kevin Junior was with his son Sean: a father taking his lad under his experienced wing. John was chomping at the bit to get started, but joked about his car to lighten the mood: "I've got just enough petrol left in the Lexus… I *knew* that hybrid engine would come in useful one day!"

"Careful John" said O'Riley "Car-Jacking has started this far out from the town."

John grinned his optimistic grin and tapped his coat pocket: "Well, I'm appropriately 'dressed' you might say… haven't fired one ah these things in years… I nearly failed my firearms course in the police yer know… ah well, too late now to wish I'd tried harder!"

"Good luck John!" said Claire giving him a big hug.

"You too old girl… we go back a long way don't we!"

Claire hugged him again as a twenty five year friendship squeezed a tear from her eye.

John sighed; it was time: "OK… well we've all got these short-wave radios: courtesy of young Kevin – not standard Police issue, but they've got good battery life – so at least we can keep in touch.

Sean took his turn: "Love yer Mum – you too Granddad: come back safe yourselves now yer hear?" She nodded more tears welling up as she held tightly on to her only son.

Then through her moistened eyes – Claire watched with a deep sadness as her son Sean, walked away to become a man…

Finally, young Kevin reached out and put his arm round his wife's shoulder. His touch was almost too much for her to bear. Turning she stumbled and fell into his arms: "Kevin! I'm so sorry, I never meant to hurt you, never; and I've never been unfaithful to you: you're the true love of my life… of *any* life, that I've *ever* had!"

"It's OK…" he whispered "I know… I understand now… You see I met *him* again, and he explained everything: helped me to feel deeply into things, and see them as they really are."

Claire raised her head from his shoulder: "*him?*"

"Yes… dad's old friend… he with the odd-coloured eyes…"

Down at the Woodside Ferry Terminal the black Mercedes S Class limousine and the Range Rover purred to a halt. Von-Hesse was first out – his pistol in his right hand – his experienced soldier's eyes scanning the shadows. When he was satisfied he nodded to *Lilith* – who casually breezed out into the cold night air – her Mona Lisa smile already broadening in anticipation of her revenge. Meier and Adler bundled the two women out of the Range Rover – handcuffed

and hooded. The last to emerge was Adam… Now feeling some existential angst as guilt pushed to break through into his trance-like state of mind.

Lilith sensed it – but was troubled that yet again her love for him blunted the deeper penetration of his mind. Stroking his face and gazing lovingly into his eyes she said: "It's for me Adam… for me *and* for you…"

Whenever she spoke to him in that way his mind sank a little more under her influence – under her influence and under that of the long-ago dead seventeenth century youth – now, reincarnated as a living 'memory' in Adam Mitchell's psyche.

He smiled as his heart melted: "This is so unreal... you are *such* a rare beauty, as beautiful on the inside as you are outside."

Of course she was... She was a beautiful *inhuman* archetype by whose values and meaning in life, everything she did was right and proper. Smiling again, she gently kissed his lips, sending a thrill of joy through his body.

Von-Hesse had gone on ahead followed by Adler and Meier dragging the women along with them – they would take the seized private yacht: *Mersey Spirit'*– all would board except for Von-Hesse, who'd return to the now concealed Pilot Boat. The next time they met would be for the fateful river rendezvous near to the Albert Dock.

O'Riley's blue Honda Legend made its way past the 'Half-Way-House' pub, driving through Oxton and down towards Ashville Road and Birkenhead Park. It was the most direct route to Duke Street and the agreed rendezvous with The Bavarian.

The streets were lawless now – the population in fear of one another: of fading resources; and of course, in terror of the plague. Abandoned cars and the occasional corpse slowed their progress but at last they arrived at the cold, dark and eerie West Float Dock. Claire's heart was racing: her maternal instincts frayed for her captive daughter and her endangered son. Light-headed she feared that she'd be too stressed to cope with what was to come.

"O'Riley shook his head: "I must confess: I don't know how we're going to save Maggie and Lizzie... it's not like last-time... we had help then."

Let's hope that Kevin and Sean manage to get to this 'soil' of hers… if that'll do any good!" said Claire trying in vain to distract herself.

O'Riley breathed hard: "Apparently it will, so long as the 'other' factor is in place too. *He* said that it had to be both."

Claire was now shaking with nerves: "Then why didn't *he* just offer to help! What use is talk and advice? May as well be a bloody counsellor or therapist – just useless words, we need *real* practical: physical help!"

The silence that followed was shattered by Claire's scream.

"Claire!" yelled O'Riley. But it was too late: Adler's gruesomely lit face, leering at her through the car windscreen; had caused her to exit the vehicle in panic.

O'Riley followed: rushing quickly over to protect her.

"Stand perfectly still!" The voice was aggressive: the cold tone of its owner; unmistakable. Von Hesse emerged from the shadows, his silenced Glock 18 semi-automatic pistol aimed squarely at O'Riley's head: "I *never* miss!"

Realising the futility of the situation: Claire and O'Riley; exchanged a resigned look and bowed their heads.

John's ultra-quiet hybrid engined Lexus halted silently behind the angle of a nearby warehouse. He'd arrived by a different route – having anticipated what would probably happen at the dock-side.

Drawing his pistol, he approached Von Hesse stealthily, from The Bavarian's blind side. Adler was looking the wrong way: and Von Hesse's attention, fully occupied with his prisoners.

There was no sign of Meier, so he must still be with Lilith somewhere: probably wherever they were holding Lizzie and Maggie.

Taking Von Hesse for the killer he was: he calculated that he had to act. It'd be now, or never…

"Drop yer gun!"

Von Hesse neither flinched nor responded. His own aim was steady, his eyes, and his pistol, focused straight ahead on Claire and O'Riley.

Tightening his grip, John squeezed the trigger…

Suddenly, Meir emerged from the shadows behind John and struck the gun from his hands. A short, brave, but futile struggle followed until at last John was overpowered by the powerful German: and brought to stand humbled, before Von Hesse: alongside Claire and O'Riley.

"That... was your *last* indiscretion!" snarled The Bavarian

Sensing John's imminent execution, O'Riley intervened to distract Von Hesse from shooting him: "Where're Lizzie and Maggie?! The deal was for an exchange; *us* for *them!*"

Von Hesse lowered his gun arm as his eyes bulged with hatred at O'Riley: "You're *powerless* O'Riley. No power, means *no* deal! Adler: search them!

The emotions amongst the ESP family were running ever higher: John felt humiliated at being searched – it was the beginning of his induction into a subservient status – the persona of this formerly powerful police-officer, parapsychologist and crack marksman: was being peeled back layer by layer. Claire, already terrified and exhausted beyond reasonable hope was fading fast under erosion from a constant flood of adrenalin. O'Riley himself – despite his renewed insight and faith in the wisdom of his old mentor, was feeling his years – he was no 'action-man' any more – his stamina, his strength, perhaps even his will-power, may not be up to this his greatest ever test...

Satisfied with the body searches, Von-Hesse continued in a surreally matter-of-fact style: "Do not concern yourselves; I will only shoot if you disobey my precise instructions. However, I promise that if it becomes necessary then it will be quick – I am a professional of some many years standing and take pride in my skills!" Then, Jerking the barrel of his gun leftwards he indicated the direction that they should go.

"Where are we going?" asked O'Riley.

"To the Pilot Boat – climb on board and make your way to the bow section – stand close together there in a group!"

Lake Hall, Oxton.

Kevin Junior went in first. Suspicious of booby traps – either physical or occult – he took the torch from Sean and scanned around the dark-wood hallway. As satisfied as he could be – he found a light switch and tried it – it worked: "The electricity supply's still on around here... unless they've got their own generator."

"Shall ah come in dad? It's dark out here!"

"Yeah come in... but stay close behind me and touch *nothing!*"

Sean's hair stood high on the back of his neck as he expected a six-foot three Bavarian to step out from every shadow.

"Up or down der yer think?"

"Wha?"

"Their 'laboratory' – all these alchemist types have a laboratory – that'll be where he keeps his precious soil samples."

"Down – in the basement, but you first" offered Sean.

"Up in the attic, and me first!" replied his dad with a grin

Sean smiled back. His father's light-heartedness and confidence were soothing his nerves. Kevin though still drew his pistol as the attic stairs beckoned...

On the pilot boat

The air around the dock was bitterly cold. John wrapped his arms protectively around Claire as Von-Hesse started the Pilot Boat's engine: "Where in hell is he taking us?" he asked.

O'Riley's intuition had already guessed: "I fear somewhere even colder and wetter than here." He cast his eye in the direction of Liverpool. Few lights shone from the world famous Waterfront – no car headlights betrayed people going about their normal business. He thought that if he half closed his eyes then the scene could be that of the Liverpool of old – smaller, colder: less-populated – perhaps even as far back as the seventeenth century – back to *her* time… hers and Adam's.

The moored Yacht

The yacht *Mersey Spirit* was moored at precisely the right spot in the great river. Von-Hesse had used a GPS grid to work out the exact required location. *Lilith* was delighted with his Germanic efficiency: "You'd think he really was Bavarian wouldn't you?" she laughed to Meier.

"Mistress?"

"Oh hasn't he told you yet? He's *French* ha ha!"

"Er… he did say something about that…"

"Oh he can be so boringly reserved about himself can't he?" she smiled "Yes, he's from the Languedoc in the south-west of France: but he likes to pretend he's German – It helped him you see, to avoid the Spanish Inquisition, and then suddenly he realised that all that Germanic stuff was so much easier to intimidate people with – they have such a militaristic

reputation don't they? I found an adopted family for him –
the Hesse's of Thuringia and Hesse– later the 'Von'-Hesse's of
Bavaria – he really thinks he is one now!"

Meier risked a smile: "I'm a blood-line Prussian on my father's
side, and Bavarian on my mother's."

Lilith smiled back: "Perhaps that explains your rude manner
with women. Now… run along and help Adler with our
hostages. After the *sacrifice* of the Lattimer woman – you may
have Maggie for your amusement – kill her if you wish – you
could even use your 'Frankfurter', ha ha!"

Meier smiled again – his Mistress would let him indulge his
lust after-all. Perhaps this was a sign of her increasing favour?

Maggie and Lizzie were being held in relative warmth in the
lower deck forward passenger cabin. Conscious, and terrified,
they had no idea what would befall them or why they were
being kept where they were.

Adam was at the door looking at them. His eyes betraying his
questioning heart: "Adam?" came the softly feminine voice
from behind him.

 "*Lilith!*" He turned to see her and was immediately
enraptured: "Oh my love… I was… looking at the women…
and for a moment I wondered why… why they had to be
hurt?"

"Hurt? Oh Lizzie will be allowed to live – I'll probably use
your sperm to fertilize a hybrid egg – hers and mine – just
enough of her to distil out that special essence she's inherited
from her father and grandfather – all the rest… me!

As for Maggie – well, if she'd been just a little younger – and
still fertile – I'd have used her as a host. She's been a very
good biological mother. But… sadly her only use now is her

still attractive body – so Meier can have her. It'll irritate poor Maximilian near to the death – won't that be delightful!"

Adam sighed: "Only for you *Lilith*, I couldn't do this for anyone else…"

Lilith sensed Adam's moral conflict – and in true spirit, reminded him of his final test: "Adam… I know that you love me – that you have always loved me since the very beginning: since you first set eyes upon me as *Lilith* Hopgood of Water Street, in old Liverpool Town…"

He smiled nodding.

"But… I know now too, that after I was gone from that time, and that place: that you went on to get married…"

Adam felt his arms slacken slightly around her waist as he recalled Sarah.

"Yes… Sarah…" *Lilith* was able to see her face in his mind's eye "and *she's* come back now too, hasn't she?"

"Claire…"

"Indeed: Claire Lattimer – direct family descendent of my enemy Nathaniel Lattimer. For that blood-sin alone she must die – but as the reincarnation of your 'wife' Sarah – well, that I cannot tolerate!" *Lilith*'s eyes had blackened sending a rippling chill up and down Adam's spine. He could be in no remaining doubt now of *Lilith*'s immutable and deadly intent towards her.

"So…" she continued "I have a task set aside for you this dark and cold evening."

"A task my love? What?"

"Claire is to be sacrificed – as I was by her ancestor, for that is what it was – *I* was sacrificed to *his* faith in *his* God as a witch! Cast right before your very eyes, Adam Teal, into the liver-dark waters of the old pool. Now, tonight, Claire will suffer as *I* was intended to suffer, but it will be *you* my love who throws *her* into the Mersey – bounded in chains – you, as proof, as final proof to me of your undying Love… Reject her then, as the *First* Adam should have rejected cursed Eve! In your soul you carry the spark of him – in your eyes, there shines his light, for you are *him* as the very soul of that first Adam moves your form and your body! Redeem him now, oh Adam Mitchell, redeem him and all descended from him, of the original sin of rejection of me, through your true love… for me… as *Lilith*.

I tell you… there will be a new Garden of Eden… I will create it from that ancient 'sacred enclosure' marked out by *Viridios* himself – 'The Green Man'… Oh yes, that little corner of English nowhere, of the Wirral Peninsula. There…will be our new Eden and there too, the new cradle of the world!"

The Pilot Boat approached the moored yacht; it was obvious now what their destination was: "A yacht! Why?" asked John.

O'Riley didn't answer instead he peered with his ageing eyes trying to make out the identity of those on board: "I can't see… but there's maybe half-a dozen people on board…"

Von-Hesse brought the boat about so that it came alongside the port gangway-rail. Adam received the ropes – securing them to the capstan gunwales. Meier was first up: "On board!" snapped The Bavarian. The ESP family exchanged a fateful glance and then led by O'Riley himself, they climbed onto the gangway. Meier waited there to greet them – if it could be called a greeting. His face was a picture of sadistic delight: "Welcome! My Mistress commands that you go to the aft passenger cabin!"

"Does she indeed!" exclaimed John unwisely. A sharp pressure between the vertebrae of his spine indicated that a pistol barrel insisted upon his unquestioning compliance. It was confirmed by Von-Hesse's voice: "To me, you are the *least* important member of your group – your life is cheap… expend it wisely!"

John slumped and followed his Claire and O'Riley into the after-cabin: "Sit down by the far bulkhead" came The Bavarian's curt command.

He stepped aside as the pre-Raphaelite visionary form of *Lilith* seemed to float into the cabin. Her Mona-Lisa smile now it's broadest and most appealing ever.

O'Riley was the first to speak: "We agreed to come here to get Lizzie and Maggie back."

"Did you?" *Lilith* replied sarcastically "You missed out one important feature of our 'agreement' Claire was to be *exchanged* for Lizzie, and so she shall: Claire dies, Lizzie…lives as my most *intimate* female companion!"

"We'll do a deal" offered O'Riley.

Lilith laughed: "What?! No deals *dear* Dr O'Riley; just your complete acquiescence: howsoever reluctantly on your part!"

"Look… you've no need of Lizzie and Maggie: you've won, what do you want them for?"

Lilith laughed again: "For a start, as witnesses…"

"Witnesses?!"

Lilith snapped her fingers. Von-Hesse raised his semi-automatic pistol as Meier went towards Claire. John stood to defend his friend.

"Do you want her shot dead where she stands?" asked *Lilith* "Maximilian is an excellent shot – it's been some years since he first executed people in this city – by gunfire anyway – his aim is quite perfect."

"I *never* miss!" reminded The Bavarian.

"John!" cried out Claire as Meier roughly manhandled her.

"John, stand still!"

Biting his lip in frustration and anger – the parapsychologist held himself motionless…

Von-Hesse grinned a deaths-head grin: "You will remain in here until summonsed. The door will be locked. If you attempt to pass through – Claire will be shot – instantly: and then, the other two!"

Lilith tilted her head in coquettish style: "A shame about you Dr O'Riley… you must have been a very handsome man in your youth. Maggie was so beautiful too wasn't she – she still is 'age-adjusted' as you might say… Ah well *Tempus fugit!*"

O'Riley replied: *Haud ullis labe labentia ventis!*"

Lilith raised an eyebrow: "Yielding under no winds?"

"We never give in!"

"Ha! Well… we shall see. *Nobody* wounds me without punishment! And that is my animus for bringing nemesis to your family: retribution Dr O'Riley, retribution!"

Lilith left, still laughing.

"Jeesh – if it were possible: looks like you just gone an' made things even *worse* there!"

"It's not over yet John…"

Lake Hall, Oxton

Young Kevin had reached the attic door. Pushing it with his foot it opened out easily: "Torch Sean!"

Sean shone the light past him: "It's empty!"

"Well, that leaves the basement – like yer said… come on…"

Creeping back down the stairs Kevin Junior and Sean found the concealed entrance to the basement: "Why hide it?" asked Sean.

"Same reason people hide their valuables in a safe."

"Me first!" Sean made eye contact with his father.

Kevin Junior smiled and nodded: "Look… we don't know what may be in there… physical or metaphysical. Still wanna go first?"

"Yeah. You and granddad are hard acts to follow, but a lad's gotta start somewhere!"

Kevin patted him on his shoulder: "Here young fellah" he said – handing him the pistol – if we get through this then Merseyside's gonna need brave new lads in its police force!"

Swallowing hard Sean lifted the stairway hatch and peered into the blackness.

Von-Hesse had handcuffed Claire's hands behind her back and shackled her legs in chains. *Lilith* circled her smirking. Well, well… how does it feel to be bound like an animal for slaughter?"

"Let my daughter go!" cried Claire with her breaking voice.

"Oh don't worry – she'll live, I have use for her."

"Use?"

"Yes… you picked your breeding partner well. Her father, young Kevin, carries something special in his blood – in his genotype to be more precise. Lizzie has inherited it from him, but *not* your son Sean: his blood is more… ordinary; just tainted by being a descendent through *you* of that accursed Nathaniel Lattimer.

Interesting isn't it? Have you any idea what it is that Lizzie carries?"

"No!"

"It comes through Kevin senior's blood-line – it's linked to the land and its power… you know what I mean now don't you."

"The… church… the church at Woodchurch. You know about that?"

"Of course! But then it's *not* the church itself is it, oh no: it's *where* it was built, and what lies beneath it –and has *always* lain beneath it. Now… I shall incorporate that special quality into my bloodline… by harvesting your daughter's ovaries!"

"No!"

"Oh but yes… Yes Claire Lattimer, I shall!" *Lilith* closed to her gently stroking her face with her porcelain perfect hand. Despite her hatred, and her fear – Claire felt herself responding sexually to the demon Goddesses touch.

"Arousing aren't I … can you feel my energy? Yes, you can…can't you. You're becoming moist and receptive Claire"

Claire's nipples erected and showed clearly through her top.

"Can't blame that on the cold can you… it's so *warm* in here!"

Handcuffed and shackled she couldn't even move as a token of resistance. *Lilith* passed her soft hands over Claire's chest running her fingers around her nipples, lightly and gently kneading her breasts–expertly electrifying her.

"Shall I, oh *Eve?* Shall I give you this one last gift – the orgasm of your life? *Lilith*'s left hand cupped Claire's pubis – her palm gently massaging her clitoris as her right hand pulled softly at her nipple. Claire closed her eyes and tried to shut out the surging ecstasy."

"No… I'll save that for your daughter. Meier, take her outside!"

Sean shone the torch down into the darkness: "Can't see a light switch dad."

"Can yer see anythin'?"

"Nope… it's… argh!" Sean had slipped and dropped the gun.

"Son! You OK?" called his father urgently.

"I've lost the bloody gun!"

"Never mind that… are you injured?"

"Ow! Just me shins…"

Young Kevin struggled past him: "Let's get the light on and find the gun!"

Adam was with Adler, Maggie and Lizzie. Lizzie's pretty face was dead with exhaustion and fear. Maggie though made eye contact with him: "Such a young man… how can you be so corrupted so deeply!"

"What? I'm in love with *Lilith!* Nothing means more to me than that!"

"So it's all about 'you' and your own gratification… emotional and physical… and screw the world if you should give a damn about anyone else eh?!"

"Silence woman!" Adler, was a pale imitator of his Master Von-Hesse.

"Think she'll let you live any longer than she has need of you: *any* of you?"

Von-Hesse himself entered: "Assemble on the gangway deck- at once!" The Bavarian's natural authority even made the 'anointed-one' Adam, jump up to attention. The group filed out into the freezing night to find Claire in shackles, crying with cold, emotional exhaustion, and pain. Von-Hesse's gun was trained on the two men – his craggy smirk the widest smile he'd achieved in years.

John's spirit compelled him into defiance of *Lilith:* "This city's survived *everything ever* thrown at it! Civil War, Hitler, riots, *everything!* It'll survive *you* too!"

Lilith laughed haughtily: " It'll be reborn! The *Pool* of *Life* and *rebirth* for *my* children!"

Von Hesse's grin widened still further. However, he wasn't going to like one bit what she was to say and do next…

Lilith wrapped herself around Adam: "Just to make certain that *everyone* knows, I now make formal announcement that Adam Mitchell — once called Adam Teal of old Liverpool Town: is my *irrevocable* and *final* choice as consort — to be my companion and lover — and father of the coming new race of -humankind. *He* is my New Adam!"

Utterly incredulous: Von-Hesse's gun arm wilted at the *extremis* of her betrayal of his loyalty, devotion: and... love for her.

John saw his arm drop: and made an ever-so-slight motion of intent. O'Riley grabbed his sleeve: "Not yet!" he whispered urgently.

Lilith continued: "In fact, it is my wish that henceforth he be known as 'Adam Kadmon' as I claim back that which was rightfully mine from old Eden! We will make our *new* Eden out of that cursed Wirral peninsula – and will there set right all that was wronged against me! It's very soil will be sewn with mine – my pure blood-red earth! Now... Adam... called *Adam Kadmon* – your final test of love for me. Go to Claire: that cursed daughter of Eve: who is also Sarah, your 'wife' of a past-lifetime: go to her, and cast forth her iron shackled body into the cruel, freezing, and unforgiving river!"

He turned and faced Claire – his face blanked of all emotion, as he took the three short steps to reach her.

Sean beat his dad to the basement light: "It's empty; the whole freakin house is empty!"

Kevin Junior silently stooped to pick up his gun: "We've wasted our time… come on *quick!*"

"Where?"

"To the West Float Dock! We might just be in time to save yer mum and sister!"

John lurched forward but was grabbed by O'Riley: "No John, wait!" he urged desperately. Adler and Meier roughly took hold of Lizzie and Maggie. Squinting and shaking his head to recover his composure: Von Hesse quickly re-trained his gun arm on John's head: "You will *all* die!" gritted The Bavarian, if you make but the slightest movement – *all* of you, including Lizzie and Maggie!" Mentally weakened by *Lilith's* rejection and humiliation of him, he had become dangerously unstable.

Claire screamed as she shook – her legs barely able to hold her up. In the desperation of her life she pleaded with her eyes to John– who was now frantically struggling as O'Riley wrestled with him, trying to stop him throwing his life away.

Adam… was with her – his face still blank as if without soul. Claire looked up and into his eyes: "Adam… it's me… *Sarah!*"

Adam's eyes blinked: "Sarah?" he whispered. Then moving his posture slightly to obscure *Lilith's* view… he extended his right hand and tenderly touched her face. A single tear moistened his cheek. His voice was soft: "'Tis the last temptation of Adam…my Sarah. Death… hath *not* parted us!"

Slowly he turned around and walked back towards *Lilith*. Alarmed, Von-Hesse re-trained his gun on him, but he couldn't bring himself to fire. *Lilith* read Adam's eyes – read his undying love for her. Her face softened: and then as they embraced, Adam stepped silently with her into the fathomless waters…

"Now John: now!"

John lunged at the astonished Von-Hesse, knocking the gun from his arm. O'Riley dashed to Claire dragging her manacled body away from the open gangway rail.

Unarmed but physically overpowering – Adler and Meier moved to force the two remaining women over the side and into the freezing black estuarine tide.

John had won the struggle for the gun. Raising it Von-Hesse had the sense to back away his hands held in resigned surrender but on opposite sides of the deck, the other two Bavarians were heaving the screaming and terrified women into position for their fall to their deaths:

"Armed Police Stop!" yelled John - and then adding - "Oh fuck it!"

Two pistol shots rang out – both found their mark.

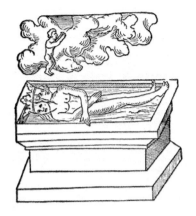

18

Animus Requiem

evin's Jaguar arrived at the dock in time to see the little orange Pilot Boat draw up near to O'Riley's parked Honda. Instinctively, he drew his gun and took cover with Sean: but at last he made out the familiar shape of O'Riley senior, tying up on a capstan: "He's back! And there's yer Mum and Sister – with John and Maggie too!"

Rushing out to meet them – they ran straight into the still menacingly proud shape of The Bavarian – his hands – now handcuffed securely behind his back. Kevin and Sean's elation was tempered by the terrible distress of the women – still deeply shocked by their ordeal – but they tearfully embraced their family: for nothing could hold back their joy and their relief.

Young Kevin smiled his old police smile at O'Riley: "Well… what happened dad? And *don't* say that yer didn't need me!"

O'Riley sat exhausted on the capstan: "She's gone… *Lilith* and Adam – both gone into the river."

"What?! How?!"

"How? The oldest magic of all, son… Love."

As that new day dawned – a figure emerged from the trees high on Wirral's Bidston Hill, looking east towards the golden rising sun and Liverpool. He raised his arms and breathed out with a thunderous wind-like breath: a roar of life and re-birth. All over the devastated city; dead trees and flowers dramatically burst forth into life: symbolizing the end of Lilith's wasteland and the recovery of the world.

The Green Man smiled: and then, slowly merged back into the living tapestry of ever-green trees.

With *Lilith* gone… a miracle happened – the contagion lifted.

Over in The Liverpool School of Tropical medicine Dr Michelle Wilson was still at her post. Drawn, weak and malnourished, she watched amazed as cultured plague bacteria and viruses spontaneously died and decomposed: "Look!" she gasped – "They're all dying!" Struggling to understand what was happening she added: "There must be some kind of limitation built it to it genetically?"

Turning, she gazed down onto the laboratory floor – there in a corner was her research assistant Laura Cunningham - stretched out on a makeshift camp bed. The buboes were fading from her neck, armpits and groin – her lungs clearing – her terrible pain... passing.

At the same instant all those afflicted and still living saw a reversal of their symptoms – fading at last like some dark nightmare before the brilliant light of that new dawn.

Young Kevin was determined that Von-Hesse be brought to justice: "Abduction will do fer starters!"

"Well we can't nail him for genocide! Who in hell is gonna believe that?" John was practical as ever with the annoying details.

Kevin kicked the cell door open at the otherwise abandoned 'Custody Suite' at the police-station in Birkenhead. "Then that'll have ter do then! This can be our makeshift base until things start to get sorted. My uniforms in the boot of the Honda – I'll put it on – we need some semblance of civilization to return!"

O'Riley was with the women. Still traumatized they hugged one another tightly. But as Claire looked over to him she saw a peace in his eyes: "You *knew* didn't you: you knew what was going to happen!"

The tired old psychotherapist nodded: "Well, kind of… you see that's what *he* said would happen… She could only be stopped by the contamination of her soil – which – when we find it we still have to do *and* by something that wasn't in my gift as he put it – 'Only by one to whom she surrenders to both in body and in heart' – and that, could only *ever* have been, Adam. In the end love was decisive. It was her now all too human love for Adam – that stopped her destroying him in that final moment – allowing him to carry her into oblivion in the dark depths of the Mersey's waters… But most importantly, perhaps, there was another love… a love between him… and you…that he could not betray. In a way then, you could say that both *Lilith* and Adam: were at last, redeemed… by love…"

Claire sobbed: "I *did* feel that love, you know… I felt it as if it were real."

"He felt it for you too Claire, in fact, he died for it – as he said: 'Death hath *not* parted us'…"

She nodded: "Yes… but… I'm 'me' I'm Claire Lattimer, and my *true* love is my Kevin, my love of this and *all* of my lifetimes!"

Outside the door, in the corridor – her Kevin heard her words and at last his heart was completely healed.

"This is the last of it John?" asked O'Riley

"As far as I can tell… we've sorted the Museum soil samples… What do we do with the skull?" asked John.

O'Riley picked it up and stared through the bony eye sockets: "Consign it to the Mersey – and her bones too. Get rid of all of it – we can't risk someone, someday, trying to bring her back."

"Claudia Moore from the Museum has survived apparently – and her child… a little blond haired green-eyed girl called Lamia. What do we tell her about Adam?"

"Lamia, that's a Greek name isn't it? Seems familiar somehow… Oh… well, we just say to her that he's one of the many thousands who went missing; and whose bodies have never been found. It's so tragic, because in the end he *was* brave John… *really* brave, and only we know the truth of it. He was given the ultimate temptation – to be the father of the whole world and become the immortal consort of a beautiful Goddess – he had all of that within his reach, and yet, he set it aside – sacrificing everything for love…"

"Maybe in some way then, it really *was* him returned to us from The Garden of Eden… The first Adam, and this, his final redeeming sacrifice, was made for all of us…" offered John.

"He chose Claire over *Lilith*, just as Adam in Eden chose Eve…" mused O'Riley.

"And his reward… was his death…"

"Truly, The Last Temptation of Adam…"

The Bavarian was at last transferred over to Walton Prison to await trial on charges of murder and abduction – no other charge could possibly stand.

Liverpool had begun to recover, despite fatalities in the several tens of thousands. The same spirit that had maintained it during the sieges of the English Civil War and the Blitz of 1940-41 rose again as the survivors of *Lilith*'s plague drew close together to rebuild their proud city. The contagion hadn't of course been contained within the *cordon sanitaire* around Merseyside... it had spread rapidly out from the city... out across Britain and into Europe, then Asia, and at last: the United States. But with *Lilith's* disappearance, it had lifted... as suddenly and as completely as it had first arisen, summonsed as a red miasmic death – out of the very earth itself.

The remaining laboratory culture samples showed nothing remarkable beyond a synergy of action between the common *Yersinia pestis* bacterium and a host of viruses - including both seasonal, and H5N1 influenza or 'Bird Flu'. But even more strangely, no survivor of the plague showed any antibodies to the infection, and even the corpses - especially those unfortunate enough to have died just before the pestilence had lifted, seemed to be free of all trace of contagion.

It was as if the pandemic had never happened...

The scientific world and the world's governmental authorities were at a complete loss either to explain the diseases sudden appearance, or even more so: its spontaneous remission. The problem would keep medicine busy for years to come.

Young Sean, though, was not released entirely from *Lilith's* emotional effect upon him. His naive heart had fallen for her, and so profoundly so, that he could not bear to destroy her last remaining lock of golden hair – given to him by her own porcelain perfect hand on their ferry journey together: o'er the wide estuarine Mersey. A keepsake to be cherished now in memory of a pure: and unrequited Love... from him... to her...

Carefully then did he conceal that coiling golden thread: tightly looped at one end about his heart... and so carefully, indeed that his conscious mind had very soon forgotten where...

In Liverpool, the prison was virtually empty – most of the previous incumbents having fallen to the pestilence. Von-Hesse was something of a star attraction for the prison officers – a proud almost 'Prussian' German, in the old continental style – quite different from their usual charges.

Today, the guards were *off*-guard. It was Christmas Day, and they had survived… Their celebrating just a little too much gave Von-Hesse an opportunity not to be missed.

His meal was delivered as usual – but this time the hooded black-brown eyes caught the unwary prison-officer and fixed him with his Mesmeric stare.

By 12.30 he was free: making his way to a secret repository where in anticipation of just such a contingency, he had safely secured some of *Lilith*'s blood-soil. Then, his implacable, iron-willed spirit: took him determinedly over into Allerton Village, in the south of the city…

The Bavarian knew what he must do. His darkly handsome olive toned features broke into a Mona-Lisa smile as he addressed the hypnotized mother: "Claudia... your newborn child has an appointment with me...and with her destiny... Here... some sacred soil for her ingestion!"

Cradling the beautiful blond-haired – green-eyed child in his arms, he said with undying love: "*Lilith*... my Mistress... it *is* you! When thou art full grown into fair and beautiful maidenhood, then, shalt I return unto thee, so that ye may yet deliver thy nemesis, once more again into the world!"

Epilogue

The Devil's Bible

Sefton Park Liverpool: midday, on Sunday 31ˢᵗ July 2011

"ou must understand, I've no one: and nowhere else left to turn to!"

Dr John Sutton, parapsychologist and deputy director of the world renowned, ESP Paranormal Research Institute, stared with compassion, at the dishevelled and terrified figure before him: "Not even..." he ventured.

"No! Especially not to them! Don't you realise what that would mean – what would happen to me?!

"But..."

"I am a Jesuit priest! An ordained member of the *Societas Iesu* - the 'Society of Jesus..' We, above *all* others, should know the dangers... the temptations... But the knowledge, the secret knowledge - it seduced me, and now I have brought damnation into the world!" he wailed.

John's brow furrowed as he tilted his head "Brought *damnation* you say?!"

"Yes, *he's* here, he walks abroad and amongst us: even now, and you don't know it, no one does, only me!"

"But who... who *is* this man?" asked John shaking his head.

The priest fell to his knees: "Today is the feast day of our blessed Saint: Ignatius Loyola" he cried – "the founder of my Jesuit Order: and yet in my most terrible shame, I am not to be found prostrate before the altar of God confessing to my heinous crime: instead I find that I am here on my knees before *you*, a secular psychologist! You *must* believe me Dr Sutton, and you *must* help me!" he cried in despair pulling hard at the psychologists sleeve. John helped him to his feet, but in his distress the priest could barely support his own body weight - clinging on desperately as if for his very life. "You see, I have the *book* – yes, I really have: and I've deciphered it!" His whole body shook as he paused and then continued with breaking voice: "I learned of its terrible secrets – and then... I read out aloud from it, the forbidden words of power!"

Something deep in John's psyche caused his spine to tingle with premonition – the priest's eyes showed fear yes, but honesty too: no shadow of delusion or insanity darkened their truth "OK... I believe you" said John slowly "I 'believe' that you're here, before me, horrified at what you say that you've done, and in fear for your immortal soul: but you *still* haven't told me just who this man is?!"

The priest's head slumped forwards: "He is called, Lucien...." he said "Lucien le Savant ... and the terror of his name, is the Light of Forbidden Knowledge..."

Characters from **Lilith** The Last Temptation of Adam

Return in

Lilith 2

The Devil's Bible

And in book two of

Tom Steven's ESP Series

Rosetta Stone

Lilith

The Last Temptation of Adam

Music

You've read the book , now listen to the music!

Maggie Reilly's song *Lilith* is the official music for Tom Stevens, epic Mythic Fiction novel, *Lilith: The Last Temptation of Adam,* and is available now on her original album: 'Looking Back Moving Forwards' from: www.maggiereilly.co.uk with the individual track *Lilith* available as an MP3 download from www.amazon.com

Maggie's song will also feature as the title track on the forthcoming *Lilith: The Last Temptation of Adam* full production feature film movie soundtrack, and audio CD: with an original music score for the whole film by Maggie Reilly and Stuart McKillop.

For more information see www.maggiereilly.co.uk

and www.greenchapelfilms.com

Lilith

The Last Temptation of Adam

Author Tom Stevens on:

The Music of Maggie Reilly and Stuart McKillop

Of all the creative arts, none are so emotionally evocative as music. For an author to have his work made into a film is a great privilege, but to have it accompanied by a music score that literally paints it, in the vivid colour palette of human emotion, is a greater privilege still.

Maggie Reilly is rightly regarded as one of the finest lyricists and singing talents of our times. The unparalleled beauty of her voice famously led to a long and successful collaboration with progressive rock musician: Mike Oldfield. But in my opinion at least, it's her later work, with her long-time song writing partner: Stuart MacKillop, that really showcases her amazing gifts.

Together, Maggie and Stuart create a very special, and perhaps unique harmony; between lyric, voice, and song: that complements perfectly what I have tried to achieve with my writing. Their music connects to the human soul, and to the living landscape, with all of its transcendent emotions: there reaching effortlessly into the heart of the listener, as no other music I have ever heard, could do.

When I first approached Maggie with the idea of a collaboration, it was for another book, the Celtic-Arthurian epic: 'The Cauldron' (special edition). But what neither of us realised at first, was that at the very same time, but completely separately, Maggie and Stuart had written and produced a song called 'Lilith' – just as I had written and published a novel by the very same name.

Moreover, when I listened to the track, I realised immediately that it fitted perfectly with my vision for the book, and for the film project, that was already then in early development, from it.

The synchronicity was both obvious and compelling – with Maggie, Stuart, and I each realising that this was something meant to happen: almost as if our creativity had been guided (outside of our awareness) towards the same goal. Then, when I heard some more of their recent material, and heard their plans for new song writing, I was frankly stunned, both by the quality of their work, and, the ideal fit, both with the book, and with the film script.

Even now, I find the beauty of Maggie's voice and the sheer talent of both her, and Stuart: to be in a class of their own. Their gift, for that is what it is: is truly a living thread of their lives, and the privilege I feel in working with them professionally, is equalled by the privilege I feel in knowing them personally.

Tom Stevens.

Lilith The Last Temptation of Adam

Image Credits

Front Cover: Freya Lund as *Lilith* © Tom Stevens 2012

Back Cover: Sumerian Terracotta relief of *Lilith* circa 2000 BC: image in the public domain.

Skull: image in the public domain.

Page

5:      Viridios - logo of Viridios Productions Ltd: © Tom Stevens 2009.

9:      Freya Lund as *Lilith* © Tom Stevens 2012.

11:     Freya Lund as *Lilith* © Tom Stevens 2012.

15:     Adam, *Lilith,* and Eve: circa AD 1210. From the base of Trumeau, left portal, west façade, Notre Dame cathedral, Paris; image in the public domain.

16:     Freya Lund as *Lilith* © Julian Baum 2011 for Green Chapel Films Ltd and © Tom Stevens 2012.

18:     Map of Liverpool circa 1600: image in the public domain.

22:     Prince Rupert of The Rhine: unknown artist circa 1640; image in the public domain.

24:     Prince Rupert and Boye: Parliamentarian propaganda pamphlet: unknown artist, circa 1642; image in the public domain.

27:     Puritan Roundhead officer: John Pettie: 1893; image in the public domain.

29:     Mark Moraghan as Dr John Sutton © Tom Stevens 2012.

32:     16th century musketeer: unknown artist; image in the public domain.

35:    Surrender of the Breda Soldiers: Diego Velazquez: 1635; image in the public domain.

37:    Glass of Wine: Johannes Vermeer: 1660; image in the public domain.

38:    Julia Amer as Dr Claudia Moore and Paul McMahon as Dr Alan Flynn © Julian Baum 2011 and Tom Stevens 2012 for Green Chapel Films Limited.

39:    'Behold, for I am Lilith and my name is retribution' reproduction ancient Aramaic script by Pauline Richards for Green Chapel Films Ltd and Viridios productions Ltd – © Pauline Richards 2010.

41:    A scene from the English Civil War: Ernest Crofts: 1911; image in the public domain

42:    Wikimedia commons: unknown artist; image in the public domain.

44:    Prince Rupert's cavalry: Ernest Crofts: circa 1911; image in the public domain.

45:    Portrait of young man: Michael Sweerts: 1650; image in the public domain.

47:    The Procuress: Michael Sweerts: circa 1655; image in the public domain

49:    Freya Lund as *Lilith* © Julian Baum 2011 for Green Chapel Films Ltd and © Tom Stevens 2012.

50:    Hermes Trismigestus: unknown artist: circa 1550; image in the public domain.

56:    Freya Lund as Lilith: © Tom Stevens 2012.

61:    Julia Amer as Claudia Moore and Matt Milburn as Maximilian Von Hesse © Julian Baum 2011 for Green Chapel Films Ltd and © Tom Stevens 2012.

63:    Liverpool Castle & Custom House in 1665: W G Herdman: 1843; image in the public domain.

69:    Stone sarcophagus: Wikimedia Commons; image in the public domain.

72:    Market-Scene: E H Beuckelaer: 1566; image in the public domain.

73:    Leiden Baker and Wife (detail): Jan Steen: circa 1660; image in the public domain.

76: Viridios: The Green Man: © Tom Stevens 2012.

77: Thomas Quilliam as Connor O'Riley: © Tom Stevens 2012.

78: Mike Mitchell as Williams The Blacksmith: © Tom Stevens 2012.

79: Terry O'Neill as Nathaniel Lattimer – Witchfinder General © Tom Stevens 2012.

80: Thomas Quilliam as Connor O'Riley and Mike Mitchell as Williams The Blacksmith: © Tom Stevens 2012.

82: Mere Hall, Oxton, Wirral: © Tom Stevens 2012.

84 (i) Peter Lewis as Hans Meier: © Tom Stevens 2012.

   (ii) Peter Collins as Gustav Adler: © Tom Stevens 2012.

87: Freya Lund as *Lilith:* © Tom Stevens 2012.

88: Matthew Milburn as Maximilian Von Hesse: © Matt Milburn 2010.

89: Imago Mortis - 'The image of death' unknown artist: 14th century; image in the public domain.

97: Freya Lund as *Lilith* with Max Jeffers as Adam Teal: © Tom Stevens 2012.

98: Max Jeffers as Adam Teal with Freya Lund as *Lilith:* © Tom Stevens 2012.

99: Max Jeffers as Adam Teal with Freya Lund as *Lilith* © Tom Stevens 2012.

101: Matt Millburn as The Bavarian Maximilian Von Hesse: © Matt Milburn 2010.

104: (i) Mike Mitchell as Williams The Blacksmith and Thomas Quilliam as Connor O'Riley: © Tom Stevens 2012.

   (ii) Mike Mitchell as Williams The Blacksmith and Thomas Quilliam as Connor O'Riley: © Tom Stevens 2012.

105: Mike Mitchell as Williams The Blacksmith and Thomas Quilliam as Connor O'Riley: © Tom Stevens 2012.

106: The Merchant's Office: unknown artist: circa 1665; image in the public domain.

111: Old Woman Boiling Eggs: Diego Velázquez: 1618; image in the public domain.

117:   Thomas Quilliam as Connor O'Riley and Mike Mitchell as Williams The Blacksmith: © Tom Stevens 2012.

118:   Freya Lund as *Lilith:* © Tom Stevens 2012.

124:   Freya Lund as *Lilith:* © Tom Stevens 2012.

125:   Matthew Hopkins: unknown artist: mid 17th century; image in the public domain

127:   Malleus Maleficarum: pamphlet by unknown author: mid 17th century; image in the public domain.

128:   Unknown gentleman: Anthony Van Dyck: 1640; image in the public domain.

132:   Unknown gentleman: unknown artist: mid 17th century; image in the public domain.

136:   Matt Millburn as The Bavarian Maximilian Von Hesse: © Matt Milburn 2010.

137:   The witchcraft trial: unknown artist: circa 1640: image in the public domain.

141:   Freya Lund as *Lilith:* © Tom Stevens 2012.

143:   Freya Lund as *Lilith:* © Tom Stevens 2012.

148:   Freya Lund as *Lilith:* © Tom Stevens 2012.

151:   Julia Amer as Claudia Moore and Matt Milburn as Maximilian Von Hesse © Julian Baum 2011 for Green Chapel Films Ltd and © Tom Stevens 2012.

153:   Eirin Jansen Hallangen-Lake as Professor Claire Lattimer: © David Jansen Hallangen-Lake 2010.

160:   Engraving from the Rosarium Philosophorum: unknown artist: 16th century; image in the public domain.

165:   Julia Amer as Claudia Moore and Matt Milburn as Maximilian Von Hesse © Julian Baum 2011 for Green Chapel Films Ltd and © Tom Stevens 2012.

168:   Julia Amer as Claudia Moore © Julian Baum 2011 for Green Chapel Films Ltd and © Tom Stevens 2012.

170:   ESP Institute: © Tom Stevens 2009.

178:   Mark Moraghan as Dr John Sutton © Tom Stevens 2012.

181:   Evil Harlequin: image in the public domain.

185:   Matt Milburn as Maximilian Von Hesse © Tom Stevens 2012.

191:   Freya Lund as *Lilith* © Julian Baum 2011 for Green Chapel Films Ltd and © Tom Stevens 2012.

203:   Bust of C.G.Jung in Matthew St Liverpool: © Tom Stevens 2012.

204:   Freya Lund as *Lilith:* © Tom Stevens 2012.

206:   Freya Lund as *Lilith* © Julian Baum 2011 for Green Chapel Films Ltd and © Tom Stevens 2012.

207:   'Hourglass' Microsoft Clipart - free to use image.

212:   Freya Lund as Lilith with Matt Milburn as Maximilian Von Hesse: © Brian McKinney Diamond Eye Movies for Green Chapel Films – and © Tom Stevens 2012.

229:   Paul McMahon as Dr Alan Flynn © Julian Baum 2011 for Green Chapel Films Ltd and © Tom Stevens 2012.

231:   Peter Lewis as Hans Meier: © Tom Stevens 2012.

242:   Sumerian Terracotta relief of *Lilith* circa 2000 BC: image in the public domain.

243   (i) Peter Lewis as Hans Meier; Matthew Milburn as Maximilian Von Hesse; Freya Lund as *Lilith;* Peter Collins as Gustav Adler: © Tom Stevens 2012.

      (ii) Peter Lewis as Hans Meier; Matthew Milburn as Maximilian Von Hesse; Freya Lund as *Lilith;* Peter Collins as Gustav Adler: © Tom Stevens 2012.

271:   Freya Lund as *Lilith:* © 2011 Gareth Richards for Green Chapel Films Ltd.

277:   Julia Amer as Claudia Moore and Matt Milburn as Maximilian Von Hesse © Julian Baum 2011 for Green Chapel Films Ltd and © Tom Stevens 2012.

279:   Freya Lund as *Lilith* © Tom Stevens 2012.

280:   Freya Lund as *Lilith* © Tom Stevens 2012.

286:   A séance: William Hope: circa 1920; image in the public domain.

288:   *Lilith:* Hon. John Collier: 1892; image in the public domain.

293: Gareth Richards as Sean O'Riley: © Tom Stevens 2012.

294: Freya Lund as *Lilith:* © 2011 Gareth Richards for Green Chapel Films Ltd.

299: (i) Mersey Ferry Royal Iris: © 2011 Gareth Richards for Green Chapel Films Ltd.

(ii) Mersey Ferry Royal Iris: © 2011 Gareth Richards for Green Chapel Films Ltd

300: (i) Mersey Ferry Royal Iris: © 2011 Gareth Richards for Green Chapel Films Ltd.

(ii) Mersey Ferry Royal Iris: © 2011 Gareth Richards for Green Chapel Films Ltd.

322: Matthew Milburn as Maximilian Von Hesse: © Matt Milburn 2010.

228: Officer: Jan Vermeer van Delft: 1657; image in the public domain.

331: Freya Lund as *Lilith:* © Julian Baum 2011 for Green Chapel Films Ltd and © Tom Stevens 2012.

343: Incubus: Charles Walker 1870; image in the public domain.

346: Eirin Jansen Hallangen-Lake as Professor Claire Lattimer: © Tom Stevens 2012.

361: Freya Lund as *Lilith* © Tom Stevens 2012.

362: Freya Lund as *Lilith* © Tom Stevens 2012.

375: Mini Cooper S: Wikimedia Commons: 2006; image in the public domain.

378: Freya Lund as *Lilith* © Tom Stevens 2012.

379: Freya Lund as *Lilith* © Tom Stevens 2012.

381: Freya Lund as *Lilith:* © 2011 Gareth Richards for Green Chapel Films Ltd.

386: Freya Lund as *Lilith* © Tom Stevens 2012.

392: Matt Milburn as The Bavarian: Maximilian Von Hesse: © Julian Baum 2011 for Green Chapel Films Ltd and © Tom Stevens 2012.

396: Freya Lund as *Lilith:* © Julian Baum 2011 for Green Chapel Films Ltd and © Tom Stevens 2012.

397: Audi R8 Supercar – owned by Hannibal Higgins © Tom Stevens 2012.

398: Engraving from the Rosarium Philosophorum: unknown artist: 16th century; image in the public domain.

406: Matt Milburn as The Bavarian: Maximilian Von Hesse: © Tom Stevens 2012.

407: Woodchurch Parish Church: © Tom Stevens 2012.

408: Peter Lewis as Hans Meier: © Tom Stevens 2012.

409: (i) Lych Gate at Woodchurch Parish Church: © 2011 Gareth Richards for Green Chapel Films Ltd.

(ii) Pool Lane near to Woodchurch Parish Church: © 2011 Gareth Richards for Green Chapel Films Ltd.

410: Peter Collins as Gustav Adler: © Tom Stevens 2012.

411: Druids Way near to Woodchurch Parish Church: © 2011 Gareth Richards for Green Chapel Films Ltd.

412: Mercedes S Class limo 'Meier': © Tom Stevens 2012.

413: Harlequin Great Dane: © Tom Stevens 2009.

421: Lady by the window: Vermeer: 1658; image in the public domain.

422: Mike Mitchell as 'The Green Man' Viridios: © Tom Stevens 2012.

428: (i) Peter Lewis as Hans Meier; Matt Milburn as The Bavarian – Maximilian Von Hesse; Peter Collins as Gustav Adler: © Tom Stevens 2012.

(ii) Peter Lewis as Hans Meier; Matt Milburn as The Bavarian – Maximilian Von Hesse; Peter Collins as Gustav Adler: © Tom Stevens 2012.

430: Matt Milburn as The Bavarian – Maximilian Von Hesse: © Tom Stevens 2012.

448: Lamia: John William Waterhouse: 1909; image in the public domain.

470: Liverpool World Museum: © Tom Stevens 2012.

479: Freya Lund as *Lilith:* © Julian Baum 2011 for Green Chapel Films Ltd and © Tom Stevens 2012.

481: Yersinia Pestis: image in the public domain.

486: Gareth Richards as Sean O'Riley with Freya Lund as *Lilith:* © Tom Stevens 2012.

501: Yersinia Pestis: image in the public domain.

506: Matt Milburn as 'The Bavarian' Maximilian Von Hesse © Julian Baum 2011 for Green Chapel Films Ltd.

510: Eirin Jansen Hallangen-Lake as Professor Claire Lattimer: © David Jansen Hallangen-Lake 2010.

526: Astral body: unknown artist; image in the public domain.

529: The Fisher King: medieval: artist unknown; image in the public domain.

540: Night club: Wikimedia Commons: image in the public domain.

542: Freya Lund as *Lilith:* © Julian Baum 2011 for Green Chapel Films Ltd and © Tom Stevens 2012.

543: (i) Liverpool Waterfront: © Tom Stevens 2012.

(ii) Liverpool Waterfront: © Tom Stevens 2012.

544: (i) St John's Tower Liverpool: © Tom Stevens 2012.

(ii) St John's Tower Liverpool: © Tom Stevens 2012.

545: (i) St John's Tower Liverpool: © Tom Stevens 2012.

(ii) Freya Lund as *Lilith* © Tom Stevens 2012.

546: (i) Freya Lund as *Lilith* © Tom Stevens 2012.

(ii) Freya Lund as *Lilith* © Tom Stevens 2012.

547: Freya Lund as *Lilith* © Tom Stevens 2012.

548: Freya Lund as *Lilith* © Tom Stevens 2012.

549: (i) Liverpool Waterfront: © Tom Stevens 2012.

(ii) Liverpool Waterfront: © Tom Stevens 2012.

550: (i) Liverpool Anglican Cathedral: © Tom Stevens 2012.

(ii) Liverpool Roman Catholic Cathedral: © Tom Stevens 2012.

551: (i) Liverpool Empire Theatre: © Tom Stevens 2012.

(ii) Liverpool Museum: © Tom Stevens 2012.

552: (i) Liverpool's Lime St Railway Station: © Tom Stevens 2012.

(ii) Hope Street, Liverpool: © Tom Stevens 2012.

553:     (i) Sun and clouds over Liverpool: © Tom Stevens 2012.

         (ii) St John's Tower, Liverpool: © Tom Stevens 2012.

554:     (i) Freya Lund as *Lilith:* © Julian Baum 2011 for Green Chapel Films Ltd and © Tom Stevens 2012.

         (ii) Freya Lund as *Lilith:* © Julian Baum 2011 for Green Chapel Films Ltd and © Tom Stevens 2012.

555:     Liverpool Waterfront: © Tom Stevens 2012.

556:     Mike Mitchell as Viridios – 'The Green Man': © Tom Stevens 2012.

557:     Fox and Hounds pub, Barnston Dale, Wirral: © Gareth Richards 2009; for Green Chapel Films Ltd.

568:     (i) Matt Milburn as; 'The Bavarian' Maximilian Von Hesse with Freya Lund as *Lilith:* © Julian Baum 2011 for Green Chapel Films Ltd.

         (ii) Matt Milburn as; 'The Bavarian' Maximilian Von Hesse with Freya Lund as *Lilith:* © Julian Baum 2011 for Green Chapel Films Ltd.

569:     (i) Matt Milburn as; 'The Bavarian' Maximilian Von Hesse with Freya Lund as *Lilith:* © Julian Baum 2011 for Green Chapel Films Ltd.

         (ii) Matt Milburn as; 'The Bavarian' Maximilian Von Hesse with Freya Lund as *Lilith:* © Julian Baum 2011 for Green Chapel Films Ltd.

570:     Matt Milburn as; 'The Bavarian' Maximilian Von Hesse with Freya Lund as *Lilith:* © Julian Baum 2011 for Green Chapel Films Ltd.

572:     'The Dale' © Tom Stevens 2012.

573:     Engraving from the Rosarium Philosophorum: unknown artist: 16th century; image in the public domain.

577:     Matt Milburn as; 'The Bavarian' Maximilian Von Hesse with Freya Lund as *Lilith:* © Julian Baum 2011 for Green Chapel Films Ltd and © Tom Stevens 2012.

578:     Woodside Ferry Terminal, Birkenhead: Wikimedia Commons: 2006; image in the public domain.

594:     Mark Moraghan as Dr John Sutton © Tom Stevens 2012.

596:     Mike Mitchell as 'The Green Man' Viridios: © Tom Stevens 2012.

597:     Freya Lund as *Lilith:* © Julian Baum 2011 for Green Chapel Films Ltd and © Tom Stevens 2012.

600:     Mark Moraghan as Dr John Sutton © Tom Stevens 2012.

611:    Freya Lund as *Lilith:* © Julian Baum 2011 for Green Chapel Films Ltd and © Tom Stevens 2012.

614:    Freya Lund as *Lilith:* © Julian Baum 2011 for Green Chapel Films Ltd and © Tom Stevens 2012.

616:    Engraving from the Rosarium Philosophorum: unknown artist: 16th century; image in the public domain.

617:    Mike Mitchell as 'The Green Man' Viridios: © Tom Stevens 2012.

618:    Merseyside Police Station at Birkenhead: © Gareth Richards 2008 for Green Chapel Films Ltd.

622:    Gareth Richards as Sean O'Riley © Tom Stevens 2012 for Green Chapel Films Ltd.

623:    Matt Milburn as 'The Bavarian' Maximilian Von Hesse: © Matt Milburn 2010.

624:    Freya Lund as *Lilith:* © Julian Baum 2011 for Green Chapel Films Ltd and © Tom Stevens 2012.

625:    Codex Gigas: Wikimedia Commons; image in the public domain.

627:    Maggie Reilly: © Maggie Reilly – www.maggiereilly.co.uk with permission.

More Books

by

Tom Stevens

TOM STEVENS

The DEVIL'S BIBLE

1244 AD in the *Languedoc* France: fallen Cathar priest and Hermetic alchemist Guy de Montpellier is desperate to escape from the siege of castle *Montségur* - taking with him the most jealously guarded secret of the Cathars: an alternative transmission of Genesis, the New Testament and the book of Revelations - the alternative account of Satan himself: a book that also contains the most dangerous of occult secrets - how to bring forth into the world - The Angel of Light...Lucifer

2011 - England... a Roman Catholic priest and antiquarian collector discovers an ancient book writ in an arcane text... Soon his curiosity becomes a compulsion as he struggles to translate the codex...

Unbeknown to him, another is seeking the book... someone to whom it once belonged... and he wants it back!

Soon the UK is being seduced by a messianic politician... a man who promises reform, a new beginning and a break from the corruption of the 'Rotten Parliament' of 2009.

Charming, handsome and utterly beguiling... Lucien is about to make his Revelation...

© 2010: Tom Stevens The DEVIL'S BIBLE

THE DEAD ROOM

TOM STEVENS
THE ESP SERIES

Book Six of Tom Stevens ESP Series

THE DEAD ROOM

"There's the Living Room, and then... there's the Dead Room"

A tale told in two centuries - the American Civil War in 1863 and the era of paranormal science in 2010.
Researchers at 'ESP' the world-renowned paranormal research institute uncover the mystery of an old Liverpool photograph from the 1860's and the awakening of a malevolent entity for whom time had stood still, only to be freed to wreak death, destruction and havoc, both then, and now...

ISBN 978-1-906983-15-4   Due in 2011

WAGS and Witches

Now in Development as a Movie Project!

The third volume in Tom Stevens epic ESP Series:

"Footballers Wives meets The Da Vinci Code!" Goddess Lilith's favourite daughter runs riot through the world of spoilt hedonistic WAGS and their wealthy friends: her mission - final retribution against the bloodline descendants of Roman Centurion Valerian - 'Keeper' of the Celtic Cauldron of Rebirth - the original and true 'Holy Grail' of ancient Britain. This, she decides, will be the final battle between Lilith's Children and that bloodline family mentored by the God of Life and Rebirth Viridios - 'The Green Man'. The final battle... for the very land and Soul of Britain itself! Originally published as The Thorstone Witches in 2008 now fully revised and updated as WAGS and Witches for 2010 - and in development as a television screenplay with Green Man Film and Media. A high-drama of mystery and adventure, but in particular of female psychology as the women in the story: WAGS, witches, paranormal researchers and the 17 yr old schoolgirl Lizzie O'Riley, come to the fore in a modern myth of redemption and self-realisation. Issues of identity, eroticism, love, power, motherhood, mother-daughter relations, friendship, ambition, creativity, men and the masculine psyche, betrayal, ageing, mortality, loss, grief, and re-birth are all addressed as an unfolding narrative of the soul's journey through a modern myth depicting timeless, universal truths.

Set against the backdrop of an occult and supernatural mystery - it is also a reflective social commentary on the times in which we live - times that echo eerily with the last days of Rome's empire in Britain: hedonism, the cult of celebrity, mass immigration, the weakening of traditional religion, and an intrusive state. The comparison is reflexive and critical: making contrasts as well as comparisons - and bringing the reader into an ever-closer communion with the characters: as they struggle with the spectre of a tragic history repeating itself - how it can be made different, and how dark psychic, as well as psychological forces, may seek to exploit the present Zeitgeist with evil intent.

The finale is action-packed, emotional and heroic, as the fate of all involved is decided at a dramatic midnight encounter at the blood-red Thor's Rock - the altar-stone to the ancient gods of thunder, set high upon the wind-swept common heath of Wirral's Thurstaston Hill.

Remote Viewing

Now in Development as a Movie Project!

Historical Fiction meets Paranormal Romance in this groundbreaking novel of Mary Queen of Scot's - the Babington Plot, time travel, the supernatural and the occult

Parapsychologists at ESP the world renowned paranormal research institute, undertake secret work for the military in a clairvoyant sensing technique called 'Remote Viewing'

The barriers of not only space but also time are breached as a Tudor Magus and Alchemist makes contact with the future in an attempt to escape his supernatural enemies. The Magus's powers are increased as his reach extends from the court of Queen Elizabeth into the first decade of the 21st century

Join ESP as they desperately battle against the Magus's evil power!

ISBN 988-0-9559656-4-7

Mythic Fiction, History and the Supernatural meet in this epic tale of Dark Age Britain!

Lilith's children return to claim The Celtic Cauldron of Rebirth as part of the great Viking Invasion of England in 937 AD. At the Battle of Brunanburgh: the descendants of Valerian are forced to ally themselves with the Saxon King Athelstan to protect the secret treasures of the land Not only from the Vikings but from The Mother of All Demons' herself...

ISBN 978-1-906983-07-9

THE CAULDRON
Special Edition

The Dark Ages at the end of Rome's empire in Britain and the origin of the Arthurian and Holy Grail myths. Volumes one (The Centurion) and two (The Cauldron) of Tom Stevens epic 'Cauldron' series combined into one special edition!

Part One

Roman Centurion Valerian is inducted into the secret mysteries of the Celtic Cauldron of Rebirth in the dying days of Rome's Empire in Britain. Volume One of Tom Stevens epic Cauldron Series: Christian Roman Centurion Valerian is left in command of the rump of the remaining Twentieth Legion at ancient Chester defending against the Pictish and Hibernian pirates that raid the western shore of Britannia. The uncertainties of his life in these troubled times are made worse by his discovery of his real origins in a pagan Druid family and of their secret inheritance as guardians of the Celtic Cauldron of Rebirth. Valerian sees the end of Rome's empire in Britain and the spreading of a dark curtain across the land as he must choose between his Christian faith and his family's sworn inheritance. Enemies both physical and supernatural battle it out against the dawn of the Dark Ages and the true origin of the myths of King Arthur and the Holy Grail.

Part Two

Dark-Age Mythic Fiction: young Celtic foundling child Arthur reaches maturity to discover his true identity as son of Uther Pendragon and his destiny to guard both the nation of Britain and The Celtic Cauldron of Rebirth or 'Holy Grail' against the invading Angles and Saxons. Book Two of Tom Stevens epic Cauldron Series see's Post Roman Britannia in the late 5th century AD. It's the age of hero's as Artorius 'Duke of Battles' leads the Celtic Briton's defence against invading heathen Anglo-Saxons led by the traitor Mordred and the Roman Warlord Dominus. Fate takes a terrible turn as the true intention of the invaders at last reveals itself - the capture of the sacred site of The Cauldron of Rebirth - the true 'Holy Grail' of Celtic Britannia. Artorius who will be remembered in myth as King Arthur meets his nemesis in the evil Sorceress Morgeuse sister of Morgain Le Fay as the fight for the soul of Britain reaches its supernatural climax. Artorius Viridios and Merlin create a new cavalry warrior-elite based at Castra Legionis: 'The City of The Legion' becoming the archetype for the 'Knights of the Round Table'. Mystery, adventure and the supernatural combine in this outstanding tale of Dark-Age Mythic Fiction.

"Landmark Literature!" Vicky Turner, Amazon.co.uk reviewer

Read how the History Channel's 'discovery' of the true location of King Arthur's fortress and 'Round Table' in 2010 were first uncovered by author Tom Stevens two years before the archaeologists and historians in 2008!

ISBN 9780955965616

© 2008 TOM STEVENS

ROSETTA STONE

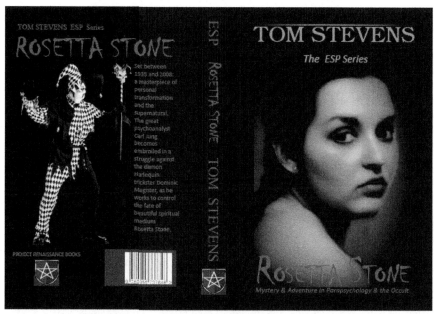

Book Two of Tom Stevens ESP Series

Who are the mysterious spiritual medium Rosetta Stone and her magician & stage-hypnotist companion Domenico Maestro di-Capella?

Join the Parapsychologists of ESP the world renowned paranormal research institute as they battle against the return of their most dangerous enemies, intent not only on personal vengeance but also on unleashing dark forces of destruction against the very land itself

Magic, psychology, the supernatural and the occult combine with ancient mythological powers in the land for an epic struggle of light against dark, good against evil

ISBN: 978-0-9557378-4-8

OXFORDS BLUES

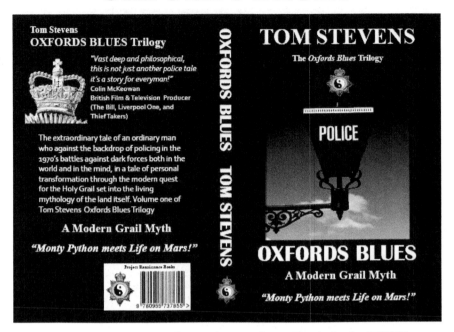

Tom Stevens
OXFORDS BLUES Trilogy

"Vast deep and philosophical, this is not just another police tale it's a story for everyman!"
Colin McKeowan
British Film & Television Producer
(The Bill, Liverpool One, and Thief Takers)

The extraordinary tale of an ordinary man who against the backdrop of policing in the 1970's battles against dark forces both in the world and in the mind, in a tale of personal transformation through the modern quest for the Holy Grail set into the living mythology of the land itself. Volume one of Tom Stevens Oxfords Blues Trilogy

A Modern Grail Myth

"Monty Python meets Life on Mars!"

Project Renaissance Books

9 780955 737855

TOM STEVENS

The *Oxfords Blues* Trilogy

POLICE

OXFORDS BLUES

A Modern Grail Myth

"Monty Python meets Life on Mars!"

Now in Production for British TV!

Monty Python meets 'Life on Mars' in this modern tale of personal transformation and self-realization

In this hilarious account of the adventures of the weirdest bunch of Coppers in the 1970's Merseyside Police: tragedy, pathos and real psychological insight mix with crime-fighting in the most innovative and witty police novel since Joseph Wamburgh's The Choirboys.

Set between 1976 and 1978 this is policing as it was in the 'golden age' before political correctness.

Written by a retired Merseyside police-officer and built around real people and events: powerful characters and multi-level plot lines entertain from beginning to end.

ISBN 978-0-9557378-0-0
© 2007, 2008 TOM STEVENS

OXFORDS CIRCUS

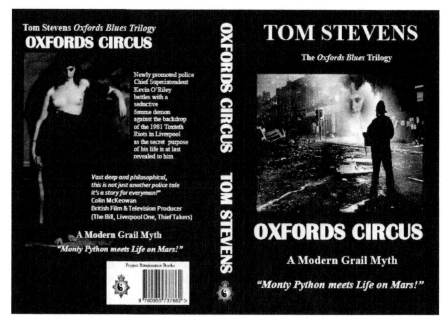

Merseyside's finest face their toughest challenge yet in the tragedy that was the 1981 Toxteth Riots – the worst urban disorder in British history.

Set between 1980 & 1982 follow the adventures of "The Birkenhead Boys" the Golf-Three Wirral sub-division and its assortment of odd-ball and ne'r-do-well front-line officers, as they live and work through the tumultuous period of political and social change of the early 'Thatcher' years.

Dark forces battle both in the world and in the mind in a modern tale of personal transformation set against a background of crime, psychology, mystery & the occult.

ISBN: 978-0-9557378-1-7

OXFORDS MISFITS

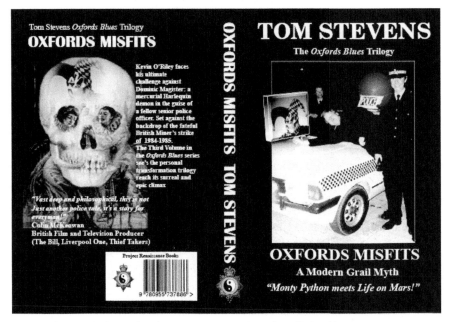

Tom Stevens *Oxfords Blues* Trilogy

OXFORDS MISFITS

Kevin O'Riley faces his ultimate challenge against Dominic Magister: a mercurial Harlequin demon in the guise of a fellow senior police officer. Set against the backdrop of the fateful British Miner's strike of 1984-1985. The Third Volume in the *Oxfords Blues* series see's the personal transformation trilogy reach its surreal and epic climax

"Vast deep and philosophical, this is not Just another police tale, it's a story for everyone!"
Colin McKeowan
British Film and Television Producer
(The Bill, Liverpool One, Thief Takers)

Project Renaissance Books

9 780955 737886 >

TOM STEVENS
The *Oxfords Blues* Trilogy

OXFORDS MISFITS
A Modern Grail Myth
"Monty Python meets Life on Mars!"

The 'Misfits' the last generation of politically-incorrect police-officers: face their final challenge in the mid 1980's Merseyside Police Force.

Set between 1984 & 1985 terrorism, police corruption, gangsters and everyday policing mix with a black Pythonesque humour as familiar characters from Oxfords Blues and Oxfords Circus return to do battle with a Mercurial force of evil, both within themselves and society

Personal transformation through the modern quest for the Holy Grail is set against a background of crime psychology; the supernatural and the occult bringing this personal transformation trilogy to its surreal and epic climax!

ISBN: 978-0-9557378-2-4

Notes

Notes